STORMS A

C000111085

BY
JULIE ANNE GATES

CRANTHORPE
—MILLNER—
PUBLISHERS

A CIP catalogue record for this title is available from the
British Library.

ISBN 978-1-9164400-3-6 (Paperback)

www.cranthorpemillner.com

Published by Cranthorpe Millner (2019)

Cranthorpe Millner Publishers
18 Soho Square
London
W1D 3QL

For my son, Matthew…

To John
with love from
Julie

De Braose Family Tree

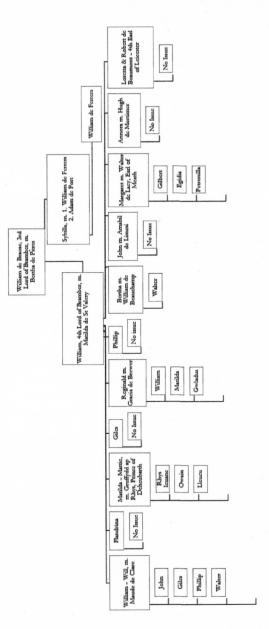

PROLOGUE

Windsor Castle, December 1210

I stand and watch them heave her body from the shadowy depths of the oubliette, hidden beneath the trap door in the Round Tower. Gently, almost reverently, she is laid on the cold flag stones at my feet, her matted hair spread around her the colour of autumn leaves against the white alabaster of her face.

You did not fail me, Ailith ...

The whisper hangs in the air, followed by a touch as light as gossamer on the wind, and I shiver. Several minutes pass in silence then, with a grunt, the body of her son is dragged through the trapdoor and laid alongside his mother, one leg broken and twisted from the long fall into the dark chamber below, a few strands of the straw that had been thrown in with them still clinging to his hair. Around us, the shadows grow deeper as the thin, wintry light slowly fades beyond the narrow-arched window frame. A ginger cat pokes its head around the door briefly, then with a sudden rise of its hackles and a sharp hiss it streaks away across the cobbles.

There is another long silence before one of the men rouses himself and gives instructions for the stiff, lifeless bodies to be carried out to the cart that waits for us in the bailey. I follow them slowly, pausing only to look at the trap door still open in the floor behind me. For a moment I think I see her standing there, but the image is indistinct and quickly it flickers and fades, and it is with a sense of loss that I step out into the cold beyond the tower door.

Outside, in the fading light, an unnatural silence hangs over the battlements. It is as if the castle is holding its breath. Waiting for something. High up in the castle keep, I think I see the face of our King at a window. A fleeting glimpse perhaps. Maybe even imagined.

I shall not let you forget, I whisper.

A thin veil of snow begins to fall, swathing their bodies like a shroud as they lie side by side on the cart. Silently, the men cover them with canvas sacks. It is getting colder now; I can feel the icy wind stinging my face, and the snow numbs my hands and feet so that I can barely feel them anymore. Still, I will stay with her to the end. For that is what I promised, and at least that is one promise I can keep. I shall stay with her whilst she is laid to rest in the little chapel in the castle grounds, alongside her beloved son. If King John knows of the arrangements then he has not said, and the chaplain has been well bribed to do his duty and fast.

At last the cart trundles across the bailey towards the chapel, and I watch quietly as she is placed in her makeshift coffin, before being lowered once more into a hole in the ground. One from which, this time, she will never leave. Then they lower her son down beside her, and the chaplain goes through the motions of the service, pausing only to let me throw a handful of muddy earth down on the coffins and whisper my goodbyes before he begins his prayers. But I cannot pray. I am all out of prayers. King John with his black heart has seen to that.

Then it is over, and I am leaving, crossing the bailey of Windsor Castle one last time to join Sam Skeet who will take me home. And home is where I shall begin my story, and you can judge for yourself whether King John truly has the blackest heart that any king has ever had ...

PART ONE

Chapter 1

Bramber Castle, England, February 1182

I remember clearly the day I first set foot in Bramber castle, accompanied only by my father. It was freezing and the north winds had already brought their promise of snow. It flurried along the causeway, not quite settling, as restless and as skittish as the horses tethered to the wooden drawbridge at the foot of Castle Hill. The tide was in and the River Adur was high as we slowly made our way across the uneven planks towards the east gate. A couple of guards ran curious eyes over us, but seeing we had nothing but the clothes on our back they waved us on. I was tired. Evening was nearly upon us and the cobbled path leading up to the castle was steep and slippery. I stumbled along it, until eventually my father had to take my arm and steady me.

'Not far now,' he said encouragingly, blinking away the snow and giving me one of his rare smiles.

Sure enough, moments later, the path flattened out and in front of us stood a small church tucked away on a natural shelf where it gazed down on the rooftops below like a father watching over his children. Giving the church only a cursory glance, my father took my arm once more and led me across a low stone bridge spanning a defensive ditch, half filled with muddy rainwater and ice. We paused on the other side for a while, our breath making wispy little patterns in the air. Above us the castle's tall gatehouse tower rose sentinel on its bank pointing to the bleak skies overhead, flanked on either side by the curtain wall of the inner bailey, its narrow-arched windows staring grimly back the way we had come. From where we stood, we could just make out the tiny figure of a guard high up on top of the keep, looking down over the marshes, towards the wide river estuary and the sea. It was a bleak, lonely place and I felt the nerves begin to flutter in my belly because from now on this was to be my home, for my uncle Jem, having called in a debt from Sir William's steward, had secured me a job as a servant to the family. Seeing my face, my father patted my arm reassuringly, then, taking a deep breath, we began the final part of our journey, both of us aware that the time for parting was approaching fast.

As we approached the gatehouse, it became apparent that there was some sort of argument in progress. A soldier stood in front of the entrance with his feet planted firmly on the cobbles, blocking the way through to the inner bailey. Emblazoned on the front of his blue surcoat was the de Braose arms, clearly identifying him as part of the garrison.

He was arguing with an older man who, despite the cold, wore only a short-sleeved leather tunic over his long woollen hose, revealing a pair of thick muscular arms corded with dark veins and sinew. A sword hung from a leather belt at his side, but although his hand hovered near the hilt, he seemed in no hurry to withdraw it from its scabbard.

Standing a little apart from the two men, sobbing distraughtly, was a dishevelled girl. She was clinging to the ripped remains of her gown with both hands. It was not hard to guess that she was the subject of the argument.

We hesitated. We were within sight now but nobody took any notice of us. Instead, the soldier ceased his shouting to kick the wheel of a nearby abandoned wagon, before turning back to the man. 'Why her, de Breauté? Why her and not some other castle slut?' he roared in an anguished voice.

'And why ever not?' De Breauté replied, shrugging visibly. 'She's as much a whore as any other woman in this God forsaken –'

He broke off as the soldier let loose another roar and launched himself at his throat. Taken by surprise, he skidded and slewed on the icy cobbles, but still somehow managed to stay on his feet as he struggled to free himself from the younger man's vice-like grip. The whole hillside seemed to reverberate with their cries, attracting a small group of spectators who gathered around them and began to pelt missiles at de Breauté's heaving back.

At last, panting with exertion, de Breauté broke free and staggering to one side he doubled over gasping for air. Deprived of his adversary, the soldier flung himself back against the wagon with a groan and began to explore a jagged cut on the bridge of his nose with his fingers.

For a while neither man spoke, then finally the soldier found his voice. 'You've ruined her reputation for good down in Bramber,' he gasped, throwing a furious glance at the girl still cowering behind him. 'Nobody's going to want her now she's been bedded by a filthy mercenary like you!'

De Breauté snorted. 'And what do you care anyway, boy? Were you hoping to get under her skirts, mayhap along with half of this lot?' he asked, gesturing towards the glowering faces of the mob surrounding them with a leer.

'You bastard!' the soldier spluttered, and would have attacked him again, but the girl flung herself at him and clinging to his arm she begged him fiercely to take her home.

For a moment the soldier hesitated, then angrily he shook her off. 'She wasn't a whore before you got your hands on her, de Breauté!' he spat, glowering at the trembling girl once more. And with that he threw de Breauté a final look of contempt, and grabbing the girl by the wrist, he began to drag her roughly down the path towards the scattered roofs of the little village below, his parting words, 'I'll kill you! Mark my words, I'll kill you one day!' floating behind him as he went.

De Breauté made no attempt to go after them. Instead, he watched their retreating figures for several moments whilst he rubbed the back of his bruised neck with one hand. Then just before they rounded the corner and disappeared, I heard him shout: 'Not if I get you first, sonny! Not if I get you first!'

Once the spectacle was over, and there was nothing more to see, the villagers began to melt away. I shivered, aware that the only thing standing between us and the gatehouse now was de Breauté. And he wasn't an obstacle I wished to tackle.

'What are we going to do, Papa?' I whispered, pulling my threadbare shawl tighter around my shoulders as though it could give me some protection.

As if reading my mind, de Breauté looked in our direction. Then in a heartbeat he was in front of us, his eyes narrow and unwelcoming. 'We don't welcome filthy beggars here,' he snarled, pushing his face so close to mine that I could smell the onions and decay on his breath.

Instantly I recoiled. Up close, he positively exuded evil: his dark eyes glittered angrily under heavy brows, and his dirty lank hair was tied back untidily, exposing a heavy jaw which hadn't seen a razor for some time. A vivid scar ran from his top lip to just below his ear; bad stitching had drawn it back from his gum giving him a permanent leer, revealing a section of decaying brown teeth. I could see the humiliation from his encounter with the soldier still burning in his eyes, and suddenly I felt afraid.

'Perhaps we should go,' I said, quietly edging around him, hoping to avoid a confrontation of our own.

De Breauté didn't move. Instead, he continued to fix us with his cold, dead stare. Then slowly he reached down and withdrew his sword from its scabbard, twisting the blade first one way and then the other as if admiring its fine craftsmanship.

'I hate beggars,' he said, turning and addressing my father as if I wasn't there. 'If I had my way, I'd string the bastards up – every last one of them!'

Immediately, the lump in my father's throat began to bob with fear, and despite the bitter chill in the air, beads of sweat broke out on his forehead and began to trickle down his face.

'Did you hear me?' de Breauté asked, almost conversationally.

When my father didn't answer, de Breauté eyed him thoughtfully for several moments more. Then, without warning, he swung the sword up and over his head, where it hung glinting for a while in the dull afternoon light, and before I realized what he was about to do, he brought it down severing his ear like a hot knife through butter.

'*No* ... Jesu! What have you done!' I shouted in horror as my father dropped to his knees, a look of surprise on his face as blood splattered like rubies against the whiteness of the snow.

De Breauté ignored me. Instead, he regarded the severed ear with interest for a moment, before kicking it aside and beginning to reign vicious blows upon my father's head and shoulders with a heavily booted foot.

'*No*! Please stop!' Wildly, I grabbed de Breauté's arm in an attempt to drag him away, but he swatted me aside as if I were nothing but an annoying insect. Then, leaning down, he grabbed a handful of my father's hair with his free hand, and jerking his head back he snarled.

'You've an excuse for your deafness now! Mayhap you'll have got the message you filthy, disgusting, whoreson beggar!'

And, throwing him face down in the snow, he suddenly began to laugh ...

We stayed like that for what seemed like hours, afraid to move or breathe in case we attracted de Breauté's attention again.

A robin flew down and began pecking at the hard earth in the vain hope that it might yield up a worm or two, oblivious to the tension in the air as de Breauté paced back and forth in front of us, kicking at imaginary objects every now and then.

At my feet, my father stirred and let out a small, animal-like moan, and flinging myself down beside him I put my arm around his thin shoulders.

'Papa, please, you have to rise,' I whispered urgently. He didn't respond. Bruises were already flowering on his arms and legs where de Breauté's boots had torn the worn fabric of his clothes, and the top of his head was a mess of blood. I tried again, this time tugging at his sleeve. Still there was no response, and I knew that I would never get him to his feet on my own.

I had just made the decision that the only way to get help was to try to make it to the gatehouse alone in the hope of raising a guard, when de Breauté suddenly ceased his pacing, and uttering a curse began to look around himself uneasily. Several moments passed in which he seemed to be listening for something, then unexpectedly a look of fear flickered across his face.

I shivered, acutely aware that the temperature had dropped a few degrees; the snow was heavier, swirling around us in flurries almost as if it was angry. The wind had also picked up - it tangled my hair around my face and whipped at my clothes like demons.

Looking agitated, de Breauté moved away from us to peer deeper into the eerie greying light as if searching for something. Just then two riders emerged through the swirling snow, spectre-like, their mantles billowing around them like ghostly sails in a storm. Seeing them, de Breauté made the sign of the evil eye with his right hand: his two mid-fingers bent inward held by his thumb. Then with a last petrified look at the new arrivals, he began to back hastily away until he was hidden in the deep shadows shrouding the gatehouse door.

A strange silence settled over the hillside; the only sound was the muffled clip-clop of approaching hooves. Even the robin stilled and cocked its head to one side, then took off in urgent flight for the safety of a rowan bush somewhere in the ditch below the castle walls.

Behind me, de Breauté began chanting fearfully, making the tiny hairs on the back of my neck rise; I could feel his terror wrapping itself around me tangibly, like a blanket, smothering and cloying.

Abandoning my father, I rose shakily to my feet. The riders were almost upon us now and I could see that they were both women, but that was where the similarity ended. One of them was old. In fact, she was positively ancient. She sat astride a stocky skewbald pony, and the hood of her mantle had blown back to reveal a face that must have seen a hundred summers or more. Her companion was much younger. The turn of her ankle in the stirrup, the long slender hands that held the gilded reins of her grey palfrey, and the beautifully manicured nails all suggested that she was a lady. My eyes lingered on those hands, strangely reluctant to move on, and I shivered again. Something uneasy stirred at the back of my mind; I had the strangest feeling that I had been here before —

Ailith …

I shook my head slowly. Had the voice been in my head?

Ailith … the voice whispered again.

I spun around. There was only my father kneeling in the snow and the two approaching riders. Of de Breauté there was nothing to be seen, though I could still feel his presence in the shadows of the gatehouse behind me.

Ailith … the voice whispered.

'No —' I breathed silently, suddenly very cold.

Ailith …

'No. It cannot be!' I said again, only this time louder, as an icy sweat broke out between my shoulder blades and began to trickle down my back. Then everything around me ceased to exist, and silence hung heavily in the air, as slowly, and inexorably, my eyes were drawn to her face …

The face that haunts my dreams …

Everything was the same and yet nothing was the same. The wheels of destiny had begun to turn and there was no escape; there was no turning back for it was written in the stars, that much I already knew. For I am the seventh child of the seventh child, and I have the Sight.

And I had already seen.

Oh yes, I have already seen …

I could hear the church bells ringing out the hour of nones as the two riders reined in alongside us, loosening their grip on the reins to allow their mounts to nose passively in the undergrowth that had sprung up along the cobbled path so that they might look for something to be had.

Matilda …

The name came out of nowhere, but instinctively I knew it was her name.

Without a word, and with surprising agility, the old woman dismounted and crouched down beside my father. After a moment she began to remove several clean rags, some salve, and some herbs from a bag fastened about her waist with twine, before gently beginning to attend to his wounds.

Still in a daze, I watched her skilfully working to stem the blood. She was as small as a bird - rather like a small, speckled wren, with skin like parchment, and shiny brown eyes like little buttons that missed nothing as she worked. Around us the silence still hung heavily in the air, broken only by the wind and the howling of wolves somewhere deep in the forest beyond us.

When she had finished her ministrations, she began re-packing her bag with small, deft movements, tucking everything tidily back into its allotted place. She was about to turn back to her pony when she hesitated, and, reaching one gnarled hand out towards me, she gently touched my face.

'*Ne pas avoir peur que le petit vous ont la force, ne la laisser vers le bas,*' she said in a low voice. Then seeing I didn't understand, she sought the words in English. '*Do not be afraid little one, you have the strength, you must not let her down ...*' Her eyes strayed to Matilda's face as she said this. Turning back to me, she fixed me once more with her bird like eyes and regarded me for a long moment. At last she nodded as if satisfied and, beckoning me to help, we lifted my father to his feet before leading him towards the little skewbald pony and finally onto the castle itself.

We did not know it then, but behind us the wind whispered nervously. Then, whipping itself into a frenzy, it skittered off amongst the trees and along the shallow plain at the foot of the rolling downs, until it became a great vortex. Here it spun for a while, before changing direction and dipping low to whisk its way up through the land, wreaking havoc amongst villages and towns on its way: *It has begun* ... it whispered. *It has begun* ...

The gatehouse was dark and broody in the fading light, a feeling that was enhanced by the deep shadows where I knew Faulkes de Breauté still lurked. I slowed down as we entered and peered around, afraid that he might suddenly appear, but he remained concealed within the gloomy depths of the cold walls, leaving only the stink of his fear lingering in the air.

Drawing her mare to a halt, Matilda turned slowly in the saddle to stare deep into the darkness as if she knew somebody was there. Meanwhile the old woman approached a large bell suspended from a rafter and rang it for admittance. Some moments passed in which no one moved, and then a muffled voice called, 'Who goes there?'

'It's the Lady Matilda and her maid, Jeanette,' the old woman answered in her heavily accented English, her voice ringing clearly in the cold air.

A few more moments passed, filled with the rattling of chains and the screech of metal. Finally, the great nail-studded doors opened, revealing a thickset guard drawing a cloak tightly around him against the cold, followed closely by another guard wielding a flaming torch who regarded us with undisguised curiosity.

Lady Matilda beckoned the torch bearer nearer to her horse so that the shadows around her dissolved to reveal Faulkes de Breauté pressed up against the wall. Making the sign of the cross, I drew back and watched warily from a distance. The atmosphere was charged. de Breauté's fear was tangible in the air; he was making strange mewing sounds and trying to back deeper into the shadows.

Slowly, Matilda pushed aside the hood of her cloak, revealing a slim face framed with long chestnut hair glinting brightly in the torchlight, and green, strangely cat-like eyes which were now fixed on de Breauté, who hastily made the sign of the cross as if to ward off evil.

'I attended a birthing today, Faulkes de Breauté,' she said, addressing him in a soft, melodious voice that barely disguised her loathing of him. Her mare took a few uneasy steps sideways and whickered through its nose, emitting a steaming breath of warm air into the cold night, and I shivered and crossed myself again.

'T'was the maid that you raped last midsummer's day. Do you recall it, de Breauté?' she asked, her green eyes flashing with unsuppressed anger as she urged the mare closer to him with her knees, causing de Breauté to back further into the shadows in an effort to keep his distance from her.

'You have no right to address me thus, madam! I shall have Sir William know of this … this slander!' He was visibly shaking now, and his voice was unsteady. 'I am a well-respected member of Prince John's retinue and Sir William's guest here - he shall hear of this witchcraft, mark my words!'

Matilda ignored him. Instead she leaned forward out of the saddle so that her face was nearer to his. 'She died cursing you, Faulkes de Breauté. She cursed you with her last breath and she will carry on cursing you from beyond the grave for the ill that you visited upon her.' Her anger was so palpable that it sparked in the air, making the torchbearer step back and look around himself in terror as if expecting demons to appear at any moment.

Still unable to free himself from her gaze, de Breauté moaned and crossed himself again, muttering, 'Jesu, Jesu, save me from this witch!' under his breath.

The mare tossed its head nervously and whickered, not liking the strung-out tension in the air, and with that Matilda righted herself in the saddle and began to undo the large silver brooch fastened to her cloak, suddenly strangely calm. 'Your child lives though, de Breauté, and I thought you would like to see him, so I brought him to you. You do want to see him, don't you?' she asked, still transfixing him with her strange green eyes.

De Breauté stepped back nervously, his blustering silenced as Matilda withdrew the brooch from the fabric and slowly parted her cloak. Then, gasping in horror, he turned, and clutching at the wall like a mad man he bent double and began to vomit in the snow.

I simply stared, my mind refusing to accept what my eyes were seeing. For strapped to her by a length of cloth wound around her body was the ugliest, most unfortunate baby I had ever seen. The child, indeed if it was a child, resembled a frog. It had widely placed protruding eyes, set beneath a broad pronounced brow. What counted for a nose was a small, unformed mound with two tiny holes, and his mouth was a wide, lipless slash with a deep cleft, drawn back to reveal the top of his pink gum where two large white teeth stuck through like baby tusks. But it was his poor hands and feet that were my undoing, for as he waved them indignantly in the air, I saw that they were webbed.

It was at that moment blessed oblivion hit me and the last I heard was Matilda's lilting voice ringing in my ears in admonishment: 'The sins of the father are always visited upon his sons, Faulkes de Breauté, and I have brought you living proof!'

Chapter 2

I woke in the busy castle kitchen with a plump, ruddy-faced woman called Merri sponging my forehead and tutting at all the fuss and commotion that had accompanied our arrival. Behind her the head cook was instructing the kitchen staff in the preparation of the food, and he didn't look too pleased to have me interrupting this obviously complicated business.

'I hear you and your father had the misfortune to meet Faulkes de Breauté on his own where he could get up to his evil mischief,' Merri commented, putting down the sponge and placing a mug of water in my hand. 'It's beyond me why Sir William keeps him here, only that he's a favourite of young Prince John, and William likes to keep in John's favour.' She wrinkled her nose in distaste at this idea, and began bustling about placing great platters of meat, hard cheeses, dried fruit and other delicacies onto a big table in the centre of the room in preparation for the evening meal, pausing only to instruct a kitchen hand to start transporting some of it to the hall where the household had gathered to eat. Immediately my mouth began to water for I had never seen such fare: great hams hung from the ceiling, and steaming pots of what smelt like mutton stew stood by a huge hearth keeping warm. Alongside them a scullion boy sat turning a pig on a spit over the fire, his face bright red from the heat, and for a moment I watched fascinated as a pastry chef placed the crust on a delicious looking pie.

Seeing my eyes following the food longingly, Merri removed some meat from a platter and pressed it into my hand. 'You're far too thin. Nothing but skin and bones, I do declare!' she said, patting her own ample stomach fondly. Her eyes widened momentarily as I greedily shoved it in my mouth, not caring that the juices rolled down my chin in oily rivulets. Chuckling, she passed me some more, her eyes twinkling merrily in the light from the kitchen fire.

'Where's my Father?' I asked between chews, mopping my chin with my sleeve.

'In the still room with my lady being stitched up, I expect,' she said. 'Oh, he'll be as right as rain, does lovely neat little stitches, does milady,' she added, seeing my face and coughing as a cloud of smoke billowed from the fire.

Glancing about to check that cook was out of hearing distance, she suddenly leaned towards me. 'Is it true about the faery changeling, then?' she asked, her face registering her disgust.

'What? Well, yes I suppose so,' I replied, remembering the child with a shudder. I glanced about myself, conscious of the strange, sideways looks I was getting from the other cooks and servants milling around the kitchen.

'De Breauté is saying it's witchcraft on the part of milady and Jeanette,' she said scornfully. 'But of course, Sir William is having none of it. He and the Lady Matilda might not see eye to eye on occasions, but he won't have her being accused of being a witch under his own roof!' she finished and picking up a platter she turned towards the fire where she began to cut thick slices of meat from the pig. 'Now,' she said, once the platter was full and she had deposited it on the table amongst the other dishes, 'Cook doesn't like women in his kitchen - though he tolerates me because he knows that I can roast a pheasant or dress a peacock as well as he can! Anyhow, seeing as you're fully recovered, we had best give you something to do, girl. You can do duty in the hall tonight, and Bertha here,' she nodded towards a plump, red-haired girl who had just slipped in through the door, 'can show you where you are to sleep later. But first things first, you'll not do duty wearing that disgusting apparel,' she said, eyeing my bloodstained homespun with a critical eye. 'So off with you both to find Hawise the chatelaine and see if she can't dig you out something decent to wear.'

And with that she shooed us both firmly out of the kitchen, shutting the door tightly behind us.

We found Hawise in a small ante-chamber away from the kitchen in the lower part of the keep scratching figures on the household rolls. She was a small, prim woman of an uncertain age – she could have been anywhere between forty to sixty I guessed - dressed in a neat brown woollen dress with a pristine white wimple over salt and pepper hair.

Hearing our request, she looked me up and down and wrinkled her nose at the sight of my bloody skirts. Then, standing, she removed a key from a chain that was slung around her waist and crossed to a large coffer wedged in a corner. Opening it, she rummaged around for a moment or two before finally emerging grasping a serviceable white shift and a dreary woollen kirtle with front lacings.

She frowned, eyeing me up and down expertly. 'These should fit you, you're about the same size as Nell was - she died of the small pox before Yuletide so she won't be needing them.'

Horrified, I snatched away the hand that I had extended to receive the clothes, and surreptitiously wiped it on my own skirt as if it were infected.

Hawise snorted, and Bertha stifled a giggle. 'You won't catch it from these, girl, they've been boiled within an inch of their life. Come on, take them,' she said waving them impatiently in front of my face. 'Nell won't be needing them where she is, so you might as well make use of them until we can get you some more.'

Feeling slightly foolish, I accepted the garments, and she nodded her approval before rummaging in the coffer again and emerging with some warm woollen hose and a pair of leather shoes that had seen better days.

Seeing that I still hadn't moved she tutted and began to pull at the neck of my gown. 'If you don't get a move on I shall send you away with those rags to be burnt!' she muttered darkly.

Realising that she was being serious, I hastily began to remove my soiled dress and put on Nell's old clothes which were, as Hawise had stated, more or less my size. 'Well at least your clean, girl! Some of you peasants come to us stinking worse than a weasel!' she said, wrinkling her nose and sniffing the air around me when I had finished, leaving me glad that my father had insisted I wet my kerchief in the icy water of the Adur before we reached castle, for if I had not, I had the impression that she would have scrubbed me from head to toe herself.

Giving me one final inspection, she waved her hand towards the door in dismissal. 'You'll do. Go and attend to your duties now, and in the morning, you can take over Nell's, which means that you will rise at dawn and lay the fires before taking the mistress some food to break her fast. After that you can spend some time helping the maids with their mending in the sewing room before attending to the children. Do you understand?'

'Yes, Ma'am,' I said, bobbing a curtsey. Then weighed down by the enormity of the tasks awaiting me, I turned and followed Bertha out of the chamber, practically running to keep up with her.

'The hall is on the next floor,' Bertha panted later, as she hurried me back outside and up a wooden staircase next to the wall of the keep. Once inside the hall she came to a sudden halt and began to smooth down her skirts and check her appearance in the metal plate that hung on the wall serving as a mirror. Then, when satisfied, she grabbed me by the arm and dragged me unceremoniously after her again, this time straight into the throng of people waiting to wash their hands in the ewers that lined a trestle table just inside the door, where she made me wash mine for the second time that day.

The hall itself I saw was a large, one-roomed structure, aisled like a church with two rows of wooden posts supporting a loft ceiling and a narrow-archway leading to a set of newel stairs at the back. Along its length rows of sconces flickered bringing light to the dark corners, and on the far right-hand wall a welcoming fire burned in a hearth.

Through the smoke, I could just make out Matilda seated on the dais behind at a long table covered in snowy white napery, and laid with silver cups, platters, salt bowls and spoons, all of which glinted brightly in the light of the candles branches that blazed above them. The cost of the candles alone was not lost on me, accustomed as I was to living by firelight with only the occasional candle if we could afford it. Alongside her sat a flaxen haired man with a florid face whom I took to be her husband, William de Braose. His back was to her, and he was deep in conversation with a clergyman who was illustrating a point by stabbing the table savagely with his finger. A squire was serving them, scooping meat off a large platter onto their trenchers, before topping up their goblets with wine.

The rest of the household sat on long rows of trestle tables along the middle of the hall, with those of a higher station, such as the knights and ladies in service to the de Braoses, seated at the tables nearest to the dais along with the eldest of Matilda's children and their nurses. Everyone was industriously transferring succulent pieces of meat to their own trenchers using the small daggers they carried on their person for the purpose. There was no silver in evidence on these tables, only serviceable earthenware and the odd wooden bowl.

Seeing me gawping, Bertha clicked her tongue, grabbed my arm, and hauled me unceremoniously over to a trestle table loaded with wine and beer pitchers. Under the instruction of the steward she handed me one of the beer pitchers, indicating that I was to make my way around the hall and top up people's cups. Nervously I glanced around and, seeing Faulkes de Breauté sitting at front with some rough looking soldiers, I resolved to stay at the back of the room out of his sight.

It was getting late when I spotted Jeannette slipping into the hall from a door concealed by a tapestry I'd not noticed before, wearing a strange expression on her face. She paused for a moment as if unsure about something, then making her way to Faulkes de Breauté's table she stooped and muttered something in his ear. Instantly his hand whipped out and, grabbing her by the arm, he pulled her closer and hissed something in her face, spraying spittle everywhere.

Immediately, a hush fell up and down the hall as people strained to see what was happening at de Breauté's table, for rumour about the child, the nature of its deformities and its relation to de Breauté was already rife. If he had thought to keep it quiet, then he had thought wrong.

One of the knights, a big man with a long bushy beard harbouring several crumbs of bread and other stray morsels of food, nudged his companion and said in a loud voice: 'Perhaps Jeanette needs help changing the babe's clout, eh – must be difficult with three legs waving at you and two bums to pad!' Then with a guffaw at his own humour, he slapped his companion several times on the back, making him splutter and knock his trencher onto the floor where it was immediately leapt on by several dogs.

Almost at once a ripple of laughter broke out up and down the hall as this sally was whispered to those who had missed it. Furiously, de Breauté looked around, his face red and contorted with anger, then throwing down his napkin he stood and stalked from the room with a nervous looking Jeanette in tow.

Up on the high table, Matilda started to rise, but was prevented by Sir William who grasped her viciously by the arm and pulled her towards him to snarl something unintelligible in her ear, causing a flicker of fear to mar her face. For a moment she looked like she might defy him, but then she seemed to think better of it, and, sitting back quietly she picked up her spoon and began to resume her meal, still throwing anxious glances at the door from time to time.

A long silence had fallen over the hall following de Breauté's sudden exit, only interrupted by the occasional cough or the scrape of a chair as someone got up to leave. This seemed to unsettle William who, banging a large hand on the table in frustration, bellowed at his squire to fetch the harpist.

The harpist, when he arrived, was young man, fair complexioned and lean, with a shock of blond hair, freckles and an engaging grin. He also had a hunched back which made him appear as if he had one shoulder higher than the other. A matter that did not deter him one bit as he settled himself down on a small stool near the dais, and after a small adjustment to his harp strings, began to play a haunting melody to which he supplied the words in a surprisingly clear and harmonious voice.

Gradually the hall settled down, and the subject of Faulkes de Breauté and the faery child was replaced by speculation about the weather, the sowing of the harvest, and other matters relating to castle life. I had almost put the matter out of my mind when, as I neared the high tables bearing yet another pitcher of wine, a lady with frizzy grey hair barely contained under her wimple, and eyes like currants in a bun, leaned towards her neighbours and whispered dramatically: 'I heard tell that de Breauté's child is a silkie child!'

'There's no such thing as silkies!' scoffed a portly red-faced man sitting opposite her, pushing aside his trencher and goblet to stare at her with dislike. 'They're just a figment of the imagination of over-wrought peasants.'

'Why ever not?' she retorted, miffed by his scornful response. 'I heard say he found her one night on his travels bathing naked in the sea - always riding the length and breadth of the land causing trouble with Prince John he is!' she added, as though this explained it. 'Anyway, he stole her skin so I hear. Stole it so that she could never go back to the ocean!' she finished, wrinkling her nose in distaste.

I paused to listen as I poured wine into a goblet proffered by a man already half in his cups. I had been brought up on tales of silkies from my grandmother. I remembered listening in awe, my eyes transfixed on her wrinkled face as she wove stories about the sleek, dark-eyed creatures from the misty days of her youth. One particular story had always stuck in my mind, and it still made my skin prickle when I recalled it.

'Silkies,' she'd said one dark, stormy night when the wind was whistling through the trees outside and rattling through the thatch, 'are seal-folk that come on to land to shed their skins and take on the human form - they can often be found dancing naked under the moon …'

That was something I already knew, but I'd settled myself down by the fire anyway, chewing a piece of dried apple from the previous year's harvest, glad to have my mind taken away from the storm.

'Anyway,' she'd confided, her voice hushed so that my mother didn't overhear and scold her for stuffing my head full of nonsense, 'if a man o' a woman sees a silkie and desires them for a husband or wife, all they have to do is steal their skin. They're trapped on land then, you see - unless of course, the silkie later finds his skin. Then, and only then, can they return to the sea …'

I remember pausing at that point, a piece of apple halfway to my mouth. Something in the tone of her voice made me shiver. I'd wanted happy stories, but the one she was telling had begun to unnerve me. My mother, sensing the atmosphere, had looked up briefly from where she was tending the babies and frowned.

'Mind, it's a bad thing to trap a silkie,' she'd continued, not noticing, her myopic eyes looking far beyond my mother, way back into the past. 'I wed a silkie, you see, so I should know. I saw a silkie man and desired him, and so I stole his skin ...'

Her eyes had filled with tears then, and I remember putting down the piece of apple and leaning forward to awkwardly pat the soft folds of her upper arm in what I hoped was a reassuring manner.

'It always ends badly,' she'd said after a while, her voice barely a whisper so that I had to lean closer to hear. 'The children, our children ... well, some said they were faery children ... on account of their hands being webbed, you see. But anyway, one day they found his skin and together they went back to the ocean. That was the last time I ever saw him. Him or my babies ...'

And with that she'd begun rocking backwards and forwards, keening in a high-pitched voice until my mother came and sang her a lullaby, like she would have sung to a child. And like a child my grandmother fell asleep. Her tears still wet on her face.

Perhaps then, that was what I had seen earlier. A silkie. A poor, helpless, little silkie. Trapped on land forever.

Shivering, I pushed the thought away, not wanting to explore it further, for there was little doubt that something of the otherworld had visited us this day.

And perhaps my grandmother was not so touched after all …

It was well past compline when Lady Matilda rose and went to say goodnight to her children who had been put to bed earlier by their nurses, and by the time the trestle tables had been removed I was exhausted for it had been a long and eventful day.

Merri saw to it that Bertha and I had something to eat in the kitchen, then she charged me with one more task before I could retire. Pulling a brick from the fire, she wrapped it in cloth and instructed that I take it up to Matilda's bed to warm it because Jennette was nowhere to be found. 'Mind you knock before you enter,' she warned me before going back to washing the pile of pans stacked on the table alongside a large pot of water.

Bertha showed me the way, yawning as we made our way back to the hall and through the bodies laid out in the rushes around the hearth where the remains of a small fire still glowed. The mingled scent of sweat and urine made me feel nauseous, and even though I had been brought up crammed into a small cottage with my parents and siblings, I still covered my nose in distaste when the man beneath my feet rolled over and emitted a small fart.

At last she pointed towards the set of newel stairs at the back of the room. 'Lady Matilda's chamber is up there,' she said, 'but you can bed down with me in here when you're finished,' she added as, stifling another yawn, she pushed aside the tapestry hiding the entrance to the chamber Jeanette had appeared from earlier, and disappeared. At the top of the stairs I paused, then knocked once briefly on the narrow oak door in front of me. Getting no reply, I knocked again, rather more sharply this time. Still getting no reply, I pushed the door open and peered into the dimly lit chamber.

Matilda was standing staring into the fire with her back to me. I coughed to get her attention, but she remained totally still, engrossed in the flickering flames. Quickly, I tiptoed to the bed and deposited the brick, before crossing and gently touching her shoulder to gain her attention.

When she still didn't respond, I moved hesitantly into her line of vision, only to recoil when I saw her face. She seemed to be in some sort of a trance: her pupils were widely dilated and her unblinking eyes were moving back and forth as if she was witnessing something taking place deep within the burning embers. Then, without warning, great fat tears began to spill out of them and pour down her cheeks, where they hung for a moment before falling silently into the rushes at her feet.

'Oh, milady! What is it ... what's the matter?' It came out in a whisper, hoarse with fear. Getting no response, my eyes roamed the room anxiously. Immediately, I felt the tiny hairs on back of my neck rise in terror. It was icy cold despite the fire, and in the corners where the dark shadows lurked, I fancied I saw something move. Then suddenly a great gust of wind came from nowhere, blowing out the only remaining sconce and banging the shutters against the wall with a resounding crash.

Uttering a shriek, I turned and was about to flee, when abruptly Matilda's hand shot out and grabbed my arm. Squeaking with terror I tried to wrench it out of her icy grip, but somehow I found myself transfixed to the spot.

Look, Ailith ... look, and you will see ...

It was the voice, the same one as earlier.

Look, Ailith ... The voice urged again.

Slowly, unwillingly, I turned my head and looked into the fire. At first, I could see nothing. Then the flames gradually resolved themselves into a shaky scene.

Faulkes de Breauté had just finished wrapping an awkward looking bundle in canvas and was tying it with rope – my instinct told me immediately that it was the faery changeling.

Feeling sickened, I watched as, reaching for a heavy boulder, he began to bludgeon the bundle repeatedly until all that remained was a red, soggy mess. At last, with casual cruelness, he weighted it down with stones before picking it up and hurling it as far into the river as possible where it sank, leaving nothing but a ripple on the surface. The look on his face when he turned around was pure evil mixed with triumph.

The scene began to flicker then, but just before it faded, I spotted Jeanette in the background on her knees praying, and I wondered if she was praying for de Breauté's soul or repenting her own sin of allowing him to do such a terrible thing.

Suddenly Matilda blinked, rubbed her eyes, and seemed to come too out of her trance-like state, giving a start of surprise to find me in her chamber. As soon as she released her grip on my arm I fled, and that night I lay awake thinking that I could not stay in the castle a moment longer.

But I did, my dearest Matilda. I stayed with you to the end. And oh, what a terrible ending it was that you had to bear …

Matilda, I learned over time, had a reputation for being fey amongst the common folk. In Wales they called her the Lady of Hay because she was said to have built the Castle of Hay all by herself in one night, carrying the stones in her apron. I knew this was fanciful, but still it sent a shiver down my spine, for there surely was a lot of the fey about Matilda I came to realise.

Sometimes, on wild stormy nights, we would search the castle only to find her high on the castle ramparts, arms outstretched, with her hair whipping in the wind and tears streaming down her face. But she never remembered, and always seemed surprised to find herself shivering uncontrollably and being stripped of her wet clothes back in her chamber.

Of course, as a young maid her strange behaviour frightened and alarmed me, and I would cross myself anxiously and say prayers for her soul believing that she was possessed by evil spirits. As I came to know her better though, she confided in me, saying that she was born under an eclipse and that she could see her own future written in the stars. And that it was dark. 'Dark, Ailith,' she would say. 'As dark as that eclipse.'

Poor, haunted Matilda. We did not know then, but the storms presaged the shadows which would haunt you in your future life. And even if we had, you could not have escaped them. For that was your fate. And we soon came to learn that fate was an ever-present mistress.

Chapter 3

September 1182, Bramber Castle, England.

It was Merri who informed me that the household was to travel to Wales for the winter. Matilda had taken to bed with a fever and had asked me to fetch some honeyed mead from the kitchen to help ease the symptoms. Jeanette's health had faded fast recently, and gradually I had taken over the role of Matilda's personal maid and confidant - a matter not over-looked by others, who regarded me with some small suspicion.

Merri seemed to like me, though, and had taken me under her wing since my father had left for home. Even Cook had got used to me appearing at every spare moment, although he would still shoo me out if there were too many people in his kitchen.

On this occasion, however, Merri was alone. She was bustling around preparing the honeyed mead, and telling me the latest gossip about Elena, a serving wench who was said to be with child by one of the grooms, when suddenly a flurry of activity broke out in the bailey, signalling the arrival of a number of horsemen who had obviously ridden very hard.

Merri broke off in mid-sentence. 'That must be Roger de Mortimer. I heard he was coming.' Crossing to the window embrasure, she eyed the men and horses milling around the yard being greeted by William and his steward Sam Skeet.

I flung a questioning glance at her hoping she would enlighten me, and she shrugged. 'I suppose you will find out soon enough that we are to visit Sir William's estates in Gwent for the winter – we are to stay at Abergavenny. From there, William will tour round his other castles collecting rents and tithes and hearing minor cases. Sir William,' she continued, and I detected a strained edge to her voice as she said his name, 'says that there are signs of insurrection among the Welsh. The Sherriff of Herefordshire, Ranulf Poer, has written to say he is expecting trouble at any moment, and that he's already in the process of fortifying Dingstow Castle in readiness. Sir Roger has further news for his lordship, I gather. His own estate is at Wigmore in Hereford - that's on the border of England and Wales,' she said, as though I should know, having never been further than Bramber.

Suddenly she shivered and crossed herself. 'Mark my words, there's bad blood between the Welsh and Sir William, for he has committed a great evil against the people of Gwent.' She turned away from the window abruptly as though she could no longer stand the sight of him. 'Rather than strengthening his strongholds he should be attending to his conscience in church!' she said rather more vehemently than she had intended, I think, and crossing herself again she glanced nervously at the door to check that no one was listening.

She paused then and seemed reluctant to say anything more. But I confess I pressed her, and perhaps I shouldn't have. But I was intrigued. I already knew that William had other estates, mostly in Wales, as messengers were often dispatched to the small garrisons of men that held the castles of Radnor, Hay, Brecknock and Abbergavenny. However, I was eager to know more about Abergavenny because Abergavenny was seldom mentioned, and when it was it was in hushed voices and with eyes made wide with fear.

And Merri knew why.

She turned away from me at that point to move around a big oak table in the middle of the kitchen laden with raw meat waiting to be put into piecrusts; ostensibly to shoo away two cats trying to steal fish from a platter in the pantry, but really to gain time to think. Then, shooing the cats unceremoniously out into the courtyard, she seemed to make a decision and, crossing herself again, she turned back to me and began to tell me the terrible tale of Abergavenny, checking every now and then that no one was eavesdropping on us.

'There was a massacre there. A terrible, bloody massacre that took place at Yuletide back in the year of 1175,' she began in a hushed voice. I saw that she had tears in her eyes, one of which had escaped and was rolling down her cheek.

'Sir William,' she continued, spitting out his name, 'invited the Princes of Wales: Seisyll ap Dyfnwal, his son Geoffrey, and some other gentlemen from Gwent to the castle for a Yuletide feast.' She paused the story momentarily to dab at her eyes with her apron, for tears were running openly down her face by then; great fat tears that rolled down her plump cheeks and threatened to soak the rushes on the floor.

Hastily I took her by the arm and led her to a chair by the fire where I poured her a mug of small beer from a jug on the table, patting her shoulder in what I hoped was a calming manner as I was not sure what else to do.

After taking a few sips of the beer, she gave a heavy sigh and continued, still dabbing her eyes with her apron every now and then. 'He murdered them,' she said in a stricken voice, looking through me as if she were in the past and reliving the horror of it. 'He brought them to the great hall, and he murdered them by hacking them to death with knives and swords. When he'd done that, he sent men to Seisyll's court where they slew his baby son and the rest of his household. Including the women and children. All except his wife Gwladus, whom they took hostage. Only a few fortunate survived, and they were Seisyll's sons and kin who happened to be pages or squires in other houses at the time. I fear that they will want revenge sooner or later.'

Suddenly she stood, slopping beer everywhere, and grabbing a cleaver off the shelf she crossed to the table and began to attack the meat still resting there. I watched in horror as bits of flesh and blood splattered the front of her apron, and flew down amongst the rushes on the floor, like a graphic re-enactment of the horrific deed she was describing.

'He hacked them to death,' she sobbed, still attacking the meat. 'Men, women and babies. Like meat for the pot. He spared no one! No one!'

Rushing to her I tried to prize the cleaver out of her grasp, for by now she was demented with grief, but she was surprisingly strong and she put up a good resistance. Quite suddenly, however, she relinquished the cleaver to me and made a small, beseeching gesture with her hand - almost as if she could make me understand the enormity of what she was telling me. And then returning to the seat she'd vacated, she laid her head on her arms and remained that way for some time.

Wordlessly, I stared at her, too shocked to speak. Finally, she lifted her head and looked straight into my eyes.

'They call him the Ogre of Abergavenny, you know – William. He said King Henry ordered it as justice for the murder of his Uncle Henry by the Welsh the previous year,' she said, her gaze never leaving my face. 'The next day, however, the Welsh rallied together and retaliated. Well they would, wouldn't they?' she questioned, shaking her head as if astounded that this obvious fact was overlooked by William. 'And for every Welshman William murdered, two Englishmen were cut down in his place in the aftermath –' She broke off abruptly then, and all I could hear was the mead bubbling on the hearth, and the occasional murmur from the men in the bailey as their horses were led away to be stabled.

Finally, in a voice so strained that I could barely hear, she whispered. 'My son, Sedwick, who was only five, and my man, Alfred, were among those massacred. They had accompanied Sir William to Abergavenny. Alfred was William's steward back then –'

Sighing, she stood and turned so that her back was to me and she was staring deep into the heart of the fire. For a moment I thought that was the end of the story, but suddenly she crouched down, her head so close to the flames that I feared her wimple might catch light. Then as calmly as if she were asking me to pass a crock pan, she said. 'They roasted my son alive, and made my sweet Alfred watch ...'

She said no more. She didn't need to. The rest hovered unspoken in the air, mingling with the soft sound of her sobs.

For a long time I stood still, just staring at her back in horror. Unable to speak as the cold of the stone floor seeped through the rushes, and rushed up through my body, until it was white in my brain …

That night I had the red dream. It was a dream I had had only once, a very long time ago. Since then I'd tried to bury it somewhere deep within the recesses of my mind; in a place where it couldn't frighten me anymore.

A woman writhed on a bed in the middle of a hot, airless chamber. Her face wasn't visible, but her distended body was arched up in strains of agony, swollen with the child she was struggling to bear. Around her, the midwife and her attendants gathered trying to ease her suffering.

Helplessly locked in my dream world, I watched in horror as with each agonizing pain she screamed. Only in my dream, as her pains got worse, her screams got shriller. And each time her screams got shriller, a new voice would join in, until finally there were hundreds of voices echoing around the chamber like banshees.

Then suddenly the scene changed, and the chamber began to fill with blood. A great tide of red, sticky blood oozing up the walls. I could smell it in my dream: sticky and sweet, but nobody in the chamber noticed it. Clutching at my bedcovers in horror I tossed and turned; desperately trying to cry out, to warn her. But she could not hear me.

Finally, she arched her back in one final spasm of agony, and the baby slithered like a fish into the arms of the midwife, leaving her to fall back onto the bed in exhaustion, the sea of blood still rising and lapping around her.

This time the dream was different, though.

As she fell back, I clearly saw her face. It was Matilda.

Merri told me much later that her eldest son Will was born on the night of the massacre of Abergavenny.

Chapter 4

Roger de Mortimer left early the next morning, leaving behind news so grave that William immediately pushed forward his preparations to take the household to Wales and fortify his strongholds there. Ranulf Poer had voiced particular concerns regarding the safety of Abergavenny, strongly advising William head to Gwent and fortify that particular garrison first.

'He writes to tell me of grave goings on,' I overheard William saying to Matilda whilst they were breaking their fast in their chamber. 'What remains of Seisyll's kin are now grown. He warns there are rumours circulating that they are burning for revenge and the constable is getting jittery.'

I noticed that Matilda made no reply, but kept her head firmly bent over her trencher. After a moment or two William threw down the letter, gave an exasperated sigh, and stalked out of the room, flinging instructions at hovering servants as he went.

Not long after that, Matilda, unable to finish her food, pushed aside her trencher, picked up the letter, and began to read.

The moving of a large household from one castle to another, I soon discovered, was no easy affair. The cook, grumbling, had to pack his pots and pans and organise food and beverage for the long journey: wastrel bread, dried meats and fruit, salted fish, (herring mainly), cheeses, wine and water skins, and nameless other barrels of food and drink that would sustain the household as it travelled, all had to be packed and carried out to the waiting wagons.

In the stables, the grooms were tasked with choosing the right horses for the journey: large, sturdy horses were needed to pull the wagons filled with household goods, whilst nimble packhorses were required to negotiate the narrow, winding mountain tracks and forests trails ahead of the main baggage train in order to warn constable of each castle to the imminent arrival its master. I watched as William's huge stallion Demon was led out of the stable towards the farrier's shed to be re-shod for the journey. Already the whites of his eyes were showing and at his side a stable boy was dodging his sideways chomps - I wouldn't have fancied my chances of getting anywhere near his hooves that day, or any other for that matter.

Merri paused on her way back from an errand to the church to watch as more servants ran between the bakehouse, dairy, grain stores and kitchen, and back again, with harassed looks on their faces. Behind us great puffs of smoke wafted from the forge accompanied by the resounding noise of hammer on metal as weapons and horseshoes were fashioned and wheels were mended ready for the carts.

'Wales,' Merri said suddenly, 'is a dangerous place to travel. Tribes of men hide out in the hills waiting to ambush any unprepared party that pass their way – Sir William is organising a posse of his most skilled soldiers and scouts to accompany us ...' This seemed to worry rather than console her, and she paused to chew on her bottom lip, a gesture I had often seen her do when she was unhappy or distressed. 'But it's Seisyll's kin I fear,' she continued after a while, picking up where she had left off. 'They have never forgiven Sir William for Abergavenny. It is they who pose the most threat. They hold grudges and will be plotting against him even as we speak. They will bide their time and then they will strike, mark my words!' she finished, crossing herself with a shiver.

Patting her on the arm, I opened my mouth hoping to say something to allay her fears just as a gaggle of enraged geese charged around the corner of the stables, honking dementedly in pursuit of a small boy brandishing a stick. He skidded past us, making us jump back out of the way as, arms akimbo, he changed direction and bolted towards the steep wooden steps leading up to the keep, a look of fear mixed with excitement on his face.

'I see young Will has been baiting the geese again,' Merri muttered, watching his sandy head bobbing as he charged up the steps. 'Just like his father baits the Welsh,' she added, so quietly that I almost didn't hear her. Then turning away, she crossed herself once more and made after Will, shooing the agitated geese out of her way as she went.

Sighing, I turned back to organise the stowing of the bed from Matilda and William's chamber onto a large cart that had been dragged into the bailey for the purpose, when suddenly I heard the sound of a commotion floating up from the bridge down over the ditch in the outer ward. Moments later men milled around, shouting at one another as two soldiers dragging a handcart made their way through the gatehouse, followed in their wake by several women wailing loudly. As they filed past me towards the family's private chapel, more people joined them, and the volume of wailing and shouting increased.

Attracted by the noise, William strode into the bailey just as the cart was deposited in front of him.

Elbowing several people out of the way, one of the soldiers grabbed hold of the edge of the tarpaulin covering the contents of the cart, and with a deft flick of his wrist it was on the floor.

Silence settled over the bailey, broken only by the soft sobbing of the women. Lying on the cart, their faces swollen and purple and their tongues protruding from blackened lips, were the bodies of the soldier and the young girl that had argued with de Breauté on the day I arrived at Bramber Castle.

De Breauté had not been seen since that night. But it was widely known that young Prince John had passed by with his retinue on his way to Shoreham some days past to meet with some important silk merchants before they set sail for the east ...

We left for Wales the next morning, after attending mass in the chapel kneeling on the cold floor where we prayed for the souls of the dead soldier and maid. I shivered. The image of their swollen faces and the rope marks around their necks would be forever imprinted on my mind. As would the image of Faulkes de Breauté the last time I had seen him, in the fire. Bludgeoning a helpless child to death.

On the alter, the communion candles guttered suddenly, sending smoke streaming down the nave just as Matilda knelt to receive the Eucharist from Ralph the chaplain. I took a sharp intake of breath. Around her the shadows lengthened, and instead of dispersing the smoke formed itself into ghostly fingers which seemed to linger over her head. Then she stood, and Ralph made the sign of the cross and started intoning a psalm, and they were gone.

But I knew that Mistress Destiny was once again singling Matilda out. Marking her as her own so that even in a place of God she was not safe.

It was bright outside and for once I was glad to leave the gloom of the chapel which usually gave me such comfort. In the bailey, the household milled about making its final preparations for the journey. The noise was deafening as people said their goodbyes. Apart from the constable and a small garrison of soldiers to protect the castle, only the youngest of Matilda's children and their nurses were staying, together with some of the infirm and those too old to ride. Flandrina, Matilda's daughter, a studious child, was setting off for a convent on the morrow where she would be educated until she was old enough to become a novice.

My search for Matilda found her standing at the foot of the wooden steps leading up to the keep saying her goodbyes to the babies. Standing dutifully behind her were Mattie, Will, Giles and Reginald, the only ones who were considered old enough to accompany us on the long journey.

Phillip, now a chubby three-year-old, was standing forlornly on the steps with his twin sister Bertha, his bottom lip wobbling as Matilda made her way down the line.

'Why can't I come?' he demanded tearfully again as she stooped to kiss John, the youngest of the brood, asleep in his nurse's arms.

Sighing, Matilda turned back to him. 'Because you're still a baby,' she said, crouching down and gently stroking a curl of soft, copper-coloured hair back from his wet face.

Like his older sister Matilda, four-year-old Philip was the only other of her offspring to inherit her green eyes and striking hair, only his hair was, if anything, even brighter than theirs. The rest of her children were grey-eyed and sandy-haired, even his twin sister Bertha, traits which were inherited from William's side of the family.

'I'm not a baby!' Phillip cried, his face screwed up in misery. 'I can ride as well as Mattie, Will, Reginald and Giles, and you are letting them go!' He threw an anguished look at his four eldest siblings.

Will opened his mouth to say something but was quickly silenced by Mattie who stepped in front of him and bent down to put her arm around Phillip's shoulders.

'Mama would like it if you would care for the puppies until our return,' she said, referring to the deerhound puppies that William the Marshall had presented to Matilda on his way to one of his tourneys a few months back.

William the Marshall was the head of the young King Henry's mesnie as well as his tutor in chivalry, and he and young Henry had built up quite a reputation on the tourney fields in France. They were always made welcome at Bramber when travelling south to sail for the far coast, and as a mark of friendship he had presented Matilda with the puppies, thinking that they would please her greatly.

'This one,' he'd said with a twinkle in his eye, handing Matilda a bundle of sleek grey fur with oversize paws, 'is Gizelle, named after a certain young French lady with whom young Henry is enamoured at the moment - although we mustn't let Marguerite know that!' he'd added, referring to young Henry's intended and winking blatantly at Matilda.'

Henry had scowled and pretended to gaze out of the window, annoyed at the teasing remark, for although he had been crowned King during his father's lifetime, he had been afforded none of the power or the responsibility that came with the title and continued to be treated as a child. A matter that he resented greatly.

'And this one,' William had continued, ignoring Henry's rigid back and depositing another grey ball of fur on Matilda's lap, 'is Roland – well you know how much I like the Song of Roland!' he'd grinned before throwing Matilda a look of apology and breaking out into a very clear tenor.

Charles the king, our Lord and Sovereign,
Full seven years hath sojourned in Spain,
Conquered the land, and won the western main,
Now no fortress against him doth remain,
No city walls are left for him to gain,
Save Sarraguce, that sits on high mountain.
Marsile its King, who feareth not God's name,
Mahumet's man, he invokes Apollin's aid,
Nor wards off ills that shall to him attai-

I suppressed a smile, remembering that he had broken off abruptly when Matilda, giving a sudden squeal, had shoved the puppy back into his arms just in time to avoid the golden arc of urine that splashed onto the rushes at her feet.

Phillip listened carefully to Mattie before turning his tearful green eyes on his mother who nodded.

'That is so, Phillip,' she replied. 'You would be doing me a great favour by looking after the puppies until I return. And of course, you must also look after your baby brother and sisters too.' Then throwing a grateful smile to Mattie, she turned and hurried off in search of William who was somewhere in the melee checking the horses and provisions, the state of the wagons, and whatever else he could think of before we set off.

After a quick meal of hard wastrel bread and equally hard cheese, the household was impatient to make a move. I made my way over to the stables where Mattie and the other children were seated on their ponies looking bored as they watched Matilda and William organise the re-loading of a wagon that had hit a rut and spilled over blocking the way to the gatehouse.

I eyed my own prospective mount warily. It was a mule, I was reliably told. A shaggy brown one to be exact. As far as I was concerned it had no redeeming features - it was barrel chested, with spindly legs and long ears that twitched and made me nervous. At my approach it lazily swung its big head around and gazed at me with a gimlet eye as if to warn me against any further advancement upon its person.

Quickly, I took a step back, only to find myself standing on the toes of the head groom.

'Steady, young lady!' he said, gingerly removing me from his foot.

'I'm so sorry,' I rushed, I –

My eyes widened and I froze in mid speech as, without warning, the mule swung its body around to join its head, and broke into a trot, keeping its brow low enough so that the hard bone impacted with a thud.

'Oof … get off you great oaf!' the muffled voice of the groom floated out from somewhere beneath the mule which was now nudging around his person frantically. Suddenly the mule's shaggy head rose triumphantly. Gripped between its teeth was a large piece of gingerbread wrapped in some old parchment.

'When are you going to learn to ask nicely?' groaned the groom from his position on the ground. 'You've just met Gingerbread, mistress,' he directed at me.

'No need to ask why he's called Gingerbread, then!' I replied.

It was later than William had anticipated by the time the household trundled noisily out of the bailey. The groom, who introduced himself to me as Simon, handed me a bundle full of the gingerbread with instructions to ingratiate myself with its namesake by giving him a piece each time I mounted. 'That way he will behave, mistress. But mind you don't hang about like I did,' he said wryly, 'else he might try to help himself again!' And with that he hoisted me on to Gingerbread's back and, giving his rump a little tap to get him on his way, he saluted me and went to join the other grooms.

The day had started cloudily, but once we were on the road it soon became crisp and clear. Beneath me, a remarkably well-behaved Gingerbread was briskly making his way over the slippery leaf mulch that covered the narrow track through the forest. Soon we would make our way along the lee of the downs and on to places that I had never even heard of before I arrived at Bramber.

Matilda made her way back from the front of the baggage train until she found me. 'Where on earth did Gingerbread come from?' she asked, frowning in consternation. 'I thought he had been put out to grass years ago – on account of cook keep finding him in his kitchen stealing his food?'

'Couldn't bear to part with him, my lady,' Simon replied for me, reining in beside us. 'Besides, he's the perfect mount for Ailith here. Perfect gent when he's had his cake! And, winking at me, he moved once more to the rear of the train.

We rode along in companionable silence for a while. Above us the sky flickered blue through the skeletal branches of oak and ash, what leaves they had left turned to gold and russet and clinging incongruously like bright jewels on the dried-up arms of old women. Occasionally, something stirred in the undergrowth or skittered away into the darkness of the forest where the thick bracken shielded it from our eyes.

'We hope to get to Winchester in a day or two,' Matilda said suddenly. 'But until then I have no idea where we will stop for the night – though there are some inns at Pulborough where we might find some beds, else we will have to make camp.'

She glanced around. The day was bright and clear, but it would be a different tale at night. Then it would be freezing and there were the wolves to think about. I shuddered and pulled my woollen cloak tighter around my shoulders.

'After that,' she continued, not noticing, 'we aim to ride to Gloucester and from there to Radnor as fast as we can. That's where we will begin to enter the deeper forests and valleys beyond the welsh borders.' She shivered and crossed herself. 'There is always danger in Wales for us,' she said, as much to herself as me. 'William did not abide by Welsh law and pay the *galanas* due to Seisyll's remaining family after Abergavenny – that's compensation,' she added, seeing that I didn't understand. 'As far as the family are concerned it's now a blood-feud. They will bide their time and wait. Then they will strike,' she finished, echoing Merri's earlier prediction. She shivered, and turning she looked me straight in the eye. 'And they have more blood-feuds to settle against us than others,' she said, before turning her gaze pointedly on William who was slowly making his way towards us from the head of the train.

Four days later our weary baggage train filed through the gatehouse at Winchester Castle and came to a halt in the large bustling bailey having, as Matilda had predicted, spent the past three nights camping or sharing flea ridden pallets at inns or begging favours at neighbouring manors along the way if we could be accommodated.

After the first day's calm weather, rain had fallen heavily, pelting over the Downs and fields, and the cold wind had cut us to the bone as it hurled wet leaves across our path. To make matters worse, the carts and wagons at the rear of the train constantly became stuck in the deep, muddy furrows made by those that had passed before, and precious time was wasted digging them out and re-distributing the loads between the remaining wagons. By the third day the unrelenting downpour meant that tempers began to grow thin. Women complained that they had no dry clothes for the children,

children snivelled because they were cold and wet, and several fights broke out over the possession of warm, dry cloaks and kegs of ale. In all it was a relief to get to Winchester, despite the fact that we were a day later than William had predicted.

Having handed Gingerbread over to Simon, I went in search of Matilda who was attending to the sick and injured. I found her over by a cart she had commandeered to transport a knight who had fallen from his horse and suffered a broken leg two days into the journey. She had located a barber-surgeon and was now deep in discussion with him about what could be done for the groaning man. After a swift examination, the barber-surgeon concluded that it was a clean break and the man would have to be taken to the stillroom to have it set properly. We were just loading the injured soldier onto a makeshift stretcher when William came striding towards us.

'It seems that the king is to arrive any minute now with the court in tow,' he said thoughtfully, surveying the crowded bailey with bright, beady eyes. 'It could be a good opportunity to ingratiate ourselves. We have been negligent where such matters are concerned and have let some good opportunities to forward ourselves pass us by, I fear.' He stroked the sandy growth of stubble that had appeared on his chin during the journey, weighing lost opportunities against future ones. 'Besides, we owe it to the children to be at court more – how else are we to secure good marriages for them without the king's favour?'

And with that he strode off to find a groom to stable Demon for the night, leaving Matilda frowning in his wake.

When he was out of sight, Matilda pushed her damp hair back from her weary face and looked around her as if seeing the heaving bailey for the first time. Men in the king's livery crowded the stables and teemed in and out of the castle preparing it for His Majesty's arrival. 'There won't be room for us all,' she commented tiredly. 'See if you can find Sam Skeet, Ailith, and ask him to arrange what accommodation he can. The rest will have to bed down in the hall or set up the tents.'

Chapter 5

Henry II, King of England, sat on the dais in the great hall of Winchester Castle and surveyed his court, his eyes straying once more to the figures of William de Braose and his wife Matilda de St. Valery, who had arrived earlier that day at the now overcrowded castle.

She was a striking woman, he mused. Far too beautiful for the likes of de Braose, who was, in his opinion, coarse and loud. Even now he was flushed with wine and laughing uproariously at his own jokes, not noticing the disapproving stares of others.

His eyes strayed back to Matilda. She reminded him of his Rosamund with her auburn hair, elfin features, and determined chin. He sighed. Fair Rosamund. His mistress. Long since dead. Her shrine watched over by the nuns of Godstow Priory who kept tapers burning and prayed for her soul daily.

Then, not for the first time, the image of Matilda de St. Valery in his bed rose and floated across his vision: her hair falling loose over her breasts, her slanting green eyes half closed as she hovered above him. Immediately he pushed the thought away. She was touched, so he had been told. Fey, or something like that.

Best leave well alone …

As if feeling his scrutiny, Matilda turned her eyes towards the dais. The king was staring intently at her with his cold, blue eyes, and immediately she felt a hot flush infuse her breasts and make its way up her neck to her face.

Confused, she tore her gaze away, but not before she saw another matching pair of blue eyes staring at her, trapping her like a rabbit mesmerised by the stare of a fox. The king's son, Prince John, had just entered the hall and was leaning against a pillar near the dais, partly concealed by the shadows. He had grown since she'd last seen him at his betrothal to Isabella of Gloucester six years previously. Still stocky, he had the look of his father: the same leonine head, the red gold hair, and the strong thighs built up from years in the saddle.

She shivered. Even back then at his betrothal, when he had been nothing but a boy, he had possessed the power to frighten her.

She remembered the moment she had first met him. Henry had sent a message as soon as they had arrived in Gloucester telling them that as soon as their tents were pitched and they had freshened up they were to attend him at court.

At last, dressed in their finest, they had picked their way through the throng of colourful tents being raised alongside theirs on the main fairway into Gloucester, and made their way to the castle where the king's lion standard rippled high up on the keep signifying that the court was in residence. Here they had found him ensconced in his chambers with William Fitzherbert, The Earl of Gloucester, and his wife Hawise, discussing the forthcoming betrothal of their daughter to Prince John, his youngest son.

Over by the hearth, Ranaulf Glanville, John's sometime tutor was settled in a chair with a goblet of wine in his hand, whilst two sable coloured dogs lounged happily at his feet.

Henry had been exceedingly gracious, crossing to take her hand and help her rise from the deep curtsey she had sunk into at the door. She remembered that he had held on to her hand for a long moment before releasing it to acknowledge William's bow with a brief nod of his head, and she had not felt entirely comfortable with that. Then he had turned back to the large table where he had been sitting with the Earl and his wife examining several manuscripts colourfully illuminated with bright inks.

The Earl had glanced up at William, then pushed one of the manuscripts towards him. 'Ah, de Braose, at last,' he said. 'I wish you to bear witness to some finalities of my daughter's betrothal,' he went on, his voice gruff with emotion. 'Tomorrow my little girl will be betrothed to a prince, a future heir to the throne, mayhap ... though of course that is only if God wills,' he said, throwing a quick glance at Henry.

Puffing up with pride at having been asked to be a witness, William had immediately reached for a quill and, dipping it in the ink, he had bent to the job, entirely forgetting her.

Amused, Henry had regarded her for a long moment, then he had taken her by the elbow and led her over to a window seat, signalling to his squire to get her some refreshment.

Matilda shuddered, for it was what happened next that would burn for all eternity in her memory, for as she sat down, he had casually cupped one of her breasts and squeezed the nipple where it rose faintly beneath the silken bodice of her kirtle.

At the very same moment the door was flung open with a crash, and a petulant looking boy, his tousled red-gold hair sticking on end, and a dirty streak down one flushed cheek, strode arrogantly into the chamber as if he owned it. Seeing them he had stopped short and eyed them up and down narrowly, the look of petulance deepening on his face as he regarded her sitting with his father's hand casually fondling her in a room full of people. Then without a word he had flung himself on his heels, and throwing her a look of unadulterated hate, he had stormed from the room as fast as he had entered it, closely followed by Ranaulf Glanville who had not missed any of the exchange.

Matilda started suddenly. Over by the pillar John had shifted. He was now leaning towards a man lingering in the shadows at his shoulder whispering something in his ear. As if sensing her eyes on him, slowly the man turned his head, and with a shock she saw it was Faulkes de Breauté.

With her heart thudding frantically in her chest, she turned and began to search for William.

Chapter 6

The candles were guttering down to their last when the old king finally rose and stepped off the dais to make his way through the mass of bowing courtiers towards his private chambers, flanked by his knights and his squire.

Merri and I gathered up our cloaks and made ready to retire as well, conscious that we had another long day of travelling to look forward to on the morrow. I yawned. Sam had managed to secure a small chamber for Matilda, William and the children. Merri and I were to bed down on some pallets outside the door.

We were just in sight of the room when suddenly the king's squire stepped forward, blocking our way, a lighted candle flickering in his hand. He bowed briefly to William before leaning forward and whispering something in his ear.

At once a broad smile broke out across William's florid face. 'It seems the king requires our presence in his private chambers, my dear,' he said, taking Matilda's arm to steady himself.

'What? Now?' Matilda asked, alarmed. 'Surely it can wait until the morning?'

'Don't be so stupid, Moll,' William snapped, his voice slightly slurred. 'This is the king we are talking about – you don't refuse to see the king when you've been summoned. Whatever the time of night!' And spinning on his heel he hastened after the squire who was now half way down the corridor, eager to deliver his charges to his master's door.

Matilda hesitated for a moment, and I thought she might refuse. But instead she gave a deep sigh and, beckoning to me, she turned and began to follow William back the way we had come.

Henry was standing on the far side of the room with his back to us, contemplating a huge wall painting when we entered his chambers. Seeing us he pulled a tapestry across the picture so that it was concealed from our eyes.

In the silence that followed, I hurried forward and took Matilda's mantle from her shoulders before retiring to a respectful distance, smoothing the soft fur absently whilst I looked around the exquisitely decorated chamber. Several richly embroidered tapestries hung from the walls lit by flickering wall sconces. They mainly depicted hunting scenes, but there was one that depicted a woman with her arm wrapped around the neck of a unicorn, whilst a knight bowed to her, one leg slightly extended in front of him.

Above us rose high vaulted ceilings with gilded plaster work, and everywhere I turned there were tall window embrasures over which the king's coat of arms was emblazoned – a gold lion on a red field, each lit on either side by a burning wall sconce. Over by the hearth stood two large, deeply padded chairs in rich red damask trimmed with gold braid. Upon one of them sat a young woman. She did not rise nor look in our direction as we entered but remained in profile, so that only the curve of her flushed cheek and the slender line of her neck remained visible from under the curtain of her gold hair.

Beside her was an ornately carved table set with silver goblets and a pitcher of wine. At her feet, three huge wolfhounds lay with their shaggy heads resting on their big paws, their jewel encrusted collars winking in the light of the blazing fire that was burning in the hearth.

'Welcome, Sir William,' Henry said as William rose from a stiff bow. 'And Lady Matilda. You are fortunate to have a wife who is still as beautiful as the day that you wed her,' he said, directing the compliment to William, all the while keeping his gaze firmly fixed on Matilda.

Turning away, Henry signalled his squire to bring them some of the wine whilst Matilda threw several surreptitious glances around the chamber, her eyes coming to rest periodically on the young woman with a frown on her face.

'I understand that you are on your way to the Welsh Marches, Sir William?' Henry said after another long spell of silence in which a burning branch broke and fell into the depths of the hearth, sending glowing ashes flying beyond the firedogs to threaten the rushes. 'I have been told that there is rumour of insurrection there and I would value some news on the matter myself – perhaps I could charge you with the task, Sir William? After all, we cannot have those Welsh rogues encroaching on baronial lands without showing some fight, eh!'

William inclined his head graciously. 'Of course, Your Majesty,' he replied, his voice slurring slightly. 'I shall have reports sent to you as soon as I have assessed the situation myself.'

Henry nodded. 'Good,' he said. 'I will send a messenger to Gloucester to inform the Sheriff and Constable of the castle that you are to be made welcome before you enter Wales. Make a list of the provisions that you need and I will send it with him. I would of course go myself,' he continued, 'but I have troubles still in France - if my sons are not rebelling against me, then they are fighting amongst themselves!'

He paused for a moment to shake his head at his offspring's perfidious behaviour. 'Anyway,' he went on. 'Now that I have concluded my business here, I cannot afford to linger anymore and I must return and try to restore order between them.' I noticed that his eyes flitted to the young woman still seated by the hearth as he said this.

Draining his second cup of wine, he handed the goblet to his squire for a refill. 'Perhaps,' he said with forced joviality, 'I shall arrange a Christmas court at Caen for a change. That way my sons might lose themselves in the Yuletide festivities and forget to fight each other - although the only comfort I have is that if they are fighting each other, they are at least not rebelling against me!'

Then turning to Matilda, he asked. 'How many sons do you have, Lady Matilda?'

'Why, I have five, Majesty,' she replied. 'Two of which are babes still,' she added, a small dreamy smile playing on her face.

'Well, I trust that your sons never turn against you as mine have done against me,' he said, fixing his cold blue eyes on her face. Then turning suddenly, he pushed aside the tapestry to reveal the wall painting he had been contemplating when we arrived. He waved a hand at it, his jewels winking brightly as they caught in the light of the wall sconces and all eyes dutifully followed.

The painting was macabre. An adult eagle dominated the composition, crouched, broken and defeated in its eyrie, with three eaglets perched, one on each wing, and the other on its back, tearing the adult's body with their beaks and talons. A trickle of blood rolled from a gash on the eagle's forehead – like a shiny red ruby to linger on one ravaged cheek. But despite the terrible injuries portrayed, the artist had still managed to convey a sense of the pride in the old bird: there remained a glint of defiance as well as something verging on the regal in the way it still held its head up high, despite of the fact that a fourth, much larger eaglet sat triumphantly on its neck, poised as if ready to pluck out an eye. Although crudely executed, the imagery was powerful. Even so, I was at loss as to why Henry had commissioned such an ugly thing when the rest of his chamber was packed with things of beauty.

I glanced at Matilda's face. She was frowning, not quite comprehending what it was she was looking at. I saw that her eyes were fixed on the eaglets, as if she could fathom out a reason for their vicious behaviour.

Henry was silent for a while as he, too, watched her face. Then he waved his hand at the picture once again. 'See how cruelly the eaglets treat the parent bird in the painting?' he asked.

Matilda looked surprised at the symbolism he'd conjured up, and she opened her mouth as if to say something.

'Well those,' Henry continued, interrupting whatever she might have said, '*those* are my sons. And that is how they will pursue me until the day I die: they will peck at me, tear me down, and claw away at my power until I am unable to resist. They will only cease when I am nothing but bones in my grave.'

I felt the tiny hairs on the back of my neck rise, and I glanced at Matilda once again. Her pale face was rigid with shock, and William was looking about bemusedly - as if he'd lost the plot of a bad play and was seeking someone to explain it to him.

'And that one,' Henry continued, pointing to the eaglet perched on the adult's shoulder ready to pluck out its eye. 'That one represents my youngest son John, whom now I embrace with so much affection. He will sometime in the future insult me more grievously than any of my other sons, I think,' he finished, his eyes going once more to Matilda's shocked face. Then after a long pause he said, so quietly that I almost didn't hear, 'As he will *you,* too, my dear ... As he will *you,* too ... one day.'

Matilda was deathly pale and, grabbing her mantle, I hurried over to put it around her shoulders. Like a sleepwalker she turned and headed towards the door, leaving William, shocked out of his stupor, to stutter his apologies to Henry and hurry swiftly after her.

I noticed on my way out that the nameless girl was no longer in her seat.

I dreamed the dream again that night. The one in which I had always known Matilda. In it she stands on the threshold of a deep precipice, her arms outstretched beseechingly to me as I try desperately to reach her. Then I am running. But I seem to be running in slow motion. And the harder I try, the slower I get, until I feel like I am wading through sticky treacle. I am angry about this. Frustrated, because I have something important to tell her but I am powerless to reach her. At her shoulder a shadowy figure stirs, and I try to scream.

To warn her of the danger. But no noise comes out. Then strong arms reach out and pull me back and I am awake and Merri is shaking my arm and telling me it is only a nightmare. But not before the shadowy figure dissolves and takes on the form of Prince John. Clearer now that destiny has brought them together.

Under the one roof ...

Chapter 7

Somewhere in the castle, Prince John lay beside the sleeping form of his latest paramour, unable to sleep because the image of Rosamund Clifford kept looming before him, her face merging with that of Matilda de St. Valery. Oh, how he had hated her, *Rosamund.* She alone had stood between him and his father's love. It ate away at him even now.

And yet, he had desired her too. But he had been rejected. Called a silly boy. Laughed at by both her and his father. He tossed and turned restlessly. Beside him his paramour let out a small snore and, uttering a curse, he shoved her brutally out of the bed and sent her on her way. Sometime later, in the distance, the bells began to ring out matins, but still he knew he would not sleep. She would be leaving today, Matilda St Valery. They were not staying for the hunting because of pressing matters in Wales, or so his father had told him. Like his father, he cannot think of her as Matilda de Braose. Cannot think of William's coarse hands roaming her body.

He scowled, remembering the way his father had looked at her in the hall earlier in the evening, knowing that he too had been drawn by the resemblance between her and Rosamund. He felt the old jealousy rear its head. The same jealousy that he had felt on the eve of his betrothal: the night when he had seen her standing with his father's hand resting on her breast, and her face all flushed. *She is a whore, like all of womankind …*

He stirred restlessly again. In his anger he had punished Isabella. After he had left the chamber, he had sought her out and locked the silly little milksop in a dark cellar. She'd not been found for hours. And when she was found, she was almost unconscious from terror because he'd told her that a troll lived in there that liked to eat little girls. He scowled, she had still been shaking during the ceremony the next day which had fuelled his hate of her even more.

Still restless, John rose from the bed and crossed to a small table bearing the remains of a pitcher of wine. He poured himself a large goblet and drained it in one gulp. How he hated his father. His father always took what wasn't rightfully his. Why, he had even sullied Richard's betrothed, Alys. Richard didn't have wind of it yet, but a secret like that couldn't be kept at court – after all, she was sister to the King of France.

Alys had told him of the conversation that had taken place in his father's private chambers last night. She had left by a door concealed behind a tapestry. She made a good spy and was keen as the next girl to warm his bed – when she could escape his father's lechery, that was. Still, it amused him to think that his father was afraid of the might of his own sons. He would tell de Breauté on the morrow.

Oh, how he would laugh …

Chapter 8

Gloucester Castle, Gloucester, England, September 1182

It was market day when we arrived in Gloucester a few days after our overnight stay in Winchester, and the town was milling with hundreds of people. To make things worse a fine mist of rain was falling across the square, making the cobbles slippery and dangerous underfoot as we tried to push through the throng past the Cathedral and on up to the castle.

Matters weren't being helped by William who, his face red with rage, was lashing out at anyone who got in his way with his whip. And that meant man or beast, regardless of size or age. In fact, he had been in a foul mood since we had left Winchester, still hung-over from the previous night's drinking, despite the fact that on our way back to the chamber he had been almost euphoric that Henry had singled them out for favour – although not a little confused at the abrupt end to the evening.

'The king's taken a shine to you, Matilda,' he kept saying, patting her arm and beaming at everybody in turn.

The next day his mood had changed, though. A squire had been sent to fetch him to the hall where Henry waited to give him some letters to distribute during his journey on his behalf. However, upon his return he could barely keep his temper. He kept glowering at Matilda as she tried to smooth the tangles in her hair, until in exasperation she threw down the hairbrush she was holding and snapped, 'Will you stop throwing those black looks at me, William – you've only yourself to blame if you have a sore head!'

William had instantly rounded on her, his face as black as his temper. 'You seemed to be mightily friendly with the king last night,' he said angrily, taking two steps towards her so that he towered over her as she sat on a stool in front of the dressing table – which was something of an advantage to him, as standing she was the taller.

Matilda had gasped. 'I seem to recall that you were only too pleased last night that I had gained the king's favour – though I had no intention of doing so, in fact I –'

She had broken off as William banged his hand down on the table and roared. 'Is it not enough that Henry has made a mistress of Richard's betrothed, Alys, without looking to ravish my wife in front of the court as well!'

Matilda had slapped a hand over her mouth, shocked. 'William, you must not say such things!' she whispered. 'Besides, it's only a rumour ...'

'Only a rumour! Only a rumour! Who do you think it was who sat so meekly in his chambers last night, eh? And this morning she is asking for you to attend her. What a scandal that would be! Well, madam, we will be leaving before terce is out. So damn well make sure you're ready!' he said and, turning on his heel, he'd marched angrily out of the room, slamming the door behind himself loudly in his wake.

It left me wondering at the quickness of his temper of late.

William was in a better temper that night as he and Matilda dined in a private chamber at Gloucester castle with the Sheriff, and Roger de Mortimer, who had delayed his departure to Wigmore so that he could impart the latest news.

'Do you think we have an ally in Lord Rhys? What chance of him intervening with Seisyll's kin in Gwent?' William asked the Sheriff when he had finished picking at the small bones of a quail.

The Sheriff considered the question for a moment, both hands cupped round a goblet of wine. 'I think he keeps the peace in south Wales with great difficulty, and then it's only because King Henry bestowed the title of Justice upon him. Anyway, when Henry goes ... well, who knows –' He left it at that.

'And what of Einion?' William asked, referring to the Prince of Elfael, another of their Welsh neighbours.

Again, the Sheriff considered the question for a moment before sighing. 'Well I think I can safely say that he will side with Seisyll's kin for sure, as has Hywel ap Iorworth, Lord of Caerleon so I hear.'

'Poer is convinced that the men of Gwent are planning revenge and will have it soon,' Roger said, deliberately not looking at William. 'The sons of Seisyll, those that were not at Abergavenny, have grown and they are burning for it. Rhys will not stop them – will not be able to stop them,' he amended after a moment.

William grunted. 'Poer's right to be worried then,' he concluded grimly. Then, satisfied he could eat no more, he leaned back in his chair.

'Well, Moll,' he said, rubbing his full stomach with one large hand and considering his options. 'I think there will have to be a change of plan, as it is obviously too dangerous to head for Abergavenny as was my original intention. Instead, tomorrow we will ride to

Dingestow and inspect Poer's new defences. It will give Poer a chance to fill me in on the latest developments whilst we call a war conference - it's about time we had a plan in place. In fact,' William continued, warming to his theme, 'he can start by pulling in a few of those devils in cahoots with Seisyll's kin and questioning them further - they have spies all over Hereford.'

'As for you,' he went on. 'I think it best that you and the children press on from there to the safety of Hay – I will dispatch a messenger to warn the constable of your arrival and tell him to batten down the gates and increase the guard until then. The baggage train needn't accompany us to Dingestow, it can go ahead to Hay tomorrow – if you are lucky it will get there first and prepare for your arrival, if not then -' he shrugged.

'But, William,' Matilda protested at once. 'I thought the plan was for us all to stay together? Surely it is not safe for the children and I to travel alone -' She shivered and broke off as William halted her with his hand.

'There is to be no arguing, Moll, I have decided. You will have an escort of twelve men-at-arms to accompany you, which should be sufficient enough guard even in these troubled times. You will be quite safe at Hay. The new castle can withstand anything that the Welsh throw at us, I have no doubt,' he finished, referring to the new stone castle built to replace the old wooden keep that had stood at the foot of the hill by St Mary's church since the early days of the Norman conquest. I saw his eyes slide suspiciously over Matilda, wondering if there was any truth in the fact that many of the townsfolk believed she had built the castle on her own in a night, earning her the name 'Maude de Haie.'

Matilda, for her part, stared him out until he could no longer hold her gaze and his eyes slid guiltily away, a moment later I saw him cross himself when he thought she wasn't looking.

And so, the next day found us riding hard for Dingestow. The baggage train was to make its own pace and head straight for Hay with what men could be spared to protect it and, outwardly resigned, Matilda pulled her fur lined mantle tighter around her and went to join William and the children who were waiting impatiently with their escort and two of the children's nurses, Lowri and Cerys, both Welsh by birth. By that evening we were in Monmouth and within sight of Dingestow castle, and by supper we were admiring the neat work of the stone mason's new drawbridge and curtain wall which replaced the old wooden palisade that had stood for so many years above the small hamlet below.

Ranulf Poer turned out to be a sinewy man of middle height, with thinning grey hair cropped very short, and faded blue eyes that missed nothing. I saw Matilda shiver, for in some respects he looked very much like Faulkes de Breauté, but despite his steely countenance he soon proved that he was an intelligent man with a dry sense of humour behind which there lurked no trace of de Breauté's evil.

Stopping what he was doing, Poer approached the small group. 'Didn't expect you to turn up with your whole damn family, de Braose!' he said, grasping William's hand tightly and grinning.

Then turning to the children, he wagged a finger at them. 'And I'll not have you children terrorising my cook for cinnamon biscuits and sweetmeats, but if you do happen to come across him ... well, make sure you bring me some!' Then, saluting them, he turned and ducked into an unfinished guard turret and settled himself down on a stool in front of a roaring fire.

Smiling, Matilda handed the horses over to the grooms and, gathering the children together, she went in search of the kitchens whilst William and Poer settled down to discuss more of the alarming rumours that the sons of Sysell were planning revenge.

'Should be all right here, though,' Poer said confidently. 'No way they can get past these fortifications – tight as a duck's arse. Nought will be able to get in or out past these walls,' he finished, surveying his new fortifications proudly. 'So, de Braose, what's your plans for Abergavenny then? You going to shore it up tight like you did Hay?'

Matilda sat down heavily on a wooden stool clutching a cup of apple juice, the remains of the harvest that had travelled with them from the orchards around Bramber to sustain them on their journey. It was nearly dawn, and she was exhausted – William had forgotten that she was meant to travel on to Hay today and had tarried with Poer for an age until she had finally made her excuses and left. But still she could not sleep. The prospect of travelling without William into dangerous territory was frightening. Every time her eyes closed she was plagued by visions of being waylaid on some lonely road and being hacked to death, or worse, by Seisyll's vengeful sons.

She blinked. Without really knowing why, she was staring into the heart of the fire. Almost absently she picked up a log and placed it on the glowing embers. Slowly, the flames flickered and began to form a hazy picture. She leaned forward and her hair fell loose over her shoulders, dangerously close to the hearth, but she paid no heed. 'Show me,' she whispered. As if in agreement, the flames caught the end of the log and ran across it. Immediately the picture resolved itself and she could make out the imposing grey battlements of Abergavenny castle rising above the huge, metal-studded gatehouse doors. The castle was under attack - she could see men and women running about in a panic as scaling ladders were thrown up from the over-grown ditch below the castle walls.

The flames flickered again, and the picture faded slightly. 'No -' Matilda whispered in anguish, 'No ... I have to see! I have to know what happens!' Obediently the fire gave a little hiss and the flames, now burning fiercely in the centre of the hearth, turned blue and leapt wildly towards the chimney.

It was a massacre. Men, women and children, still in their night-shifts were being brutally cut down as they tried to flee, their screams mixing with the ugly shouts of their attackers. Matilda moaned in horror as a young woman with long, dark hair clasping a child to her breast tried to dodge her assailant, only to have it wrenched from her arms and thrown to the ground, before being run through viciously with a sword. Moments later the man took her head from her shoulders with a clean, savage stroke, sending it spinning through the air, eyes still wide open with shock, leaving him covered in spurts of thick arterial blood as her body hit the ground behind it.

Silent tears ran down Matilda's cheeks. She had recognised Fion, the wife of one of the garrison soldiers who had been stationed at Abergavenny on William's command. She had been a kind girl, always ready to be friendly to her mistress when they were in residence, and when last Matilda had seen her, she had been excited at the imminent birth of her child. Callously, her attacker kicked the bodies aside and strode on, looking for his next victim, still wiping the blood from his sword on the edge of his tunic as he went.

The flames flickered again, and the scene changed slightly. Apart from the few guards on the battlements still in full armour, the rest of the men were in disarray as they wildly tried to regain control of the situation. But it was too late she realised, as tears continued to course their way unchecked down her face. The bailey was running with blood now and the Welsh were singing a victory song and blowing their trumpets loudly as the bodies piled up.

Matilda's eyelids drooped and the scene faded slightly. Then suddenly it was clear again and the castle was burning as the men threw lighted torches into the thatch and the stables ...

Matilda woke with a start. The smell of burning flesh lingered in the air all around her. Sweet and pungent. Like pork roasting on a spit. Immediately the bile rose in her throat and, grabbing the hem of her shift, she ran to the garderobe and vomited into the privy.

Later, she wondered wearily if she should tell William. But no. William was superstitious and untrusting, believing her a witch if she told him. And anyway, there was already a messenger on the way.

I awoke stiff from a night on an uncomfortable pallet to find Matilda already awake, sitting looking at the new fortifications from the window seat in the chamber we had been allotted. She turned to me and I saw the fear in her eyes and the dark smudges below. Of William, there was no sign. Matilda stood hastily and pulled her fur lined mantle tightly around her slight form.

'Ailith,' she whispered, looking about as if fearful of eavesdroppers. 'We must make haste for Hay!' She shivered and clutched her mantle even tighter. 'All is not right here. The children, they are not safe. And Abergavenny. Well, Abergavenny has already burned …'

'What?' I whispered. 'What do you mean that Abergavenny has already burned. That's not possible … how … how could you know?'

Matilda fixed me with her wide, frightened eyes, and I felt a chill run down my spine. 'We must make haste, Ailith,' she repeated. 'All is not well. They are coming. Ranulf Poer is a dead man. For all his defences!'

The messenger arrived muddy and exhausted just as we were mounted and ready to leave. William stood shocked and angry in the cold bailey, as the fall of Abergavenny was recounted by the breathless man. According to the messenger, the sons of Seisyll had hidden themselves in the overgrown ditches of Abergavenny castle the night before. Earlier in the day one of the party had actually ventured forth and joked to the constable that they intended to scale the walls that night. In light of this the constable and the household had stayed on guard, refusing to take off their armour until dawn when they deemed it safe to retire, but as soon as they had retired then the attack had begun. The constable and his wife were captured, but there were many dead the messenger finished, crossing himself fearfully.

Matilda shivered, and I saw William look at her long and hard with suspicion, then he shook himself.

'Make haste for Hay, Matilda, you and the children will be safe there. Head through Gwent, then make your way towards the Black Mountains. But keep away from Offa's Dyke, it's much too exposed. If you have to stop, then make for Llantilio castle. It's in much the same state as here as Henry is having it fortified, but they still have a large garrison to protect it. From there head for Llanthony, and if you can, beg shelter at the Priory for the night. The Prior will welcome you, I'm sure, but give him this purse to assist with the restorations there anyway,' he said, handing her a heavy purse of silver. 'It can only be a day's ride after that, but whatever you do give Abergavenny a wide berth for they will still be in the area!' he finished.

Matilda nodded and swallowed. 'Please follow soon, William – promise me that you will follow soon? I ...' she hesitated. 'I have a bad feeling, William ...' she trailed off again as William narrowed his eyes and looked up at her with suspicion once more. Then turning on his heel, he strode off with a puzzled Poer in his wake to make arrangements to pick up several known associates of Seizyll's that Poer's spies had reported were in the area.

Rumour was that Dingestow was next.

It was raining heavily as we rode out of Dingestow accompanied by our escort of twelve men-at-arms. Back at Gloucester, Matilda had found a sturdy little pony more suitable to the terrain to carry me for the rest of the journey, and so Gingerbread had been despatched with Simon and the baggage train to Hay.

Before we left, Matilda had pressed a small dagger in my hand which had frightened me. 'Don't be afraid to use it if you must,' she said, her face grim. I shivered, aware that there was danger all around us. Matilda had armed herself with two daggers: one in her boot, and the other in a sheath tucked into her girdle which she fingered nervously as we made our way down the narrow, winding hill tracks that took us through Gwent – avoiding villages on the way – and on towards Llantilio where hopefully we would take refuge in the castle for the night.

We stopped once at a rickety old cottage where we bought provisions from an old woman tending some chickens in a muddy yard. She looked at us suspiciously, then seeing the silver piece that Matilda offered she reluctantly handed over some hard bread and cheese.

We stopped once more in clearing some distance from the cottage so that Matilda could share out the provisions that Poer's cook had provided, supplemented with the bread and cheese purchased from the old woman, all the while glancing around as nervously as a cat protecting her kittens.

After that we picked up the pace and rode hard. The only sound was the squelch of the horses' hooves in the slippery mud, and the crash of birds' wings as they took fright and careered through the trees to take refuge elsewhere, calling to their fellows in alarm as they went. Only when we reached Llantilio Castle did we stop as William had instructed. Once there an exhausted Mattie had to be lifted from her pony and carried into the castle by one of the men-at-arms, her sleepy form huddled uncomfortably against his armour whilst the other children followed disconsolately in his wake.

The constable of the castle made us welcome, fussing over Matilda and expressing his shock at the fate of Abergavenny, before showing us the alterations that King Henry had ordered to be carried out to strengthen the castles defences. The feeling at Llantilio was the same as at Dingestow; the Welsh were restless and the fall of Abergavenny was surely only the first sign of more trouble to come in the Marches. Finally, after a simple meal of fish and vegetables, we retired to gain strength for the next leg of the journey, though none of us slept well at all.

Early the next morning we were once more riding hard across Wales. A weak, hazy sun had broken out behind the fine mist of rain that always seemed to accompany us and a rainbow now shimmered in the distance, iridescent in the sky, its bright colours making the children exclaim in delight.

By late morning we had found the river Honddu, and we began to follow the path northwards knowing that it would eventually deliver us to the safety of the Priory. In places the noise was deafening as the river rushed and eddied past us back the way we came, swirling angrily over and around the small boulders that packed the shallower parts, and tumbling down into deeper pools with a crash.

In other places the banks were too steep to traverse, and any trees that clung to them leaned precariously low over water as if reaching desperately for the other side.

Time and time again we crossed small streams that poured down from the black mountains to join the Honddu, with the horses' hooves kicking up the muddy red earth so that our hems and boots were soon stained the colour of rust.

By late afternoon the sky had darkened once again, but grimly we plunged on into the valley between the dark, steep mountains, heading upwards towards the Vale of Ewias and Lanthony Priory where we hoped to gain shelter once more for the night with the good fathers there.

Above us the clouds clung to the mountain peaks which were dotted with the rusts and browns of dying heather, the only vegetation to survive the harsh welsh winters at such a height, and the only sound was the moaning of the wind and the occasional exclamation from one of the men-at-arms. Everyone was tight lipped; the forest seemed to close in around us and, Matilda, certain that we were being watched, drew her dagger from her girdle and kept it concealed beneath her mantle.

By midday we found ourselves on a narrow track so overhung by trees that we were forced to ride single-file with the men-at-arms positioned strategically between us, and at the front and rear with their swords drawn ready against the ambush they were sure would come, but there was no such ambush. Then suddenly we were out in the open once more, and with a sigh of relief Matilda reined in her horse, dismounted, and began to unpack the provisions that had been provided for us by the cook at Llantilio castle.

Matilda sighed. She didn't want to tarry too long, but the men were hungry and thirsty and the horses would be blown if they pressed on now. So, suppressing her irritation she strode down to the river bank and dangled her fingers in the cold icy water of the Honddu, leaving the men to eat their pasties and some leftover cheese, lounging on some rocks a little way above.

After a while she relaxed. The air here was full of the pungent scent of wet earth and pine needles. It was pleasant, she realised. Almost calm, after the brooding silence of the dark, shadowy forest.

Leaning back, she closed her eyes as, one by one, the children, led by a curious Will, made their way along river bank to where a group of rocks lay just beyond the fringe of the forest, followed idly by Lowri, Cerys and Ailith.

The attack, when it happened, was swift and sudden.

There was a party of twenty or so men, their swords drawn and bows ready. Matilda leapt to her feet realising that the children were the closest target to the Welsh party as they exploded from the trees.

Some of the men-at-arms leapt onto their horses and urged them towards the little group who were now milling about frantically, the shrill screams of the children echoing around the valley.

Almost casually, one of the Welsh bowmen raised his bow and let loose an arrow. It struck the nearest rider in the thigh with a sickening thud, penetrating the tassets of his leather tunic, before driving on down through flesh and bone and pinning him to his saddle. Maddened, his horse reared and he tugged it around in a half circle, his face a mask of surprise and pain. Without pausing the Welshman raised his bow again, letting loose another bolt, this time striking the same man in his other thigh and sending his now terrified horse bolting for the woods with him pinned to his seat from both sides.

Amidst the confusion of their companion's misfortune, some of the other men had reached the children who were now huddled behind a rocky outcrop with Ailith and the two terrified Welsh girls, their swords drawn defensively in front of them. Others, more unfortunate, had fallen where they stood, shot through by the deadly shafts.

Matilda realised she was shaking. How had it happened? They had only let down their guard for a moment - but it had been enough, she thought, glancing frantically round to where two more men–at–arms stood separated from the others, their hands resting helplessly on the hilts of their swords knowing that they were hopelessly outnumbered.

One of their ambushers stood out from the others. He was richly attired in a long, vibrant blue tunic over his hauberk and chausses, with elaborate gold trim at the hem, neck and sleeves, and an elegantly tooled leather belt with an ornate silver buckle at his waist. Above the tunic his face was dark and lean, with a neatly clipped moustache and a close–cut beard that hugged finely sculptured cheekbones. He also had a haughty blue gaze which was now lingering on Matilda's frozen form.

'*Da ddiwrnod*, Lady de Braose,' he said, urging his mount forward to where she stood and lowering his sword. 'You are without your husband, I see,' he observed wryly, switching deftly to fluent English. 'A mistake, I think, to leave such a beautiful young woman and her children vulnerable in such a hostile place and with such inadequate protection.

Matilda drew herself up to her full height, anger suddenly taking over where fear had been a moment before.

'I am Hywel ap Iorworth, Lord of Caerleon,' he continued. 'I had heard that you were making for Hay. These are dangerous times, I think, what with the kin of Seisyll burning for revenge - perhaps it was not wise of you to have ridden out alone and with such an unsatisfactory escort?'

Matilda flinched, remembering that his name had been linked with the raid on Abergavenny. 'Is that a threat? she asked, keeping her voice as steady as possible and trying not to show any fear.

Hywel leaned forward and placed the tip of his sword directly under her chin so that she was forced to look up at him. It was so sharp that she felt the tip of it break the tender skin at her throat. Immediately a trickle of blood ran down her neck and began to snake its way down between her breasts.

Matilda swallowed as a rising tide of fear threatened to engulf her, wondering how long her traitorous legs would be able to support her trembling body. Behind her, her men-at-arms growled angrily in the knowledge that they were outnumbered and completely at the mercy of this man.

Suddenly, Will broke free from the restraining arms of Ailith where they had remained huddled by the rocks with the others. Without more ado one of the Welsh bowmen kicked his horse into action, but Will was too swift, and darting neatly past the horse and rider within moments he was at Matilda's side, his little face flushed with anger.

'How dare you, sir! How dare you treat my lady mother so?' he demanded, his voice shrill with fear.

Slowly, Hywel lowered his sword and regarded Will with interest as if he was some rare specimen that he had just come across. Then he laughed. It was an ugly laugh that echoed round the valley and, gathering Will to her breast, Matilda covered his ears and buried her face in his hair, not wanting it to be the very last sound that her beloved son might hear.

Time seemed to stand still as Matilda waited for the final blow that would end their lives, and when at last she dared to look up, it was to see Hywel's retreating form vanishing in the distance, closely followed by his men amidst the slowly diminishing echoes of his laugh ...

The Prior of Llanthony Priory was riding towards them as Matilda made her way towards him with her stricken party in tow. He was accompanied by a number of his black robed canons, a look of intense worry etched on his ruddy face. 'Lady de Braose!' he exclaimed. 'I was beginning to think the worst – your man was brought to us – he was found by a woodsman who took pity on him and fetched him to us.'

'Oh, thank God!' Matilda whispered. 'How is he, Father?' she asked. 'We have been searching for him ... following his trail ... There are two others, both dead ...' she tailed off, and her eyes filled with tears as she took in the look of compassion on the Prior's kindly face.

'Do not distress yourself, my lady,' he said gently. 'He did not suffer much in the end, and he is now in God's safe keeping.'

Matilda covered her face with her hands as black despair filled her heart: where was this all going to end? And where was William, the man who had started it all? Suddenly a vision of her father, Bernard de St. Valery, floated into her mind as she had seen him on the day that he told her she was to wed William de Braose.

'He is a good man, Matilda, God-fearing and kind - he will protect you when your mother and I are no longer able to ...'

Suddenly Matilda laughed bitterly, shocking the Prior and making her men-at-arms glance at her suspiciously. 'Oh, how wrong you were, Papa,' she whispered, 'how very wrong you were!' And with that she wheeled her horse around and made ready to follow the good Prior back to the safety of his Priory.

Chapter 9

Hay Castle, Wales, September 1182

Hay was bathed in watery sunlight as we pushed our mounts along the steep path that led to the gatehouse, exhausted and drained from our perilous journey and the knowledge that but for the grace of God we might not be here at all. The watch, seeing our approach, let down the drawbridge and we crossed it with relief, the horses' hooves clattering loudly on the sturdy timbers as we went, shattering the peace of the castle.

Matilda dismounted wearily then, smoothing down her skirts, she turned to the constable who was waiting to greet us.

'Bad business, Abergavenny,' he said, shaking his head in disbelief. 'Can't see how it could have happened, forewarned as they were.'

Matilda grimaced. 'But what of Dingestow?' she asked, wringing her hands suddenly in agitation. 'As we were leaving Lanthony, word came to the Prior that there is a pitched battle going on there – have you news?'

'No, my lady, I'm afraid not. But I will dispatch men immediately to seek word if that is what you wish?'

'Please,' she said. 'I must have word of William – he delayed at Dingestow.' She faltered. 'I must know if he is saved or not.' Then beckoning to me, she turned on her heel and made her way towards the steps leading up to the keep, leaving the constable to wonder if she desired good or bad news of William, and knowing that if the Welsh did capture him they would offer no mercy.

Unable to sleep, Matilda was up early the next morning, and after a quick search I found her in the castle's herb garden adjacent to the kitchens from which an overriding smell of fish wafted. As I approached her, she broke off a sprig of lavender from a well-established bush bordering the roughly paved path that wound through the beds, and immediately the pungent scent was set free into the atmosphere. Turning to me, she waved it in front of my nose.

'This should help me sleep ... calm me, Ailith,' she said, sighing deeply, 'but it does not. It disquiets me ... heightens my senses ...'

I hovered uncertainly, intuitively knowing that there was more.

'Jeanette is dead,' she whispered. 'I feel it in my bones ...'

I touched her arm gently, not sure what to say. I had not known Jeanette well because she'd been mostly confined to her bed chamber since the incident with Faulkes de Breauté when I first arrived.

'Ailith,' she began again, hesitantly. 'I know that you see things ...' she tailed off for a moment before continuing. 'I only wish to know. Could ... could things be different if William were to die now?'

I did not know how to answer her. In my dreams she was always hovering on the precipice of a dark pit. There was no light to guide her. I was not even sure why I was chosen to accompany her on her journey, only that I had a purpose. But what? That even I did not know, and so I could only stare mutely at her.

She sighed. 'Forgive me, I should not have asked,' she whispered.

'There are riders approaching,' Matilda called, looking down from her chamber where it overlooked the main route into Hay. It had been two days now without news of William, in the meantime the baggage train had arrived untroubled and we were now in the process of unpacking it so that piles of Matilda's bliauts, tunics and wimples lay heaped on the huge bed which was now installed in its rightful place in the room.

We watched as the constable crossed the battlements and enquired of them their business before instructing the guards to allow them entry. Minutes later Rhiannan, a local girl employed to assist Matilda, could be heard running up the newel stairs, her slippers making loud slapping noises against the stone steps as she went. Breathlessly, she poked her round face through the door.

'*O na, madam!*' she said, a pained look crossing her homely features as she saw that Matilda was not yet dressed. '*Mae'r Archdderwydd yma i'th weld di - mae'n rhaid i ti frysio a gwisgo!*'

Then, seeing that Matilda didn't understand, she grabbed the nearest bliaut and girdle and thrust it at her. 'The Archdeacon is here to see you, madam – you must hurry and get dressed,' she repeated in English, her singsong voice rising a few octaves in agitation as she glanced once again at the dishevelled heap of clothes on the bed, in the hope that it might offer up something less travel creased.

For a moment Matilda hovered uncertainly, and I saw dawning understanding cross her face. The Archdeacon was an important man, and it was unlikely that he was just passing Hay and had spontaneously decided to drop in. Whatever he had to say it clearly concerned recent events, and for a moment I thought she might refuse to welcome him. But then, grabbing a clean chemise, she nodded to Rhiannan and hastily began to get dressed.

Gerald, Archdeacon of Brecknock, was reclining in a chair in the private solar that Matilda used to greet her visitors. A bright fire burned in the hearth, and he was holding a goblet of wine in one hand whilst he stared thoughtfully at something in the rushes. Seeing us, he put it down beside him and stood and bowed over Matilda's hand briefly. He was a good-looking man: tall and lean, with dark wavy hair and clear grey eyes topped with the shaggiest eyebrows I had ever seen.

'Ah, Lady Matilda,' he said, his eyes roaming her face kindly. 'I have just ridden over from Llanddew – I know that I could have left word at Brecknock and have the constable ride over, but I heard that you were at Hay and I wanted to impart it myself ... I have grave news.'

'What of William? The battle of Dingestow?' Matilda asked sharply, accepting the hastily poured goblet of wine that I thrust at her.

'William was involved in the battle at Dingestow, yes, but as far as we know he was not amongst the dead. Never-the-less,' he continued, 'he has not been seen since Ranaulf Poer was killed, and I thought you should know.'

'Ranaulf is dead?' Matilda asked, looking shocked, but at the same time clearly not surprised that the kindly grey-haired man who had accommodated us for the night and made the children laugh was now dead.

'Yes,' Gerald continued. 'I did not want you to hear wild rumours from the numerous messengers that are galloping around the country spreading them. For all we know, William is safe and being harboured somewhere before making his way to you – it has been a bad business and now they are laying Radnor to waste, from what I hear. And you, too – I hear that you encountered Hywel on the road here?'

'Yes,' Matilda replied, putting down her goblet and turning away to look into the flames. 'He must have been heading for Dingestow. I wonder,' she said, glancing at Gerald. 'Why did he not kill us – although he had every opportunity?' She shivered, and unconsciously her hand went to her throat where a small scab was all that remained of the encounter.

Gerald pondered a minute or two, then sighed, 'I cannot tell you why he chose to spare you – by all accounts he can be a cruel man and then there is the blood-feud – but still, God works in mysterious ways, does he not?'

Outside, a dog began to howl, and I crossed myself, for I knew that death at the hands of Hywel ap Iorworth, Lord of Caerleon, was not the fate that Mistress Destiny had in mind for Matilda de Braose.

Chapter 10

Matilda breathed in, allowing Rhiannan to pull the lacing of her bliaut tightly over her chemise, so that the material fitted snugly under her bust and accentuated her still slim waist, before falling in folds down to the floor where it skimmed the top of her soft kid shoes. I knew that she had chosen the dress with infinite care. It was not of too rich a fabric. Flemish cloth to be exact. The colour of fine Burgundy wine, offset by intricate gold embroidery at the neck, hem and the boat shaped sleeves which fell below her hips. Around her waist she wore a loose gold embroidered girdle, and her hair was covered by a simple gauzy white veil held in place by a woven fillet of silk.

It was Michaelmas day and as there was still no word of William. She would have to oversee the collection of tithes, the settling of debts and the land transactions, as well as deal with the minor transgressions on the part of William's tenants. As lady of the castle, it was important that she looked the part.

Satisfied with her work, Rhiannan bobbed a curtsey and, going to the window, she began to pack away the discarded distaff and wool that lay on the narrow window seat there.

'They are beginning to arrive,' she exclaimed, peering out of the window at the steady stream of people drifting slowly into the bailey to form an orderly queue in front of the steep wooden staircase leading up to the hall.

Matilda swallowed hard and, knowing that she was nervous because she had never been involved in the collecting of tithes or presiding over the petty squabbles that occurred amongst William's tenants, I picked up her mantle and together we began to make our way out into the corridor where a squire waited with two armed guards, ready to escort her to the proceedings.

The room was buzzing when we finally stepped over the threshold and looked around, taking stock of the trestle tables that had been set up along one side of the main body of the hall. At one of them a clerk was busily preparing the bundle of parchment rolls upon which he would record the transactions and verdicts of the court during the day's proceedings. Alongside him were the tally sticks. These were Hazelwood sticks carved into flat batons and used to record transactions between the lord and his tenants where one of them owed money to the other – most commonly the tenant when they could not afford to pay the rent on their land or were advanced money by William in lean times. The sum owed would be marked by a series of notches and then the stick would be split down the middle, one half being retained in the castle treasury, and the other half by the tenant upon which the loan was made. Most usually these were only given if the person receiving the loan was illiterate, as it was a simple matter to match one half of the stick to the other as proof of the transaction, thus avoiding the sort of argument that occurred when a suspicious tenant was shown a piece of parchment that he could not decipher.

At last, steeling herself, Matilda took my arm and together we crossed the hall to the dais, our skirts swishing over the rushes to where Sam Skeet was already seated at the table from which she would preside over the proceedings. Alongside him sat several other manor officials that I could see she recognised from past visits.

Ralph the bailiff was present, as was the heyward, Herbert Pinkerton, a ferrety little man in charge of the hedgerows and fences who I found out later she did not trust. Then there was the reeve, William de Blois, whom I soon learned was responsible for the organisation of the manorial assets: land, grain, livestock and buildings, as well as the hours that William's tenants were required to work his fields. Beside them sat several other well attired men that she didn't appear to recognise, but she nodded politely to them anyway.

As we stepped onto the dais they stood, and Sam moved round to pull out one of a pair of ornate chairs similar to the ones at Bramber so that she could sit. In the silence that followed all eyes turned on Matilda. I could see the superstition etched on each and every one of their faces, and for the first time since we had arrived, I felt a ripple of discontent flow through the room. Matilda was said to have built Hay all by herself in one day. And what the Lady of Hay was said to have built in one day, I could see the people of Hay believed she could undo in another.

The morning's proceedings were straight forward enough. Tithes and rents were collected, some paid by coin, and some by goods: bushels of corn, or sacks of flour, all of which was recorded by the clerk so that Ralph could write up the accounts later. Then the business of land transfer was begun.

Half way through the proceedings Matilda yawned discreetly, it was obvious that William's men were quite capable of conducting business without her – and in truth it looked like she was finding it all a bit tedious really.

The clerk bent his head and scratched across his parchment. 'Dyved, son of Dyved of Glasbury, fined 4d for leave to take one acre of new land from the copse adjacent to his cottage, to hold to himself and his heirs ...'

I saw that Matilda's eyes were drawn to the doors of the hall. Outside there was a scuffle going on and she frowned before instructing a page to go and find out what the problem was.

'Henry, son of Amabel of Hay, fined 2d for leave to purchase ½ one acre of existing land from his neighbor, Robert Spittlewode ...' intoned the clerk as he wrote.

Just then a man broke free of a restraining guard and, pushing past the queue, he strode arrogantly into the hall. I could see that Matilda vaguely recognised him as one of their Brecknock tenants, though she told me later she had seldom ever spoken to him.

'My lady,' he said, bowing low in front of the dais and ignoring the outraged looks of the villagers and officials seated alongside her. 'I have news of Sir William.'

At once Matilda's hand flew to her throat and she stood, knocking over the goblet of wine that she had been toying with on the table in front of her. Ignoring the spilt wine, she turned to the men that now surrounded him with their swords drawn, and with her hand still to her throat she bid them to withdraw.

Seeing that he had obviously distressed her, the man adopted a kindlier voice. 'I am sorry to barge in like this, my lady, but you might remember me. My name is Trahaearn Fychan, Lord of Llangorse, and I have news of your husband, but ...' he said, looking around, 'perhaps this is not the best place to impart it ...'

The solar was cold and damp and whilst I built up a fire, Matilda beckoned Trahaearn Fychan to sit. Then she instructed a page to pour him some wine and fetch him some food from the kitchens whilst she steeled herself for the worst.

Trahaearn smiled kindly. 'Do not distress yourself, dear lady,' he said when the page had left the room. 'Sir William is quite safe, but as yet unable to travel too far.'

Matilda let out her breath. 'What happened?' she asked, her voice barely a whisper above the sound of church bells in the distance.

'William and some of his men escaped the battle of Dingestow,' Trahaearn said carefully, 'but he sustained some injuries – nothing life threatening,' he added hurriedly when she paled visibly. He paused for a moment to let her compose herself before continuing. 'I believe that he was trying to make for Hay. But the countryside is overrun with those out baying for his blood and they must have been watching all the roads leading to the castle.' He sighed. 'To cut a long story short, he sought refuge at my manor in Brecheiniog. We took care of him until he was able to move and we could place him in the capable hands of your constable at Brecknock castle where he could be tended to properly. He is safe there, I assure you.'

The logs in the hearth suddenly spluttered to life, giving off a warm glow that went some way towards taking the chill out of the air. Slowly, Matilda raised her head so that she was looking at Trahaearn properly for the first time since he had arrived; I could see her taking in his coal black hair and lazy brown eyes. He still exuded an air of arrogance, but there was honesty in the way he carried himself, and the broad hands resting on his lap looked solid and comforting. He was a very attractive man, and I wondered that she had never noticed before.

'But why did you shelter him?' Matilda asked suddenly, for like me she sensed that Trahaearn did not like William all that much.

The question hung between them for a long moment, then Trahaearn said at last. 'Sir William is my liege lord, and therefore I was duty bound to assist him. But enough of that. I wonder, do you like hawking, madam? Sir William told me that you have a marvellous mews here at Hay. I have a mind to see it if you would give me the pleasure,' he finished, holding out his arm and smiling winningly at her.

'Yes, yes, of course!' Matilda replied, her face immediately brightening as she cast a look in my direction. 'The court can do without me for the rest of the afternoon, can't it, Ailith?' And taking his arm, she smiled up at him, William quite forgotten as she stood drowning in Trahaearn's twinkling brown gaze.

PART TWO

Chapter 11

March 1188, Hay Castle

The day had dawned fresh and bright, and outside a light breeze propelled fluffy white clouds across the blue skies above the Wye valley. Down in the bailey, small clusters of daffodil and crocus poked their heads up, and tiny buds awakened on branches recently laden with snow. From the window of the solar, high up in the keep, I could see the fields beyond the curtain wall where new-born lambs unsteady on their spindly legs nuzzled their mothers greedily. In the vineyards beyond, I could just make out tiny figures moving along the rows, pruning and grafting the vines ready for the growing season to begin.

Down in the small township of Hay there was a distinct air of excitement. This was due to the unexpected arrival of Gerald and Baldwin, the Archbishop of Canterbury, who were touring Wales at King Henry's command: enlisting support for a third crusade to the holy land where, even now, Saladin held Jerusalem in his grip. Every now and again, excited shouts drifted up towards the keep as men scuffled and jostled one another, eager to throw themselves at the Archbishop's feet and pledge allegiance to the cause.

Sometime later Baldwin and Gerald entered the solar where Sir William, resplendent in a blue silk tunic edged with silver, waited to greet them with Matilda. Later we would all assemble in the great hall where Gerald and the Archbishop were to be honoured guests at supper. Even now I imagined Merri's round figure running back and forth across the bailey, and to and from the bakehouse, making sure that only loaves made from the finest flour graced the Archbishop's table.

Once the introductions were finished, the servants began to make themselves busy handing around the sweetmeats and wine whilst my gaze drifted idly over to where the Archbishop and Gerald were now standing in front of one of the narrow-arched window embrasures. William was in full fettle, gushing on about the latest plans he had for a new castle at Dinas. Beside him, looking bored, were Richard, the Earl of Clare, and his wife, Amice. They were visiting on their way back to Tonbridge with Will, who had for the last year been the Earl's squire. Maude and Gilbert, their children, were kneeling at their feet laughing delightedly over the dogs who were happily thumping their tails against the rushes, pleased with all the attention.

I couldn't help noticing that Maude was an exact replica of her mother, only in miniature. She was wearing a bliaut in a soft shade of blue which exactly matched her eyes, and her long, dark hair which hung loose, had the same blue-black sheen as her mother's which was demurely tucked beneath a wimple. But what enchanted me the most was the circlet woven of spring flowers that adorned her hair, adding to the air of innocence and maidenly perfection that radiated from her.

At my elbow, Matilda said in a low voice. 'I could never get Mattie to stay looking like that at her age – isn't she sweet!'

Despite her comments about the child I could see that her attention was fixed elsewhere, for her eyes kept straying to the only other guest in the room who had not put in an appearance at Hay until long after Baldwin's sermon. Trahaearn Fychan had ridden over from Llangorse with the purpose of escorting the party into Brecheiniog on the morrow, having heard that was where they were headed. I regarded Matilda unhappily. It was a blessing that frequent travelling between castles over the years had meant that the she'd not seen much of Trahaearn Fychan since he'd sheltered William in the aftermath of the battle of Dingestow. But it was obvious from the way her features softened and her face glowed on the occasions they did meet that she had formed an attachment to him, and I glanced at William, afraid that he too could see the longing in his wife's eyes.

At that moment the children entered the solar accompanied by their nurses and tutor. Immediately Matilda began fussing around them, straightening tunics and tucking stray locks of hair back into ribbons ready to present them to Archbishop Baldwin.

Bertha, now ten years old, and so like her father in appearance, was presented first, and after bobbing a pretty curtsey she responded to the Archbishop's questions politely enough before returning to her nurse. Then Margaret, the youngest of the girls, was led forward and after managing a small curtsey she promptly ran to her mother and hid behind her skirts where her flaxen head peeped out shyly from time to time to observe the proceedings.

Then the brothers came forward: Will, the oldest of the boys, reached his mother's shoulder, was as thin as a whippet and possessed his father's clear, grey eyes. He bowed gracefully to the Archbishop and answered his questions well enough before stepping aside. Next, Reginald, Giles, Phillip and John, the youngest still at seven, with his round, apple-like cheeks now flushed from the heat of the solar, stepped forward.

The Archbishop suppressed a smile as his eyes alighted on Giles. The boy was clearly bursting to say something; he kept shuffling his feet and looking pleadingly at his mother.

'You must be young Giles?' he said, having been forewarned by Matilda that Giles had a mission.

'Yes, Your Grace,' Giles squeaked.

'You have something to tell me?'

The boy drew himself up visibly to his full height, and after a moment's hesitation said. 'I wish to enter the church, sir – when I am old enough. But –'

'Carry on,' prompted Baldwin.

'Well –' he hesitated again, and Matilda stepped forward and put her hand on his shoulder.

'What he is trying to say, Your Grace, is that he would like your blessing. He feels that it will help him keep the faith until he is old enough to enter the church – his sister Flandrina has already taken the veil. She is with the nuns of Godstow Abbey, and Giles believes he too has a calling.'

Immediately, the Archbishop bent down towards the little boy, made the sign of the cross on his forehead, and intoned: 'I bless thee, Giles, in the name of the Lord God Almighty, and trust that your faith will remain true, and your heart remain dedicated, until the day that you are old enough to enter the holy offices of the church and carry out His good works.'

Only when the Archbishop had finished did Giles let out the breath he had been holding, and I saw Matilda dab her eyes surreptitiously before leading the children back to their nurses, satisfied that they had all conducted themselves well in the presence of their important visitors. The only one conspicuous by her absence was Mattie. She could not be found anywhere in the castle and it soon emerged that she had taken her mare Floret out for a canter, accompanied only by a groom and two guards.

Williams's face was dark with anger. He had left explicit instructions that she was to be present with the other children when they were presented to the Archbishop and not on one of her reckless cavorts across the countryside. Throwing a glare at Matilda as if she was to blame in some way, he turned his back on her and signalled to the servants to bring more wine.

The light was beginning to fade in the solar and by my estimation the bell would soon ring nones, the time when we would make our way to the hall for supper. The nurses had already taken the children back to the nursery to wash and dress for the meal, and Will had made himself scarce, off to the stables no doubt.

Everyone else had gathered around the Archbishop who was recounting the journey through Hereford and Radnor prior to their arrival at Hay. Ranulf de Glanville, Chief Justiciar of the kingdom, had accompanied them as far as Radnor Baldwin explained, and there they had met with Rhys ap Gruffydd, Prince of South Wales, and Gerald's kin, who himself had made a pledge to take the Cross.

Gerald dipped his head in acknowledgement at this, proud of his noble birth and the fact that he was related to a line of Welsh princes. 'Lord Rhys takes Saladin's threat to Christianity very seriously and is determined to join Henry in his bid to reclaim Jerusalem for Christendom – as does his daughter's husband, Enion,' he said. And drawing himself up to his full height, he regarded each person gravely in turn, his eyes coming to rest on William who everybody knew had made no such pledge.

Immediately, a tide of red washed up William's face and neck at Gerald's quiet reprimand and turning away he signalled to a servant to top up his wine whilst he struggled to contain his anger.

'Tomorrow we hope to continue our journey on towards Brecon, but we will stop at Llanddeu and preach there. Gerald has promised to show me his marvellous house where we hope to spend the night - which means that we probably won't make Brecon until the following day.' Baldwin interjected into the silence that followed.

'I have already sent someone ahead to prepare the house for your Grace,' Gerald said, bowing slightly towards the Archbishop. 'I would not have you turn up to an empty larder and cold bed.'

After a little more conversation, the Archbishop broke off and went to speak with his servant who had just entered the room to enquire about sleeping arrangements.

Suddenly William loomed over Matilda and drew her to one side. 'He is an insufferable character,' I heard him hiss, gesturing towards Gerald who was now deep in conversation with the Earl of Clare. 'Do you know that he means to write a book of his travels around Wales with Baldwin? And in it he means to allude to Abergavenny - you know, what happened there in seventy-five!'

'The murders you mean?' Matilda asked, fixing her shrewd green eyes on William's face which was now suffused with anger.

'It was done on the order of King Henry,' William spluttered hotly. 'To show the Welsh who is their true overlord –' He broke off suddenly, realising that he was attracting unwanted attention, and slamming his goblet down on the window embrasure he went off in the direction of the garderobe to let off steam.

By the time William returned to the solar, Matilda was deep in conversation with Gerald. She was dressed in a pale ivory chemise, over which she wore a vibrant green silk bliaut with trailing sleeves. The latter was trimmed with gold thread at the hem, neck and wrists, and laced tightly at the hips where a belt of twisted gold sat emphasising the soft folds of the skirt as they fell to the floor. On her head a simple white silk wimple secured by a gold fillet hid her hair, although some had escaped to curl beguilingly around her face. For a woman who had so many children, she still turned heads. Even Gerald was not immune.

Glancing across at them, William scowled and went to join the Earl of Clare. Then in a loud voice he began to enquire if the Earl would find a match between Will and Maude a suitable arrangement in the future. This came as no surprise to me. Matilda had already hinted that William thought the pair would be a good match as they had come to know each other well during his time as squire in the household. But still, I saw Amice raise her finely arched eyebrows and frown at her husband.

Gerald, sensing the atmosphere, glanced at William's stiff back. Then taking Matilda's arm, he led her out of his hearing, signalling for me to bring her goblet and a pitcher of wine. 'I heard William speak of my intention to write about the foul atrocities that happened at Abergavenny in my next book, "A Journey through Wales", which I mean to write after this tour,' he said when they were safely ensconced in a corner.

He paused then, pondering how to put it delicately whilst I topped up his goblet with William's fine Burgundy.

'Please reassure him,' he continued when I had finished, 'that it is not my intention to paint him in a poor light, for I believe there are others who are more deeply involved than he - people about whom I cannot speak freely of yet, having no firm evidence. However, I must ask your indulgence if I state the blunt truth in my writing, for without it, history loses all authority and ceases to be worthy of its name. In short, Matilda, I know that I will anger people, both Norman and Welsh, when I recount matters that have happened here in our lifetime, but -'

He broke off once more to pet Giselle who, bored with the children, was trying to get his attention by licking his hand. 'But,' he repeated firmly, 'I must tell the truth as best I know it and not be prejudiced by what others think.'

Matilda inclined her head at the end of Gerald's long speech. 'You must take care though, Gerald,' she said quietly, and I could hear the urgency in her voice. 'William can bear a grudge as keenly as the Welsh. It would not be good for you to make an enemy of him –

he has influences in high places, remember, and he could make things difficult for you,' she finished softly.

After a short silence in which they both contemplated how capable William was of cruelty, Gerald said, 'I have already completed my first book entitled "A Topography of Ireland". You probably already know that some years ago, King Henry appointed me to accompany Prince John to Ireland as his Chaplain and advisor? The trip was a complete and utter failure – he can be such an arrogant young man – do you know that he actually poked fun at the way the chieftains dressed and wore their beards?' he finished, still shaking his head as if John's arrogance were still a mystery to him all these years later.

Matilda stiffened at the mention of Prince John and threw me a swift look. 'I'm sure it's a fine book,' she said quickly. Then, 'Did you see the way the men of Hay charged out of the church in pursuit of his Grace this morning all eager to take the cross following his inspired sermon, Gerald?'

'Yes,' Gerald said, shaking his head incredulously, the subject of Prince John already forgotten. 'Now, that *would* be a good story to include in my new book of our travels around Wales, would it not!'

Matilda's lips twitched, pleased to have diverted his attention from a subject that disturbed her. 'Ah, yes ... but did you see their wives and sweethearts?' she enquired sweetly, putting her goblet down on a small intricately carved table beside her and crossing her arms inside the trailing sleeves of her bliaut.

'No, what about them?' Gerald asked, a surprised look appearing on his handsome face suggesting that he had paid them no attention at all.

'Well,' she said, keeping her face as straight as possible. 'Let's just say that they now have a surfeit of warm cloaks for next winter – on account of the fact that their men had to wriggle out of them to escape and keep up their pursuit of his Grace.'

Seeing he didn't understand, she sighed and, letting her smile slip, she said gently, 'Not everyone was moved by the Archbishop's speech, Gerald. Some, the women mainly, are not so keen for their menfolk to disappear off on a crusade – no matter how important that crusade is to Christendom. They fear for their families. How are they to feed them? What of the hard labour that has to be done? How will they survive without a man during the long, cold winters?'

Gerald pondered this for a moment, turning it over in his mind, then he patted her on the back of her hand where it rested beneath her sleeve, and said. 'I shall pray for them, Matilda. You and I shall pray for them. God will surely provide. I shall speak to my kin and the king,' he went on enthusiastically, 'and a way will be found – prayers, alms, poor tax. No king in Christendom would leave his loyal subjects to starve to death!'

At that moment the bell rang for nones, summoning us to supper in the great hall below, cutting off any reply that Matilda might have made and silencing us all. In the corner of the solar a candle guttered and went out, plunging it into semi-darkness where a shadowy image stirred.

No king in Christendom would leave his loyal subjects to starve to death ...

It was barely a whisper, followed by a caress on the back of the neck as light as a feather, and then the ghostly spectre was gone.

For a moment nobody moved. Then Matilda spun around, her shocked white face gleaming at me as she picked up her skirts and ran from the room in a flurry of petticoats.

William and the others stared after her in surprise. 'Well, I guess that's the signal for supper!' William said eventually, forcing a note of joviality into his voice. Within moments the room was empty.

Crossing myself I looked around. Then picking up my own skirts I quickly ran down the narrow winding stairs after the retreating party, the soles of my soft kid shoes slapping each one in turn, the sound ringing in my ears like the laughter that followed me as I went ...

The hall was buzzing with gossip and excitement as the household washed their hands in the ewers provided at the entrance and settled themselves down at tables spread with snowy white linen which would soon be strewn with breadcrumbs and soiled with wine and sauce.

Peering across the smoky hall I saw that William and Matilda were already seated at the high table on the dais, with Gerald and the Archbishop on either side of them as their honoured guests. Further down the table Richard de Clare sat with Amice, Maude and Gilbert, all erect and shiny as new pins. Maude, I noticed, had perked up. She now looked slightly flushed and was throwing shy glances from under her lashes at Will who sat the other side of Gerald. She had been told of the possibility of betrothal, I assumed.

Mattie was the last up on to the dais. She was dragging her feet, but I was relieved to see she had finally shown her face - though she'd positioned herself as far down the table as possible and hadn't bothered to curb her unruly hair.

It was stuffy in the hall and the children, seated at one of the lower tables, were fidgeting with hunger and boredom by the time I made my way through the throng to sit beside them.

Seeing that people were ready to eat, William signalled the servants to begin bringing in the food, and a silver goblet encrusted with rubies and emblazoned with the de Braose coat of arms was passed along the honoured guests seated at the high table, signifying the beginning of the feast. Whilst serving maids and pages ran back and forth to the kitchen, the butler and Sam organised the distribution of jugs of the best Rhenish wine for those seated on the dais and for the knights of William's mesinie. Ale brewed from last year's barley made its way to the lower trestles where the rest of the household sat.

It was simple fare because it was well known that Gerald deplored gluttony: a stew of salted venison, dried peas and beans, and freshly sliced boar straight from the spit arrived first. This was followed by an open pie of chicken, pigeon and mushrooms and, finally, lamb stew liberally seasoned with sage and parsley. The rich smells mingled with the smoke from the fire in the hearth; apple-wood from the log hut in the bailey, gathered before the long winter had set in the previous year. To round off the meal there was dried fruit and cheese from the dairy and frumenty: a gruel of wheat boiled with milk and flavoured with spices – a favourite of the children.

Throughout the meal the soft notes of lute and harp floated down from the minstrel's gallery, accompanied by the dulcet tones of one of the travelling troubadours that had attached themselves to the Archbishop's company as they made their way into Wales.

Not to be outdone, Owen, William's harpist, joined them and began plucking the strings of his own instrument, his strange hunched back throwing a macabre shadow on the wall behind him.

It was late, and I must have dozed, because the hall was half empty and people were pulling their pallets out and preparing themselves for sleep. Rubbing my eyes, I glanced up at the dais. I frowned, surprised to see that Mattie had left her seat further down the table, and had slipped into a vacant one alongside Gerald whilst Matilda and William were deep in conversation with Archbishop Baldwin. She had passed nearly sixteen summers and was the image of her mother, with hair the exact same shade of chestnut, and the same slightly tilted green eyes that were now brimming with tears. Right now, her hand was resting on Gerald's sleeve and there was an imploring look on her face that no man, clergy or otherwise, could resist.

Sensing trouble, I rose and began to make my way towards the dais, still rubbing my sore eyes, when William suddenly spotted her. Immediately, his face flooded with anger and he stood abruptly, knocking over a goblet so that wine filled his trencher and overflowed onto the rushes on the floor.

Matilda also leapt to her feet, her face flushing with embarrassment as William strode round, grasped Mattie's arm, and tried to pull her bodily out of the seat. There was a hushed silence in the hall as all eyes turned on the dais, wondering what the sudden disturbance was about. It made a strange tableau as, for several long moments, William and Matilda stood with their eyes locked in unspoken battle over the head of their stricken daughter.

Then suddenly all the anger left William and, releasing Mattie's arm, he turned on his heel and strode from the hall. The silence was unnerving, then all at once there was the buzz of excitement as people turned to each other to discuss this turn of events with relish.

Ignoring their audience, Gerald patted Mattie's hand and drew her gently back down into the chair. Matilda threw several nervous glances over her shoulder in the direction that William had departed, but she didn't follow him. Instead she pulled her chair closer to Gerald and Mattie's and glancing quickly down the length of the hall she whispered, 'William plans a betrothal between Mattie and one of your kin, Gerald. Gruffydd ap Rhys to be precise. He plans to have it agreed in the next few weeks before we return to Bramber and she will be married the following year.' Matilda sighed wearily. 'William and I have not seen eye to eye on the union.'

'Ah, I gathered as much,' Gerald said succinctly. 'But the Welsh are not all ruffians,' he added, turning to Mattie. Then seeing that she was still very distressed he took her hand. 'He will treat you kindly, my dear, you may have my word on it – I am not completely without influence, you know, despite the fact that I carry a cross rather than a sword.'

Mattie's tears had brimmed over by now; they were making their way down her face and plopping onto the table linen where they were lost in the sea of crumbs and spilt wine.

Sighing, Matilda glanced once again down the length of the hall, and seeing the furtive glances still being thrown at the dais she threw down her napkin and said, 'Perhaps it would be a good thing to have this conversation in the solar rather than in public.' Then catching my eye, she signalled for me to follow.

William was standing in the solar staring into the hearth when we arrived, a goblet of wine in his hand. I slipped past Mattie who was the last to enter the room and poured the same for Gerald and Matilda before making myself discreet in the corner. Baldwin had tactically stayed in the hall and struck up a conversation with the Earl of Clare.

William turned, and putting down his goblet he crossed to Mattie saying gruffly, 'It will be a good union, child. It will make us allies with Lord Rhys. He is, after all, the ruler of Deheubarth. It is better to be allied to him rather than be his enemy. Can you not see that?'

'But I will be so far away from you. Amongst people who are –' Mattie hesitated. 'Among people who hate us, Father. Who hate us because of Abergavenny,' she finished, her voice little more than a whisper.

William's face flushed in anger at this subject, but he gainfully managed to suppress it as he regarded her through narrowed eyes. It was no secret that she had never been the dutiful daughter he wanted, or that he blamed Matilda for letting her have too much freedom. But it seemed that he was only just beginning to realise how much of a wedge his volatile daughter could put in his plans.

'Gruffydd is not one of Seisyll's sons,' he said at last, trying to keep his voice level. 'And, therefore, he will not hold a grudge like they do. Besides, the king demands this marriage, and so we must obey.'

'But, Father -'

'No!' William shouted. 'Your mother has been far too lenient with you! I will hear no more.'

'By the grace of God, Gruffydd's father has taken the cross with us – I was only telling your mother and father a couple of hours ago,' Gerald said quickly, interrupting William before his temper could get the better of him once again. 'He's a good Christian gentleman, my dear - he will look after you, you have my assurance of that.'

Then throwing a conciliatory look at William, he drew Mattie's hand through the crook of his arm and led her towards the table where he began to pour her a goblet of wine. 'I know it's hard, but it is your duty to marry where your father wishes – where it will be for the greater good. Can you not accept that, my child?' he asked gently.

Suddenly Mattie let out a loud chocking sob, and snatching her arm out of Gerald's grip, she spun on her heel and ran from the solar, her hair flying like a banner behind her. It was clear that her bid for an ally in Gerald had failed.

The room was silent for a moment, and I saw William contemplating Matilda from his position by the hearth with hooded eyes. On his face was a look of fear mingled with desire. And beneath the surface, barely disguised hate.

Later that night William dismissed me curtly from Matilda's chamber where I was brushing out her long hair by the light of a single rush sconce, and the next morning she did not appear to take leave of Gerald and Baldwin. I found her later in the privy being sick. Her robe had fallen off her shoulders so that I could see the evidence of William's cruelty. Cruelty which I knew to be borne out of fear, and his desire to bend her to his will.

Llangorse, Wales, July 1188

Matilda reined her palfrey in before the old hunting lodge tucked away on the edge of the woods at Llangorse. This was the first time that she had ever disobeyed William and ridden out alone. And if he found out, he would flay her within an inch of her life. But the short exchanges in the hall or in her solar were no longer enough for her, especially when those exchanges were carried out in front of Ailith, from whom she could hide nothing, she thought guiltily as she remembered the knowing look on Ailith's face when she had insisted that she that she would ride out that morning on her own. No, she just had to see Trahaearn Fychan alone.

Tied to a tree near the entrance of the lodge was Trahaearn's favourite grey stallion. He whickered when she approached and, dismounting her own horse, she tied it up deftly alongside his. Then with her heart thumping in her chest, she picked up her skirts and headed up the path. It was quiet and still when she pushed open the door and entered, stopping just inside to allow her eyes to become accustomed to the dark after the brightness of the sun outside. It took a moment for her to recognise Trahaearn silhouetted against a window at the back of the room, but when she did, she immediately felt the familiar surge of longing that only ever gripped her when he was near. With a groan Trahaearn took three long strides and, pulling her into his arms he buried his hands in her hair, seeking her mouth and crushing his lips to hers greedily.

'No, Trahaearn, we must not,' Matilda whispered, pushing him away. 'I should not have come here. I must return to Brecknock Castle. William will be there soon and I must not dishonour him. To do so would be a great folly, for he is a cruel and unforgiving man and if he ever found out he would kill me.'

'You would not have come here if you did not want me as much as I want you,' Trahaearn said, smiling gently as he pulled the pins from her veil. 'It's torture whenever I see you sitting next to him and not being able to touch you. I long for you so much, my love.'

Turning away to hide her confusion Matilda looked around the lodge. Someone, perhaps Trahearn himself, had taken a great deal of care to make it welcome. The hearth had recently been swept and the floor was newly strewn with a mixture of fresh rushes and herbs. Over in one corner there was a wide wooden bench covered with furs, and in the middle of the room Trahaearn's sword and scabbard lay discarded on a table, alongside two goblets and a flagon of wine. All at once the overwhelming urge to throw caution to the wind and give into her desires took over. She knew that she wanted him as much as he wanted her, and suddenly she found herself trembling with the need.

As if sensing her uncertainty, Trahaearn pulled her back into the circle of his arms, his grip more insistent now; she could smell the scent of wine on his breath, and she was helpless, unable to resist as she felt the throb of his arousal through her skirts.

'If you were mine, I would never let you out of my sight,' Trahaearn whispered. 'William is a fool and a brute and he does not deserve you.'

Matilda moaned as one of his hands slid beneath the neckline of her gown, seeking her nipple. Immediately, she felt a tugging sensation deep down in the pit of her belly and between the juncture of her legs. The smell of sex was in the air, heady and powerful.

Picking her up suddenly, Trahaearn carried her to the bench and laid her gently on it. Then he was above her, fumbling with the hem of her gown as he released one of her breasts from the confines of her bodice, capturing the nipple between his teeth. Without another thought Matilda arched her back. Urging him on. Wanting him to take her quickly. Needing him to satisfy her desire. Then, before they both knew it, her skirts were up around her waist and he was inside her.

He moved slowly at first, and she began to moan as she matched his rhythm with hers, meeting each of his thrusts with one of her own. Trahaern's back was slick with moisture; she could see the veins on his neck standing proud as he concentrated on bringing her pleasure. Then at last, as if sensing that she was on the cusp but not quite there, Trehaern moved his hands to her hips and raised them.

For a moment Matilda stared into his eyes. She had never felt such intimacy, such closeness to a man before. William's advances had been crude, rough and thoughtless beyond the knowledge that he needed to beget a child upon her. As if sensing her thoughts, Trahaern hesitated and, dropping a kiss on her forehead, he pulled back a little. For a moment Matilda thought that he might stop and she made a small, breathless noise of protest which was cut off suddenly as with a groan he began to move once more. Faster this time, with his hand beneath her buttocks and his fingers caressing the soft slippery flesh at their base.

He didn't stop until wave after wave of pleasure had engulfed her, sweeping her away on a tide of ecstasy from which she never wanted to return. But although it was his name she called with a final shuddering cry, it was William's face she saw when at last she fell back against the furs. And it was dark with fury and rage.

When she finally opened her eyes again, Trahaearn was still trembling above her.

'If William finds out,' Matilda whispered, 'he will kill me.'

'He won't find out,' Trahaearn said, stroking a stray lock of hair from her forehead. 'Come,' he offered, taking her hand in his. 'I suddenly find that I have a vast appetite, I have some of the best wine from my vineyard and apricots like you have never tasted before straight from my orchard in my saddlebag.

Matilda smiled. 'I must not tarry for long,' she said, 'or they will send a search party out for me and we will be discovered.'

Nevertheless, she took the goblet of wine, and ate the apricots he offered her. And all the while the

storm clouds gathered on the horizon as Mistress Destiny
continued to weave her sticky web.

Chapter 12

Brecknock Castle, Wales, May 1189

I helped Matilda slip the blue silk bliaut over Mattie's head and pull it down over her fine linen shift, beneath which her silk hose gleamed. Carefully Matilda arranged the soft drapes over the girl's slim waist and adjusted the side lacings, as she once more tried to draw her into conversation. Seeing the set of the girl's head, Matilda gave up, and sighing she turned and lifted one of her own jewelled girdles from a coffer beside her before fastening it loosely over her hips.

'You must eat something at least,' she said finally, picking up the wreath of flowers woven by Margaret that morning which was to be the last touch to Mattie's wedding attire.

A tear rolled down Mattie's pale face. The closer it had come to the allotted day of her wedding, the less she had eaten and the more she had ridden out, unattended and defiant of William's wishes. But it had all been to no avail as the day had finally dawned when she would be handed over to Gruffydd and made his wife.

Gruffydd had not been unkind to her – after their betrothal the previous year he had constantly sent her gifts. First to arrive had been a casket of jewels which, he said in his letter, befitted the princess she would one day be. A spirited pony had followed that, then a pile of furs, and finally a skein of the best silk and a reel of gold thread from which Rhiannan and Matilda had fashioned her wedding gown.

The only request that Mattie had made was that she might take Cerys and Lowri, her old nurses, with her to her new home, and to this Matilda had happily conceded in the knowledge that she would have alongside her people she loved, for there was no doubt that love her they did.

Downstairs in the chapel, Lord Rhys, Gruffydd's father, and his mother, Gwenllian, waited in the front pews. Alongside them sat several other members of the family, including a clutch of Gruffydd's brothers and, of course, Gerald, who had travelled from his house in Llanddew to witness the wedding. Sitting on the other side of the isle were Margaret, Bertha and John. Will, Giles and Philip were all absent serving as pages or squires in different households and could not travel home for the wedding. Filling the remainder of the pews were Trahaearn Fychan and his plump wife, along with several other of their close neighbours, and at the back of the chapel were as many of the household that could be crammed into the small space remaining.

Gruffydd himself waited with Hugh the chaplain and William outside the chapel door where the vows would be exchanged, nervously smoothing his thick, dark brown hair back from his forehead, his topaz eyes flicking constantly over his shoulder as if he was afraid that his bride was not going to appear.

Matilda sighed again, then putting down the floral wreath she drew her daughter into her arms. I knew that her heart ached for her as any mothers would seeing her daughter so unhappy. But a woman was but a chattel and she must marry where she was told. Even her beloved Mattie.

Feeling like an intruder, I turned and left the room to wait outside, my own heart heavy with guilt. For I knew that there was worse to come.

Rows of sconces lit the hall. The feast had been underway for hours, and now the real revelling had begun, with tables and benches being pushed to the side for dancing to commence. Up on the dais, Mattie sat alongside Gruffydd sharing his platter, although she ate scarcely anything at all. Outside in the bailey it was as noisy as it was inside, for William in a sudden act of charity had provided some food and barrels of ale for his villeins, including some who had travelled by foot from as far as Hay and Radnor to see Mattie wed, because, despite being William's daughter, Mattie was much loved by those who knew her. Every now and then Gruffydd would bend his head close to Mattie's and whisper something – once I thought I almost detected a smile cross her flushed face. Then when the tables had finally been cleared, he shyly offered her his arm and led her out into the centre of the hall to join in the dancing, his eyes never leaving her face.

Seeing this development, Gwenllian leaned towards Matilda and whispered something in her ear. At once a look of understanding dawned on Matilda's face, and for the first time that day I saw her smile and glance towards the high tables as if seeking someone out. Almost imperceptibly Trahaearn Fychan raised his goblet to her, and I felt the hairs on the back of my neck prickle. The look of longing that flitted across her features was so plain that I wondered how I had not guessed before, and suddenly my heart began to thud loudly with fear. Mistress Destiny was meddling again. And it was clear that Trahaearn Fychan was the next fly she intended for her web ...

At last the bells rang the hour of compline and it was time for the newlyweds to retire. Up in the gallery the troubadours had run out of roundels to play, and the revelling had ceased for the night.

Without realising it, Mattie suddenly found herself being propelled towards the newel stairs leading to the wedding chamber by a bunch of giggling maidens. Behind her, Gruffydd was similarly being propelled by a bunch of drunken young men shouting bawdy jokes and lewd suggestions to the girls dancing ahead of them.

Once in the room Mattie found herself being stripped of her clothes. Protesting, she tried to fend the maidens off, but to no avail. Before she knew it, the wreath was torn from her head and deposited on the head of a giggling young girl, and then she was being thrust naked into a large bed covered with thick pelts of soft white miniver and strewn with spring flowers.

Moments later Gruffydd was thrust naked into bed alongside her, and a fat priest was sprinkling them both with Holy water.

It was her worst nightmare, and Mattie averted her gaze from her new husband as a hot tide of embarrassment rose up from her breasts to flood her face. Then, when she felt the ever-present tears begin to well behind her eyes, she bravely tilted her chin and waited for the unwelcome guests to finish having their fun and leave.

When they did, Mattie wished they had left sooner.

From the dais, William watched Matilda with narrowed eyes as she danced a slow pavane with Trahaearn Fychan. When they had finished, Trahaearn courteously led Matilda back to her seat and returned to the dance floor.

William scowled as he toyed with the hilt of his jewelled eating knife. He was not unaware of the ill-concealed looks that the damned man had traded with his wife all through the evening, making a cuckold of him in his own hall. He watched as Trahaearn led his own wife into a lively galliard, trying to put his finger on why he had disliked the man so much even before he'd caught him trading looks with Matilda.

It was true that Trahaearn had sheltered him at his manor at Llangorse after the battle of Dingestow, probably saving his life. However, during his stay William had gained the impression that Trahaearn was a reluctant host. Once, when he was drifting in and out of fever, he thought he heard Trahaearn and his wife quarrelling over him, but afterwards he had put it down to his overwrought imagination. As he regained his strength, though, he had needed less rest, and on several occasions, he had noticed Trahaearn receiving and dispatching messages under the cover of darkness as if he did not wish him to know.

William put down the knife irritably as he considered the matter. Since then he had made discreet enquiries about his neighbour, and it had come to his attention that not only was his wife a distant niece of Lord Rhys, she was also related to the Prince of Powys, and he wondered why Rhys had mentioned neither fact to him considering that they were to be related by today's marriage.

William drummed his fingers on the wood beneath the soiled napery, the sound imperceptible above the din in the hall. Perhaps Rhys didn't think it important. After-all, Mattie's marriage to Gruffydd was to ensure King Henry's wish for peace between the Southern Wales and England, and, if that were the case, Trahaearn's kinship didn't really matter at all. Or did it?

William was almost certain that it did.

After several more days of feasting following the wedding, the time had finally come for Mattie to accompany Gruffydd and his family to Dinefwr Castle, their principal court in Deheubarth. The day had dawned bright and clear, and already Mattie's possessions and wedding gifts had been loaded onto a wagon ready to take its leave later.

Strangely, since her wedding night, which Matilda had been sure would end in tears, Mattie had gone around with an oddly wistful look on her face and could frequently be seen to be throwing flirtatious glances at her new husband – the very same man who only three days before she had professed to hate with every bone in her body.

Matilda sighed. Although she would miss Mattie greatly, she confessed that she was much heartened that her first born daughter seemed to have found something in her marriage to her liking. The morning after the wedding she had teased her over her change of attitude. However, in spite the rising tide of heat that had snaked up her neck, Mattie had still retorted spiritedly that she would not be bent to Gruffydd's will, and that she had already made it quite clear to him that she was nobody's chattel. Gruffydd, upon hearing this, had surprisingly replied that that was exactly what he liked about her — her strength and her spirit. 'A princess of Wales,' he said, 'must have exactly those qualities in order to survive.'

For a moment Matilda's mind lingered on the word 'survive.' She knew little of Gruffydd and his family and had been alarmed to hear only that morning that he had an ongoing blood feud with his older brother Maelgwn who had not been present at the wedding feast, and immediately a familiar fission of fear had curled down her spine. Still feeling slightly unsettled, Matilda went to look out of the window to where the other children were playing. She was left now with only the four youngest. Before the newlyweds had left, William had made an agreement with Gruffydd that when John was old enough he would follow Mattie to her new household and become his page. And so, she would soon lose yet another of her children, and she realised that she harboured some resentment against William for that.

But still, it would be uncommonly quiet without Mattie she thought, watching as Merri's bulky form crossed the bailey with some cinnamon biscuits for John and Loretta who were now playing with the puppies that Giselle and Roland had recently surprised them with. Then, with that thought still on her mind, she turned reluctantly on her heel and made her way back to the now quiet hall.

Chapter 13

28th August 1189, Marlborough Castle, Wiltshire

In the fields surrounding Marlborough Castle, brightly coloured pavilions were being thrown up as the royal court flocked to attend the wedding of Prince John and Isabella of Gloucester.

A shocking series of events had rocked the land, ending in the death of old King Henry in Chinon, France, the month before, leaving the throne for Richard to seize. Some said he died from a broken heart, for on the 5th of July, Henry's vice-chancellor, Roger Malchat, had brought him a list of those who had joined Richard and Phillip Augustus against him. The name at the top of the list was Prince John's. The only son to remain loyal to him at the end was his bastard son Geoffrey, according to William's messenger.

Matilda shivered, remembering the interview that she and William had been summoned to by Henry in Winchester all those years ago. The one in which he had showed her the wall painting of several eaglets ripping an adult eagle to death. Could it be that he had really predicted his own end at the hands of his sons?

Even now, as John prepared himself for his nuptials, Matilda wondered if he felt any remorse. She doubted it very much, for he was selfish to the core; spoilt and over indulged by the father that had loved him to the very end. Immediately her heart began to thud at the thought that she must sit through the long night of feasting ahead, and then attend his wedding on the morrow ...

He will, sometime in the future, insult me more grievously than any of my other sons, I think. As he will you, too, my dear ... As he will you, too. One day ...

The words seemed to float freely in the air, barely a whisper and as light as gossamer in the breeze. Was that day now? Matilda wondered, casting her eyes around frantically for Ailith as her heart began to pound.

I bent down and began the task of unpacking the heavy coffer that had accompanied William and Matilda to Marlborough castle.

Matilda had been very subdued since arriving. William, on the other hand, was striding around like a prize cockerel, having been told by John's steward that he and Matilda were to sit at the Reward table during the feast. This was the table nearest the dais where they, along with a selection of other favoured courtiers, would be served with dishes from John and Isabella's own table.

He had received the news that morning, just before he and Matilda had joined the ranks of courtiers crammed into the great hall at Marlbourgh Castle to pay their respects to the pair, Merri told me. It was a great honour, she said. But I shivered to think whether it was William that John was honouring, or Matilda he was planning on dishonouring. My spine prickled when I recalled the predatory way in which he had eyed her curtsying form, before finally moving on to the next courtier waiting to greet him.

I had nearly finished unpacking the coffer, when two soldiers fought their way through the billowing rectangles of silk that covered the entrance of the tent. They were carrying a large bed adorned with brightly coloured sheets which they deposited behind the panels demarking the sleeping quarters of the pavilion from the living quarters.

'Compliments of Prince John,' one of the soldiers said with a leer. 'Be more comfortable than those pallets!' he finished, nodding to where they now lay, pushed back against the rear of the pavilion.

After they had gone, I stood and contemplated the bed in consternation. In the distance, I heard the raucous laugh of a soldier, and the soft murmurings of a maid, occasionally joined by the shouts of a pie man selling his wares. Other than that, all was quiet. Far too quiet for my liking. And, despite the oppressive August heat, I suddenly felt very cold ....

Prince John paced the length and breadth of his private chambers, his eyes narrowed, his hands clenched behind him. 'Is it all prepared, then?' he demanded of Faulkes de Breauté who was lounging on a deeply padded chair, the remains of the late August sun highlighting his grotesque leer so that he looked like he was wearing a mummer's mask.

'It is,' de Breauté confirmed, one hand lazily stroking the head of a huge hound lounging at his feet. 'The bed is delivered, and the potion secured – poppy juice, just a few drops in her wine. All that remains is to get William in his cups and remove the maid somehow – that shouldn't prove too hard.'

John shivered in anticipation, and he felt his loins stir.

Behind him Faulkes chuckled, but it was not a nice sound. 'So, you are to have her at last,' he murmured, 'I trust that you will reward me well, my old friend ...'

Matilda paced the pavilion chewing her bottom lip. 'But why did he send us a bed?' she asked me anxiously for the umpteenth time. 'It is most uncommon – what will William make of it?'

Just then William entered the pavilion to ready himself for the evening's events. 'Where have you been?' she demanded of him angrily. 'While you've been gone, we have been delivered of a bed – from Prince John no less! If you had been here, you could have sent it back – we have no need of such gifts!' She finished, her eyes blazing in indignation.

William regarded the offending article for a moment, then he shrugged. 'Well, Moll,' he said thoughtfully. 'You can't very well reject it for that would appear churlish, wouldn't it?' Then glancing approvingly at her new green gown embroidered with gold thread, he slipped behind the panels to get washed and change his tunic.

Later that night, when Matilda and I returned alone, leaving William still waiting on Prince John, Matilda demanded that I sleep in the bed with her, and as an extra precaution she had the guard doubled at the entrance.

29th August 1189, Marlborough Castle, Wiltshire

Matilda pushed aside the tapestries that concealed the door to the Duchess of Gloucester's chambers where she was to wait on Isabella for the morning. Inside, Isabella sat on a stool in front of a dressing table staring into a mirror, her small face reflecting miserably from its uneven surface. Behind her, her mother attempted to arrange her hair with the help of one of her ladies who was making a sow's ear of it.

Angrily, Hawise threw down the comb. 'Why did that useless girl have to sneak off last night, drink too much, and get sick?' she demanded of no one in particular – 'I swear I will have her flayed within an inch of her life – this is the most important day of our lives. I just will not tolerate it!'

A couple of other ladies in the room threw their hands into the air, demonstrating that they had no hairdressing skills either.

'Here, let me,' Matilda said, taking up the comb and signalling me to help her. Between us we made a decent job of combing the girl's fine brown hair and twisting the flowers proffered by her sister Avisa into her tresses. 'You see,' Matilda said, standing back to admire her handy work. 'You don't need anything elaborate … she is still but a maid.'

I saw Isabella flinch and turn her pale face away from the mirror so that no one could see her expression, and I was reminded of Mattie on her wedding day.

A while later the girl was still saying nothing, but she stood up meekly when her mother ordered her to so that she could adjust the girdle and the bodice of her bliaut to show the pleats to good effect.

'Now you know what you have to say, don't you?' Hawise demanded of her. 'The last thing you want to do is make a fool of yourself in front of everyone – well, speak up girl!' she finished.

'Yes, Mother,' Isabella said this time. Then with tears brimming in her eyes she looked like she would say some more but, seeing her mother's face, she gave a small hiccup and fixed them on the floor instead.

There was a moment's awkward silence before Avisa sat down on the vacant stool and began to primp herself in the mirror, pursing her lips and pinching her cheeks with her fingers to bring colour to them. With her long dark tresses, and periwinkle blue eyes, of the two youngest Gloucester girls she was by far the prettier. She also possessed a boldness that her sister didn't, and I couldn't help wondering if she might not have been the better match for John. Unlike Avisa, there was something all too innocent and endearing about Isabella that made you want to treat her with great care - like you would treat a timid bird perhaps.

Turning around, I began to gather up the pins and comb, aware that a lump was wedged in my throat. She would not get that sort of care at the hands of Prince John and glancing at Matilda, I saw my own thoughts reflected on her face.

Just then the tapestry was pushed aside again, and Amice de Clare bustled in with Maude, Will's betrothed, in tow. Amice, being the eldest of the Gloucester girls, and married to Richard de Clare for ten years now, was clearly about to give her younger sister the benefit of her advice, judging by the business-like way she was appraising Isabella.

Sighing, I carried the pins and comb over to the open coffer and packed them away. Whatever happened, Isabella of Gloucester was going to be married to John today. But I detected a dark shadow surrounding her, and not for the first time I wished that I hadn't the ability to see deep into other people's souls.

Chapter 14

The wedding feast seemed to go on interminably. The hall was hot and sticky, but the guests, dressed up like peacocks in every hue and colour, the feathers on their caps waving jauntily, refused to give in and retire.

Up on the dais, Isabella sat white faced and tight lipped, the strain of the day's events showing clearly as she picked at the food from the platter she shared with John. Alongside her, he toyed with his wine goblet, breaking out occasionally in ribald laughter at some jest delivered by one or other of his companions, most of whom were deep in their cups by now.

Below them, Matilda sat alone at the Reward table close to the dais. In front of her, untouched, sat some of the gilded marchpane soteltie of an eagle that had been the highlight of the feast, even more spectacular than the swan and pheasants carried in earlier, each adorned in its own feathers.

William, she knew, in some befuddled part of her mind, was somewhere in the body of the hall making merry with some of his acquaintances. Slowly, she lifted the goblet of wine to her lips. Her hand was unsteady, and she felt light headed and strangely detached from the events going on around her. Surely, she had not had too much wine?

Carefully, she replaced the goblet on the table. It caught the edge of her trencher, knocking the remains of the soteltie onto the floor. For a moment she thought she heard her own voice from far away asking for Ailith, but then she half recalled that she was on one of the low tables with some of the other maids.

Feeling numb, she fumbled awkwardly at the tablecloth as she tried to stand. Then strong hands seized her and steadied her ...

Up on the dais, John watched as Matilda struggled to rise. Then he turned and nodded to Faulkes de Breauté who muscled his way towards her, signalling to a couple of soldiers on the way to give him a hand. Within moments she was leaving the castle unnoticed by the postern gate and being carried towards her pavilion, which was helpfully landmarked by the de Braose pennant flying reproachfully from its silk roof.

Back at the castle, John turned to his new wife. 'Time to retire, I think, my dear ...'

Much later, in the small hours of the morning, the side panels of Matilda's pavilion stirred and John entered stealthily. He had left Isabella lying rigid and white faced in their wedding bed, having made little effort to be gentle with her. When he had taken his leave, she had barely been able to disguise her relief, turning her back on him and uttering a tiny sob of despair.

He paused for a moment, looking around to check that Matilda was indeed alone. Somewhere in the castle William lay in a drunken stupor, and if everything had gone according to plan, her maid had been slipped an equal measure of the poppy juice in her watered-down wine. As a final precaution, Faulkes had made sure that the guards were bribed with coin and drink. And so, he was left undisturbed.

Sighing, John placed the candle on the coffer at the foot of the bed and sat on it to study her. Her eyes were wide open. Her pupils dilated and unfocused. He stayed like that for a while, taking in the bright auburn streaks in her hair, which, freed from the confines of her wimple, now lay spread like a fan across the pillows, and the slightly parted lips that revealed her small, dainty teeth. Then, sliding his hands under her skirts, slowly he began to raise them.

'*Trahaearn* ...?' Matilda's voice, slurred and uncertain, cut loudly into the silence.

John stilled. So, there's someone else. Another man, he thought angrily.

'*Go away, silly boy* ...' For a moment Rosamund's voice echoed inside his head; he could see her face and hear the sound of her laughter tinkling in the air above him, joined by his father's short bark as he clipped him about the ear and sent him on his way.

Why is there always someone else – Why did nobody want him? his childhood voice asked resentfully.

For a moment John's anger made him impotent, and abandoning Matilda's skirts around her waist, he leaned forward and placed his hands either side of her slender throat. Immediately, he felt an overwhelming surge of power come over him. He could smell the perfume in her hair and feel the tender pulse at the base of her neck which would be so easy to break, and suddenly he was consumed by a mixture of desire and hate in equal measure, for both this woman and the one who still haunted his past. He wanted to hurt her. But at the same time his loins ached with a different need.

How you hated Rosamund, your father's whore ... his childhood voice taunted. Angrily, he increased the pressure on Matilda's windpipe as Rosamund's face floated across his vision again ... *Laughing with his father at something he'd said* ...

Beneath him, he felt Matilda stiffen slightly. *'Trahaearn? William -?'* her voice came out a pitiful, strangled croak. He looked down at her. She was staring up at him, trying desperately to focus her gaze on his face as it hovered above hers. He could see her head swimming with the effort and her eyes beginning to bulge from the strain.

'Why is there always someone else? Why are all women whores?'

He wasn't aware that he had spoken out loud, but the sound of his voice roused Matilda and frantically she tried to cry out, only to gag instead as the sour smell of wine mixed with the musty odour of sex assailed her nostrils. Taking this as further rejection, John threw his full weight down over her body, crushing her deep into the mattress and deliberately cutting off any further sound she might have made. For a moment she froze, and he felt a surge of triumph as he saw that, too late, she had recognized the cold blue eyes glittering dangerously above her face. Horrified, she tried to wriggle sideways out from under him, but he was stocky and strong, and grasping her wrists he clamped them above her head easily.

'Be still! Another move and I shall have to take steps to silence you, my lady. Do you want that?' He could feel her fear now, a tangible thing in the air spurring him on and, grinding his mouth down on hers, he forced his tongue between her lips and probed it hard against her teeth.

'All whores,' he muttered again, his breath hot on her mouth.

At last, as if realising that it was too dangerous to struggle, Matilda gave a small sob and went limp beneath him. 'Good girl, that's better,' John said, smiling coldly into the darkness above her. 'Now, let us enjoy our sport. Mayhap you will find me better than this Trahaearn you speak of ... or even your husband, William.' Then, levering himself up onto one elbow, he took a handful of her gown, and with a wrench he ripped it from the bodice down to the waist. Within moments his mouth was on her breasts, his hands pinching, grasping and hurting her as they travelled down her body. Only once did she cry out, and that was when he forced her legs apart with his knees and drove himself deep inside her.

Time and time again he took her. Punishing her, bruising her, humiliating her, as he'd wanted to punish, bruise, and humiliate his father's whore all those years ago. Sometimes he called her Matilda, sometimes he called her Rosamund. But most often, he called her whore.

It seemed to go on forever. Then suddenly his desire reached its peak and, throwing back his head, he let out an animal groan, his mouth drawn back in an ugly rictus as at last he spilled his seed into her.

Total silence hung over the pavilion, punctured only by the shriek of a small animal as it was born away by an owl, before John finally came to his senses. Slowly the anger left him, and he looked down at Matilda. She was staring up at him, her green, cat like eyes luminous with tears in the early morning dawn, and contempt written all over her face.

'It needn't have been like this. You could have given yourself to me freely, instead you chose this way,' he said as, caught up in a sudden and uncharacteristic wave of guilt, he attempted to turn the blame on her.

Matilda said nothing. She simply turned her head and stared at a point somewhere past his shoulder as the tears began to course there way down her face. After a while, he climbed off the bed and began to pull on his hose and tunic. Then fastening his dagger to his belt, he turned towards the side curtains and flung them open.

Outside the pavilion, Faulkes de Breauté lounged against a tree, but as soon as John appeared, he straightened up and fell into step beside him. When they were far enough away from the camp not to be heard, John paused and turned to de Breauté.

'Find out if de Braose knows someone called Trahaearn for me,' he instructed, his face dark with hate. 'I want all the information you can glean. But be discreet about it, I don't want him to suspect anything. The information could be useful to me in the future.' And with that, he set off once more for the castle.

I am running again through my dream to where Matilda stands on the edge of the precipice, her hands held out beseechingly towards me. This time in my dream, however, there is great clarity of colour: everything is bright, as if someone has spilled paints of every hue on a palette and let them mingle at will. I am aware that something is very wrong, but I want to laugh. I feel extraordinarily happy, and incredibly sad at the same time.

In my dream, Prince John reaches out, touches Matilda's shoulder, and hands her a cup of wine laced with the poppy juice. He is much clearer now. I can see that his face is twisted and dark, and his eyes are very blue. I shiver with fear and try to cry out. But the words are stuck in my throat in the manner of dreams. I toss in my sleep. Restless, uncertain, and afraid. I want to go to her, but I am too tired to try to run anymore. Instead, I can only watch as John engulfs her in his dark embrace and pulls her towards him so that their bodies are as one.

Then I am falling. Tumbling in my dream into a great, wide chasm. And my head is filled with a loud humming noise; like a hive of bees gone mad. Dark despair threatens to overwhelm me, and I hear myself cry out loud. Yet it is not my voice but Matilda's that echoes back. Desperate with fear.

Then William is at my shoulder. I can smell the drink on him and see the stubble that blurs the lines of his chin and frames the bitter grooves of his mouth.

'All women are whores,' he says with contempt.

'But you can stop him,' I say.

'Nay,' says William bitterly. 'What Prince John wants, Prince John takes.' Then he is gone, and I am left with only the faint whisper of his words still hanging suspended in the air, waiting to echo down the channels of time and back again to haunt us.

Then suddenly I am awake, lying on the rushes looking up at the ceiling of the hall. I try to sit up, and instead I knock over the remains of my cup. I pick it up gingerly and sniff it. It smells bitter. It smells of watered wine, and something else I remember from my dream.

Poppy juice, a small voice whispers. And I am sure that I hear the faint hint of a giggle ...

Matilda and I sat huddled on the bed as at last the sun began to peak shyly from behind the clouds, half expecting John to return but he did not. Despite the humidity in the pavilion, she had pulled a warm mantle round herself because she could not stop shivering. We had not spoken of what had passed – me because I was ashamed of the fact that I had failed her, and Matilda because she did not want to re-live the horror of the night. I had stuffed her lovely ruined gown into an old sack and would find somewhere to burn it later away from prying eyes.

When the sun had risen fully, Matilda stood numbly and crossed to her clothes pole, and with her back to me she said. 'William must never know of this.'

'But –'

'No,' Matilda interrupted me. 'It would serve no purpose, none at all. If he makes a fuss, it would shame me, and it would shame Isabella. No,' she finished firmly, 'he cannot be told.' And with that, she pulled a deep green bliaut off the pole and handed it to me, bidding me to help her dress whilst she summoned up the courage to go and face John in the great hall.

The great hall was crowded when Matilda entered, and all eyes turned towards her as she hovered in the doorway. For a moment, she wavered, and almost turned to flee as her resolve threatened to desert her. John, however, had seen her, and he beckoned her forward with a single gesture. Swallowing hard, Matilda picked up her skirts, and made her way down the gap between the trestle tables with as much dignity as she could muster.

When she reached the dais, John waved a hand benignly towards a free chair alongside Isabella's at the high table; several eyebrows were raised at such an honour. Isabella did not look at Matilda once, but continued to pick at the platter in front of her. Dropping a deep curtsey to John, and then to Isabella, Matilda mounted the platform and sat down. The smell of food made the bile rise in her throat, but she managed to hold it down, desperately hoping that her fear and disgust did not show on her face for the rest of the hall to see.

'I trust you had a restful night,' John enquired of her pleasantly. Underneath his brows his blue eyes mocked her, and Matilda felt a shameful flush suffuse her face, but she held her head high.

'I am seeking Sir William, sire,' she said. 'He did not return to our pavilion this morning, and I was worried.'

'Still sleeping off the effects of last evening's reverie, I believe,' John replied, helping himself to another portion of cold pheasant, and breaking some bread from a loaf in front of him.

Shakily, Matilda took the goblet of wine proffered to her by John's squire and raised it to her lips, then taking several large gulps from it she sat back on her chair and took a deep breath. 'I wish permission to return home, sire,' she said, ignoring John's barb and keeping her voice low and steady. 'I have had word that there is an outbreak of small pox in Hay, and I wish to remove my children to the safety of Brecon.'

John frowned. 'But you are to accompany your husband and the rest of the court to Winchester for Richard's coronation, are you not?' he enquired, a note of warning in his voice.

Matilda's eyes held John's for a long moment. 'I think it best, my lord, that I attend to my children. I would be sorely sick if one of them were to die in my absence. Besides, as you know, because Richard is not wed women are not invited to attend the coronation – or the feast afterwards – save Queen Eleanor,' she finished. Then, seeing that he was still undecided, she pressed: 'I am sure that you would not be so cruel as to deny a loving wife and mother to be with her children in a time of crisis.' She placed extra emphasis on the word 'wife,' and John looked away in discomfort.

'Very well,' he said suddenly. 'So be it, return to your children.' Then pushing back his chair he stepped down from the dais and, flanked by his knights, he strode arrogantly down the body of the hall to prepare for the day's hunting. All the way down the length of it, Matilda's eyes bored into his back as if they could penetrate the very centre of his soul and expose the evil buried there.

But if John felt them, he did not falter.

Brecknock Castle, September 1189

Matilda, in need of air, was making for the stables when the messenger arrived, but she paused when he announced that he had come straight from Archdeacon Gerald's house at Llanddeu with a message that was to be placed in none but the Lady Matilda's hand. 'I am Lady Matilda. Pray tell, what of the contents?' she asked, handing her switch to a groom.

'I am afraid I'm not in the Archdeacon's confidence regarding the contents, my lady, only that he bid me make sure that it fell into your hands alone.'

Matilda nodded distractedly, wondering what could be so important that it had necessitated Gerald to dispatch a messenger so urgently. Turning to Ailith who had just left the bakehouse, she instructed her to show the messenger to the kitchens so that Merri might give him a bite to eat and drink before he embarked on his return journey. Then, picking up her skirts, she made her way across the damp bailey and into the herb garden, where she sat and took a deep breath before breaking the wax seal on the roll of parchment with shaking hands.

Llanddeu 14 September, the year of our Lord 1189

My dear Lady de Braose,

I am afraid that in Lord William's absence I must acquaint you of the perfidious actions of my kin Rhys ap Gruffydd, the Lord Rhys, father of Gruffydd ap Rhys to whom your daughter Matilda wed with my assurances not long ago. Despite my earnest pleas to the contrary, it seems that Lord Rhys no longer finds himself bound to the oath that he forged with King Henry when he was alive, and he is now undertaking to renew attacks on the Marcher lordships with vigour, driven by his sons who are at once in conflict with both their father and each other.

It is not my intention to alarm you, in fact I am writing to reassure you on behalf of your daughter that she is safe, as are you for the time being. I have recently visited her myself at Dinefwr and so you can be assured, dear lady, that this is so and that she is in the rudest of health and is expecting her first child next year. However, I must warn you that Lord Rhys is much manipulated by his sons, particularly Gruffydd, who encouraged him to hand over his brother Maelgwn to him as prisoner (you of course know of the ongoing blood feud between them which has not improved much over time).

Furthermore, to add to this treachery, Gruffydd seeks to encourage Lord Rhys to annex the lordship of Cemais held by his own kin William Fitzmartin who, as you know, is wed to his daughter Angharad, and take Llanhyver castle from him, despite swearing by the most precious of relics that his indemnity and security should be faithfully maintained. For this reason alone, I feel that you and Lord William should be cautious in your dealings with the Lord Rhys and his sons. Blood ties are but tenuous threads in these turbulent days that can easily be broken at a whim like silken threads when one party has the blood lust upon them. Therefore, dear lady, please do not be complacent. The treaty through marriage between yourselves and Lord Rhys affords you some protection but remember that wolves sometimes wear sheep's clothing.

Having warned you, dear lady, I will say that although Gruffydd is undoubtedly a cunning and artful man, I myself have witnessed the strongest affection for your daughter and I beg you have no fears on that score, but I fear that you will need all your strength for the future. Please be assured that I have written to Lord William on the matter and hope that my messenger can intercept him on his way back from Winchester.

May God go with you, my dear Lady de Braose.

Gerald, Archdeacon of Brecon

So, Gruffydd had persuaded Rhys to hand Maelgwyn, his own brother, over to him as a prisoner and they were planning further treacherous acts together.

Matilda shivered. Despite the hot late summer sun that flooded the herb garden, she suddenly felt very cold, and from far away she thought she heard the distant cries of a war horn and the shrill screams of a battle float in the air. Then suddenly she was in the herb garden no more. Instead, she was surrounded by men milling around her, their swords clashing loudly together as the sinews of their arms strained under the weight of shield and sword; she could smell the stench of the battle and see the fields running red with blood, and she knew with sudden certainty that they, too, would face the might of the Lord Rhys one day.

'Oh, William ... what have we done,' she whispered.

Chapter 15

Brecknock Castle, late September 1189

Several sennights had passed since Matilda had received Gerald's letter, and although she had confided a little in me, I thought she must have forgotten about it when we heard the shouts and clatter of horses' hooves crossing the drawbridge below the gatehouse, where she had gone to get some peace.

Putting down the clothes we were packing away in a coffer, I crossed to the window and looked down. Above the noise of the drawbridge being raised, I recognised William's voice shouting orders, but without straining to see I couldn't make out who accompanied him. Moments later I heard the final bang as the drawbridge shut, followed by the screech of the great wooden gates being opened, before men and horses began to pour through into the inner bailey.

Crossing quickly over to the other side of the tower, I peered out into the early evening gloom. Joining me, Matilda gave a sudden, strangled gasp of horror. William was making his way towards the stables. Behind him was Prince John, the jewels on his fingers and the hilt of his dagger flashing ostentatiously in the light of the flickering torches.

Without another word, Matilda picked up her skirts and flew down the newel stairs and out into the bailey, with me following closely in her wake. Giving the men and horses milling by the stables a wide berth, she made for the wooden steps at the side of the keep and dashing up them she ran through the great hall towards the stairs leading to her chambers.

Once there she sat down on to the bed and covered her hot face with her hands.

'Dear God, Ailith,' she whispered as I sank down beside her, 'I don't think that I can face him this soon after.' Then letting her hands fall to her stomach, she covered it protectively. For as I had already guessed, and Matilda knew with a woman's certainty, she was with child ...

William beckoned Matilda onto the dais where he and John sat, each with a goblet of spiced wine in their hands. John put his down on the table as Matilda dropped into a low curtsey and accepted his bejewelled hand to kiss.

He bid her rise. 'I trust I find you in fine fettle after all the excitement of the wedding, Lady de Braose,' he asked, his eyes sliding down to her stomach where her girdle spanned her waist, still narrow and flat.

Matilda froze. Without knowing why, she knew that he had guessed her secret, knew that she was with child by him, and at once she felt the familiar sick churning in her stomach that she'd come to associate with the presence of Prince John.

Sensing her discomfort, John smiled a cold, cruel smile that reflected the coldness of his blue eyes before releasing her hand.

'Prince John will be staying with us for a few days, Moll,' William said. 'He is undertaking a military expedition against Lord Rhys on the orders of King Richard – as you know, Rhys does not set the same store by Richard as he did King Henry, and he is once again attacking our Norman lordships along the borders. Prince John will stay as long as it takes to negotiate suitable terms with Rhys, a mission which will hopefully be accomplished before Yuletide when Richard plans to return to his lands in France.'

There was a long silence in which Matilda nervously toyed with the carved ivory cross that hung between her breasts. William smiled sourly and produced the letter that Gerald had written to him, the twin of the one that she had received.

'It seems that even Archdeacon Gerald has grave concerns about his kin at the moment.' He sighed and, hooking his thumb through his sword belt, he regarded Matilda thoughtfully from under hooded eyes in much the same way as a falcon would eye its prey.

With an effort, Matilda pulled herself together. 'You are welcome, sire,' she said tightly.

John smiled his cold smile again. 'I look forward to renewing our acquaintance, Madam. Tonight, at dinner mayhap.' For a moment his eyes held hers, and the message was clear. She was expected to attend more than dinner, and when she did, this time he would see that she did not fight him.

'You don't look well, Moll, what ails you?' William's voice broke irritably into the silence.

''Tis nothing, William,' Matilda said tiredly. 'Only I beg your leave to go to the kitchen and discuss tonight's meal with Merri as we now have extra guests to feed.' And with that she turned on her heels and left.

Later that night, as William slept where he fell in the hall, Matilda stood in front of John in obedience to his summons. This time she did not fight him. This time she did not scream, even when he pinched her flesh cruelly and bit her. This time she endured, rather than suffered, the wretched pain and indignity of rape. She endured his hands roaming over her body and probing her most secret parts. Not once did she cry out. Not once did she think to tell William, for in the dark recesses of her mind she knew that he would blame her if he lost favour with Prince John. Oh yes, she played the game by Prince John's rules this time. She closed her eyes tight and she endured. Even when he forced her onto her front and took her cruelly from behind, no better than an animal in a barn. And she closed her ears when he called her Rosamund, and wished, like her, that she was dead.

Prince John and his party stayed for five long days and five long nights, and a dark cloud settled over the castle. William rode out with him each day, and duly returned each night after negotiations had ceased with Lord Rhys, or one or other of his emissaries. Each evening, William and John drank deeply whilst Matilda played hostess with brittle falseness, studiously avoiding Prince John where she could.

And I watched. I watched as the dark clouds gathered around us all. I watched as Mistress Destiny wove her web and entrapped us firmly in her snare. I watched as William basked in Prince John's approval, and slowly won his favour, not knowing that the price of that favour was his wife. And I watched as the flesh fell from Matilda's bones, as surely as the leaves fell from the trees outside in the bailey. And I did nothing, for there was nothing I could do.

One afternoon, Trahaearn was summoned from his estate at Llangorse to pledge his allegiance to King Richard. And I saw as clearly as Matilda did, the shadows that hung over him and the dark fingers that beckoned him towards his fate as he forsake his own kin to pledge himself with William and treacherous Prince John for Richard. And I watched as John leaned towards William and whispered something. And I saw as clearly as Matilda did, the dark storm shadows gathering in William's eyes, and the calculated cunning in John's as he turned his sharp blue gaze on her.

And I dreamed.

Oh, how I dreamed.

As usual I was running hard through treacle. Ahead of me Matilda was standing on the edge of the precipice, her belly now swollen and fit to burst with Prince John's ill-begot, bastard child. Then next she was holding a new born baby in her arms; a silvery slip of a thing still covered in vermix, and William was urging her to throw the child into the pit, for if she did that their son would be saved. And then John was standing beside me, his blue eyes glittering with malice. 'It is to no avail,' he says conversationally. We cannot change our destinies any more than we can change the colour of our skin.'

'But why?' I say. 'Why Matilda?'

'Because she is a whore!' says John. 'All women are whores!'

But I didn't understand then as I did later, for I was an ignorant girl still, and so I did nothing. Then on the fifth day, Prince John and his entourage left to join the Lord Rhys and ride to Oxford where they were to meet with King Richard and make a truce.

On the fifth day, all our steps were lighter. William was riding high, boasting that his skills had ensured that a truce would be made at Oxford; that King Richard would make his peace with the Lord Rhys, and all would be as it was in old King Henry's time.

But Richard would not bend like old King Henry. Richard did not even bother to go to Oxford to meet with the Lord Rhys, and so our cause was lost before it had even begun. And during the long weeks that followed, Matilda grieved for Mattie. Matilda grieved for her child that had been forced into a marriage with a man who was soon to become her sworn enemy. And Matilda grieved for the child that was to come. A child forced on her by an arrogant prince with cold, blue eyes, and an even colder heart.

Oh, how Matilda grieved … for wasn't that Mistress Destiny's plan?

Brecknock Castle, Wales, October 1189

Matilda looked up from the book she was reading. She could hear the sound of the portcullis opening down in the bailey, and she wondered who it could be, for William was absent, riding with Prince John to Windsor where they hoped to try and persuade King Richard to re-consider and meet with Lord Rhys. She didn't expect him home for a few days yet. It was a while before the door to the solar opened and Rhiannan entered looking flustered, closely followed by Trahaearn Fychan.

'He insisted on seeing you, my lady, though I told him Sir William was not at home,' she said, looking from one to another and not missing the tide of red that had crept up Matilda's neck to suffuse her face.

'It's all right, Rhiannan, you may leave,' Matilda said, putting the book down beside her.

'But, my lady,' Rhiannan said, scandalised.

'I said, it's all right,' Matilda said sharply, 'I had a message sent this morning. I have some bulls to sell, and William told me before he left that Trahaearn might want one. So, it's purely business,' she finished.

Rhiannan bobbed a curtsey and turned towards the door, but the troubled look remained on her face, leaving Matilda wondering how much the servants knew about her and Trahaearn. Nothing, she hoped. But still she felt an icy finger of fear run down her spine.

When Rhiannan had gone, Trahaearn crossed the room, and putting his hands on her shoulders he drew her to him. 'You did not come,' he said. 'I waited at the lodge as usual, and yet you did not come.'

Matilda pulled away from him and went to stand by the window. Down in the bailey several dogs squabbled over a bone and she could smell the aroma of freshly baked bread wafting from the kitchens.

'I could not,' she said, turning around to give him a tight little smile. 'I am with child.'

Trahaearn looked taken aback. 'Is it mine, Matilda? Is that why you didn't come – because you are you angry with me?'

'No, Trahaearn, it's not yours. And neither is it William's. It's Prince John's,' Matilda finished.

'I ... I don't understand,' Trahaearn said softly. 'Are you in love with Prince John, Matilda, is that it?'

'No!' Matilda cried passionately, going to him and taking his hand. 'No, never think that, Trahaearn. It's you that I love. Prince John forced me. He takes what he wants without a thought for anybody else, and this time it was me.' She dropped Trahaearn's hand. 'Does that disgust you, my love?' she whispered, seeing the appalled look on his face.

Trahaearn shook his head fiercely. 'No Matilda, never think that! Never say that again, it was not your fault! Have you told William?' he asked.

'No,' Matilda said. 'He would blame me, he would believe Prince John's word over mine and look elsewhere for the father!' She shivered. 'William believes the child is his,' she whispered turning away in shame. 'I allowed him in my bed.' She shivered again. 'It was shameful, I allowed him to maul me night after night – I tricked him into believing that the child is his, Trahaearn, and I pray that he never finds out the truth!'

Trahaearn gathered her in his arms and Matilda realised that she was crying; soaking his tunic. But she could not stop.

Chapter 16

Brecknock Castle, England, November 1189

Matilda flinched as William, her husband, stormed into the room and flung the door shut with such force that it nearly flew off its hinges. Dismissing Ailith and Rhiannon, moments later he was standing in front of her, his face as dark as thunder as he watched her lower herself into a chair unsteadily, before placing her hand protectively over the soft, round curve of her belly where the child had begun to stir.

'What is it, William? What has happened?' Matilda asked, suddenly feeling sick with fear.

'Is it true? Have you lain with Trahaearn Fychan?' William spat, ignoring her question. 'I am a laughing stock in the servant's hall! They snigger behind their hands at me and call me cuckold behind my back and say that you lay have lain with him, one who claims kinship with Gwenwynwyn, Prince of Powys! God's bone's, Matilda, he is married to Lord Rhys' niece, and despite the marriage binds between Mattie and Gruffydd, we are still for the time being Rhys enemies - at least until Richard comes to his senses and deals fairly with him!'

'Who says this?' Matilda whispered.

'That is none of your business,' William retorted angrily. 'But I have been told that you have met him on several occasions on your own and in my absence. Do you deny this, Moll?'

Matilda grabbed William's arm and desperately dragged herself back onto her feet. 'It is no secret that I have met Trahaearn on business in your absence, William, but there is nothing between us, I swear it!' she cried desperately. 'Dear God, you must believe me, husband, or you will go mad! We will all go mad, for it is all lies, I say!'

'Do you deny then that the brat you carry in your belly is his! That you bewitched me into not seeing what is before my very nose – that you carry another man's bastard child!' William shouted, shoving her away from him with such force that she fell back against the arm of the chair sending a sharp, stabbing pain coursing through her hip.

'Yes!' Matilda cried, ignoring the pain. Then seeing that William didn't believe her, she hauled herself upright and, grasping the intricately carved ivory cross that always hung between her breasts, she gripped it tightly between her fingers and thrust the tiny, tortured figure of Jesus before his face. 'I swear on the cross of Christ that, as God is my witness, Trahaearn Fychan is not the father of this child,' she sobbed, hoping that God would grant her mercy in the truth, but forgive her for her other lie, for if William guessed he would surely kill Trahaearn. 'You have to believe me, William!'

William looked at the figure on the cross for several long moments, then he lifted his eyes to her face. They were still bitter and angry. 'Do you? Do you swear it, wife? I will have you flogged if you lie to me!

'Yes,' Matilda said fiercely. 'I do, William. I swear it on the bible and on the heads of my own children - *our* own children. You must believe it!'

William looked at his wife for a very long time, the heat of anger still burning in his cheeks. 'Well it matters not at all now,' he said slowly. 'From now on you will be a good wife - and you will not be alone with Trahaearn Fychan again,' he added warningly.

Matilda shivered, it had grown cold in the chamber and the shadows were gathering in. Seeing her fear, William pulled her closer and began to undo her girdle and loosen the laces on her bliaut. 'I think we shall begin our first lesson in being a good wife now,' he said, pushing her down onto the bed so that she was on her back with her belly pointing towards the ceiling.

'No, William, we cannot,' Matilda said frightened. 'Think of the baby … it is not good for the baby!'

William ignored her. Instead, panting, he pushed down his braes so that she could see his erection jutting from between his short stocky legs. Then before she could move or protest further, he pulled off her gown in one swift move, and forcing her knees apart he rammed into her.

May 1190, Bramber Castle, England

It was dark. Matilda had already been in labour for some hours, and the strain was starting to show in her drawn face and laboured breathing. Heedless of her patient's discomfort, the midwife shuffled around the chamber laying out the tools of her trade, before instructing a serving girl to go and find hot water and clean sheets. On the other side of the room, Matilda groaned and gripped the bed pole as another wave of contractions gripped her belly, the muscles squeezing and twisting her insides until she thought she could bear it no more. The midwife clucked and, crossing to the bed, she pulled up Matilda's shift and began to press her thumbs, none too gently, into her groin. 'Not long now,' she prophesied, 'the head's in place at any rate.' After several more contractions, Matilda fell back exhausted onto the pillows. She was too old to bear children, and she resented her body being put through this agony because of the lechery of one spoilt little princeling, who was fast gaining a reputation for raping barons' wives.

Although the room was hot and oppressive, mercifully the contractions began to subside for the moment, and Matilda leaned thankfully back against the pillows hoping to doze for a bit. After a while, she felt someone touch her shoulder. A touch as light as gossamer, and the hairs on the back of her neck rose. For a moment she lay still, and then she opened her eyes. Standing beside the bed was the figure of a man, already fading and indistinct. Briefly, their eyes met, and Matilda smiled sadly. Then, slowly, she raised her hand in farewell as the vision disappeared. Only when it had completely gone, did she allow the hot tears to slip and roll down her face.

'Now, now,' said the midwife, lifting her shift again. 'There's no time for tears, you can begin pushing …'

'What will you call her?' I asked.

'Annora,' Matilda replied without hesitation.

I looked at Annora. She was pale and ethereal. All Matilda's other children were robust and sandy haired, or red headed, but Annora broke that mould. The little cap of hair that clung to her head was pale gold and so fine that it felt like silk, and her eyes were as blue as the sky – King John's eyes.

'Not like the others, is she?' the midwife muttered darkly. She was a dried-up old biddy who had apparently attended all Matilda's births. She was also prone to castle gossip, so I knew that her opinion would be all round the castle in a matter of moments once she left the chamber.

Matilda ignored her, and I could see that her heart was filled to overflowing. 'She is special,' she whispered. 'Dear God, she should not be, but somehow she is.' As if realising that she was being discussed, the little girl waved a small fist in the air and let out a little mew sound. Immediately, Matilda put her to her breast where she rooted for a moment, before finding a nipple and industriously beginning to suck. After a while Matilda raised her head and looked at me, and I saw that she had tears in her eyes. 'I had almost forgotten, Ailith,' she whispered. 'My father passed away this afternoon.'

Hastily, I crossed myself. One did not need to ask Matilda how she knew these things …

Much later on, whilst Matilda slept, William crept quietly into the chamber and stood staring down at the new born baby in the crib. He knew instinctively that it was not his, but he could see no signs that it was Trahaearn's, either. Without knowing why, he suddenly shivered. There was something unsettling about the child as it lay there unmoving, staring up at him with its wide, blue eyes. It was a changeling. And if Matilda had not begot it by Trahaearn, then he did not like to think how else she might have conceived it, and suddenly he was afraid. With a shudder, he turned and left the room.

Over in the crib, Annora began to cry.

Chapter 17

Hay Castle, spring 1192

William strode into the hall where Matilda was supervising the changing of the rushes with the chatelaine, wearing only his padded gambeson and hose. Behind him trailed two squires carrying between them his hauberk, a surcoat emblazoned with the de Braose coat of arms (three sheaves of wheat on a field of red and blue) and his riding cloak and boots.

He was not unaware that the last couple of years had been hard on Matilda, for the strain showed in the dark rings under her eyes and the faint lines on her forehead. After Annora's birth, he had left Bramber abruptly and returned to Hay without her, leaving the household scandalised. Then without giving her any warning, he had summoned her back to Wales. Not because he missed her, but because in her absence he had decided that the best way to keep her under his control was to keep her with child. It had pleased him greatly to witness Matilda's dismay when she found out that her secret store of penny rule and willow that she had gathered with Ailith had not prevented her conceiving again. And now, along with Annora, the nurses had baby Loretta to care for.

'I am off to hand over Maelgwn to Rhys at Llandovery according to arrangements,' William said, throwing a dark look at Annora who was playing with her nurse whilst Loretta slept in her cradle. He scowled, for several long years he had been Maelgwyn's gaoler after Rhys, fearing for his son's safety in Gruffydd's hands, had demanded that he hand him over to his wife's father. Now, all of a sudden, Rhys had demanded that Maelgwn should be released back into his care, perhaps because he thought that he might end up as a hostage because of his increasingly brutal raids on the Marcher barons.

'Will you carry some letters and some gifts I have made for little Rhys Ieuanc and Owain?' Matilda asked, referring to Mattie's sons, neither of which she had seen yet.'

'Yes, yes,' William said impatiently as the weight of his hauberk was lowered onto his shoulders and adjusted by his squires, quickly followed by his surcoat and his sword belt.

'I worry for Mattie,' Matilda said, perhaps for the hundredth time. 'I wish she could visit at least so I can reassure myself that she is safe.'

'How many times have we discussed this, Moll?' William said testily. 'Mattie has two fine sons now, both of whom share Norman and Welsh blood. Consequently, there is no reason for either her or the boys to be harmed, for they ensure the succession. Anyway, you know that whatever his faults, Gruffydd has great regard for Mattie – he will do everything in his power to keep her safe.'

Secretly, William was not so sure that this was the truth anymore. King Richard, it was rumoured, was to sponsor a marcher invasion of south Wales, and if he did, then William was secretly planning on annexing the cantref of Elfael and taking Painscastle for himself when the time was right – the only problem being that the sons of Einion, to whom the canteref had fallen when Cadwallon its ruler had been assassinated, had the powerful patronage of Rhys, his daughter's father-by-marriage.

For a moment William mused on the personal safety of his daughter should he take such action, then he pushed the thought away. Nothing, not even his own blood, would stop him taking what he wanted. Then grabbing the waxed package that Matilda proffered, he threw one last look at her and made his way out into the less stifling proximity of the bailey.

The day was bright but cold as William rode into the bailey at Llandovery Castle where Rhys was currently in residence. At his side, Maelgwn puffed out a breath of frosty air and rubbed his hands together, glad to be free for the time being and willing to be conciliatory to his father. Rhys had deemed that Gruffydd and Maelgwn be kept apart, so Gruffydd had remained at Dinefwr where Mattie had just been delivered of her third child, a baby girl.

Stamping his feet to restore some feeling, William followed Rhys' steward into the great hall where his host sat. Rhys did not ask William or his entourage to sit, and he did not offer them the hot spiced wine that was being served to others in the hall. Instead he sent them a pitcher of small ale, leaving William bristling with anger at the lack of hospitality, whilst he spoke in low tones to Maelgwn.

After what seemed like ages Rhys nodded curtly to Maelgwn, and beckoned William to follow him into a small anti-chamber, just off the main chamber, where a scribe scratched away at his accounts. Here Rhys barked out a few instructions to the scribe in his guttural Welsh, before turning to William and indicating a seat.

'I will come to the point, Sir William,' he said reverting to English. 'I have word that you are planning to annex Elfael, and I warn you that no alliance that we have made in the past will stop me from raising an army against you if you should try.' He paused. 'Gruffydd will succeed me and he too will make a powerful enemy should you oppose him. Don't think that because of marriage ties I will allow you any liberties with my lands, and don't make the mistake of thinking that your daughter would do anything but side with her husband.'

William had no choice but to acknowledge the threat for what it was and understand the truth behind Rhys' words. Mattie was one of theirs now, she had made her choice, and she would side with Rhys and her husband if it came to a fight.

Well before the bells rang the hour of nones, William took his leave of Rhys armed with letters from Mattie and news of her new baby daughter, Lleucu. He had the feeling that this was probably the last time that he and Rhys would stand in the same room now that Maelgwn was returned, and that it would be even longer before anyone saw Mattie again, except under a truce.

But unlike Matilda none of that worried him at all. What worried him was who was passing sensitive information about his future plans to Lord Rhys? Only one name came to mind – Trahaearn Fychan. And once more hate for the man twisted in his breast like a knife.

✝

Hereford Castle, Wales, Autumn, 1192

I looked across the solar to where Matilda sat by the light of a window embrasure, sewing an intricate pattern along the hem of a new blue court tunic for William in gold silk thread. Annora tried to clamber on her lap but was prevented by the slippery fabric draped over her legs, and so she plopped down in the rushes instead and began to play with an ivory rattle that had once belonged to Will.

Alongside her, the children's wet-nurse sat quietly feeding Loretta whilst her own child lay in a woven basket at her feet, waving her hand and examining her five chubby pink fingers with interest, occasionally making a grab for her mother's shawl which dangled just out of reach from the back of a chair.

Other than Loretta's rhythmic sucking, and the occasional gurgle from the basket, the room was unusually quiet. We were in a sombre mood for word had come that King Richard had gone missing whilst travelling home from the crusades, and Queen Eleanor was beside herself with worry and grief. It was believed that he might be in the hands of Phillip of France, with whom he had quarrelled when he had broken his pre-contract agreement to marry his sister Alys the previous year, to marry instead Berengaria of Navarre, in Cyprus.

Phillip of France had, of course, been furious as Richard had effectively declared his sister soiled goods and given credibility to the rumour that she had been Henry's mistress.

I remembered with sorrow the lovely young girl we had seen at Winchester Castle all those years ago. She had become a simple pawn in the game of kings: King

Louis, her father, had sent her to King Henry of England to be betrothed to his son Richard, but Richard had rejected her because of her alleged affair with his father.

If rumour was to be believed, even John had not passed her over, and so she would return to France in disgrace.

Annora offered up a small carved effigy of a bird in her chubby pink fist. 'Bird,' she lisped, then tottering to the window embrasure she clambered onto a chair and pointed outside. 'Bird,' she repeated turning to look solemnly at us with her large blue eyes.

Just then William strode into the chamber dressed in a long tunic of madder trimmed with a deep gold border and intricately sewn in a herringbone design.

'I will be at the last of the court sessions all afternoon, Moll,' he said, eyeing the child with his customary dislike. He had, only this year, been awarded the post of Sheriff of Herefordshire and he took his duties very seriously, dressing grandly for his appearances in the court rooms.

Annora scrambled down off the chair, ran to Matilda, and buried her face in her skirts.

Knowing that she already sensed her father's animosity keenly, I went over, gathered her up, and handed her to Rhiannan to take downstairs to the kitchens where Merri would spoil her with ginger biscuits and sweetmeats.

Matilda watched them go sadly, then turning to the wet-nurse she plucked Loretta out of her arms and carried her over to William, hoping for at least one of her offspring to have some kind words before he left.

William studied her for a moment before giving a satisfied nod and continuing. 'I have plans to ride over to Wigmore after the court sessions to see Roger de Mortimer. I have business with him regarding Annora's betrothal to his son Hugh – I shall be gone for a few days'

Brought out of her reverie, Matilda looked at him sharply. 'You are to arrange Annora's betrothal so early without consulting me?' she asked in a shocked voice. 'But William, she is yet but two years old – why the rush?'

'I will try to arrange for her to have her tutelage under the watchful eye of her new mother-to-be as soon as is possible, that way she can become accustomed to her new family,' William continued as if he had not heard her.

Then without so much as a farewell, William turned and ran down the staircase, his spurs echoing on the stone as he went, leaving a stunned Matilda standing in his wake staring mutely after him.

Llangorse, Yuletide, 1192

Outside the old lodge at Langorse it was beginning to snow. Inside, Matilda lay on the pile of soft furs carelessly strewn in front of the hearth, watching as wispy tendrils of smoke rose from the embers and snaked towards the thatched ceiling. Beside her, Trahaearn lay naked toying with a lock of her hair, twisting the curl around his finger absently.

'This must be the last time that we meet like this,' Matilda said sadly, knowing that she should have ended their secret trysts a long time ago as she had intended after Annora was born. Even meeting Trahaearn this last time, she was selfishly risking his life, for since William's visit to Rhys' court to return Maelgwn, he had once again grown moody and suspicious of his Brecknock tenant.

'William is to send Annora away,' she said sadly. 'I think he still suspects that she is yours, but I could never tell him the truth of the matter ... Prince John,' she shivered. 'Prince John is ruthless, he takes what he wants when he wants, sparing no thought to those whom he ruins along the way. I am not the first or the last wife of a baron that he has raped. To tell William the true circumstances of Annora's birth would serve no purpose at all. Indeed, if King Richard is dead, as many people now believe, then we will have either John, or Arthur of Brittany on the throne, and as William has sworn fealty to John already, he must have no quarrel with him if he is to remain in favour.'

'No, I must not see you again,' Matilda repeated, her bottom lip trembling. 'Sweet Jesus I cannot bear it, but I must not, for William now looks to prove you a traitor through your kinship with Gwenwynwyn and Rhys.' She paused. 'William believes that someone is passing valuable information on to Rhys. Rhys' raids are well planned and his growing teulu is well trained and equipped if the travelling minstrels who pass our way are to be believed. In short, William is suspicious, Trahaearn,' she finished quietly. 'And I think he suspects us, though he has not got a shred of proof.'

'So, William thinks that I pass secrets on to Rhys and maybe even to Gwenwynwyn which I get during love trysts with you?' Trahaearn said in amusement. 'Well he's right to be suspicious on one count, you are my paramour, but does the man really think that I would spend time in idle gossip when in bed with you? He must be a very boring bedfellow himself if he does.' Trahaearn finished his amusement breaking into laughter

'Listen to me Trahaearn, this is no laughing matter. You don't know William, he is a cruel man and he has spies everywhere!' Matilda said fiercely, glancing around the room quickly as if she might catch someone listening at that very moment to their conversation. 'His heyward, Herbert Pinkerton ... I am sure that he has no proof about us, but he is shifty and for a piece of silver he will pass lies on to William.'

Trahaearn sighed. 'But surely, Matilda, if he has no proof about us, and we are careful –'

'No, Trahaearn,' she whispered, cupping his face in her hand, 'no we must never be alone like this again – for our own sakes. I must go now,' she said, and standing, she crossed to the fire and began pulling on her shift and bliaut. 'William is due back from Hereford for the yuletide feast and I must be there when he arrives. Besides, I must put my children first from now on, Trahaearn. I could not bear it if William were to punish me through them – which is what he is doing by sending Annora away.'

Trahaearn stood and tried to draw her into his arms but Matilda shook her head. For a moment, she hovered, taking in every detail of his face, then stepping forward she kissed him for one last time, before drawing her mantle tightly about herself and disappearing through the heavy oak door of the hunting lodge. Outside she untied her mare's reigns and rode away without once looking back.

Back in the lodge, Trahaearn bent to pick up his tunic, when his eye caught something glinting in the light of the fire. Bending once again, he retrieved it and rubbed it lovingly between finger and thumb. Then pulling on his tunic and hose, he pushed it into the little pouch that hung from his belt, before donning that.

Finally, grabbing his mantle and pushing his feet into his soft leather shoes, he ran outside after Matilda. But she was long gone.

✝

May 1194, Castle Dinas, Wales

Heavy rainclouds hung over Castle Dinas as William rode into the bailey, having spent a period of time at court in England with King Richard who was now newly restored to his throne. The events of the last few years had been turbulent and had wrought a deep scar upon the loyalties of Richard's subjects in both England and France. After the initial fears that the king had been murdered on the road back from the crusades, news had finally seeped through to England that he had been captured by Leopold, The Duke of Austria, whom he was said to have offended during the crusades by casting down his standard from the walls of Acre, claiming that he had played no part in the city's fall. Shortly after that, they learned that Richard had been passed over to Henry VI, the Holy Emperor of Rome, and apart from demands for a ransom, no more news had filtered through and the country had been left in turmoil. Matilda had to swallow her bile when she thought of the trouble that Prince John had stirred up in King Richard's absence, and in which he had embroiled them.

John had been in France when Richard's incarceration became known and, after drumming up a certain amount of support there, he had sailed back to England in the Lent of the previous year intending to take the throne in Richard's absence by force if necessary. Matilda grimaced as she remembered him arriving at Hay with his band of mercenaries demanding William's fealty once again. His cruel blue eyes had wandered over to her as she sat on the dais challenging her to prevent him, but Matilda had not had the courage. Shortly after that, John had gathered together his mercenaries and the barons that had sworn fealty to him, and he had ridden to London. And one of those who accompanied him was William.

Once in London, John had quickly spread rumours that Richard was already dead and demanded that the regency council surrender their powers to him. Queen Eleanor, not trusting her youngest son however, had already foreseen such a move on his behalf, and had installed a council of trusted men, including William the Marshal, and Geoffrey of York, in her absence, and John had not succeeded in swaying their loyalty. Angry, and out of control, John had ridden with his band of mercenaries and rebel barons to Windsor and captured the castle. It was only after much negotiation that terms had been met on the understanding that, if Richard did not return to England, then John was a better prospect to succeed the throne, rather than the seven-year-old Arthur of Brittany, whom Richard had named in his will according to the strict rules of primogeniture.

Matilda turned away from the window, she could feel a headache starting at the thought of Prince John. Would he never leave them in peace? William had been forced to beg pardon of Richard and swear fealty to him once again, otherwise they might lose their lands, but she knew that as soon as Prince John showed his face again, William would change allegiance at the drop of a hat.

After a while Matilda's thoughts turned to Trahaearn Fychan. It had been a long time since she had last seen him, for these days he seldom showed his face in the hall when they were in residence at Brecknock if his business could be conducted by his steward instead.

Nervously, she fingered the fur trim on her mantle. She was aware that now William had made his peace with the king, he would once more be at liberty to look to Trahaearn for treachery. She shivered, remembering how angry William had been when Trahaearn had failed to lend support or men to Prince John in his campaign for the throne.

For a moment, she wondered why Trahaearn had acted so - he must have been aware that it would cause people to talk, and rumours to abound, regarding his loyalty to William, his liege lord, and once again she shivered.

Picking up her mantle she decided that she would summon Ailith and they would walk. Ailith who saw everything but would say nothing. For, like herself, Ailith saw nothing but trouble ahead.

Chapter 18

Hay castle, June 1197

The streets of the little township of Hay lay silent and still, with none of the usual bustling trade in the market or booths along the main street. Even the Inns remained shuttered and bolted, and the customary laughter that usually spilled out of their windows and doorways was a ghostly remembrance of the past. The only signs of life were the scraggy dogs that still roamed the deserted roads foraging for food, and the odd mangy cat slinking along walls, and down alleys, in the hope of trapping some small unwitting bird far from its nest. As if sensing the mood of the township, the sun hung oppressively over the hills and deserted fields beyond Hay, and there was the promise of thunder in the air and more rain to flatten what was left of the corn.

Inside the solid walls of the castle, Matilda kept a vigil by Loretta's bed, every now and then bathing her fevered brow with a damp cloth or holding a bowl for her while she vomited the thin stream of blood and bile that was all that was left in her stomach. Over in the hearth, a small brazier burned, adding to the heat of the already stifling room, but the windows were kept firmly shut as instructed by the kindly physician William had summoned. He had been back at daybreak to inspect the hard, suppurating boils that had risen in Loretta's groin and under her arms, and he was of the opinion that she was one of the lucky ones who would recover, for it was those whose swellings turned inwards that were likely to die.

Loretta opened her eyes and called weakly for her mother, before once more being swept away on a tide of delirium and fever as her small body was wracked with pain and spasms, and not for the first-time, Matilda felt tears on her cheeks as she looked down at the now emaciated face of her small daughter for whom she could do nothing, and wondered if God had deserted them.

The year of 1197 was cursed it seemed. First the crops had failed, and then famine had come. Then, in quick succession, the plague had spread through the villages and townships of Wales. Already the dead were being carted out to hastily dug pits to be cast one on top of the other, for there was no time for proper burials to be arranged.

Matilda wondered if they might have avoided the plague, had not one of the canons from Llanthony Priory arrived with the message that Lord Rhys had been struck down with it, and died not five days since. The canon had refused a meal but had stayed the night. He was found in the morning feverish, and in a great deal of pain, but it was only when she had visited him and learned the true extent of his symptoms that they realised he must have carried the illness with him. And now Rhiannon lay dead, as did William's heyward, Herbert Pinkerton, though for him she could not summon any sorrow. Even Ailith, her loyal, capable friend and confidant was lying seriously ill confined to her rooms along with a handful of other servants.

Loretta moaned again and Matilda leaned forward to bathe her forehead with fresh water that a frightened young maid handed her and adjust her pillow so that she might be more comfortable, then she gently lifted each of her arms and began to resume the task of cleaning away the sticky pus that continued to ooz from beneath them and the top of her thin thighs. The faint clink of a rosary was the only other sound in the room as Nerys, the child's nurse, murmured prayers over the beads in between the occasional sob.

As Matilda worked her mind turned to her other children and she sent silent prayers that they were safe.

Already William had sent messages where he could that they were not to come to the castle, the gates had been closed and they would remain that way until the worst had passed. It was fortunate that only Reginald and his new wife Gracia had been visiting, although Gracia was heavily pregnant, but as far as she was aware, they were safe in another part of the keep and being tended by the servants that hadn't fallen sick.

The others were, like Mattie and Reginald, nearly all wed now to the sons and daughters of high-ranking barons, each chosen with care by William for the prestige and power that would come to him through such connections.

On the same day that he had been knighted, Will had finally married Maude de Clare and they now spent their time administering several of William's estates between Sussex and Radnor in Wales.

Bertha was now married to William de Beauchamp, and only last year Margaret had married Walter de Lacy of Meath. As for John, the youngest of her boys, William was engaged in talks with Amabil de Limesi's father for him, but he was currently safe accompanying Phillip, Bertha's twin, on the tourney circuit in France, practicing their newly acquired knight skills there. That left only Giles who was studying theology at Oxford, Flandrina who was now ensconced in Godstow Priory where she had taken her vows, and Annora who had been dispatched to live under the watchful eye of her intended husband's mother at Wigmore as soon as William could decently achieve it, and she had heard nothing of her for some time. She hoped again that they were safe and well.

Matilda felt her eyelids flicker. She was hot, her head ached badly and she had not slept for days, so she was exhausted, but fear for her daughter's life had kept her going. The room was acrid and thick with the smell of vomit, but slowly tiredness got the better of her and her head began to droop, until at last it was resting against the soiled feather mattress and she dreamed of the last time that she had seen Lord Rhys.

Painscastle.

A series of new conflicts between Rhys and his sons had finally culminated in them capturing and imprisoning him in Nevern Castle, leaving his realm open and vulnerable to attack, and William had immediately seized the opportunity to march into the cantref of Elfael and take Painscastle as he had planned to for so long. Matilda had pleaded with him not to directly attack Rhys's territories – she had argued that to do so would endanger Mattie and her children, but he would not listen. And then he had argued with Trahaearn Fychan. Matilda didn't know exactly what they had argued over for she had ridden in just as Trahaearn had stormed out of the great hall at Brecknock Castle, but she suspected that William had called Trahaearn before him and demanded troops from him as a test of his loyalties.

William's face swam in and out of her dreams, twisted and bitter in his rage. *'Traitor... Our enemy now ... Once sworn to us ...'* His voice droned on, cold and angry, buzzing in her head. *'Traitor ... Enemy ...'* A picture of Trahaearn kneeling at Prince John's feet loomed. Then shadows ... Suddenly she remembered dark shadows – Whatever oath Trahaearn had sworn she now realised that destiny had not meant him to keep it ...

Matilda groaned. She could hear Nerys' voice talking to someone. She thought it might be William and she wanted to tell them to save her children, ride with them away from the castle to somewhere safe, but her mind slipped away again, back into the past and William's devious and cruel plan to make her lead the army that he was to send into Elfael; a plan that would make her Rhys' enemy and, more cruelly than that, it would mean that she would be Gruffydd's and Mattie's enemy too.

The sky outside was dark when Matilda next opened her eyes, and the shutters had been opened to let some cool air in. She could hear Nerys instructing someone not to close them again no matter what the physician said, then she was lifted onto the bed and a cool compress was laid over her forehead.

After a while she dozed fitfully once more, and the dark countenances of Hugh Say and Roger de Mortimer rose before her. Both cruel and ruthless men, they had accompanied her on the invasion and they had marched the army fearlessly into battle, and the slaughter that followed had been terrible. Thousands of Welsh had been cut down, men, women, and children, taken by surprise by the huge army that poured down on them.

With Rhys imprisoned and his sons still fighting one another their army had been invincible, and she had been responsible for the slaughter.

Matilda felt the hot angry tears squeeze out between her eyelashes and trickle slowly down her cheeks as she recalled what the Welsh had said of her. They had said that William's army was led by a witch, a giantess; *Moll Walbee*. The name rang in her head taunting her ... They had said that she rode a horse of fire and summoned a host of demons to do her work at Painscastle. She was made into a gorgon, a witch, and a horror ....

Matilda's hand clutched at the coverlet. There had been no mercy ... *no mercy* ... The words echoed round her head, gentle hands tried to restrain hers. 'No mercy,' she whispered. The army had given no quarter and now the ghosts of the men they had slaughtered haunted her fevered dreams as they pointed accusatory fingers at her, the author of their destruction. Once again Matilda saw the fires and smelled the burning flesh as they stormed and won, first Colwyn, and then Painscastle, just as William wanted.

And he had called it "Matilda's castle ..."

More tears squeezed out from under her eyelids. 'Oh, William, how you must hate me,' she whispered, for the name would always remind the people of Wales of the slaughter that was unleashed in her name, and she could never forgive William for that.

But their victory had only lasted a year before Lord Rhys was once again free and vengeful. Within months, he had razed Colwyn and New Radnor Castle to the ground and then, having defeated Hugh Say and Roger Mortimer's army in a bloody battle with the loss of forty knights including Hugh Say, Rhys had then laid siege to Painscastle with catapults and engines.

Hugh the chaplain continued his low incantation at Matilda's bedside, but Matilda was oblivious to his prayers as she relived the shouts and the screams and the roar of the catapults as Rhys ordered still more rocks to be hurtled towards the castle's half-finished fortifications, laying them once again to waste whilst they shook with fear inside the crumbling walls.

And finally, they had had no choice but to surrender the castle to Rhys. Matilda remembered the humiliation of standing in the great hall in front of him and handing him the keys. Mattie had stood at his shoulder, her eyes glittering with anger and barely suppressed rage as Rhys made his conditions. He would hand them back the keys if they swore upon the heads of Mattie's children that they would cease hostilities against him - William had already marched into Ceredigion with Will and burnt part of Cardigan, which was one of Rhys' main seats, and Rhys, although desirous of revenge, recognised that he needed a bargaining point with William in order to restore the peace. Still, it had been humiliating. Once again Mattie's face swam once more before her; bitter and angry, her small fists curled into balls at her side.

The tears coursed down Matilda's face as she remembered the last occasion she had seen Mattie. She had sensed a change in her: the coldness that had not been there before. Mattie would never trust them again, and inside she grieved. For Painscastle was not prize enough for losing the love of her daughter.

Then Matilda remembered again that Lord Rhys was dead, taken by the plague, and she had the feeling that she was going to follow soon …

Matilda sat by the window wrapped in blankets, for despite the heat of the day she still could not get warm and her head ached abominably. Loretta sat beside her, pale and thin still, but thankfully recovering with the robustness of a child. Although still weak myself, I helped Matilda sip some hot posset and tried to encourage her to eat from the meagre platter cook had prepared in the kitchen – food was still rationed, but William and his men had been out hunting and had managed to bag a couple of hares, which, with the addition of some wild garlic, had been the makings of a meal.

Opposite her sat Archdeacon Gerald, staring out of the window, a perplexed look on his handsome face. 'Do you know that Rhys died excommunicate after a quarrel with the Bishop?' He asked Matilda, referring to the Bishop of St. David's, Peter de Leia. 'The Bishop had to have his body scourged in posthumous penance before he could be buried in St David's – the quarrel was over the theft of some horses,' he said, seemingly mystified as to how such a thing could lead to excommunication in the first place.

Matilda shook her head. 'I never did understand Rhys. I mean did you ever ask yourself why he returned Painscastle to William after he won it back so spectacularly – why besiege it at great cost to himself, if all the time he meant for William to remain its castellan? No,' she said, 'I never really gave credence to the idea that if William retained the castle he would cease hostilities. William is a warmonger and Rhys must have known that even though he pulled out of Ceredigion, given the opportunity he would attack him again.'

Gerald shook his head, 'It's likely we will never know either. Rhys was a mystery unto himself, and yet his death has not solved anything as his sons still fight one another even though Gruffydd's succession has been confirmed by the Archbishop of Canterbury.' Gerald sighed, he had ridden with Gruffydd on that occasion and had witnessed the Archbishop, Hubert Walter, confirm Gruffydd as Rhys heir in his capacity of Chief Justiciar of England, but Maelgwn would not stand down and accept the succession, even at his own urging.

Matilda frowned. 'Will Maelgwn not have to accept Gruffydd as Rhys's heir eventually, though?' she asked.

'When have you ever seen a Welsh prince accept anything that stands in the way of what he rightly believed was his?' Gerald asked. 'No, I have known Maelgwn since he was a boy and I know he will never accept it.'

Matilda sighed. 'It's been a terrible year,' she said, her voice still gruff with the fever. 'So many dead.' She sighed again. 'Nearly every family has lost a loved one. Still, it's worse when it's a child. The miller lost all six of his children, I hear - to both famine and fever. When I'm able to ride, I will visit him and any other family that has lost someone – perhaps we could have a special service ...'

'It can be arranged,' Gerald said nodding. 'Once you are strong and well, my dear lady, we will arrange services to be said for the dead in every parish church, God rest their souls.'

'Do you have any regrets, Gerald - in this life I mean? When Loretta lay so ill and I myself succumbed, I wished that I had stood against William when he married Mattie to Gruffydd. Mattie refuses to speak to me or answer my letters, and I am kept apart from my grandchildren as punishment for Painscastle, I think,' she finished, her voice hoarse with emotion.

'My only regret is not being made Archbishop of St. David's,' Gerald said sadly. 'I once thought it was in my grasp, but well –' he sighed, 'I was offered others, but never my heart's desire – though I suppose it's never too late ...'

Matilda's eyelids drooped, and seeing that she was nearly asleep Gerald stood, and smiling wryly, he quietly left the room.

Outside on the stairs I heard William's page, Richard de Bohn, ask, 'Is it true, your Grace, that male beavers mutilate themselves to prevent the hunter from cutting of the most prized part of his anatomy – you know his ...'

His voiced had dropped to a whisper, and after a minute I heard Gerald reply that there were many things in heaven and earth that we did not understand.

'And,' Richard continued, loudly again this time, 'is it also true that a knight called Gilbert Hagernall gave birth to a ...'

His voice drifted away as they disappeared further downstairs. William, I knew, would not like it that his steward read out loud sometimes from Gerald's book when the staff gathered in the kitchens, as he had not painted him in a good light when recounting the story of Abbergavenny. I therefore resolved to find the copy as soon as possible and hide it away before William got wind of it and went into a rage.

✠

Brecknock Castle, Wales, October 1197

Outside in the bailey, the shouts of servants running to and fro between the castle, the bakehouse, and the brewery preparing for the evening meal carried up to the solar where Matilda had been ensconced all afternoon. Ordinarily she would have enjoyed the sound of so much activity, and perhaps even have gone down to help. Now, though, she looked down at the letter in her hand and sighed. It was from Archdeacon Gerald and it contained bad news, but instead of seeking William out as she knew she should, she put it to one side and turned to gaze out at the rain clouds gathering over the mountains instead.

Autumn had come upon them fast and, as usual, it was so much worse in Wales than it was in Sussex. Next year she vowed to go back to Bramber where the milder weather suited her better and her bones didn't ache day in and day out.

After a while her thoughts turned, as they so often did, to her children: Margret in Ireland with Walter tending his estates, Bertha at Elmley with William, Will and Maude, now expecting their first child, John recently betrothed to Amabil de Limesi, and Reginald and Gracia with their first-born son William on her father's estates in Devon.

Of the others, William was in talks with the Earl of Leicester for Loretta now that she was well, and

Annora was still at Wigmore. Giles, though, was for the church, whilst Flandrina remained incarcerated in her convent in Godstow and Phillip continued to tour the tourney circuits in France.

Were they all happy, she wondered? And was Mattie the only child that she had need to worry over? her conscience asked, as without warning her daughter's angry face rose before her eyes.

Gerald's letter suggested so ...

William strode into the solar to find Matilda looking wearily out of the window. It was a dreary day, the rain had not let up once, and he was soaked from constantly walking a horse with colic round the yard. It was one of his best stallions and he had been afraid he would lose it, but it seemed to be over the worse now and Simon his head groom had taken over.

'Gerald has written,' Matilda said, nodding towards the letter lying on a small table by the blazing hearth. 'Maelgwn and Gwenwynwyn joined forces and they have taken Aberystwyth. Gruffydd, Mattie, and the children are now Maelgwn's hostages.' She sighed. 'It's a bad business this fight between brothers with Mattie stuck in the middle of it all.'

Picking up the letter William quickly scanned it for himself. Gruffydd had chosen Aberystwyth as his main seat thinking it well able to withstand attack from Maelgwn's quarter, but obviously, he had not counted on an alliance between Maelgwn and Gwenwynwyn.

'What will happen to them?' asked Matilda quietly. 'Will he treat them fair or will they be killed or worse, murdered at his hands?'

'There are already plans for them to be taken to Corfe Castle and held there as hostages,' William said after a pause. Matilda looked at him in surprise, 'You mean you already know of their capture and you did not see fit to tell me?'

'Yes, I already know about Gruffydd's capture, and I thought it best not to tell you because I did not wish to enter into another round of recriminations based on Mattie's marriage.'

And with that he turned to the hearth and began to warm his hands, no longer interested in Mattie's fate. Matilda stared at his back for a moment, then turned to gaze sadly out of the window once more. She had long since ceased to be surprised by William's cold ruthlessness. Even when that ruthlessness extended to his own family.

Brecon, Wales, March 1198

Faulkes de Breauté sat alone in the small tavern room he'd hired just outside Brecknock, and waited patiently, taking only the occasional sip from the mug of ale on the table in front of him.

After a while there was a knock on the door and a tall, thin man of middle years with pockmarked skin entered. His bloodshot eyes darted around the room, missing nothing. Then, without asking, he pulled out a chair and sat down opposite de Breauté.

Concealing his irritation at the man's impudence, de Breauté nodded towards a jug of ale and a second mug on the table, waiting until the man had filled his to the brim and taken several deep draughts before asking, 'Do you have them?'

The man nodded and, wiping the back of his hand across his mouth, he delved into the leather satchel that hung at his side and produced a bundle of letters which he thrust towards de Breauté. 'I made two copies of everything,' he said. 'Trahaearn never suspected.'

Fulkes didn't touch the letters, instead he watched with an implacable look on his face as the man proceeded to top up his mug again.

'I have something else,' the man said after an awkward silence, and returning to the satchel once more, he thrust his hand inside it and produced a second item with the flourish of a mummer producing a rabbit from a hat.

'What's this, then?' de Breauté asked, picking up the item and studying it. 'Well, well, well,' he said. 'Where did you get this, eh?'

'Let's just say that Trahaearn was careless with it, shall we?' the man said, reaching for his mug and drinking deeply.

Faulkes watched him for a while, never once topping up his own mug before asking. 'You've been in Fychan's employ for some years, have you not?'

The man looked at him blearily and blinked.

'So, why betray him now?'

The man blinked again. 'Coin,' he said. 'I'd sell my own granny for a bag of coin.' Then, as if realising he had not been paid, he stood, drained his mug, and held out his hand.

Faulkes stood, too, and producing a pouch, he handed it to the man who opened it and tipped the contents on the table.

'I think you will find it's all there,' Faulkes said in an amused drawl.

The man grunted and began to drop the coins back into the bag. Then, without another word, he turned, flung the door open, and began to make his way unsteadily down the steep stairs.

Faulkes waited until another man entered the room. 'You saw him leave?'

'Yes,' the man confirmed.

'Make sure that he gets no further than the outskirts of Brecknock. And make it quick and clean!'

Satisfied, Faulkes poured what was left of the pitcher of ale into his mug and leaned back. He would see to it that the evidence of Trahaearn's treachery fell into William de Braose's hands by tomorrow morning. And this time he was sure William would deal with the man effectively. The image of Trahaern's estate at Llangrose came unbidden into his mind. Along with that of his plump little wife. He meant to ask Prince John if he could have them as trophies. After all, Trahaern's impending fall had been no mean feat to arrange. And he had done it for him ...

Chapter 19

Brecknock Castle, Wales, March 1198

William strode from one side of his chambers to the other, his face contorted with rage. Then, crossing to the table, he picked up the letters which had been delivered that morning by an unknown messenger who had left before he could question him. Plucking one particular letter out from the pile, he re-read the part in which his neighbour, Trahaearn Fychan, pledged support to Gwenwynwyn in his latest campaign to: *"restore Painscastle and Elfael to the Welsh people at any cost."* Of course, it had been in some sort of code against the possibility of it falling into someone else's hand, but his scribes had not taken long to decipher it.

Angrily, William flung the letter down again and shouted for a page to bring him a goblet of wine which he downed in one go before sending the boy away for more. Gwenwynwyn was fast becoming a thorn in his side. With Rhys dead, he had expected to nurture strong links with his daughter's husband Gruffydd as the new Lord of Deheubarth. Instead, Gruffydd was rotting in Corfe castle along with Mattie and the children, leaving him to face the combined threat of Gwenwynwyn and Maelgwn with only a handful of Marcher barons. Of course, pledging support to Gwenwynwyn was not the same as joining forces with him, but – William slammed his fist down on the table hard. 'Damn you, Fychan,' he whispered. 'Damn you to hell.'

Just then, the sound of the gates being closed and the drawbridge being raised drew William to the window where he stood for a while looking down at

Matilda. She was handing her mare over to a stable boy, having just returned from visiting a family of sick cotters in the outskirts of the village. At her heels sat one or other of Giselle and Roland's descendants, sniffing a proffered bone hungrily. William's already black mood darkened as her companion, Archdeacon Gerald, offered Matilda his arm and began to escort her in the direction of the kitchens for refreshment, an attentive look on his face as she said something to him.

As if sensing his scrutiny, Matilda looked up and, seeing him glaring down at her, she hesitated before commencing on her journey to the kitchens, a troubled expression marring her bow. Behind her, the stable boys milled about shouting to one another as they re-stabled the horses and put away the tack. Over in the bakehouse, a window was thrown open against the heat and a sudden cloud of smoke billowed out. William saw none of this as he looked down at the object that he gripped in his left hand. It was a silver earring fashioned in the shape of a crescent moon, set with a single moonstone in the middle. He knew it well. He had had the earrings made as a gift for Matilda after the birth of Will, and he knew that its partner still lay in the little silver box that they had come in for he had checked.

The page returned with the wine and, crossing to the table, he topped up William's goblet, spilling some of it on one of the rolls of parchment as he did so. With a roar, William crossed the room and clouted the boy round the head with his fist, knocking him to the floor where he lay shaking with fear until William returned to the window and his back was to him once more. Only then did the boy crawl fearfully out of the chamber making as little noise as possible.

Turning to look down into the bailey again, William saw Matilda lifted her head to the sky before entering the kitchens on Gerald's arm. The sun was very hot, but never-the-less he saw her give a little shiver as a sudden rumble of thunder rolled across the mountain – or was it the old God's that her maid Jeanette had once believed in?

Later when he was very drunk William had Simon, his head groom, saddle his horse. Matilda had stayed out of his way for much of the afternoon, ensconced in her solar deep in conversation with Gerald. Armed with a piece of rope, William was sure that by now Trahaearn Fychan would have received his summons to meet him down by the tavern at the crossroads, on the way into the town of Brecon. Summoning his men, he checked that his sword was in his scabbard and, dragging brutally on the reins of his horse, he wheeled the beast around and roared for the drawbridge to be lowered.

Up in her solar, Matilda put her hand to her head which was buzzing furiously as if it had been invaded by a swarm of bees. She wanted to look in the fire, but it was too hot for a fire at this time of year. Gerald's voice came from afar. 'Are you all right, my dear?'

'Yes, yes,' she whispered. 'Nothing but a silly turn.'

'Here, let me get you a goblet of wine,' Gerald said solicitously.

'Just a silly turn,' Matilda repeated again. But she found that she was shaking.

Down by the crossroads, Trahaearn Fychan approached William, a wary smile on his face, for as yet he was unsure why he had been summoned. Above him the black clouds gathered and rumbled a warning, but he did not notice, or maybe he already knew what they heralded.

I watched the scene as if it was happening in slow motion. As if from afar. As in truth it was. For that is the way of destiny; I had already seen Trahaearn's fate a thousand times, and there was nothing I could do.

And so, I watched in sorrow as William and his men seized Trahaearn and dragged him brutally off his cob, then binding him by his hands they fastened him to the tail of William's big war horse. Trahaearn's handsome face registered shock, and he might have shouted in protest, but I was too far away to hear, and his men were too few to defend him.

A crowd was now gathering around the group. Children were throwing taunts and running excitedly to and fro, attracting the attention of others. A group of women huddled together, chattering ten-to-the-dozen, some with looks of horror on their faces, and some alight with malice.

Then William signalled his men forward and kicked his horse into a trot. Trahaearn gamely tried to stay on his feet, but William cruelly spurred his horse into a canter so that he fell hard to be dragged through the streets of Brecknock, desperately twisting and writhing in a vain attempt too free himself.

I felt the wet tears roll down my face. Destiny was a cruel mistress who was now extracting the nastiest of revenge on the kindliest of people. Then, picking up my skirts and forgetting the pies I had come to buy, I followed the crowd who were flocking to see what the Ogre of Abergavenny meant to do with Trahaearn Fychan.

The crowd gathered at last in front of the village gallows where William had finally come to a halt. A young boy in the stocks, stained and spattered with the pulp of the decayed fruit that had been pelted at him all day, strained to see what was happening, glad that attention had been diverted to some other poor unfortunate.

Trahaearn lay bruised and battered on the ground in front of William who had dismounted from his horse. His tunic was ripped to shreds, the blue fabric stained in a gaudy, mockery of red from his shoulders which now resembled a piece of meat on a butcher's slab, and one ear, torn from the side of his head, now hung like a flap across his cheek by only a thread.

Cutting Trahaearn free from his horse, William's men dragged him to a felled log which had been turned on its end to serve as a makeshift block, where they shoved him to his knees. For a moment Trahaearn's sad brown eyes met mine and held them before turning to seek out William's.

'Are you not going to tell me for what sin am I about to die without so much as a trial in which I can defend myself?' he shouted.

At the sound of Trahaearn's voice, the crowd grew silent and watchful. William did not answer. He was incandescent with rage and seemed to be incapable of speech. Then, with a nod at one of his men, Trahaearn was pushed face down on the block and held there.

'Will you not tell me for what I am about to die!' Trahaearn shouted again, desperately struggling too free himself from his captor. The mood of the crowd was changing. There was an angry buzz, a feeling of unrest, resentment even, that a Norman Lord could treat one of their own in such a fashion.

Just then a woman pushed her way through the crowd and, clinging to William's sleeve, she pleaded clemency for Trahaearn. I recognised Trahaearn's wife. William, unmoved by her sobbing entreaties, flung her off so hard that she crashed to the ground with a bone jarring thud. Then with a final enraged roar, he raised his heavy sword and brought it down hard, striking Trahaearn's head from his shoulders with a single stroke.

The crowd watched in eerie silence as it flew from his shoulders, bounced once, and then rolled to lie buried in some deep grass out of sight. Moments later Trahaearn's body slid bonelessly to the ground at William's feet where it lay twitching silently in a pool of its own blood.

There was an angry rumble amongst the crowd as they looked from William's dark face to the body of the Lord of Llangorse. Once again, this arrogant Norman had dished out a hard and undeserved punishment on one of their own. One man slid a dagger from his belt and the crowd swayed as if it might move towards William, but the sound of swords being drawn from scabbards was enough to prevent any folly, and after a moment they began to slip away to the safety of their own homes, leaving Trahaearn's widow still sobbing on the ground.

William's eyes still glittered with malice as he looked down at Trahaearn's corpse. 'Have him hung upside down on the gallows as a warning to anyone else that this is the price of treachery.' Then, turning, he spotted me and holding my gaze for a moment he said, 'That, and taking what belongs to another ...'

In the solar Matilda stood unnaturally still, the buzzing in her head was getting worse. She was standing under the light of a window and without thinking she looked down into her wine and moaned.

A picture was forming.

She could see Ailith standing amongst a crowd of maybe twenty or more people – she recognised the gallows and stocks beneath the willow. Then the surface of the liquid rippled, and Trahaearn's image appeared bound by his hands to the tail of William's horse; his back was bleeding and torn and one of his ears hung loosely down by his cheek. The wine rippled again, only this time Trahaearn was kneeling in front of an upturned log; she could see the sadness in his eyes as they sought and found Ailith's, before, like great birds of prey, shadowy hands grasped him by the shoulders and pushed him down.

Her mouth formed a silent, *no ...*

Over in the corner Gerald, who was watching Matilda with deep concern on his long, gentle face, quickly crossed over and removed the goblet from her stiff fingers.

But not before Matilda saw William's huge battle sword rise and fall, taking Trahaearn's head clean from his shoulders so that it bounced and rolled into the deep grass beyond the gallows.

That was when Matilda began to scream ...

Matilda lay on the bed in her chamber where Sam Skeet had carried her once she had been calmed down. A maid had infused some herbs which had finally sent her into a troubled sleep. There was no fire in the room, but a servant had lit a small brazier in the corner where a single sconce burned brightly.

Whilst she slept, William entered the room and stood looking down at her. His eyes were narrow slits and his face was hard and bitter. He had been drinking heavily and the hate that gnawed at him had not been assuaged by the events of the afternoon. Instead, it lingered like the ache of a pulled tooth.

Matilda moaned as if sensing his presence. William scowled, then he walked towards the end of the bed and, removing something heavy from a sack, he placed it carefully upon the coffer. Finally, he pulled something out of a kerchief and laid it alongside. Then with a nasty smile he turned and left the room, closing the door softly behind him.

On the bed, Matilda moaned again as her mind gradually struggled to assert itself over the effects of the herbs. How William could do such a terrible thing was beyond her, but at least now she truly knew that she loathed him. Slowly, she sat up. She had to go to chapel and pray for Trahaearn's soul, and for William's for he would surely burn in hell.

Her mouth tasted foul, and when she opened her eyes the brightness of the brazier and the sconce in the corner made her head ache. Pushing the coverlet down over her knees, she paused – there was something on the coffer at the bottom of her bed. Feeling suddenly sick, she rubbed her hand over her face, blinked to clear her vision, and looked again.

Perched on top of the coffer, looking straight back at her, was Trahaearn's severed head. Matilda stared at it for a long time, taking in the details of his once, lively brown eyes, now glazed and vacant, and the thin, white lips drawn back from his teeth where, Matilda noted numbly, he had recently lost a molar.

Then her gaze turned to the little object lying beside Trahaearn's head, winking in the light of the brazier. It was a silver earring in the shape of a crescent moon.

For the second time that day, Matilda began to scream ...

Chapter 20

March 1199, Hay Castle, Wales

Rainclouds hung heavily in the sky above the small party approaching the gates of Hay Castle. The portcullis had only just been raised when a huge clap of thunder, accompanied by a fork of lightning, struck the ground in front of them, making Matilda's mount rear and nearly dislodging her from her seat. Immediately, one of William's guards ran forward and grabbed the reins, moments later he had calmed the horse sufficiently enough to lead it into the bailey, leaving the rest of the party to follow cautiously behind on their own wild-eyed mounts.

As she dismounted, Matilda thought she saw a dark shape fly over the wall and settle itself in the huge oak on the far side of the bailey, and she glanced surreptitiously at Annora. As if sensing her looking, Annora caught her eye and smiled, then pulling the hood of her mantle up against the rain she ran lithely in the direction of the nursery hoping to find her siblings. Matilda let her go. The longer she delayed her meeting with William the better. She had no wish to see her husband in a hurry. In fact, she didn't care if she never saw him again.

The year following Trahaearn's death had been terrible and traumatic. Amidst the rows and recriminations over the manner of Trahaearn's demise, fighting had broken out in the hills around Brycheniog, following which Gwenwynwyn had amassed a huge army and besieged Painscastle. William blamed her.

Matilda sighed, and rubbing the rain out of her eyes she began to make her way to the still room where Jeannette had kept her herbs. It was there that she had hidden the huge, leather-bound book of spells and remedies which travelled everywhere with the old woman, mostly out of nostalgia, but also, she reminded herself, because it still occasionally had its uses.

As she walked, her mind drifted back to Gwenwynwyn. After a series of failed attempts to settle the siege without force, William asked that Gruffydd be released from his imprisonment at Corfe Castle to negotiate on their behalf. But instead of being of assistance, Gruffydd had been resentful of everyone around him, blaming them for all his misfortunes. In the end he had only managed to make matters worse, and finally he had withdrawn to lick his wounds.

Then there had been the sudden and unexpected arrival of Geoffrey Fitz Peter, the new chief Justiciar of England, with a large army to save the day. The fighting that had followed in the foothills of Painscastle had taken its toll on the Welsh, and with over three thousand now dead, Matilda wished that she had never had the misfortune to set eyes on the place.

Arriving at the still room, she crossed to a coffer and, extracting a ring of keys from the hessian pouch at her side, she inserted one into the rusty keyhole. After a lot of wiggling and rough turning she managed to spring the lock and reaching in, she removed the huge leather-bound book she was looking for, reflecting that the latest set of events to befall them was likely to make the next year or so equally as unpleasant.

Early in February, Matilda had received a letter from Isabel de Mortimer asking them to visit Wigmore.

The letter had not been specific, but Matilda sensed that Isabel had concerns about Annora, and along with a small band of men and a handful of servants, she had immediately ridden to find out what they were. Upon her arrival Isabel de Mortimer had greeted her warmly enough, and she was relieved to see that Annora seemed to have been well cared for. However, what Isabel told her was a little disturbing, and it was soon agreed that Annora should spend some time with her family before she wed Hugh so that Matilda might get to the bottom of it. Brushing a layer of dust off a stool, Matilda settled herself down and looked at the book reverently. Then, opening it, she began to flick through the pages until she found what she wanted.

It was an account of a woman that Jeanette had treated many years ago – a woman who had a familiar in the form of a bird ...

PART THREE

Chapter 21

Bramber Castle, England, April 1199

'King Richard's dead!' Matilda looked up from the letter she was reading in horror, her face ashen. It had arrived that morning from the Limousin in France where William was with the king suppressing a revolt by Viscount Aimar of Limoges.

'He can't be,' I said stupidly, feeling an icy finger creep down my back. 'Why, Sir William only wrote a few weeks ago to say that the army is laying waste to the Viscount's lands … that they are certain to win …'

'I'm afraid it's true,' Matilda said, her voice barely a whisper as she looked down at the letter in her hand again. 'I know it's hard to believe, but according to William – and I see no reason why he would lie - once Richard had dealt with the Viscount, he laid siege to the neighbouring château of Châlus-Chabrol, apparently with the intention of seizing a treasure trove reportedly discovered by a peasant in a field nearby.' She swallowed, and I could see her biting back the tears. 'It seems that whilst there, a skirmish ensued. Richard, thinking little of it, carelessly ventured out with only his helmet and shield and was wounded in the shoulder by a stray crossbow bolt fired from the château walls. He died two weeks later on the 6th April in his mother's arms. Not from the wound itself according to William, but from mortification due to lack of care – William blames the butcher of a surgeon who tried to remove the arrow head …'

We stood in silence for a while, each of us lost in the turmoil of our own thoughts.

'There's more though, Ailith,' Matilda said after a moment, and I saw the lines around her mouth tighten as she struggled with the words. 'On his death bed, Richard bequeathed his kingdom and all his treasure to his younger brother: Prince John is to be our new King …'

I looked at her aghast. King Richard had always supported Arthur of Brittany's claim to the throne following the death of his father, Geoffrey of Brittany, in a tournament in Paris some years past.

'But why?' I asked.

'William writes that his mother, Queen Eleanor, finally persuaded him on his death bed that it was safer to entrust England and its Angevin holdings to a grown man rather than to a mere boy - Arthur is, after all, still only twelve.'

'But I still don't understand,' I said doggedly.

This wasn't how it was supposed to be, Arthur should have ruled first …

Matilda shook her head in exasperation. 'Queen Eleanor always supported John for the throne - even when he was trying to snatch it out of Richard's hands when he went missing on his way home from the Crusades. I wouldn't put it past her to lie and say that Richard changed his mind at the last if it suited her purpose and ensured John's succession.' She turned away again, not wanting me to see how distressed she was for she, like me, had not expected John to come to the throne so soon and in such unexpected circumstances.

'I suspect there will be trouble,' she said tiredly. 'Many of Richard's barons will likely lend support to Arthur of Brittany - Phillip Augustus almost certainly will. John is not well liked, and therefore he will not have an easy ride to the throne, despite the fact that Richard bequeathed it to him in the end. At any rate, it doesn't matter what I think,' she said, glancing at me again. 'The last few lines of William's letter make it quite clear that he was among the first to swear fealty to Prince John in France, and he has promised to be among the first to swear fealty to him when he is crowned King at Westminster.' She shivered. 'If John had power as a prince, then how much more will he have as a king, Ailith? It doesn't bear thinking about!' Then, throwing down the letter, she sighed. 'I had better send for a scribe to inform the steward at Knepp to be prepared. Bramber will be the first port of call for John and his retinue on the road to London. Oh, and Ailith, send Sam Skeet to me please,' she said, as, knowing that she would like to be alone for a while, I turned to leave. 'We will need to send to Horsham and Steyning for supplies. For if John's retinue does stop here they will surely eat us out of house and home.'

Bramber Castle, England, 25th May 1199

William stood with his back to the burning fire. He was watching the newly titled Duke of Normandy play chess with William Marshall on a small table at the back of the hall. The Marshall was, he noted, letting Prince John win, mostly because it was widely known that John was a poor looser and he had inherited the Angevin temper.

Matilda hovered nearby, nervously gripping a pitcher of wine. For some reason John had demanded that the lady of the house serve him personally, and it seemed to amuse him to send her off on errands for sweetmeats, books, his mantle, or for whatever else he happened to desire. Occasionally he threw her sly looks, and now he beckoned her forward with his finger and said something to her in a voice so low that she had to stoop hear. The Marshall affected an air of disinterest as he leaned down to pick up some chess pieces that had fallen to the floor, taking his time over it as if he was embarrassed about something.

William signalled for a girl to top up his goblet and yawned. It had been a long day, what with the crossing from France being rough and him not travelling well by sea, but at least they had set sail knowing that John's continental lands were secure for the time being in the hands of Queen Eleanor. Taking a few sips of his wine, William reflected on the excitement of the last few weeks. There had been, and still was, plenty of resistance to John's succession to the throne of England amongst the French lords. As soon as John was crowned King of England, he would have to return to France to try and win over those that, like King Phillip of France, were proclaiming twelve-year-old Arthur of Brittany as the true successor to Richard's empire, according to his previously declared wishes.

Normandy, it was true, had declared for John without a fight, preferring a grown man to a mere boy, but Anjou, Maine, and Touraine had declared for Arthur, resulting in several uprisings having to be suppressed before John had been able to sail to England for his coronation. At any rate, in two days' time John would be the King of England as well as the Duke of Normandy and Maine, and like many other English noblemen, William was pretty sure that he would have a difficult time trying to balance the two and keep the peace in France.

Over in the corner, Faulkes de Breauté roused himself from his chair and helped himself to more wine, before joining William by the hearth. William didn't trust the man one bit, but as John kept him constantly by his side, he had no choice but to grin and bear it and offer him hospitality when he was under his roof. Faulkes gave William a twisted smile that looked more like a scowl before picking up one of the sweetmeats that sat on the table beside the hearth. It was warm and sticky, but he popped it into the gash in his face that he called a mouth and chewed.

William shifted his weight so that he was slightly leaning away from the smell of de Breauté's breath, trying to contain the irritation he always felt when he was near him. Then he turned his attention back to Matilda, hoping that de Breauté might leave if he declined conversation. He frowned. John was openly fondling her breast; Matilda was flame red and weakly trying to fend him off, but William couldn't hear what she was saying because of the blood ringing angrily in his ears.

'You didn't think Trahaearn Fychan was the only one tupping her, did you?' de Breauté said lazily at his side.

William turned to him angrily. 'What the hell do you mean, man?' he hissed.

'I mean what I said,' de Breauté said, reaching for another sweetmeat. 'Only you can't cut off a prince's head, nor a king's for that matter, for tupping your wife – you might well remember that before you act too rashly. Besides, even you must know John's penchant for his baron's wives, particularly if they are comely – you can't possibly think that he would have overlooked yours, surely?'

William spluttered into his wine, speechless.

'You know,' de Breauté said conversationally, 'when de Vesci's wife took Prince John's eye he put a whore in her bed rather than let him seduce her. Then, when John boasted to him about how good his wife was the next day, the stupid man told him the truth. John went into one of his rages – have you seen him in one of his rages, lying on the floor with his mouth full of the rushes and howling like a baby?'

'Yes,' William said shortly.

'Well,' he continued. 'The whole family had to flee the court, so if you are thinking of doing or saying anything, then think again, for you will lose his favour – besides, he only got the one bastard on you, and think of it man, you might get an Earldom out of it ...!'

In a daze, William looked at Prince John; his friend, a prince of the realm, soon to be king, as his stunned mind struggled to take in what de Breauté was saying.

De Breauté was saying that one of his children was not his. One of his children was the next King of England's child; a bastard, a cuckoo in the nest. And he knew which one, but he had never suspected the real truth of the matter - or maybe he had, but he had just not wanted to see what was really in front of his face. With a shudder, William put down his goblet and left the room, unable to look at his wife any longer.

He didn't see de Breauté smile darkly to himself as he went. Nor did he hear him say that if de Braose thought that he was the only baron in England and Wales who didn't pay for John's favour, then he was a truly stupid man, to the unfortunate girl he took to his chamber and beat half to death a moment later.

I sat and watched as Prince John openly fondled and leered at Matilda in front of his host, the servants, and the guests. Up until now he had been more discreet; but now that he was the Duke of Normandy, and soon-to-be King of England, he could take what he liked and none could refuse him. So why be coy about it?

Faulkes de Breauté had joined William by the hearth and I could see by the look on William's face that he had confirmed his worst suspicions for he looked mutinous. I looked back to where Matilda was still being fondled by John and I shivered. A sconce had gone out throwing him into shadow and sitting there in the shadows he looked like the Prince of Darkness. Was that what he truly was then? The Prince of Darkness himself? Suddenly I recalled Matilda telling me that Angevin kings were spawned by the devil, and at that moment I truly think I believed it. I shivered again and crossed myself before going to re-light the sconce - I had the strangest sensation in the pit of my stomach – the wheels of fate were turning fast and gathering speed, and I was afraid ...

William was waiting in Matilda's chamber when she entered that night, and he was boiling with anger. 'So, you've been opening your legs for a prince and will you still do so for a king?'

'Not now, William,' Matilda said tiredly.

'Not now? When, then, if not now?' William retorted angrily. 'Do I have to make an appointment with the Prince's whore now?'

'I never meant for this to happen, William. Dear God, but I did not. I would sooner that he had overlooked me - that I had been plain and never taken Prince John's eye. But it is done and there was nothing that I could do. John takes what he wants and there is none who can refuse him - not even you.'

'And what of Annora, is she his?' William enquired coldly, knowing all the while that she was. How blind he had been. She was so different to the others with her oh so blue eyes – Prince John's eyes - he saw that now, and her soft gold hair. And to think that he had once thought her Trahaearn's and hated him for it!

Matilda nodded once and then sat down tiredly on the bed.

'I always knew she was someone else's bastard and not mine, I just never looked so high for his father! William said tightly. 'Well, no matter, he will be gone soon, back to France, and I will travel with him. You will return to Wales and we will contrive to keep you out of his way in future, although I think you are getting a little old for bedroom dalliances!'

Then, turning his back on her, he left the room to seek his own solace for the night.

John stirred restlessly in his chamber. She had not pleased him so much tonight. Oh, she had been compliant enough, turning this way and that to accommodate his needs. But he had noticed that she was getting old. Not that she looked old. No, she was still beautiful and alluring, and she still had a way of making him hate her whilst at the same time making him want to touch her. But she had been ill a while ago, and there was stiffness in her joints, and some silver in her hair. Rosamund had not grown old – not that he remembered anyway. She had died with her beauty intact, in a nunnery of all places. What a place for a king's whore to die; in a nunnery repenting of her sins. And oh, what sins she had committed – sucking and moaning and opening her legs for a king so that she could wear silks and sparkle with gold and gems!

He moaned as his loins stirred again. Oh, how he had hated Rosamund. And oh, how he hated Matilda. But still he could not resist her. And if William wanted reward for helping him gain the throne, then there was always a price to pay ...

Shoreham, England, 20th June 1199

Matilda watched as the small fleet of ships bearing John and his army of barons, including William, sailed slowly out of Shoreham harbour, bound for France to begin raising support against Phillip and Arthur.

John had been crowned King of England on Ascension Day at Westminster Abbey, amidst much pomp and ceremony, followed by several days of feasting. Matilda noticed that Isabella was conspicuously absent from the occasion, and no mention was made of her being crowned queen, which did not bode well for her, she thought remembering the sad little girl that John had married all those years ago. Neither was there an heir for Isabella to try and keep him with her, and so Matilda supposed she would be somehow thrown aside by John; discarded, rejected, and humiliated as the barren wife that he should never have married. Perhaps if Isabella had borne him a son, John might have been more kind to her – maybe even set her up in a castle somewhere where she could be at peace with a small allowance for her and her ladies to live on.

Sighing, Matilda walked a little way down the beach and shielded her eyes, watching as the small fleet slowly became tiny dots in the distance. Even in his short time as King, John was not proving widely popular. He was a suspicious and crafty man, and yet, she had to grudgingly admit, he had readily rewarded those who helped sit him on the throne of England. Hubert Walter had been made Chancellor, and William Marshall was now the Earl of Pembroke. Even her husband harboured high hopes of gaining much reward himself, though it was yet to be bestowed.

Anyway, she thought, it would be good to see the back of John for a while. France would not welcome him; he was an evil, greedy little man who was always seeing a plot where there wasn't one, and always taking what he wanted with little thought for others. She had no doubt that he would cause further harm during his reign as King of England and Duke of Normandy. And, if his expedition to Ireland in his father's time was anything to go by, she had no doubt he would lose his lands in France sooner or later.

When the fleet was out of sight Matilda turned and, mounting her horse, she began to make her way back to the castle. Now that there was no longer a court to attend, she would find Ailith and together they would pack the up the household and head for Hay. There she would gather her children around her in the knowledge that she would have a few months of peace and freedom. Yes, she thought with finality, she would do as William had bid. She missed Loretta who was still at Hay undertaking her lessons, and it would be a good opportunity to talk to Annora whilst William was out of the way to find out if anything was worrying the girl.

Chapter 22

Hay Castle, Wales, July 1199

Hay was a place of calm and peace in William's absence and I think we all secretly begrudged the day he would return. Gerald had called on Matilda that morning and he had settled himself in the same seat he always sat in when he was in her solar. It was almost ritualistic, and I saw her smile at him indulgently before handing him a goblet of wine.

On the far side of the room, Annora sat demurely on a cushion in the window embrasure staring out across the hills at the blue afternoon sky, and Will, who was visiting from his duties at Radnor, sat nearby engrossed in a game of dice with his squire.

Pulling up a seat herself, Matilda sat down and leaned towards Gerald. 'May I ask you something?' she ventured, resting her hand briefly on his arm.

Gerald smiled. 'Of course, you know you can always talk to me.'

'It's about Annora,' Matilda said, throwing a quick glance at Annora to check she wasn't listening.

Gerald nodded briefly.

'Her betrothed's mother, Lady de Mortimer, believes that she has a familiar -' Matilda paused to take in Gerald's reaction, but beyond the slight raising of his eyebrows she appeared to see nothing to say that he was shocked or disturbed by this statement. 'I myself have noticed that there's an owl,' she continued, encouraged by his silence. 'It made its home in the grain store on the night I brought Annora home, I don't like to give credence to such things, but-'

Gerald nodded once. 'And does Lady de Mortimer think she's practicing the dark arts or has fallen into some kind of sin perhaps?' he enquired.

'No, nothing like that,' Matilda replied. 'Quite the opposite in fact. She seems to like Annora well enough and treats her like her own. She's just worried that it's not natural - although even as a small child Annora had a fascination for birds. No, Annora is to return to them soon and I think Lady de Mortimer just wants to be sure that all is well - for both her and for her son.'

Privately, I thought that Matilda was being too kind about Isabel de Mortimer. She might have been very polite to her face at Wigmore, but she had stopped by Hay on her travels with her husband recently, and I had the feeling that she disliked Annora immensely and was looking for a way out of the marriage contract.

'And are you worried for her?' Gerald asked, stroking his chin thoughtfully.

'No, not at all,' Matilda replied immediately. 'There has always been a bit of the fey in my family – you must have heard that the people of Hay call me a witch and a giantess and say that I built the castle all on my own in one night?' She grimaced, reminding me how horrified she'd been that such rumours could be built around her reputation.

Gerald smiled and patted Matilda's hand. 'Rumours, dear lady, naught but rumours. We're a superstitious lot you know, the Welsh. I myself have witnessed many miracles and strange occurrences, and I have heard of many other similar happenings on my travels, which, as you already know, I have written about in my books: there's the story of the water fowl that only sing when the natural prince of the country orders them to do so, and the one about the mare that belonged to the hermit Illtud - it's said that she was mated by a stag producing the most wonderfully fast creature resembling a horse behind and a stag in the fore. There are many things on this earth that cannot be explained, and if as you say Lady de Mortimer loves the child as her own, I am sure with a little reassurance from yourself she will soon put the matter of her fears for the child aside.'

Matilda sighed then, seemingly satisfied, she changed the subject. 'But I am being remiss, Gerald, in burdening you with my worries. What of you? What brings you here to my solar on this sunny morning?'

Gerald leaned forward and I saw that his eyes were suddenly shiny and wet with tears. Immediately, Matilda rose, and crouching down she covered his hands with her own.

'What is it, Gerald? You can tell me. Has something terrible happened?'

'No, dear lady, no! Far from it, for I do believe my greatest wish is to be granted as King John proposes to accept me as Bishop of St David's and I was elected by the full chapter of St David's at the end of June! My star is rising, Matilda! Finally, my star is rising and I am to have the see of St David's at last!

For a moment Matilda looked confused but then she broke into a delighted smile. 'Oh, but that's wonderful news, is it not!'

'Yes, but it has been many months since Peter de Leia died and there has been much conflict – I am constantly refused; my family are too powerful, the Archbishop of Canterbury opposes me because I wish for Wales to be free from subservience to Canterbury – I could go on!'

Matilda was sitting back on her heels now and frowning. 'But if the Archbishop of Canterbury is against you, surely he will refuse to consecrate you, despite John's wishes? Oh, that would be terrible!'

'No, listen! I am to be consecrated by the Pope. In Rome. That is what I have come to tell you. I am to travel to Rome immediately!'

Matilda grasped his hand again. 'Oh, Gerald, that's wonderful – at last you will have your heart's desire. May God grant you a good journey, though I shall miss you.' Then releasing his hand, she turned away, and I could see that her eyes were shimmering with unshed tears. Rome was a long way to travel and Gerald would be gone for weeks, perhaps even months, and the journey might be dangerous.

'I only hope that God will keep you safe, Gerald,' I saw her whisper into the air. And suddenly I realised that Gerald was perhaps her only real friend.

Hay Castle, Wales, August 1199

'Thank you,' Matilda said as the messenger handed her the latest packet of letters from William who was still in France with King John. Then waving him away to find refreshment in the hall, she made her way out into the bailey and towards the small kitchen garden to read them.

The sun was already high in the sky, and the only sound was the coo-cooing of doves in the dovecote beyond the garden wall. A kitchen maid crouched down between the rows of carefully cultivated vegetables, digging up salad leaves and chives to marry with the fresh pike that had been caught in the River Wye that very morning. Brightly coloured marigolds and nasturtiums dotted the beds with colour: the marigolds kept the slugs at bay, and the nasturtium seeds, brought from the east by a merchant and grown for the first time this year, not only kept black fly away from the vegetables, but also made very good eating she'd been assured – though Merri was yet to be convinced.

The thought was still in her mind whilst Matilda made herself comfortable on a wooden seat built around a walnut tree at the back of the garden and began to open the dispatches one by one.

The first one contained the usual news, mostly centring around John's latest negotiations with King Phillip and his nephew, Arthur of Brittany. John and his party had arrived in Rouen in June, and his French barons had immediately rallied around him to offer their support. John, William wrote, was now deep in negotiations with Phillip who couldn't afford to finance another war and, so far, he had managed to negotiate an eight-week truce with him without a single visit to the battle field. More talks would come later, William observed.

Folding the letter and putting it aside, Matilda picked up another one. It irritated her that William's correspondence was constantly dotted with phrases like, *"praise be to God,"* or, *"if God so wills."* He'd even been known to slip his scribes extra gold coins in their salaries to insert the phrases in his official correspondence. The one she had in her hand began:

Dearest wife,

I trust to God in his kindness that you are well and in good health ...

She snorted, and the kitchen maid threw her a startled glance - since when had William ever cared about her health! Smiling apologetically at the girl, Matilda began to scan the rest of the letter quickly. Much of the content was in the same vein as the first and held little interest, but she stopped abruptly as Isabella of Gloucester's name jumped out at her.

I have some news to trust to you. Our King has in his wisdom had his marriage to Isabella of Gloucester annulled by the Bishops of Lisiex, Bayeux, and Avranches on the grounds of consanguinity, and Isabella has not contested the action for she knows full well that it is a sin before God to marry your cousin and that her punishment for such a sin is that she is without issue, may God forgive her soul ...

A bee alighted on Matilda's hand but she barely noticed. So, Isabella was free. She recalled that at the time of the marriage, Baldwin, the Archbishop of Canterbury, had made a formal protest declaring the union invalid because John and Isabella were close cousins. He had also warned that the marriage should not be consummated because it would be a sin, but nobody had taken a blind bit of notice of him at the time.

'It's ironic that all these years later John decides to heed the late Bishop's concerns when it most suits him!' Matilda muttered to herself darkly, before turning her attention back to the rest of the missive, which mostly concerned the ongoing negotiations and various grumbles regarding the poor accommodation and food in France.

But try as she might, Matilda could not concentrate on such trivialities when her mind kept going back to the thought of Isabella ... free at last to make a life for herself.

Hay castle, Wales, March 1200

Will strode into the great hall and crossed to warm himself before the hearth. It was freezing outside, but although snow remained on the mountain tops it was beginning to melt in the valleys, and the roads would soon be passable enough for him to begin his journey to his wife's father's estates in England which he had agreed to manage whilst he was abroad.

Matilda wandered over carrying his youngest son Giles tenderly in her arms. John, his sturdy two-year-old, was happily sitting in the rushes playing with a stack of wooden toys that one of the grooms had given him. Maude, who was pregnant again, was nowhere to be seen.

'Do you have any news of Father's return from France yet?' Will asked. 'I saw a messenger arrive – though how in God's name he got through in this I don't know.' He coughed deeply and winced. He'd recently taken a fall from his horse and broken several ribs, and it was the danger of infection that had prevented him accompanying William abroad in the service of John the previous year, but he still harboured hopes of joining him later.

Matilda nodded. 'Yes, I received word this morning. The letters are of old news as they have travelled slowly in this inclement weather, I think. He gives no word of his plans to return yet, and as far as I can tell he intends to keep himself close to John at all times. He believes that John will reward him well for easing his path to the throne.' She paused to adjust Giles' weight in her arms before continuing. 'He also tells that Phillip no longer supports Arthur's claim to the throne of England, and that he has accepted John's succession as valid at last.'

Will nodded. 'I heard something of this just before Yuletide straight from the mouth one of the Marshall's messengers. He had just returned from Normandy and was on his way to advise the council of Westminster of the turn of events in John's favour – though he did say that he is beginning to earn himself the rather illustrious name of "*softsword*" because he is giving too many concessions to Phillip in order to pave the way – let's just hope it doesn't stick and follow him into battle!'

'Yes,' Matilda said, wrinkling her nose as she recalled that he had once been known as "*lacklands*" for his lack of land in old King Henry's day when his brothers were all secure in their own. But they were all dead now, including young Prince Henry, or rather young King Henry, for Henry had very unwisely crowned him against the advice of Thomas Beckett sometime before he died. She pushed away the memory of the handsome youth so often to be found standing in her solar at Bramber all those years before and wondered how fate had managed to deliver the throne of England into Prince John's hands. She shivered. Fate was a devious and twisted mistress who always had a plan … and that plan was threatening to overtake them all.

'Anyway,' Matilda continued, stroking Giles' soft mop of dark curly hair tenderly, 'William says that John has ceded Brittany to Arthur and the boy has accepted terms, if not a little ungraciously, as Phillip bids him do homage to John for it. He also says that John is once again discussing a treaty with Phillip that recognises his rights to Anjou, Maine, Aquitaine and Normandy, although he has had to concede the Vexin and the Norman county of Evreux to Phillip – still, it means that our Norman properties survive. Phillip is demanding 30,000 silver marks, so we can be sure that John will raise taxes once again!'

'Well,' Will said, relieving her of Giles who was already beginning to wriggle from her arms. 'As soon as I am recovered, I mean to join the king and Father in France - Maude is more than capable of running her father's estates whilst I am away. Trust me, Mother, the future is bright for us de Braoses - Father is rising high in the king's esteem, and I mean to do the same!' Then turning away, he went to meet Maude who was entering the hall at the far end, leaving Matilda to fight back the sudden tide of fear that threatened to overwhelm her at his words. In the hearth the fire guttered suddenly, and for a moment Matilda thought she glimpsed the dark countenance of John, followed by that of a younger man.

Afraid …

I listened to Will and Matilda's conversation, knowing that Matilda feared for Will constantly because of the circumstances of his birth. With a shiver I remembered the red dream and its omen of death, an omen that hangs over our heads like an axe daily. Trying to shake off the feeling of impending disaster that comes when I think of the dream, I turned to where young John was still sitting quietly in the rushes with his stack of wooden toys. His eyes were following his father as he crossed to meet his mother, intrigued by the way in which the shadows trailed after him; reaching out to touch him at times with their long, wisp-like fingers. Then, dropping the wooden top he was holding, he giggled and stretched a grubby pink hand out to grab one. But within moments they were gone ...

Somewhere in France, King John stirred restlessly in his sleep as the image of Matilda de Braose rose once more to haunt his dreams. In his dream, Matilda had her back to him and her long chestnut hair hung down to her waist in a braid thicker than a man's wrist. John moaned as beneath the covers his loins stirred with desire; he ached to reach out and touch it, and, from afar, he heard himself calling out her name in a voice that even to his own ears sounded too plaintive, too pleading.

John woke suddenly. His mattress was soaking wet; drenched with the sweat of his fear. All around him the sound of Matilda's laugh still lingered in the air; mocking him, teasing him like the whore that she was as he lay shaking in the cooling passion of his desire. Afraid, John gripped his coverlet. She was a sorceress like Rosamund was before her; a sorceress, a witch and a whore. Around him the chamber grew darker and he lay still and waited, cowering like a child under the covers.

Rosamund's voice, when it came, as he knew it would, was little more than a ghostly whisper ... *what are you afraid of, silly boy* ... followed by her laughter ringing around the chamber, mocking him from the grave as, with a shaky hand, John reached for yet another goblet of wine ...

Chapter 23

Guildford Castle, December 1200

Large snowflakes flurried around our small party as we rode into the bailey at Guildford Castle where, at the last minute, King John had arranged a Christmas court to present his new wife, Isabella of Angoulême, to his most prominent barons. I waited alongside Matilda who sat atop her dappled mare watching the servants running to and fro from the bakehouse to the brewery whilst William conducted business with the castle's steward as to where we were to be housed. High up on the wall-walks I could see groups of sergeants and guards surveying the surrounding countryside, hollering every now and then when a new party approached, adding to the air of excitement that hung over the proceedings.

Despite all this I knew that Matilda hated the fuss that surrounded Christmas courts, and would have preferred to have been at one or other of their estates with her children gathered around her, but even I knew that was no longer an option with William having risen so high in John's favour of late. Already, he had been rewarded with the right to take as much land around their barony of Radnor as he could, and there was talk that he would soon be given the county of Limerick in Ireland as well.

I knew that the only pleasure that Matilda would have from our visit to Guildford was that Will and Maude would be attending, as would John, Bertha, and Giles, whom King John had appointed Bishop of Hereford in September – a singular honour as William kept reminding us all. Bertha, Matilda told me whilst we waited for William, was only coming because she was seeking to pay a fine against a petition not to be married again – her husband having died three years previously – preferring to dedicate her widowhood to her only son Walter. She glanced sideways at me as she said this, for we both knew that although she had loved him, her late husband's fondness for wine had made him short of temper and overly fond of the village wenches far too often, and the real truth was that Bertha had no wish to endure such a marriage again. John, on the other hand, she continued, her face brightening at the thought, was here under more pleasant circumstances, for he was to be knighted before travelling home to marry his betrothed Amabil de Limesi.

After a while William returned and stood watching as Matilda dismounted with the help of a groom. 'It's a good thing that we are high in the king's favour at the moment as it wasn't hard to secure some decent rooms with a bit of extra coin,' he said, rubbing his hands together and grinning at her smugly as the groom helped her step down from the mounting block.

I saw Matilda try for a smile, which quickly turned into a grimace instead as she spotted William's sister, Sybilla, bearing down on us like a large ship in a storm.

'Matilda,' Sybilla rasped, throwing William a quick nod of acknowledgement. 'You must come with me instantly!' And securing Matilda's arm in a punishing grip, she nodded at me and began propelling her towards the wooden stairs leading up to the keep at a pace that belied her size, leaving William standing staring after us in surprise.

'I have been given leave to escort you to attend the new queen immediately,' I heard Sybilla say as she deftly steered Matilda around a pack of dogs snarling over the remains of a bone. 'She's naught but a chit of a child and not only that she's rude and petulant to boot, but King John is besotted with her! No good will come of it, mark my words!' she grumbled, tutting occasionally so that the rolls of fat under her chin wobbled, reminding me of a blancmange as she threw orders over her shoulder for me to keep up.

I scowled, but obeyed, quietly confident in the knowledge that even if Sybilla paused long enough to hear it, she would get no reply from Matilda for she had already refused to speculate on the child that, if it were to be believed, John had kidnapped from under the nose of her betrothed Hugh de Lusignan, a wealthy and influential French Count, before being whisked away to marry to him against her will. Even a maid like myself could not fail to feel shocked by the scandal it had caused on both sides of the Channel. Although another Isabella, the spoilt daughter and heiress of Count Aymer of Angoulême, she was rumoured to be the complete opposite of the mouse that was Isabella of Gloucester, and tales of wickedness and witchcraft to keep John infatuated in bed whilst others planned the fall of his French empire dodged her every step to the throne. Nevertheless, Matilda, despite the unfavourable reports pertaining to John's new bride, confided in me that even if she were the most spoilt, petulant child in the world, the thought of her in John's hands was still enough to make her skin crawl.

'It's a complete scandal,' I heard Sybilla say, oblivious to Matilda's silence. 'Not only has John made enemies of the de Lusignans, but he also threatens the truce between King Phillip of France and himself which he worked so hard to gain – Indeed, I've heard that he spends half the day in bed mauling her. It's most indecent, and she's not much over twelve summers!' she finished, tutting her disapproval again.

At last, after negotiating the steps up to the keep, Sybilla led Matilda across to a set of newel stairs hidden behind a richly embroidered tapestry at the back of the great hall. 'The queen has her rooms up here,' she said turning her fleshy face briefly towards mine again before continuing on up the narrow winding staircase.

Pushing aside the sudden tide of disquiet that threatened to overwhelm me as we stood at the foot of the stairs, I fussed over the train of Matilda's fur lined peliçon which she wore over a gown of fine blue wool, now stained and dirty from travelling, then wearily I followed her and Sybilla up to face the spoilt child who was now the Queen of England.

Isabella was sitting on an ornate chair surrounded by her attendants when we entered the room. And she was indeed everything that Isabella of Gloucester had not been: dressed exquisitely in green shot silk, her small, dainty feet were propped up on a padded stool, exposing the delicate turn of her ankle above the gold embroidered shoes that she wore. Her face, which turned to Matilda as she entered the room, was heart shaped, her lips full and pink, and her corn coloured hair fell unchecked by a wimple down to a waist so small a man could span it easily with both hands.

But it was her eyes that stopped me in my tracks, for they were a deep, hyssop blue which should have enriched the child's beauty. But instead they were cruel, knowing eyes; the eyes of a woman much older, who'd seen much of the world, and much of it was to her distaste.

Indicating that Matilda and I should wait at the door, Sybilla crossed to Isabella, whispered something in her ear, and then withdrew. For a moment Isabella studied Matilda, the look concealed by her lashes, then waving a well-manicured hand she indicated that she should step forward.

'So, you are Lady de Braose?' she asked, watching as Matilda sank into a deep curtsey before her. The Braose part came out as *Bwoase*, but apart from that Isabella's English was very good, and even I could tell that she had been well schooled. Isabella stuck out her bottom lip petulantly. 'You know my husband well, I think.'

I saw Matilda blink. It was a statement and not a question, but before she could reply Isabella rushed on.

'He is cruel; he stole me from my betrothed, and *they* made me marry him.'

"They," I took to mean Isabella's parents who, seeing the opportunity to put a crown on their daughter's head, had gone along with the plan to send Hugh on a fool's errand abroad whilst they whisked Isabella off to marry John in secret – Of course it was not really kidnap, but nevertheless Isabella would not have had a choice; girls were merely chattels, especially one as beautiful and desirable as Isabella who, although young, would attract older, more ambitious suitors because of the fact that she was also an heiress. That she had been promised elsewhere was of no consequence. Particularly when a king came courting.

'Hugh, my betrothed,' Isabella carried on doggedly, determined to make her feelings known to all and sundry, 'was not cruel, and he was not fat; he was handsome, and he gave me a kitten.' The last part of the statement revealed how young Isabella really was, and for a moment I felt a twinge of sympathy for the child, but then Isabella suddenly spat. 'And *he* pokes me! Poke! Poke! Poke! All the time!'

Matilda blanched and went so pale that for a moment I thought she might faint.

'Poke! Poke! Poke! With his nasty sausage thing!' Isabella continued, deliberately ignoring Matilda's discomfort.

I looked around. None of Isabella's ladies seemed prepared to chastise the child who could bring great trouble on her shoulders if John heard of this conversation. Indeed, they looked bored by it. Only Sybilla looked as if she was sucking something sour.

At last Matilda pulled herself together long enough for me to hear her say in a low voice. 'I beg you take care, my lady … you don't know who might be listening –' but before she could finish Isabella chimed. 'And he has poked you, too, Lady de Bwoase.

Behind me Isabella's ladies in waiting gasped audibly, their interest suddenly piqued by the malice in Isabella's voice, and over by the window Sybilla covered her mouth in horror. I hardly dared move. The child was glaring at Matilda now, her mouth set in a mutinous line.

'Don't deny it,' Isabella said cruelly, her eyes never leaving Matilda's face. 'I know he poked you, because he has nasty dreams and he says that you cause them – and then he has to poke me to be rid of them!'

The silence in the chamber seemed to go on forever with nobody daring to breathe. Then, without warning, Isabella stood, and letting out an unholy scream she picked up a skein of silk and threw it straight at Matilda. Moments later she was gone. Running from the room in a flurry of skirts, her hair flying behind her like a golden banner in the fading evening light.

Up in the gatehouse tower Matilda, having managed to rid herself of both Sybilla and Alith, stood alone surveying the town of Guildford unhappily. Unlike many Norman castles, Guildford castle was not perched defensively on a hill, instead it was built just outside the town overlapping the town ditch, for its purpose was to provide a base and a meeting point for when the court was travelling through the south of England.

At the moment it looked very fine – as many as a hundred torches burned along the wall walks illuminating the narrow-curved street leading up to the drawbridge where the townspeople had set up their booths. She knew that nearly as many illuminated the rich tapestries in the hall and burned down the sumptuous corridors and in the private chambers where John's barons and their wives readied themselves for the banquet that was soon to start.

But Matilda had no appetite for the feast. She just wanted to curl up and die. She would never have thought that a child as young as Isabella would have the power to upset her so much, but the interview that afternoon kept flooding back into her mind. Now she dreaded seeing John, for she didn't understand how, in the few short months of her marriage, Isabella had found out about her, or why she had taken to hating her so hard. What in God's name had John said to her? And what did she mean about nasty dreams?

After a moment William appeared in the doorway and seeing that she was nowhere near ready for the banquet he frowned.

'Has something upset you, Moll?' he asked. 'Perhaps it's that you are to see John again after all this time?

'I expect so,' Matilda replied listlessly.

'Well, have no fear,' William responded testily. 'I can guarantee that he will not have eyes for you as he is besotted with his child queen. Even now he has her on his lap whilst she chooses the Lord of Misrule, and I swear her skirts are much higher than they should be at the back!'

Matilda grimaced. 'Are we to endure twelve days of this, William?' she asked angrily.

'Yes,' William snapped. 'You will put aside your feelings for twelve days and behave impeccably as the wife of a baron high in John's favour should! Now, go and find a maid to help you get changed. We have a feast to attend!'

The hall was crowded when Matilda eventually took her place with William at one of the lower tables with Will, John and Bertha alongside them. Giles was in the chapel where he would probably stay and offer up prayers, such was his devotion, and Matilda did not expect to see him before he left for Winchester Cathedral on the morrow, where he was to have the honour of taking Mass. Up on the dais, the newly elected Lord of Misrule was ordering that Isabella cut up his food and feed him, whilst King John sat beside her grinning with delight. He was one of

John's squires - a handsome young man who, having discarded his tunic, was now dressed in finest of silks and jewels straight from the king's own coffers, leaving his mock court, each dressed equally as gaudily, to run around after him preparing the stage for the evening's entertainment. Leaning towards Matilda, Bertha whispered that by the end of Christmas the Lord of Misrule would be twice the size he was now, if Isabella carried on stuffing food into his mouth like he was some sort of pet.

As William had observed earlier, John seemed to be completely smitten with Isabella and took every opportunity to touch her, and although Matilda knew from her outburst that she hated John, Isabella endured his attention in the manner drummed into her by her parents. Evidently her bitterness was reserved for more private moments.

It was getting late by the time the food begun to arrive from the kitchens to be delivered to the tables where the trencher bread was already in place. John and Isabella were the first to be attended to by the pantler, who laid their trenchers carefully before them, along with a large ceremonial salt cellar, several silver knives with which to cut up their bread, and a spoon each for the main courses. Other servers bustled around, tasked with setting bowls for salt along the lower tables before the service could begin. Finally, the carver and cup-bearer advanced towards the dais with towels and napkins draped over their shoulders, where they proceeded to begin the tasting ritual. Matilda grimaced. Out of all of old King Henry's sons John probably had the most to fear from poisoning, and she couldn't help the treasonous thought that if she were Isabella, she might harbour thoughts of doing it herself.

When the bread and wine had been sampled, the rest of the food was carried into the hall on large silver salvers. First came a whole suckling pig, gilded to perfection with a shiny red apple in its mouth. This was immediately transported to the dais where the carver proceeded to slice dripping cuts of meat onto a large platter. Again, the pantler tasted it before allowing the rest to be divided between several smaller platters and placed at intervals along the high table. King John and Isabella would share one messe, but others further down the table might have only one between three or four of them from which to transfer the succulent meat onto their trenchers. Further dishes followed, with a stew of venison being carried out in a large cooking pot upon the shoulders of two sweating kitchen boys, along with a tray of ducklings and tiny roast partridges to be accompanied by the various rich sauces that were the speciality of the cook. Finally, the first course ended with dishes of buttered vegetables, followed by a large pike with galentyne sauce, and lampreys, a favourite of John's which immediately brought back bad memories of pregnancy to Matilda.

In the lull between courses, Matilda looked around, hoping to see some friendly faces at the tables surrounding her. Immediately, she spotted Sybilla and her husband, Adam de Port, seated at an adjacent table alongside William's nephew, William de Ferrers. William the Marshall, the Earl of Pembroke, and his wife, Isabel, had the honour of being seated on the high table with John and Isabella and the Archbishop of Canterbury. At another table she saw Hugh de Lacy deep in conversation with Roger de Mortimer and Richard de Clare, with their wives, she noted, regarding each other warily as they picked at the food on their trenchers. Dotted elsewhere were the faces of the Cliffords, the de Lacys, and Reginald's father by marriage, William Brewer. Matilda shivered, so many of those faces were related to them by marriage. She should feel elated that they had formed such prestigious and important connections, but instead her heart began to beat faster as she wondered which, if any of them, she could trust.

Up on the dais a round of applause had broken out with the discovery that the shiny red apple gracing the mouth of the suckling pig, was in fact meat formed and painted to resemble the fruit. This seemed to delight Isabella, who promptly began to feed it to the hounds that lay at her feet.

Matilda noticed none of this. Neither did she notice the shadows slowly gathering around her, their gossamer fingers reaching out … *caressing … touching … choosing …*

The feast was nearing its end. The peacock dressed in its own feathers had long since been consumed with relish, along with dozens of capons, frumentys, dried fruits and nuts. And the subelty that had once been fashioned in the shape of a castle was now just crumbs on the once snowy white table linen.

Up on the dais John sat alone, his goblet of wine half empty before him. Isabella had long since made her excuses and retired to her chambers, leaving him disgruntled. For a while he watched Matilda de Braose chatting to her sons before finally bidding them goodnight and making her way towards her own chambers. William remained in the hall, participating heavily in the wine as usual. In the past, on such an occasion, John knew he would have taken advantage of this and summoned Matilda to his own rooms, but lately his desire for her had been dampened by bad dreams.

He shivered as he recalled the overwhelming surges of desire and the tugging at his loins that beset him each night in his sleep. A desire which, once fuelled by lust, was now tainted with fear and hate, and was threatening to drive him over the edge.

Picking up his goblet with a shaky hand, John downed the contents in one, hoping that if he drank enough before he retired that night he wouldn't dream.

Temptress ...

Sorceress ...

The words came unbidden into his head, buzzing around like a thousand bees, followed closely by the image of Rosamund and the sound of her voice ringing in his ears ... *What are you afraid of, silly boy ...?*

Abruptly John stood and, beckoning to his squire, he turned and left the hall, knowing that the only way to forget his madness was to bury himself deep in Isabella ...

Matilda seated herself on a chair as near to the dais as she could and let out a sigh of relief. It was Twelfth Night and the Christmas court was almost nearing its end. To round off celebrations people had gathered in the hall to watch the two young men kneeling at John's feet become knights, after which they would receive their golden spurs, swords and lances; gifts from the king himself. Matilda watched with tears in her eyes as her beloved son John rose first, followed closely by the son of a French baron who had impressed the king, having ridden at his side to secure the treasury at Chinon in the wake of Richard's death.

Beside her, Bertha gripped her arm and watched her brother proudly in the knowledge that they had both got what they wanted: he was now a knight of the realm, and she had John's written word that a new husband would not be forced on her in the future.

Matilda knew she should be elated. But instead she felt a fission of fear and quickly she looked around for Ailith, eager for her to begin packing so that they could return home.

Up on the dais Isabella of Angoulême watched Matilda from under her lashes knowing that if her mother was there she would have known instantly that she was up to mischief. Fortunately, however, there was only a handful of her tiring women and her old nurse, who by rights should have been retired to a cottage by now to live out her days, but instead had insisted that she make the dangerous crossing to England armed with the potions and spells with which she could ensure Isabella's safety.

After a while the old nurse stood and nodded to Isabella before beginning to make her way towards the chamber occupied by Matilda de Braose. Once there, she looked around briefly to ensure that no one was about. Then, when she was certain that she was indeed alone, she slipped inside and closed the door before making her way to the dressing table where she hurriedly searched for what she wanted. Seeing it, she quickly loosened a few strands of chestnut hair from its teeth and, removing a small object from her apron, she deftly attached the hairs to it, taking time only to mutter a spell before thrusting it into a coffer at the foot of the bed and hurrying from the room.

I left William and Matilda in the hall eagerly making preparations to travel the short distance back to Bramber where they planned to wait for the weather to improve before heading for the Marches once more. Then, as instructed, I made my way to their chamber's to pack. Opening one of the travel coffers, I began by folding some of Matilda's newly washed chemises. Laying them on top, I used the flat of my hand to smooth them out, enjoying the feel of the clean linen when, unexpectedly, I encountered something small but solid beneath my fingers. Pulling back the chemises and some of William's clean court tunics, I drew a deep breath. Buried amongst them was a tiny wax doll, no bigger than a man's finger but intricately carved in the form of a woman. Stuck to the head of the little doll were four or five hairs, deep chestnut in colour which, even as I knelt on the floor of the chamber, I knew instinctively had come from the comb that lay on the dresser. My hands shook as I reached in and picked up the little doll; it felt alive in my grip, I could feel the power radiating from its little body like a tiny furnace waiting to explode. I shivered. Whoever had made it had invested it with great evil, and suddenly I was very afraid ...

Chapter 24

Bramber Castle, Sussex, January 1201

William strode into the hall with a look of satisfaction on his face. 'It's signed and sealed at last, Moll,' he said. 'I am finally to have the honour of the county of Limerick in Ireland – as a mark of my growing status in King John's eyes.'

Matilda glanced at me and put down her sewing tiredly. Although she had not voiced her fears to me directly, I knew that she had serious concerns about the way William was acquiring their newly found wealth and status by the means of bribery. 'Do you not think we are over reaching ourselves, William? Can we not be content with what we have and not owe everything to John? There is Giles's position as Bishop of Hereford, the numerous grants of land to us – not to mention the concessions to expand still further into Radnor, which I confess worry me the most for I do not feel safe in Wales. Must we owe everything we have to John?'

'Oh, rubbish,' William said crossly, and I saw him glance at her suspiciously as was his custom whenever Matilda ventured her fears to him out loud nowadays. 'You know as well as I do that one can never be high enough in the king's favour. As for Radnor, it's in John's interest to have his major barons protecting the Marches – what with the Earl of Chester in the northeast, and William Marshall once more in Pembroke, John sees to it that the Princes of Powys are contained within an iron circle of our making, and therefore they will not be so willing to make mischief as they have been in the past. Besides, I have plans for Will to push further into

Radnor and Builth, and I mean to fine for the land of Shoreham – think of that, Moll, not only will we be rich in lands in the Marches, but also on our own doorstep in Bramber. Oh, and before I forget, Walter is asking that I fine for the custody of his lands now that he and Margaret are so often in Ireland. I thought that John could handle those estates when he is married to Amabil – he needs a challenge and a bit of stability, he's had too much time on the tourney circuits with Phillip, if you ask me. Mark my words, Moll, we are rising fast. Not even the king himself can infringe upon the lands we shall gain, particularly those in the Marches! Anyway, I must not tarry if I am to re-join the court on its travels to the north,' he concluded as the sound of horses being led into the courtyard interrupted his flow. Then, turning on his heel he made for the door once more, leaving Matilda standing staring after him with a look on her face that I was rapidly becoming accustomed too.

A look that was part way between resignation and fear.

Bramber Castle, Sussex, March 1202

A gentle Sussex breeze stirred the wild daffodils poking their heads up along the bank below the castle keep, and beyond them tiny buds were beginning to appear on the trees that rose protectively behind the castle walls. Along the shores of the River Adur, at the foot of Castle Hill, there was a bustle of activity as a cog moored itself alongside the jetty to offload its merchandise, before turning and floating serenely away downstream on its smooth glassy waters, heading once more for the sea. It made a lovely sight, with the gulls swooping and wheeling in its wake and its sail billowing before it. But Matilda had more important things on her mind than the view beyond the window embrasure.

In the May of the previous year William had returned to France, accompanied by Will, to do knight service for King John. The Lusignans, still angry at the manner in which Hugh had been robbed of his bride, had finally openly revolted against John, and he now was constantly being forced into petty little battles in his effort to maintain control of his lands there. Matilda sighed, thinking that nearly a year on things were no better. King Phillip of France no longer considered himself tied to his truce with England and had sided openly with the Lusignans' cause, demanding that John appear at the French court in Paris to answer charges laid against him. And if that wasn't bad enough, Arthur of Brittany had sided with them too, and the outcome now looked even bleaker than before.

Matilda shivered as once again cold fingers of fear crept down her spine, making the hairs on the back of her neck rise. Then, shaking herself out of her reverie, she turned back to the small oak desk in the chancery and surveyed the books with their lines of neat figures that needed her attention.

Bramber did well enough for itself – the rents were adequate and on good years they brought enough corn in to feed their villeins for the winter. The harvest from the fruit orchard had been good that year too, and the apple cellars were now full to the brim with the brewer making apple cider from the rest.

Matilda ran her finger down the kitchen ledger. Listed were the miller's fee for grinding the corn into flour, a keg of herring, mackerel, a side of beef along with salt, various expensive spices, some barrels of ale and wine, and other culinary necessities that had to be obtained from beyond the estate - either in Horsham or Steyning, or from the travelling merchants who stopped at the castle. In addition to this, Matilda knew that the newly planted vegetable patch in the kitchen garden would yield enough vegetables to feed the household for many months to come, and meat, such as wild boar, deer, rabbit, duck and squirrel, were all caught on the estate. Another page revealed that the income from the wool that year had also been good, and that they had traded cheese and animal pelts, and even a litter of pigs to a neighbouring farmer. But even so, Bramber did not bring in enough revenue to pay the mounting fines for the lands and castles so recently bestowed on them by John, and Matilda knew that she would have to return to the Marches soon without William, to deal with the husbandry of the estates there in order to fill their coffers.

Sighing, Matilda wished again that William had refused the honour of the county of Limerick as his father had done before him. Five hundred marks a year was a lot of money to find, and before long they would add to it the cost of the marriage fees for John to marry Amabil de Lemisi — around a thousand marks! For a moment her brow creased with worry, then she pulled herself upright. If they did not have the money immediately, then John would have to wait until they did. At any rate William often paid his fines late. It was not an uncommon practice among John's favoured barons, and he never harried them for it. Still, it went against the grain to owe John anything.

Pushing the thought of their depleting coffers aside, Matilda picked up her pen. She had written to Mattie only once since Rhys' death, and she had not received a reply for her efforts. But whatever Mattie thought of her there was now need of a letter, for word had come that Gruffydd had died the previous July and had been laid to rest in the little abbey of Strata Florida. Matilda had no particular feelings about the death of her daughter's accursed husband, but she owed it to Mattie to send her commiserations, even knowing as she did that Mattie would not bother to reply as she had already put it off for too long. She also had a duty to offer her daughter and grandchildren a home if needs be, but as much as she yearned to have her oldest daughter back home with her, there was too much water gone under the bridge to ever truly believe that it would happen. With a sigh Matilda picked up her quill and dipped it in the ink, but even as she set the first mark upon the parchment all she could see was Mattie's face glaring back at her, and those of the grandchildren she had never even seen, laughing as she led them away.

Chapter 25

Le Mans, Normandy, France, 30 July 1202

King John waved the dispatch in front of William as soon as he entered the canvas tent that had been erected on the road to Chinon, where Isabella, now under the charge of Richard's widow, Berengaria, awaited him. 'Arthur is besieging Queen Eleanor at Mirebeau. His own grandmother of all people!' he said incredulously.

William's eyebrows rose even though he found it hard to be quite as incredulous as John, for since arriving back in France the previous May relations had gradually deteriorated between the king and the Lusignans. John had refused to appear before the French court in Paris to answer for his deeds, declaring himself both King of England and Duke of Normandy, and therefore not answerable to the courts of France. King Phillip had responded by demanding John attend the court as Duke of Aquitaine, Count of Poitou, and Count of Anjou, which again fell on deaf ears. Inevitably, Phillip, now firmly on the side of the Lusignans, had declared John a traitor, and the tenuous truce between them had been broken. Then, as a final insult, he had confiscated all John's French lands, save Normandy, which he proceeded to go to war with.

William sighed. It was no more a surprise to him or any other of John's barons, that Arthur, now an ambitious fifteen-year-old, had taken up the sword against John at Phillip's urging and set siege to his own grandmother; or that he sought to hold her hostage and barter with John for the return of the mortally spoilt Queen Isabella. The boy was foolhardy and rash. But still

William couldn't help but admire him just a bit for his stand against John, or for his audacity in thinking that he could outwit the formidable Eleanor who had a lifetime of subterfuge and trickery tucked under her girdle.

Walking angrily to a small desk that occupied the rear of the tent, John poured himself a goblet of wine without offering any to William, whose mouth was as dry as tinder.

'Phillip's to blame for this! Only he would encourage the little runt in this latest outrage. Not only does he hand over my rightful territories to him and begs him do homage for them, but he has betrothed the pup to his daughter Marie and given him two hundred knights to add to his Brittany men to try and goad me to war!' John said, sitting down heavily on a chair and glaring into his wine.

'Will we fight, then?' William asked lazily.

'Yes,' John said grimly. 'We leave tonight, and we won't delay until we get to Mirebeau – I doubt he will harm his own grandmother, but we cannot take that chance. Very soon we will have the yapping puppy under our control.'

William felt a rush of new adrenaline at the prospect of a good fight, and there was every chance of good plunder too. Arthur was young and inexperienced in the ways of war and John was, if not the great lion that Richard had been, at least as cunning as the old fox King Henry in his time

Suddenly losing interest in William, John turned away from him and broodily begun to sip his wine, leaving William to go and find his mesnie and advise them of the change of plan. There could only be more rewards on the horizon if things went the king of England's way.

✝

Mirebeau, France, 1st August 1202

The walls of Mirebeau were bathed in the eerie light of dawn, and William saw King John smile grimly. It had taken two days of hard marching to get his army of barons and mercenaries here so swiftly, which was a feat in itself. Queen Eleanor had managed to get word to William de Roches, the seneschal of Anjou, and he had joined them en-route offering to lead the attack on the castle if John promised not to deal viciously with the boy. Only William had seen the glitter of malice in John's eyes as he clasped the other man's hand in agreement, and he'd felt a faint tingle of disquiet run down his spine. He would do well in the future to remember not to cross John.

Turning to his men, John surveyed their wary faces. They'd spent the hours before daybreak resting in the woods on the outskirts of the town, and after a brief war meeting with William Roches, John and his council of barons had decided to take full advantage of the gloom and strike just before the sun rose fully. A scouting party had reported an unsecured gate in the city walls which, if they stormed through it, would give them advantage of taking Arthur's men by surprise whilst they were unarmed and breaking their fast.

Nodding his satisfaction, John turned to William Roches and issued his orders. Roches' eyes glittered as he pulled the guard to his helmet down, raised his sword, and signalled his men to begin the first wave of attack. William's own sword arm itched, and hearing screams and clash of swords coming from inside the city walls, he felt the old familiar blood lust come upon him. But King John held back, along with a company of his best knights and mercenaries, including William's own men. They would enter the city after the first wave of fighting was over, flanked by a group of John's most trusted soldiers. Their goal was to find John's treacherous nephew, Arthur of Brittany, and take him alive. William glanced at John astride his great war destrier. His face was grim and determined, and for a moment he pitied the boy Arthur for his folly in making John his enemy.

Then at last came the signal for them to strike. The main gates were opened and William, keeping abreast of John, galloped through them and into the melee beyond shouting a blood curdling war cry. Arthur's men were putting up a good fight, but they were no match for John's army, caught by surprise as they were. Whinnying loudly, William's horse side-stepped a pile of bloody corpses. In the midst of the heap a man groaned for mercy, but the sound stopped abruptly as one of John's mercenaries ran him through with his sword. To William's left, John immediately engaged himself in battle with a group of men who were being driven back towards a stable block. The men, seeing that they were outnumbered and surely beaten, threw down their swords and begged for mercy. With a yell for his men to follow, William turned his horse around and galloped down the street, leaving a group of foot soldiers to prod the group into the stables with the points of their swords. Rounding the corner, he heard the whoosh of thatch going up in flames and the agonising screams of those trapped inside, but by now he was immune to the sound.

Slowing their horses to a trot, William and his men headed north of the city. Even beyond the main square the streets of Mirbeau were awash with blood and corpses. A woman lay slumped with her back to a wall, her head cleft in two and the whitewash splattered with blood and brains. Beside her, still squalling, was a new-born baby. William gave it a casual glance, then at his signal a knight strode over, grabbed the infant by its foot, and dashed it viciously against a door. Immediately the squalling stopped. At his side, Will looked as though he was going to vomit, but he merely whispered, 'Jesu' into his sleeve

Ignoring his son, William surveyed the remains of the smoking city, oblivious to the smell of roasting flesh which assailed his nose and stung his eyes. Apart from a few screams, the streets were now completely silent; William vaguely registered a group of mercenaries tying a half-naked girl over a barrel. Her eyes were already dead from the horrors of the morning and she, too, no doubt, would be dead by the end of the day. But none of this made any impression on William; he had come here for one reason and one reason only, and that was to capture Arthur of Brittany. Turning his horse towards the castle, William urged it forward; he was sure that if he handed Arthur over to John himself there would be great reward. Yes, he mused, John would reward him well for he was certain that Arthur of Brittany was the key to his future ...

✠

Mirebeau, France, 2nd August 1202

Arthur of Brittany stood before King John in the great hall of Mirebeau Castle, frightened and bowed in the face of John's anger. For a moment John studied the boy, disliking the way that his large grey eyes seemed as luminous as a girl's, the lashes spiked with unshed tears. Suddenly he seemed to be truly what he was: a snivelling fifteen-year-old child. With a grunt of disgust, he turned to William who stood beside the shackled lad.

'You did well, de Braose. The fighting was tough, but you secured the greatest prize for yourself, and I see the insolent puppy no longer yaps but rather leaks tears of shame for trying to wage war with his uncle, the king!'

William bowed to John. 'He will no longer be a thorn in your side, sire, and neither will those two,' he added, referring to Hugh and Geoffrey de Lusignan, standing weary and battle worn alongside Arthur,'

'No, that he shall not be,' John said darkly, glancing back at the boy, 'I have decided that the young whelp shall go to Falaise under your guardianship, de Braose. Once there you will pass him into the custody of the castle's warden, Hubert de Burgh, until I arrive and decide what shall be done with him in the future.'

Behind John, on the dais, Queen Eleanor stirred and coughed to gain John's attention. 'I trust that I may have your word that no harm will come to my grandson whilst he is under your protection?' Eleanor stressed the word "protection" so that the entire hall might note its warning, and although she was now eighty years of age Eleanor's querulous voice still held authority. Behind her, partly concealed in the shadows, Faulkes de Breauté alone saw the truth that lurked in John's eyes, as yet unrecognised by John himself. Arthur of Brittany would be safer if he was lodged with a pack of wolves in the forests outside Falaise, than confined within the walls of its castle with his uncle.

Slowly a smile spread across his ruined face - things were looking up already.

✠

Brecknock Castle, Wales, 30th August 1202

Reaching for a stool, Matilda dragged it nearer to the bed where Will now lay having returned from France carrying news of the battle for Mirebeau and Queen Eleanor's freedom, following a bout of dysentery. Once settled she began to read William's version of the discourse which John had sent to his English Barons and was already been pinned up triumphantly in every church and cathedral across the land.

Know that by the grace of God we are safe and well, and God's mercy has worked wonderfully with us, for on Tuesday, the feast of St Peter ad Vincula, we heard that the lady our mother was closely besieged at Mirebeau, and we hurried there as fast as we could. And once there we captured our nephew Arthur and all our other Poitevin enemies, and not one escaped. Therefore, God be praised for our happy success.

Matilda shivered, remembering the recent glimpses of a boy in the flames; a boy with large, grey eyes, fringed with dark lashes.

Afraid ...

Pushing the image aside, Matilda glanced anxiously down at Will's white face. 'How goes it for Queen Eleanor since her ordeal?' she enquired, secretly glad that he had returned home safely even with his illness.

'Still tall and feisty as ever, despite her age!' Will replied his voice tinged with tired, but grudging admiration. 'She held her own council where her grandson was concerned, bidding John do no harm to him or his sister Princess Eleanor, who I believe is now being confined at Bristol Castle well out the way of her brother's scheming influence.'

Matilda frowned. 'I hear bad reports of John's treatment of his prisoners. Its alleged that he's starving many to death, both here at Corfe Castle, and over in France when he could demand a Knight's ransom for them from their families.' Suddenly Gerald's voice floated down from the past, making the hairs on the back of her neck rise ... *no king in Christendom would leave his loyal subjects to starve ...*

Dear God, Matilda thought, I shall drive myself insane ... *but they had not been loyal, had they ...?* a small voice whispered.

'Go away,' Matilda said. 'Go away and leave me alone!' Then realising she had spoken out loud she looked down at Will, afraid that her outburst might have shocked him. But he was fast asleep.

I awoke with a start from my dream. *The dream.* The one in which there was now a boy; a young man, handsome, with luminous grey eyes fringed with thick, dark lashes. He is peering into the pit which is slowly filling up with water, grey and murky, and deep. Very deep. At his shoulder a figure hovers, and I recognise King John wearing the usual look of contempt and scorn on his face that he reserves for those that he has condemned. The boy looks around, confused and afraid; I can feel his fear and see the tears in his eyes. Big, luminous, grey eyes filled with tears of pitiful fear and a dawning understanding ...

I lay still for a while staring at the ceiling in the dark. I would not fall asleep again. I would not have to see the twisted face of Faulkes de Breauté as he hovered in the background like a wolf waiting for the kill. There is much pain ahead. So much more suffering to be endured before Mistress Destiny has had her fill. And I feel my heart twist in my chest in despair. Because there is also so little time ...

Chapter 26

Hay castle, Wales, November 1203

Gerald sat once more in Matilda's solar at Hay. But he was a different man from the one who had left for Rome four years previously. The eyes that once glowed with compassion and humour, were now dulled by exhaustion and failure. And where he had once been tall and lean, Gerald was now stooped and gaunt.

I watched as Matilda served him personally, handing him a goblet of wine and offering him some sweetmeats which he declined with a brisk shake of his head.

'So, John was not true to his word,' Matilda said sadly, pulling up another chair by the fire and holding out her hands to warm them.

Gerald smiled grimly, showing evidence of some missing teeth, and I saw the compassion in Matilda's eyes. She was not the only one who had heard harrowing accounts of Gerald's journey to Rome and back, for I too had heard tell of the things he had endured on his travels.

'It was not all John's doing,' Gerald said tiredly. 'In truth, I believe now that it was never to be, that it was always to pass me over. Perhaps if Hubert had not been the Archbishop of Canterbury ... well, I will never know.'

'But to put you on trial, Gerald. You of all people would never have stirred the Welsh to rebellion. That was just a rouse on Hubert and John's part to sully your name so that you had to flee to Rome again.'

I remembered the fuss the previous year. Gerald, having returned from Rome and without the promised support of the Pope, was accused of plotting a rebellion with several prominent Welsh princes, causing him to have to flee abroad again.

'St David deserted me,' Gerald said bitterly. 'I had to travel in secret, rely on the beneficiaries of friends of whom I have many, thankfully. However, when I tried to return to Wales again I was captured by John of Tynmouth, the castilian of Châtillon-sur-Seine, and thrown into prison with no money or food. Luckily, I was released the next day by the seneschal of Burgundy who was passing through and heard of my plight – he then had the castilian thrown in the dungeon as a lesson,' he finished with a self-depreciating smile.

'What will you do now?' Matilda asked. 'Will you carry on fighting for what you believe in?'

'Nay,' Gerald said, 'I have made my peace with the king - well, a peace of sorts. I appeared before him in Elbeuf and stated my case again, but he was more pre-occupied with his wife than with my dilemma.' Gerald sighed. 'He is fast losing his empire to Phillip. Normandy will go next, mark my words. The rumours surrounding Arthur's disappearance have enraged even those who were loyal to John – they say that John had the boy's eyes put out and his body thrown in the Seine. Then there's the way he treated his prisoners after the battle of Mirebeau. He has earned himself a reputation of being both capricious and callous, and many of his lords are now deserting him.'

I felt my skin crawl at the mention of Arthur of Brittany. The rumours that Gerald spoke of had spread through both England and Europe faster than the plague, for he had simply disappeared overnight and any demands for him to be handed over to King Phillip ignored. Gerald fidgeted a bit as if he wanted to enlarge on Arthur's disappearance and I wondered if he wanted to say something about William's rumoured involvement in it. But if he did, he thought the better of it.

'Anyway,' Gerald continued, returning to the topic of his failed trip to Rome. 'Geoffrey de Henelawe, the prior of Llanthony Priory, has been pronounced the new Bishop of St. David's and I am not going to fight it. I shall perhaps go on pilgrimage once more, then I shall take up my writing once again as I have much neglected it.' Matilda smiled sadly, and Gerald quickly changed the subject.

'But what of you, my dear? I trust that you fare well?'

'Yes,' she said. 'In all it has been a good year, Loretta married her Robert but he is sorely ill after being wounded in France and we are worried for him ...'

I sighed and left the room to go and see that a chamber was made ready for Gerald, sad that he had suffered such depredations in his search for the one thing that would have fulfilled his life.

Hay Castle, Wales, December 1203

'So, the rumours are true, Arthur is dead!' Matilda gasped. William stood in front of her. He had just returned from France with King John who was trying to salvage some support from his English barons after losing

the loyalty of the vast majority of his French nobles –
mostly due to the rumours surrounding Arthur's
disappearance.

'Yes,' William said tersely. 'The rumours are
true'.

Matilda sat down slowly in a chair and picked up
her goblet of wine with shaky hands. It was cold in the
solar and William crouched down by the hearth to warm
his hands in the fire, and for a moment she thought she
saw a gleam of malice in his eyes. He was enjoying telling
her she realised. He wanted to shock her.

'How …?' she asked, her voice catching with
sudden emotion; a mixture of anger and acute sadness
for the fate of the boy.

William shrugged. 'There is little to tell. It was
the Thursday before Easter and John had Arthur taken
from his prison in Falaise and moved to Rouen where
he could keep a better eye on the lad. I had already told
him that I could no longer be the boy's nursemaid – that
it was becoming awkward –' He left the sentence there
whilst he put another log in the flames, and Matilda
wondered what was awkward about trying to protect a
defenceless child. She took a sip of her wine hoping it
might quell the sick feeling that was rapidly developing
in the pit of her stomach.

'John had already ordered Hubert de Burgh to
blind and geld the boy at Falaise,' William continued
suddenly. 'But the boy wept and pleaded with him, and
de Burgh refused like the lily-livered coward he is.' He
shook his head in disgust. 'He would have been
incapable of trouble if it had been done then, and John
would have forgotten all about him until such a time as
he was a useful bargaining tool with Phillip Augustus.

Anyway, John later heard rumours that Arthur was plotting to have him ambushed and killed. He was drunk, and ordered the boy brought before him for interrogation. In the end it was Arthur's refusal to acknowledge him as his king and pledge his allegiance to him that sent John into his final rage. John was certain that Arthur would never stop plotting against him if he was allowed to live. De Breauté and I were the only witnesses. John made us swear on the Holy Bible that we would never reveal how Arthur died,' William finished with a shrug.

'But ... what ... what did you do to him? How ... how did you kill him?' Matilda whispered, horrified and shocked that William could have partaken in such a horrific act of cruelty, but still needing to know the truth at the same time.

William rocked back on his heels and glanced at Matilda. 'John blinded him with a poker and then strangled him with his bare hands. I don't think I have ever seen John in such a rage, and Arthur, well he blubbered and pleaded, but ...'

Matilda frowned.

'It was done in a drunken fit of rage, Moll. I don't think John knew what he was doing. When he sobered up a bit he had us weight Arthur's body down with stones and we put him in a boat and threw him in the Seine - we had hoped that was the end of it, but several days later a fisherman found his corpse tangled in his net.' William tutted. 'Nobody could have recognised the corpse. But some guessed, I suppose. And that was when the rumours started.

'There is no doubt that the boy deserved to die, Moll,' William continued defensively as he finally registered the look of disgust and horror that was gradually replacing the look of initial disbelief on Matilda's face. 'At the end of the day he was a traitor and a usurper. John was right, he was never going to stop scheming and plotting against him. In short, he was trouble.'

He said this so matter-of-factly that Matilda jumped to her feet angrily. 'I can't believe that you did nothing to stop him, William! It was murder! King John did a vile thing and you assisted him in this disgraceful act! You are an accomplice in the murder of Arthur of Brittany!' Her voice was shrill with disgust and anger, and suddenly she felt nothing but hate for her husband, King John, and Faulkes de Breauté who had taken the life of a young boy without, it seemed, any remorse what so ever.

'Oh, pull yourself together,' William said, suddenly tired of the whole matter. 'We're to get reward for it; we are to have the city of Limerick and John has promised me Glamorgan and Gower as well - there we will be the custodians of, not only Llangenydd, but Oystermouth and Swansea too! But you are to mind your tongue, woman. It would not be good to encourage more gossip about Arthur of Brittany's fate. That's to be kept our secret!' Then turning on his heels he swaggered out of the chamber, leaving Matilda alone with the memory of a pair of large grey eyes, fringed with dark lashes ...

Chapter 27

Canterbury, Kent, Christmas 1203

John held a dismal Christmas court in Kent that year, depressed at his losses in France and unable to gain the support of his barons in England as he'd hoped. He sat now, hunched on the dais, wallowing in the knowledge that only Château Galliard and a few other regions held out against Phillip. And they were likely to fall along with the rest of Normandy soon. Many of the barons that had stayed loyal to John had lost lands and estates in Normandy. Indeed, William had lost the family caput in Rouen, and other property that he had never even visited. He had grumbled in private that if John had spent less time trying to fight his way out from under the bed covers, and more time fighting for his kingdom, their losses might not have been so great. But the truth of the matter was, that it was the rumours surrounding Arthur's disappearance that had alienated him from his kingdom, rather than his amorous attentions to his sulky young wife.

'Look at the way that William preens in front of John like some sort of popinjay,' Matilda whispered to me in disgust. 'He told me the other day that John has promised him more castles and lands as reward for his loyalty, despite the fact that he is fast running out of gifts to give. More castles indeed! More fines to pay, more money owed to the treasury that we can't pay, and more trouble, more like! But William doesn't see it that way. Soon he will be expecting an Earldom!'

I watched William for a moment; he did indeed exude an air of self-importance and conceit as he flirted freely with the ladies of the court and drank copious amounts of wine.

Suddenly, a flurry of activity on the dais caught our attention as King John rose unsteadily to his feet. For a moment, he swayed, then, wiping a smear of sauce from his mouth with the back of his hand, he raised his goblet.

'Tomorrow we shall hunt,' he shouted. 'But first –' he signalled to a soldier, who disappeared briefly behind a tapestry concealing a door at the back of a hall. After a while, the man returned, dragging behind him a young lad. The boy was so beaten and battered that I nearly failed to recognise him as the squire that Isabella had chosen to be the Lord of Misrule at the Guildford Christmas court four years ago. A deep hush settled around the room as those gathered waited expectantly up and down the lines of trestles. Up in the minstrel gallery, the music petered out as the players realised that there was better entertainment happening below.

'By God, tis his squire - de Brun's whelp,' whispered a portly man behind me before a jab in the ribs from his wife silenced him.

John's eyes glittered as he surveyed the broken young man kneeling before him. After a moment, he raised them and addressed his silent audience in silky tones. 'Some of you might recognise this scoundrel here as my former squire,' he said, jabbing him viciously with his boot. The boy flinched and drew back fearfully, and I wondered what appalling treatment he'd endured in John's dreadful dungeons.

'He shall answer to some charges before you all,' John continued. 'Grave charges.'

Taking this as his cue, the soldier bent down and, grabbing the boy's arm and a handful of his hair, he hauled him to his feet. The lad could barely stand, so great were his injuries, and looking at the rapt faces surrounding me I suddenly felt sick.

'This boy,' John said loudly. 'Has defiled the queen!'

A collective gasp emanated from the audience and behind me I heard a titter as one of the court whores whispered, 'Likely it's her that defiled him, she's more sex craved than any court slut!'

John held his hand up for silence. 'He was found sneaking out of the queen's bed chamber.'

The boy opened his mouth as if trying to speak, but only a croak came out.

'Hang him!' came a shout from the back of the hall.

'Yes, hang him!' came another. 'Yes! Yes! Yes!' they chorused, and the stamping of their feet made the hall floor shake.

Matilda's face had gone white. Her body tensed with fear for the boy, and I knew that she was thinking of Arthur; thinking of his blind, sightless eyes staring at us in reproach from his watery grave.

After a moment, John held up his hand once again for silence. 'Nay,' he said. 'There shall be no hanging!' A roar went up and I felt myself jostled by a group of courtiers behind me, indignant that they should be so deprived.

'What then?' shouted another. 'Shall you behead him in front of the court as a lesson to other squires who may pay the Queen lecherous attentions, sire?'

The crowd went still; I could see a pulse beating at Matilda's throat.

'I shall do no such thing,' John said, holding his hand up once more for silence. 'He will be returned to his family in disgrace. I shall not take his life - though he deserves such punishment. I am not a murderer of children.'

At this the hall went silent, and then suddenly a shout went up. 'God save the king, for he is merciful! God save the king!'

For a long moment Matilda stared at John, a look of disgust on her face. Then, picking up her skirts, she turned and left the hall without once looking back.

✟

Bramber Castle, Sussex, December 1205

'John has given me custody of the three castles of Grosmont, Skenfrith and Llantilio,' William said, striding into the room and throwing his mantle to his squire.

Matilda blinked, startled out of her reverie by his unexpected arrival. 'Is not Hubert de Burgh castilian of those castles?' she asked, glancing at me before putting down her sewing to look at him more closely.

'Not anymore,' William replied with relish. 'Word has it that he has been captured abroad.'

I felt my stomach tighten warningly. The last few years had seen William showered with gifts of land and titles at a rate which even I was aware was beginning to cause tongues to wag at court.

'But William, do you not think we are over-reaching ourselves, what with –' Matilda began, standing up agitatedly.

'We have had this conversation before, Moll, and I don't intend to have it again,' William said, cutting her off before she could finish and gesturing to his squire to bring him a goblet of wine. 'Besides, it's not women's business and I am tired and weary from my ride from the court,' he added, running a hand irritably through his hair and sitting down on the stool she had just vacated.

Matilda turned to the window. Outside fog was beginning to fall, blurring the distant tree line and the view towards the village where William's villeins toiled along the saltings and the fields and downs beyond, and from the set of her shoulders I knew what she was thinking – that they too must be aware of the tension that hung over the castle and threatened to bring it down upon us all like a house of cards.

'Are we not too much in debt to the Exchequer?' Matilda asked at last, flinching as she turned back and saw the tell-tale signs of anger beginning to settle themselves on William's face.

William scowled. 'You're like a dog with a bone,' he retorted, reaching for a tray of sweetmeats languishing uneaten on a table nearby. 'Leave the matter alone. All you need to understand is that by rewarding us well John is showing us great favour. We have a status, Moll, and I need castles and lands to reflect that status and to show others how high we are in the king's favour. Besides, I mean to have an Earldom out of this,' he added, pausing to inspect one of the sweetmeats now sticky from the warmth of the fire, 'for it has always been my intention to stand alongside de Claire as his equal.'

Matilda stared at William aghast. 'You have always yearned for an Earldom, William, but I had not realised how much until now,' she said bitterly, and I could see the fear in her face as she wondered how far John would allow himself to be pushed by William's greed before he slapped him down hard and we all suffered, for like Matilda I knew that the only thing that prevented John from reining in William's power was that William had witnessed Arthur's murder at his hand, and the price for stilling his tongue was to reward him with castles, lands and fiefs which they could little afford.

How long then before John decided that the price of William's silence was too high?

Winchester Castle, October 1207

It was unusually warm for the time of year and we had ridden to join the court at Winchester where John and Isabella had retired to celebrate the birth of their first child, Henry, at the beginning of October. Isabella had shocked the court by refusing to be churched and arranging instead several long weeks of festivity to mark the occasion. King John, pleased with his new heir, had indulged his wife, and after three days of tournaments he had decreed a day of hunting in her honour, a pastime that Matilda particularly enjoyed. The last few years had been tough for Matilda, marred as they had been by the unexpected death of her son John in a riding accident at Bramber, leaving Amabil no sooner a bride than a widow. That had been followed by further worries about Will's health which had prevented him from travelling very far abroad – the only good outcome of which was that Will and Maude now had three boys for her to fuss over, the youngest being Phillip, with yet another on the way. Despite her troubles, however, she had seemed much happier once we had entered city walls and were heading for the castle, telling me that she was determined to relax and make the most of the balmy weather ... even if that meant she would have to endure Isabella's company for the next few weeks.

Left alone in Matilda's chamber, having cleared away the remains of the previous night's supper, I stood for a while looking down at the runes I had just thrown. The room felt freezing despite the watery sun that slid through the narrow-arched windows. Down below I heard the sound of a hunting horn calling the hunt to order, and the loud baying of the hounds eager to be out for the kill. But still I could not tear my eyes from the runes. Scattered on the table before me they told a secret that I knew well. Pushing them aside, I went to the window and stood looking down. If there ever was a day that I wished the runes did not speak true, or that I did not have the Sight, then this was the one.

Turning back to the table I swept them onto the floor. In the distance I heard the sound of the hunting horn fade into the forest. And in the room, I heard the sound of Mistress Destiny's laugh ...

Out in the field, Matilda ran a finger over the head of the little brown merlin perched on her wrist. 'You might be small, but you're deadly, my lovely,' she whispered. Beside her, William shifted in his saddle, impatient to fly his buzzard, a gift from John's own falconry that very morning, and next to him John himself sat with a magnificent gyrfalcon on his gauntlet, waiting for the rest of the court to gather. At last, just Matilda was beginning to think that he was never going to give the signal, John wheeled his horse around and gave orders for the dogs to be set free. Almost immediately a couple of hares shot out of the undergrowth. John could barely contain his excitement as, pulling the hood from his gyrfalcon's head, he released her from her jesses and flew her. Around him the court held a collective breath as the bird soared high up into the cloudless blue sky, before plummeting down with breathtaking speed to snatch one of the hares from the ground in mid-run.

'It's a kill!' John yelled excitedly.

At his side, Isabella looked around, already bored with the hunt.

'It's only a hare,' William muttered beneath his breath.

'Shush,' Matilda whispered, knowing that William was only being testy because he had been forced to lose at chess against John the night before.

With the hare in the bag, John signalled the party to move forward across the meadow towards the river Itchen. Moments later a swan was flushed out of the reeds, and with a jangle of bells John released his bird once more for the kill. Matilda narrowed her eyes against the glare of the sun, watching as the gyrfalcon took the swan down before it had any real chance of flight, leaving it only for an elated John to send in the dogs and bring back the catch.

Then William had his chance. John beckoned him forward, and once again the dogs flushed out half a dozen ducks, sending them flapping and quacking indignantly into the air above the water. With a toss of his arm and a shout of delight, William sent his buzzard after them and within moments they had another bird in the bag.

After watching William for a while, Matilda went and joined a group of ladies who had broken away from the main party and were sending their merlins after smaller prey such as wood pigeon and rabbits, and very soon she too had added to the bag. Another hour passed pleasantly enough, but the weak, early morning the sun which at first had been so pleasant, was now beginning to turn hot. Passing her merlin back to one of John's austringers, Matilda took a deep breath of fresh air. Then, urging her mare into a trot, she headed for the coolness of the trees overhanging the water away from the main party, hoping to clean some of the dirt from her hands and face before the picnicking began. Behind her, the sound of the hunting horn signalled that John had spotted bigger prey to chase. A heart probably, Matilda thought.

Once down on the river bank, Matilda dismounted and, tethering her mare to a tree, she made her way down to the water edge, where she kneeled and scooped some up with her hands and splashed it onto her hot face. Then sitting back on her heels, she watched a kingfisher – a flash of iridescent blue and green – dive beneath the glittering surface before breaking back through again with a silver fish in its beak. After a while she stood and, brushing off some dry twigs that clung to her gown, she moved to sit in the shade of a willow tree, idly chewing on a blade of grass. Somewhere in the forest the sound of the hunt carried to her, and she wondered if William had joined it yet.

She must have dozed for a while because she was woken by a giggle and the chatter of a girl's voice and the deeper, more strident tones of a man's coming from behind the group of trees beneath which she was sitting. Then abruptly the chatting stopped and, embarrassed, Matilda realised from the sounds that followed that the couple were now engaged in something far more satisfying than idle chitter-chatter. Standing, she was about to leave when it suddenly occurred to her that to do so she would have to pass right by them - unless she could sneak downstream - but to do that she would have to cross a clearing and, even occupied as they were, they were bound to spot her.

Covering her mouth to stop herself laughing, Matilda decided that there was nothing else to do but sit back down and wait. After a while the sounds stopped. A moment later there was a rustling noise as the long hanging branches of the willow tree were pushed back and Isabella appeared, hand-in-hand with a handsome man of about twenty summers or more whom Matilda recognised as one of John's favourite grooms. Matilda wasn't sure who was more shocked, her, or Isabella, who immediately dropped the man's hand like it was a red-hot coal.

'How long have you been sitting there?' Isabella demanded angrily.

Matilda leapt to her feet. 'My lady, forgive me, I did not know it was you!' she cried, unable to disguise the look of disgust on her face as she took in the sight of the girls flushed cheeks and crumpled gown. 'But, my lady,' she continued, her outrage mounting as Isabella hitched up her skirts and began to adjust her silk hose. 'Did it not occur to you to stop and think about what happened to the last person upon whom you bestowed your favours? He was just a boy! A boy who was nearly beaten to death because, rightly or wrongly, it was suspected that the two of you had become lovers!'

Isabella gasped. 'How dare you! How dare you speak to your queen in such a manner!' she hissed, dropping her hems and looking wildly at the groom for help, before turning back to glare at Matilda with such venom that Matilda could have bitten off her tongue in an instant. Isabella, the beautiful, dishevelled young woman who stood in front of her, was no longer the spoilt, petulant child-queen who had nearly been the cause of an ignorant squire's death. She was now the adored mother of the King's son, who in turn was heir to the throne of England, and that gave her power and made her a very dangerous adversary indeed.

'Isabella — my lady,' Matilda managed at last, trying keep her voice steady and aiming, if not for friendliness, then at least for some hint that she might actually care about the girl's welfare. 'I am not trying to talk to you as a queen. Please believe me when I say that I am simply trying to advise you as one woman to another to employ some caution when it comes to … to …' quickly she sought about for the right words, '… to the manner in which you conduct your liaisons in future. I think, my lady, that it would be wise to remember that John is not *just* your husband. He is more than that. He is also a king, and a jealous one too —' She broke off, biting her lip, her heart pounding as she saw the blind fury in Isabella's face at the mention of John's name. 'But of course, that was impertinent of me, I should not have presumed to —'

Matilda gave a sharp little cry as Isabella flew at her, snatching at her veil and tearing it from her hair in her fury. Shocked by Isabella's behaviour the groom grabbed her from behind, pinning her arms to her side, but not before Isabella had got hold of a fistful of Matilda's gown, ripping the bodice from the neck almost to the waist. It seemed to take forever, but at last the groom succeeded in dragging Isabella to one side where she stood a little apart from them both, still panting hard and shaking with anger. For a moment nobody said anything at all. Then suddenly the willow branches were pushed aside again, and Matilda was horrified to find King John standing in front of her, his expression murderous as he took in every detail of her appearance, down from her wildly cascading hair to the soft curve of her creamy white breasts, exposed now beneath the ruined fabric of her gown. Behind him, William clutched the reins of their horses with an appalled look on his face. Horrified, Matilda's hands flew to her bodice, her fingers groping at the torn material in an attempt to cover herself up, but before she could open her mouth to speak, Isabella had run to John and grabbed his arm.

'Look at what I had to walk into!' she cried. 'They were at it like a couple of peasants out in the open. It was disgraceful, my lord, they should be flogged!'

Matilda gasped. 'But, sire, that's not true –'

John silenced her with his hand, and from the set of his lips and the cold, hard anger in his eyes, Matilda knew that there was nothing she could say or do in her own defence. John had already drawn his own conclusions.

Without a word, John turned on his heels and, taking his horse's reins from William, he mounted the animal and rode away. He didn't once look back at her or Isabella who, throwing a look of triumph at Matilda, quickly hitched up her rumpled skirts and made after him.

Only William was left, still clutching the reins of his horse, and he couldn't conceal the look of bleak hatred in his eyes.

Of the groom, there was nothing to be seen.

Hearing the sound of the hunt returning, I picked the runes up one by one and tipped them back into their bag. Outside the sun had dropped and the forest had gone still. As if in a dream I wandered to the window and leaning out over the deep sill I looked down into the moat beneath. Then, knowing that I would not be needing the stones again, I slowly released them one by one into the murky depths below before turning away to begin the task of packing up Matilda's coffers. For even if they did not know it yet, Matilda and William would be leaving the castle later that day. That much I knew for sure.

Bramber Castle, Sussex, England, November 1207

'I don't understand,' William said as the messenger from the Royal Exchequer fidgeted awkwardly in front of him, red faced and embarrassed. 'Why demand payment of my debts in full now?'

'Payment for what debts, Father?' Will asked, striding into the hall and looking round at the frozen faces of his brothers, Reginald, Phillip and Giles who was taking a break from his ecclesiastical duties in Herefordshire.

'The exchequer has written that we must repay all our debts to King John.' William ran his hand through his thinning hair in agitation and passed the offending roll of parchment over to Will to read.

'But how have your debts risen so high, Father?' 'Surely you have been making regular payments against them to the king's exchequer?' Giles asked, rousing himself enough to usher the messenger out of the room and returning to look anxiously over Will's shoulder.

Will threw him a quick glance before turning back to the piece of parchment in his hands. 'It says here, Father, that you haven't paid for the honour of the city of Limerick for five years when you were required to pay five hundred marks a year. King John appears to want you to settle the debt in full now. That's five thousand marks in total, is it not, including arrears? It also says that you have not settled for Munster according to the terms of your agreement with John, and there is a long list of other debts,' he finished, handing the document over to Giles.

'Damn it, man,' William shouted, 'what baron *can* afford to pay all the fines, taxes, knight's fees, and other expenses that John heaps on us? And why this demand and now and only from me? Why has he not called in debts from Richard de Clare or the Marshall? Tell me that!'

'Do you know that he has not?' asked Phillip.

'No,' William replied. 'But even so this is impossible to pay! It would ruin me – it would ruin a nobleman of even the Marshall's standing!' William snatched the parchment back from Giles hands – 'Look, he even demands that I pay the fine for not escorting King Alexander to the English Court two years ago! A sum of ten bulls and ten cows! Why on earth would he be so petty when in the past he has overlooked my debts?'

'Have you done anything to offend the king?' Phillip asked tentatively.

William glowered, but said nothing for he would not be humiliated in front of his sons by repeating the story of Matilda's disgraceful behaviour at the hunt in Winchester, although he knew they must have heard rumour of it by now, for upon his return to the castle John had been incandescent with rage, calling Matilda a whore, him a traitor, and repeatedly slapping Isabella. After that they had been asked to leave.

'Have you spoken to Mother?' Phillip asked.

'Not yet,' William said shortly, knowing that if he did, he would probably wring her neck because he blamed her entirely for his fall in favour with the king.

Just then Matilda entered the hall and began to fumble with her wet cloak before handing it to one of her ladies. Noticing the awkward poses and long faces of her men-folk, she crossed the room with a look of concern on her own. 'What is it, William? What on earth has happened?'

Without a word, William thrust the parchment into her hand. Matilda read it in horror, the colour slowly draining from her face as she took in the full meaning of words that swam before her eyes. 'But we can't pay this, William. Why, he is demanding the five thousand marks in full for Limerick immediately ...' she whispered.

'Well you should have thought of that before you started a cat fight with Isabella at Winchester,' William hissed, not missing the sharp glances his sons traded with each other over her head.

Will coughed. 'Do you think we can meet some of the debt, Mother?' he asked gently. 'Mayhap we can raise some more money from the estates in the Marches?'

Matilda sat down tiredly on the seat Giles offered her, accepting a goblet of wine with a shaky hand while she considered. 'Well, I will admit that we have had good husbandry at Hay and Brecknock this year,' she paused. 'But Dinas is too new a castle and so out of the way that it has not yielded much, but there is some gold plate there. I should think that we can offer John a few hundred marks until we can gather the rest. Perhaps that would appease him for the moment?'

'There are the herds of cows at Brecknock and Hay,' Will suggested. 'And we can sell some of the horses and sheep, can we not?'

'All that takes time,' 'William snapped.

'Still, it's a start,' Giles said calmly. 'First things first, Father, you must write to the king and send him some money in lieu of your debts – beg him for more time to pay, I am sure he will see reason.'

William disappeared to do as Giles bid, still grumbling and muttering under his breath. He was frightened at John's sudden and irrational demands - of course he had known that there would be repercussions for Matilda's behaviour, but he had not thought to incur such a backlash, nor did he expect to have to pay off all of his debts at once.

Meanwhile, Matilda took the ring of keys from her girdle and bid Will to go and get the gold. There was enough there to appease John for the moment. At least she hoped so. But John's face swam before her. Angry and hard. And she knew there was no longer any room for forgiveness in his heart, even if they were to settle their debts in full.

The letter lay on the table, a great gulf between us all. The king, not at all appeased by the sum of money and gold plate that Matilda and William had sent, now meant them to pay their debts in full. And soon. Starting with William handing over Gower and Glamorgan to Faulkes de Breauté. A look of startled shock was fixed on Matilda's pale face at this insult, and William, his shoulders drooped and his face ashen, suddenly looked like an old man.

'I must go to John and throw myself on his mercy.' Matilda said at last

'I will accompany you.' Adam de Port, Sybilla's husband, unfolded himself from the shadows where he had been listening, and came to stand at her side.

'And I.' Will Ferrers, Sybilla's son by her first marriage, and staunch supporter of his mother's kin stepped forward. 'I have many friends at court who might perhaps be persuaded to speak on your behalf if you will let me accompany you.'

Tears of gratitude began to prick Matilda's eyes. Their immediate family had all rallied round and helped where they could, shocked at the speed in which William had lost favour at court, only to be replaced by other barons lately risen in John's esteem. On the dais, Will sat with Maude, Reginald, and Gracia, looking worried – Gracia sat with her hand on the evidence of her third pregnancy, glancing at the door through which her children had been taken to play in the nursery along with their cousins. Loretta hovered by the hearth with her husband, the Earl of Leicester, who evidently regarded the recent turn of events with distaste, judging by the look on his face. Those missing were Annora who had recently married Hugh and remained at Wigmore, Bertha, who was sick and being tended to on her dower lands, and Margaret, who was in Ireland. Giles, too, was missing as he had suddenly and abruptly returned to Herefordshire with Phillip as an escort following a visit to Flandrina at her nunnery in Godstow.

Reginald scowled. 'What mercy? The man has no heart!'

'Nevertheless,' she said tiredly, 'I must try.

Back in Matilda's chamber we laid out the clothes she wanted packed from the clothes pole, then she pulled an old coffer out from behind the bed. 'I think I have some jewelled girdles in here,' she said. 'I will get one of the maids to help me remove the gems so that we can sell them. Mayhap we will get a decent price, even if it is not their real worth. Meanwhile, I think we will have to arrange to have anything of value stowed away somewhere safe for the moment. We cannot leave ourselves without means, and I have a feeling that King John is going to demand every penny that we have – I will talk with William about the best place to store it, although it might be best if we send it into Margaret's safe keeping in Ireland for the time being.'

Matilda rummaged around in the coffer for a moment, and then she suddenly froze.

'Ailith –' she said. In her hand lay the little wax doll that I had found all those years ago in her coffer at Guildford castle.

'Where did you get that?' I whispered, my stomach suddenly tightening with fear. 'I had that destroyed and stripped of its power by a wise woman of my acquaintance at Bramber.'

'But where did it come from?' Matilda asked, glaring angrily at me. 'Why did you hide it, Ailith? Is it some trickery of yours!'

'No! No, my lady!' I cried. 'I tried to destroy … thought I *had* destroyed it … years ago after I found it among your things at Guildford castle. It was Isabella's doing, I swear … she had that witch of a nursemaid place it there, I –'

Matilda flung the little doll on the bed angrily, interrupting my stumbling explanation, and then she burst into tears. 'Go, Ailith,' she said, and her voice, as cold as ice, brooked no argument.

And so, with a heavy heart, I turned to take my leave. But not before I saw the little doll open its eyes and smile.

Chapter 28

Gloucester Castle, Gloucester, England May 1208

It had taken several days of hard riding in bad weather for Matilda, William de Ferrers, Adam de Port and her attendants to reach Gloucester Castle where the king was in council. Here they hoped to be given the opportunity to petition him in person; to beg him to grant William some reprieve from his debts, perhaps even restore his standing somehow in the king's eyes. But Matilda held out little hope.

Drawing her cloak more tightly around her, Matilda stood patiently staring out of a window in the great hall, watching the rain pouring down into the courtyard outside whilst Adam de Port spoke with the usher.

'We've quite a wait,' he said when he finally reappeared at her elbow. 'We're being offered no favours and there are others before us.'

Matilda nodded, barely seeing the masses of people milling around her waiting impatiently for the king to summon them to his presence chamber. She was too afraid.

William de Ferrers crossed to her side bearing a trencher of food. 'You must eat,' he said gruffly, depositing it on a bench beside her before sidling away to do business with some barons of his acquaintance.

Matilda barely noticed the food or cared when a hound came and devoured it, trencher and all. Then, after several long hours of agony, when they finally received their summons, Matilda promptly fainted.

John was standing by a chair when Matilda de Braose and her companions entered his presence chamber, waiting for the ushers to clear the room of curious clerks and scribes, all reluctant to miss the interview between their King and the wife of the baron whose very name made him roar.

Matilda's looked pale and wan, and had he had a heart John thought he might actually have felt sorry for her as he watched her stumble through the door and take several deep breaths to calm herself. He only hoped that she was not in the habit of fainting because he had been informed about her earlier attack of vapours. Beside her, William de Ferrers, whom he vaguely recognised as a nephew of some sort, shifted awkwardly from one foot to another, obviously anxious for the interview be over. And on her other side, Adam de Port, her brother by marriage, and an increasingly troublesome attendant at court, laid a supportive hand on her arm and squeezed it encouragingly. A small gesture for which she threw the corpulent, grey-faced old baron a grateful look, before returning to study him fearfully once again from beneath her lashes.

At last, impatient for the interview to be over, John beckoned them forward, his smile grim as he watched Matilda sink into a deep curtsey, unable to disguise the plethora of emotions that flitted across her face as she sought the words with which to address him.

It was William de Ferrers who finally spoke, however, after bowing before him in supplication for the third time in a row. 'My lord, I do not wish to insult you by pretending that you don't know why we are here.'

John sat down on an ornately carved chair and lazily swung one expensively boot-clad leg up so that it rested on the knee of the other. Then, selecting a piece of crystallized fruit from a bowl on the table beside him, he popped it into his mouth and began to chew, his eyes pinning his three unwanted guests to the spot with a glare so stern that they dared not move. After a while, he addressed Matilda as if the other two men were not in the room. 'I am assuming that you're here today to plead on behalf of your husband, madam?'

'Yes, sire,' Matilda replied. 'I am here to press William's cause and throw myself on your mercy.'

John stood, and stepping off the dais, he crossed to Matilda and picked up a lock of hair that had escaped from beneath her veil. 'You're still as lovely as ever, I see,' he murmured, before letting it drop with a shudder.

'Leave us,' he said to William and Adam, who were studying the gilded roses decorating the length of the petition table in embarrassment.

When they had left, John examined her again through hooded lids, wondering at her audacity in appearing before him after last summer's fiasco. He shivered, despite her initial discomfort, her wide, slanting green eyes were suddenly strangely calm.

The eyes of a witch ... A sorceress.
Just like Rosamund before her.

'And you wish me to release your husband from his debts?'

'Sire,' Matilda sank to her knees. 'I beg of you give us more time. We have animals and gold plate which we need to sell first in order to re-pay you - we just need your leniency so that we may arrange it - that is all I ask of you.'

John looked down at her, shuddering as he recalled the times that he had bedded her; she had been as cold as a fish between the sheets, but still, he couldn't help but feel a throb of desire.

She is nothing but a whore.

All women are whores.

Turning his back on her abruptly, John strode across the room and poured himself a goblet of wine. 'And what if I do allow your husband more time?' he asked, hardly noticing as some of the content splashed, as red as old blood, onto the front of his tunic. 'He will only come crawling back to me begging for more favours to replace those lost through his own greed and foolishness. William is far too ambitious, madam. Far too greedy for his own good. Why, it has even been hinted that he was banking on an earldom by Yuletide this year!'

Hearing the rustle of rushes, he turned and watched as Matilda hauled herself to her feet once again. 'William has learnt the error of his ways, sire. His fall from your favour has shocked him to the core. He is like a child that has lost the love of his father and he will do anything to get it back. I beg of you, give William another chance to pay and you will not regret it.'

John surveyed Matilda through narrowed eyes. 'Very well, my lady, you shall have your way one last time, but if William fails to pay then the penalty will be high. But for now, as a mark of your obedience, you will surrender Radnor, Hay, and Brecknock castles immediately. You may continue to dwell in the others whilst I decide who the new castellans will be, but only until then.'

Then, as if suddenly bored with the whole subject, John dismissed Matilda with a wave of his hand, waiting only until she had dropped one last curtsey before stopping her as she headed for the door.

'And, Lady de Braose.'

Matilda hesitated, then slowly she turned back to John.

'As you know, my refusal to accept Stephen Langton as the Archbishop of Canterbury has meant that all of England is under a papal interdict.' John said, watching her reaction carefully.

Matilda nodded. It was common knowledge that the number of bishops fleeing England to join Stephen Langton in exile in France was growing due to the disagreement between John and the Pope. Meanwhile, John was busily seizing all the churches treasures and income to bolster his war treasury as if it was of no consequence at all.

'I trust that I can count on Giles' co-operation in handing over Hereford's Episcopal properties to me as soon as possible?' he asked, making no attempt to hide the triumph on his face as he did so.

Matilda swallowed. 'Sire, I am sure that Giles will trust to his own conscience and that whatever decision he comes to it will be the correct one,' Matilda said, holding her head high and meeting John's gaze squarely. 'After all, now that he is a grown man, he is no longer in my keeping but in God's.' Then turning she made her way out into the long corridor that led back to the hall, leaving John staring after her with his pale blue eyes boring into her back.

✠

Windsor Castle, Windsor, England, June 1208

'God's teeth,' yelled King John, 'I would but that wretched family could give me no more trouble, but yet they still plague me with it!' His face had taken on a blotchy red hue, which was generally an indicator that he was working towards one of his more violent attacks of rage; the kind that usually involved hitting out at those nearest to him in the room, or rolling around in the rushes spitting venom.

Faulkes de Breauté unfolded himself from the ornately carved chair in which he lounged, and relieved John of the parchment he was waving furiously in the air. Whilst de Breauté read the words that had so enraged the king, John signalled his squire to bring him a goblet of wine. Then, sitting down at his solid oak desk, he picked up a quill and ink and began to scratch angrily on a piece of parchment.

When he'd finished reading it, de Breauté rolled up the letter, and placing it on the desk beside John, he eyed him thoughtfully. 'So, Giles has fled to France to join the other Bishops in exile.'

John didn't answer.

'It seems that treachery within the de Braose family is catching,' de Breauté continued, unfazed by John's angry silence. 'I trust that you will deal with them accordingly?'

'First,' John said through gritted teeth. 'I am sending Peter Maulue to Bramber to demand that they send hostages immediately – I know they're in residence there, for I have heard word of it.' He scratched away furiously again for a moment, then he raised his head and looked Faulkes de Breauté squarely in the eye. 'I shall not tolerate this sort of insurrection among my barons, Faulkes,' he said. 'William and his wife have risen to great heights at my expense. He is a greedy, odious little man, and if he thinks that Giles' defection to France will improve his current position, then it needs to be made quite plain that it has in fact done the reverse!'

Faulkes grinned. Peter Maulue was another of John's mercenaries whom he had charged with the post of equerry. He was also a diligent messenger, whom, if he did not receive the answer that was required by his sovereign, was often known to extract it by other means. Fair or foul.

John finished the letter with a flourish, and then pouring sealing wax onto it he stamped it with the royal seal.

'Ride with him, Faulkes. See how the land lies. I will have your report immediately upon your return.'

De Breauté nodded his abeyance at once and, turning on his heel, he left the chamber, delighted that he would once more get to see William and his upstart of a wife squirm.

☦

Bramber Castle, Sussex, June 1208

'There's two of the king officers in the hall wishing to speak with you, my lord,' William's steward said, entering the chancery where I had set about trimming the candle wicks as part of my daily rounds.

William scowled, and deliberately attempted to delay the interview by ordering the clerk attending him to add a footnote to the letter he was dictating.

Minutes later, Matilda entered the room wringing her hands. 'You must come, William! The king's men are impatient to be gone – and I wish they were gone, too, for they carry more bad news if the look on their faces are anything to go by.'

Sighing, William delayed a moment more by handing the clerk a coin before dismissing him and sealing the letter himself with his signet ring, then he stood and steeled himself for the coming confrontation. Anxiously, I followed them down the newel stairs with the remaining untrimmed candles in my hand, and towards the bottom I overheard Matilda hiss. 'One of them is Faulkes de Breauté, William.'

William reddened angrily. 'He should be thrown out like the dog that he is,' he said, pushing aside the tapestry at the foot of the steps and striding across the hall to where his unwelcome visitors stood side-by-side at the foot of the dais.

Ignoring de Breauté, William addressed Maulue alone, recognising him for the king's equerry and official messenger. 'Well, what is it, man? What does the king want now? I have already relinquished castles and am now busily mortgaging my land to pay him back –'

He broke off as Will, Reginald, and Phillip burst into the room, alerted to the officers' arrival by the presence of a small contingency of the king's soldiers down in the bailey. 'Yes, tell us what the John wants now!' Reginald sneered, throwing his gloves down on a nearby table. 'Perhaps the tunics off our backs, mayhap?'

Paying no attention to Reginald, Maulue handed William the document he was holding with the king's seal on it. Then he came straight to the point. 'The king feels that he now needs some surety of your loyalty – in light of Giles' dereliction of his duties here in England. And so, he requires hostages. In the form of your eldest son, Will,' he inclined his head in Will's direction, 'and two of his sons – your grandsons - John and Giles de Braose. The other two will be spared,' he said, referring to Phillip and Walter who was only a baby and far too young to be of use to John. It's all there,' he added, nodding to the document in William's hand.

'*No!*' Will sprang to face Maulue and, thinking that he was going to attack him, Reginald grabbed his arm, but Will shook him off angrily. '*No!*' he hollered again, tears of rage standing out in his eyes. 'If the king requires hostages then he can take me gladly - but I'll not let you take my sons – I'd rather die than give my children to you!'

There was a long silence, broken only by the distant sound of hammering coming from the forge beyond the castle walls and, like everyone else, I held my breath afraid of what would happen next.

It was Matilda, eyes blazing, and her hand pressed to her chest as if she could still the beating of her heart, who spoke first. 'How dare you, sirs! How dare you stand in my hall and request my son and my grandchildren be hostages of that ... that *monster!* A man so low that he murdered his own nephew by foul means when he was in his care at Rouen. And don't you deny it!' she continued, her voice shrill with fear and anger. 'He's a monster! And the whole of England knows he's a monster!'

'*Matilda* –' William voice was heavy with warning.

'Oh, shut up!' Matilda hissed, turning on him in fury. 'This is all your fault, don't you see? You with your vile little secrets and your greed! And if you think I would entrust *any* of my family to a common murderer to save you, then you are very much mistaken!'

An appalled silence fell over the hall in which everybody remained rooted to the spot, paralysed by Matilda's outburst, but powerless to retract it. Finally, an ashen faced William stepped forward. 'Please ignore my wife,' he whispered, his voice low with fear, 'she is obviously upset and I fear that she knows not what she is saying. We will pay. But no hostages, please. Not just now, I beg of you.'

There was a triumphant laugh as Faulkes de Breauté, who had remained silent during the exchange, drew himself up to his full height. 'I have no doubt that the king will learn soon enough of your wife's high opinion of him, de Braose. Perhaps you should have considered curbing her tongue when you had the chance. Anyhow, we shall leave you now to think over the terms and prepare yourself for our return. You have one week.' Then, turning to Matilda, he bowed and began making his way towards the door of the hall, followed closely by Peter Maulue who looked perplexed by the swiftness with which Faulkes de Breauté had taken over and concluded the situation.

Only Reginald and Phillip reacted to their leaving, their hands flying to their swords as they made to go after them, but William stopped them in their tracks. 'Don't be stupid,' he said tiredly. 'Your mother has done enough damage this day, let them go.'

The silence seemed to go on forever after they had left. At my side, Matilda stood as still as a statue, her anger gone, replaced by numbness as the reality of the situation took over.

'We must fight,' Reginald said suddenly. 'We have no choice.'

'No!' Will rounded on him. 'That's not the way. If we take up arms against the king, it would ruin us all.'

'But don't you see, we're already ruined.' Reginald said furiously. 'What else would you have us do, just sit back and take the tyranny our King dishes out to us?'

'That's treason!' Phillip interrupted, looking around. 'Mind you the servant's ears, please!'

William roused himself. 'No, Reginald's right. John's fast becoming an ogre and we must stand against him. And we can begin by taking back the three castles, Radnor, Hay and Brecon that he confiscated from us. That way we'll convince him that we cannot be subordinated. After that, we'll show him that we are willing to repay our debts to him. But on fair terms. He must understand that we barons will not be suppressed and belittled by the will of a King – we have rights, and we must stand by them. And that begins today.'

'No,' Matilda said dully, speaking for the first time since the king's officers had left. 'No, I will send a gift to Isabella. We have a herd of much prized cows, and a handsome white bull with red ears. I will arrange for them to be dispatched immediately. Perhaps then John will see that we mean no ill.'

Suddenly William turned on her, enraged, and I saw her flinch visibly at the look of naked hate on his face. 'For Christ's sake, woman!' he shouted. 'This is all your doing – if you'd only kept your mouth shut. Do you think that a herd of cows and a pretty white bull would appease John after what you said!'

'No, William. I don't think that,' Matilda said tiredly. 'Only it was your own greed that brought us to this place, and I struggle to see any end but the worst.'

She turned to me then. 'I'm tired, Ailith,' she said. 'I shall go and get some rest now whilst my husband plans yet more treasonous plots against the king – plots which will, no doubt, be one more nail in my coffin.'

Even though it was hot enough to fry an egg on the walls of the bailey, I shivered. Dark clouds were gathering above us and I could hear the distant rumble of thunder in the air. Soon, I knew, the storms that Mistress Destiny meant Matilda de Braose to call down upon herself would follow. And then the shadows would begin …

Chapter 29

Hay, Wales, September 1208

'Gerald, what are you doing here?' Matilda exclaimed in surprise as I ushered him into the small solar at the top of the keep.

Gerald looked ill at ease, glancing around the room quickly before he spoke. 'I'm afraid that I come bearing bad news, dear lady,' he said bluntly. 'Unfortunately, I had the misfortune to be in Hereford with the king when word came that Sir William and your sons unsuccessfully attempted to take back the castle of Radnor by force. When they failed, they sacked Leominster and burnt it to the ground before they were forced to flee by the Constable.' Gerald paused. 'I fear that the king will never forgive your husband this, my dear.'

Matilda let out a little sob and turning to me she grasped my arm fiercely. 'Ailith, go and find Sam Skeet, quickly! Go! Go!'

I hurried away to do as she bid and returned to find her pulling out the small stash of plate and jewels that she'd kept hidden from William in case of such an emergency whilst Gerald stood looking anxiously on.

'Sam,' she said, seeing him hovering in the doorway. 'I must have horses saddled immediately – all is lost, William has sacked Leominster and I fear King John is marching against us even as we speak! But first, take this and hide it in the place we spoke of last week. I know I can trust you.' She paused to thrust the last of the jewels into a leather satchel, before pushing it into his arms and issuing him with further instructions.

Gerald turned and pretended to look out of the mullioned window towards the Wye Valley so that Matilda might conduct her business with Sam in private. When Sam had left the room, he swung back to her. 'If you tell me where you're headed, I will get word to William and your sons.'

Going to her friend, Matilda took his hands. 'Oh, Gerald, how has it come to this? I tried to warn William that it would be folly to attempt to recapture the castles. But to sack Leominster! If John was our enemy before then, what is he now? He will never forgive us. I fear we will be outlawed!'

Gerald said nothing, obviously considering words of sympathy to be empty and pointless. Instead, he went and poured her a goblet of wine whilst she sat down on the nearest seat and laid her head in her hands in despair.

'There are people arriving,' I said, taking Gerald's place at the window and peering down into the bailey as I heard the rattle of the drawbridge and the sound of hooves on the cobbles below.

Matilda turned pale, 'You ... You don't think ...'

'No!' Gerald said firmly, handing her the goblet of wine and coming to look over my shoulder. 'For a start, there are only two of them, and one is a woman. They're talking to your man now –'

Without waiting to be asked, I ran down the newel stairs and across the rough grass to where Sam stood speaking with Robert of Coombe, one of William's gentlemen tenants from Glamorgan. His horse was saddled and he was clearly impatient to carry out Matilda's orders because he kept glancing towards the gatehouse.

Standing quietly alongside them was a beautiful young woman with long fair hair. It took me a moment to recognise her, for I'd not seen Annora since her marriage to Hugh.

Turning to me, Sam said grimly. 'You'd best take Richard up to the mistress, Ailith. Tis more bad news. King John has officially declared Sir William a traitor and appointed Gerald d'Athee to ride to the borders with a declaration that his tenants and vassals be released from their allegiance to him. William's followers have deserted him almost to a man to pay homage directly to the king. There's now only myself and Robert here who has ridden to offer his services in helping the mistress escape.' He nodded at Annora. 'He found her travelling alone on the road. It seems that her husband's family have allied themselves with the king, and so she fled to warn her mother.' He shook his head, saddened by this turn of events.

Up in Matilda's chamber she and Annora embraced quickly, whilst Robert recounted what I had already learned in the bailey.

'I have a manor farm at my disposal in Pembroke for which we can depart straight away,' he said grimly when he'd finished. 'From there you can make plans – you will almost certainly have to flee. Perhaps to France, where you can be with your son Giles. Or to Ireland – William Marshall would offer you shelter, as would your daughter Margaret and her husband, the Lord of Meath. If all else fails, I'm sure his brother, the Lord of Ulster, would offer you safe house, too. I doubt the king would be foolish enough to attack Ireland and incur the wrath of the Irish lords. Not only are they're too powerful, but half of them are married into your family,' he concluded with a wry smile.

Matilda sank shakily down onto a chair. 'So, we are now officially outlaws,' she whispered, covering her face with her hands.

'Where's Phillip? He wasn't with William and your other sons,' Gerald asked suddenly.

Matilda wiped away a tear and frowned. 'As far as I'm aware, Phillip left for France with messages for Giles. Reginald asked him to take Gracia and the children with him, but it wasn't safe for her to travel in her condition and so he took her home to her family instead. Bertha couldn't go because she is too ill to travel anywhere, and I wasn't able to get word to you or Loretta in time to tell you of our situation,' she said, turning to Annora.

'I will arrange to have my steward ride with messages for William as soon as I can,' Gerald said, swatting a fly impatiently aside with his hand. 'I doubt it's safe for him to travel here. Best you meet with him in Pembroke, I think.'

'And what of you, Annora?' Matilda asked, turning her worried green eyes back to her daughter again. 'You should really return to your family, shouldn't you. You would be safer there where they cannot accuse you of being a traitor?'

'*No!*' Annora said sharply. Then seeing our faces, she took a deep breath. 'My husband calls me a witch and has turned them against me - I suspect they side with King John to spite us.'

'But I don't understand?' Matilda said, gripping the back of a chair for support. 'What happened, child? You must tell us!'

Annora sighed. 'Hugh raised a riding crop to me one night – to chastise me for speaking out against his mother – Lady de Mortimer doesn't approve of my knowledge of herbs and medicines taught to me by a wise woman in the village. She says it's unseemly.' She sighed. 'Anyhow, Hugh was riding home from the village one night when an owl swooped down on him suddenly. He tumbled from his horse and broke his arm – Lady de Mortimer said that I had summoned it deliberately using the black arts. She claims that it is my familiar.'

'And is it?' Gerald asked gently, and I saw that his grey eyes were full of concern and not judgmental as others might have been.

'No,' Annora said fiercely. 'I just have a way with birds. They come to me. They trust me. Sometimes in my sleep I dream that I'm flying with them – out over the mountains and down in the valleys. It feels so real,' she sighed. 'It's only then that I feel truly free …'

Gerald simply nodded. He'd heard enough strange stories in his time. But I saw Robert give her a curious look before turning to us and issuing orders that we pack lightly and dress warmly as bad weather was on the way. After that I often saw him making the sign of the cross when he thought she wasn't looking.

Pembrokeshire, Wales, October 1208

We left early the next morning before the sun had risen fully. Sam Skeet stayed behind, released of his duties, and it was with tears in her eyes that Matilda bade him goodbye. I stood wordlessly by as they embraced briefly, then he turned and kissed me gently on the cheek. 'Look after the mistress, Ailith. If you have any need of me, I can be found in Hay, for it's my hometown.' I nodded and turned away before he could see the tears in my eyes, then mounting my pony I followed Matilda and her tiny retinue over the drawbridge, knowing that it was for last time.

The ride to the manor farm was fraught with danger and difficulty; the king's troops were everywhere and it was too dangerous to travel on the open road. Instead, we found ourselves navigating treacherous footpaths and tracks through the densely forested mountains in the knowledge that we could be ambushed at any moment. Now and again we found a few days respite sheltering with friends or family who were sympathetic to our plight, but mostly we took shelter where we could: some coins slipped into a goatherd's hand got us a shed for the night, and at other times a kindly monk or a priest would hide us and share their meagre supply of food for a few days until we were able to move on. Occasionally we glimpsed some of the many outlaws that had made their homes in the rocky outcrops along the way, but as if sensing that, like them, we had reason to hide, they melted away back into the trees like ghosts, leaving us to continue on unmolested.

I counted five days before we finally crossed into territory familiar to Robert Coombe, just as heavy snow began to fall, and it was another day before we finally arrived on the edge of his estate where the manor farm he had told us about was hidden, deep in some woods near a tiny village with an unpronounceable name.

Exhausted, Matilda hunched over her saddle and clung to the mane of her horse in an effort to stay in her seat as we traversed the final road that led to our destination. She had chilblains from the freezing winds sweeping down through the mountains, and the long hard ride through the driving rain had soaked her to the bone, causing her joints to swell painfully beneath her sodden mantle. The others had fared little better. Despite having a thick curling beard, Robert's face was still chapped and reddened from constant exposure. And although Annora had wisely worn a barbette which she had adapted to cover her nose, her eyes peered out from beneath lashes spiked with crystals of ice, and her cheekbones were sore and pinched above the silk.

As we neared the house itself, two men stepped out onto the frozen track and I recognised Will and Reginald. They wasted no time greeting us. Instead, with a quick nod to Robert, they took the reins of Matilda's horse and led us into manor's outer ward where a stable boy sat hunched on a barrel observing us curiously from beneath the rim of his felt cap. Once there, Will gently lifted Matilda out of her saddle and wiped away the silent tears that had begun to slide down her frozen face, before half leading her and half carrying her through the huge wooden doors and into the hall with Reginald on his heels shouting for William. Only when they were out of sight did the stable boy rouse himself enough to assist Robert in helping Annora and I dismount, and together we followed them in, our feet dragging and our cloaks steaming as the warmth of the fire enveloped us.

The inside of the manor house proved to be sparsely furnished but homely. It was seldom used,

Robert said as he warmed his hands by the fire, mainly because it was too far away from a large town to be of interest to his wife who was a socialite and not given to country living. Therefore, he concluded, it was the ideal place for us to rest and make plans because it was unlikely that anybody of significance would be passing by and visiting unannounced.

It was William who, with one look at Matilda's grey, exhausted face as she sank onto a stool with the help of her sons, had a maid show us to a room where I rubbed salve into her swollen fingers and eased her boots from her feet. Later we returned to the hall, but she was too tired to do anything except sit in a chair by the window and pick at some food that had been laid out for us, whilst she explained briefly to Reginald that Gracia and the children were safe with her father, before giving a brief account as to the whereabouts of the others.

'It's best you put them out of your mind for the time being,' she said when Reginald protested later. 'They are safest where they are and I fear that we have a long and arduous journey ahead of us which will be tough enough without having to worry about Gracia's pregnancy and more children,' she said, throwing a worried glance at John, Giles and Phillip playing quietly in the rushes with Maude and baby Walter, before glancing over to the hearth where Will was in deep discussion with his father and Robert over plans to flee to Ireland before John's spies located us. Robert, I learned as I set about putting more logs on the fire and topped up their goblets with wine, proposed to make arrangements to sell the horses as soon as possible, for not only were they thoroughbreds, they were also a burden that we could ill afford. He would pose as a horse trader whilst he made discreet inquiries at the nearby ports about passage, he said, running his hands through his hair in a gesture of anxiety that we were becoming all too familiar with.

It was only when they had a possible plan ready to put in action that Robert and William came and joined us by the window where, after drawing up a chair, William grimly told us that not only had the de Mortimers chosen to support the king rather than their own kin, but incredibly Maude's family had too, with Richard de Clare demanding that she and the children be sent to him. Will put his arms around his wife's shoulders as he told us flatly that were he to send the children to Maude's father he was certain that he would immediately hand them over to John as hostages, and I was sure that I was not the only one to see the shimmer of tears in her eyes as Maude turned and buried her head in the crook of his neck. Not only was she now the enemy of the king, but, like Annora, she was also now the enemy of her own family. A family divided by loyalty. I shivered, despite the heat of the hall I felt cold, and I felt her sense of loss and sorrow as keenly as if it were my own.

It was several days after this revelation that Robert found a captain who was willing to take us to Ireland. During this time, we feared discovery or worse, betrayal from one of the servants, but it appeared that Robert had scrupulously vetted his staff and the few servants that attended us showed us nothing but care and concern. If they had any idea as to who we were, they kept it to themselves.

Several more days passed in agonising slowness. I sat with Matilda as she ate a bowl of broth listening to the *thwack, thwack* of the woodsman's axe as he chopped logs outside in the courtyard. Over by the window Maude sat on a bench with Annora, watching the children playing with some crudely carved wooden figures a kindly maid had found for them.

There was a crash as the door opened and William entered the room, his face red with exertion from the stairs. 'I hope you're feeling better,' he panted, coming to stand in front of Matilda.

'A little,' she replied, turning her head away listlessly.'

'William frowned. 'Come, come. You must rouse yourself. The captain has sent word – a thaw has set in and the wind has dropped. We will soon be able to travel to the coast where conditions will be right for us to set sail for Ireland. You must be prepared, Moll,' he said in a cajoling voice, 'for he thinks it might be in the next day or so. Tis a rough journey, but at least we'll be out of harm's way across the sea. John will not pursue us and risk the wrath of the Irish lords. We shall be safe. Does that not please you?'

At this, Matilda handed me the bowl she'd been eating from, and for the first time in days I saw some colour begin to return to her cheeks. 'Oh, thank goodness,' she whispered, the ever-present tears beginning to form in her eyes. 'I shall be glad to leave this accursed place. I grow ill with fear when I think of John's troops searching for us. He will pursue us forever, I just know he will. We will never be able to return to England or Wales again. Not until he's dead!'

'What of Garcia and the children?' Maude asked from across the room.

William sighed. 'Thankfully Reginald has seen sense and decided that it is too much of a risk to take them with us as Gracia is too near her term. She will stay with her family until he sends for her.'

Maude nodded. 'I'm glad. The delivery of baby Tilda was nearly the death of her. I feared that a long journey oversees to a foreign land might prove to be too much. I imagine she can join us later when it is safer, can she not?'

William nodded. 'Yes, I expect so,' he said, throwing a neutral look her way from under his lashes.

When William had left, Matilda turned to me, her eyes bright with anticipation. 'Perhaps we shall be saved yet,' she whispered. 'Perhaps we shall outwit King John after all. Oh, say it will be so, Ailith … please say it will be so.'

After a moment she fell back on her pillow exhausted. Shortly after that she was fast asleep, her hair fanned around her shoulders like a young girl's. It was only then that I let the tears come. And they were hot and bitter on my cheeks. For I knew that I was powerless to stop the shadows as they moved in to claim their own. Powerless to stop the storms that would blow her from one end of the land to another before King John was done with the chase. For, like with a game of chess, King John never liked to lose.

A few nights after the conversation with William we stood concealed by a copse of trees watching as two little boats nosed their way into the cove. The horses had been sold discreetly to a farmer who had offered half of what they were worth, and the few possessions that William and Matilda still owned had gone ahead of us to be loaded onto the ship that was to take us to Ireland. I glanced behind me nervously; even now John might have got word of our flight and at any moment I expected to see a long line of men in the king's livery file down the track and arrest us all. I looked down at little John standing beside his grandmother, staring solemnly out to sea, not really understanding what was happening. Will stood beside Reginald holding Giles in one arm, his hand curled protectively around the little boy as he slept, whilst he fiercely gripped Phillip's small fist with his other. I could just make out Robert down by the shore making his way into the shallows, leading Annora and Maude towards one of the boats with baby Walter held tightly to his chest.

Then a cloud passed over the moon, blotting out what little light it provided, plunging our little group into inky darkness. I shivered. The world seemed to have tilted off its axis. Everything seemed different from how I imagined. As we stood silently waiting, listening to the roar of the sea clashing against the rocks, I couldn't help wondering if we would even know if the king's men surrounded us.

Then at last the cloud drifted away to reveal the women scrambling onto one of the precariously bobbing boats, their skirts hitched up to their waists. Once they were safely aboard, Robert handed Walter over to Maude, before turning to give the signal for us to follow. Quickly, we ran down to the sandy shore with the children, keeping close to the shadows of the cliffs for cover. I could sense Robert's impatience as he half pulled, half pushed us up on to the little vessel, before guiding the little flat-bottomed boats out to sea where we were rowed swiftly towards the larger vessel that was waiting to take us to Ireland. Above us the sky was still as black as a cinder. Only a sickle moon still hung there, its ghostly light the only thing that might reveal us to a watching enemy.

It seemed like forever before, having traversed the icy water round several dark, eerie little coves, the little boats pulled up alongside a wooden jetty where a larger fishing boat was moored.

Robert of Coombe did swift business with a leather skinned sailor with dark glittering eyes and a red bandana wrapped round his greasy hair, who I assumed was the skipper of the boat. Then we were all ushered on to the wide beamed vessel by means of a narrow gangplank. Once aboard, Matilda clutched her mantle tightly around her shoulders and sat down heavily on an upturned crate, leaving me to trail after Maude and the children, to be shown into a tiny deck cabin which was all that could be spared for the crossing.

After checking the rigging, the skipper declared the boat seaworthy, and as soon as the rope was neatly coiled on the deck, the craft began to nose its way out of the narrow inlet towards the sea, where it caught a wind in its sail and began making its way west towards the safety of the Irish coast.

'Not what you be used, too, I'll be guessing,' one of the shipmen said a while later, a hint of malice glinting in his eyes as he turned to us, 'What wi' you being fugitives, as I hear!'

'Mind your tongue,' Maude said sharply.

'Ha!' he retorted. 'You be a feisty one then, and that be no word o' a lie!' And with that he turned on his heel and made his way to the aft where Matilda stood with the others gathered around her, staring back towards the rugged coast of Wales, which only a little while before they had called home.

'King John can't reach us in Ireland, Ailith,' Matilda said to me later as we huddled together out of the wind wrapped in the thick sheepskins Robert thought to provide us with before we left. 'In a few weeks' time we shall all be safe in the bosom of Margaret and Walter in Meath. I long to see Margaret again. I've never seen her children, so perhaps one good thing will come out of this and I shall get the chance to be a proper grandmother to them.' She sighed, 'I'm tired now, Ailith, I must get some rest.'

I watched her go, electing to stay on the deck with Robert of Coombe who was deep in conversation with the skipper, whilst one by one the rest of the family slipped away to make the best of the cabin and its sparse facilities for the night. The hours passed slowly as the ship's bow cut through the black glassy water towards our destination. The rocking motion made it impossible for me to get any sleep save the odd nap, and so I lay listening to the gentle lapping of the waves and the creak of the planking as the sailors went about their business instead. It seemed like forever before the darkness faded into a grey streaked dawn. In the distance the sun struggled to rise behind a bank of cloud, tingeing the horizon fiery red, and I saw the skipper purse his lips and muttered something about a 'red sky in the morning,' but I took little notice as I wrapped my serviceable home spun cloak around me and stood and stretched my aching limbs.

It seemed none of us had slept much at all; William was hunched on a barrel, fear and worry blurring the features beneath the sandy grey stubble that now covered his face. I peered into the little cabin where Will and his wife sat huddled together in one corner with their luggage scattered around them, whilst in another the children dozed with their nurses with the babies cradled awkwardly in the crook of their arms. The whole cabin stank with the odour of vomit and unwashed bodies. Of Annora and Reginald there was no sign.

Sighing, I moved to the bow of the ship and looked out towards the horizon, but it was too early to see land after only one night. After a while Matilda appeared beside me like a ghost out of nowhere, her green eyes sparkling with joy, and the sea spray clinging like jewels to her lashes.

'You seem to have better sea legs than my offspring,' she said with a mischievous smile, running her hands through her hair to free the tangles, and looking towards the aft where Reginald and Annora had just appeared and were leaning over the rail taking deep gulping breaths of fresh air.

'It's not too rough out there yet,' I replied, 'though there are clouds gathering on the horizon,' I cautioned, pointing them out to her.

One of the sailors stopped what he was doing and tugged at his forelock in what I supposed was a gesture of greeting. 'There'll be a storm before the day is out, mark my words,' he said.

Matilda smiled and went to talk to her children, leaving me to continue to stare out over the water absently.

As the sailor had predicted, before the morning ended the winds changed dramatically, and the clouds that had gathered ominously on the horizon were soon rolling towards us. Before long the ship began to list and buck like a bull stung by a bee as it rose and fell on the waves and troughs with such force I thought it would break.

'Jesu, I never thought to see such a squall,' Matilda shouted, returning to my side and grabbing my arm to stop me falling as the ship hit another wave.

I was beginning to feel frightened. But Matilda just laughed; the hood of her mantle had blown back and her hair, whipped by the wind, clung in damp tendrils across her face as she hung on to the rail exhilarated by the mood of the ocean. Around us crewmen struggled to keep the boat from being blown back towards the rocky coast of Wales, and possible disaster, as huge, sweeping dark waves crashed against her hull, sending gallons of foaming green water crashing onto the deck. Finally, we were forced to take refuge in the dank little deck cabin, huddled together with fear as we realised that it was not just a little squall that we'd entered, but a full-blown storm.

For two whole days the wind whistled through the rigging and tore at the canvas sail whilst we listened to the shouts of the crewmen running to and fro across the deck outside. Maude, overcome by the smell of stale sweat and vomit, was soon doubled up over the leather bucket by the door, and I felt my own stomach turn in sympathy. As time went on, we were no longer sure if it was noon or night outside. Then suddenly there was a commotion as, with a sharp rending crack, the main mast fell, hitting the deck with a crash. The screams of the unfortunate men trapped beneath it were whipped away on the wind, along with the frantic cries of their shipmates as they tried to drag the ruined pole aside. After that we heard nothing for a while, and we began to fear that the sea had taken them. Pulling a rosary out of a tangled mass of objects that had rolled into the corner where she was huddled, Annora began to pray frantically. Very soon we all joined in. The children, frightened and tearful, were passed between ourselves and the terrified nurses whilst we took it in turns to kneel on the floor of the foul little cabin and pray to the blessed saints and the Virgin Mary that we would be saved.

Then God answered our prayers, and as suddenly as it had started the storm abated. Exchanging twin looks of gratitude and relief, Will and Roger went out onto deck to see if they could help the skipper, leaving the others to try and make some order of our belongings, and me to wonder why God had answered our prayers, only to send us out to weather a worse storm.

'What will Phillip do?' Matilda asked Will later as, having recovered from the storm, they stood side by side on the deck scanning the horizon for signs of land. 'Do you think he'll follow us after he has delivered his message to Giles in France?'

'Not immediately,' Will said, leaning against the ruined mast. 'He has pledged to return to Wales. Once there, he plans to hide in the mountains and start negotiations with the Welsh princes. See if he can get some of them on our side. Personally, I don't hold out much hope, although Prince Llewellyn might be persuaded. No, our best chance is to lie low in Ireland until John forgets his grudge.'

'He won't do that,' Matilda said softly, remembering a pair of fine grey eyes. 'Will,' she said, 'You met Arthur of Brittany, did you not?'

'Yes,' Will said, nodding.

'Did he have grey eyes?' Matilda asked. 'Grey eyes fringed with thick, dark lashes?'

'Yes,' Will said. 'Yes, he did.' He said no more. Instead, pulling Matilda into the crook of his arm, he hugged her fiercely. 'I won't let any harm come to you, Mother, trust me.'

Matilda let the words blow away on the wind.

Chapter 30

Waterford, Ireland, October 1208

'Land ahoy!' came the shout from the rigging.

Eagerly Matilda picked up her skirts and made her way to the bow of the boat with Annora and me in tow, and between us we strained to see beyond the horizon. It was Annora who first made out the craggy outline of Ireland rising out of the mist ahead and overcome with emotion she hugged her mother briefly before disappearing to tell the others. It seemed like hours before the skipper finally guided the injured vessel into the mouth of a small estuary leading to the river Suir, and by noon we were approaching the busy little port of Waterford where we could see the tiny shapes of people at work on the wharf. Then at last, ignoring the gulls that shrieked and wheeled above the us, the skipper carefully guided his craft towards its moorings, navigating the plethora of bobbing fishing cogs and larger ships that crowded the harbour with the consummate skill of a seasoned sailor.

'The Marshall is residing at Kilkenny Castle at the moment. I've had word that he is sympathetic to our plight, so perhaps he will accommodate us for a few days until we can continue on to Trim rested,' William said, joining us on deck as the crewmen folded the heavy canvas sail and stored it alongside the damaged mast for repair. 'Maude is getting the children ready to disembark. Mayhap she'll feel better soon with her feet on steady ground,' he finished, nodding at Will and Reginald who were leaning against the cabin watching dry land approach with cautious smiles on their faces.

'Whose castle is that?' Matilda asked, pointing to an imposing wooden keep, rising from an island in the middle of the river.

'Belongs to the Fitzgeralds, my lady,' the skipper said, coming up behind her. 'You'll no' find sympathy with them. They're the king's men. But there's no one in residence at the moment, that's why I brought you to this port. 'Tis but a short ride to Kilkenny from here,' he added, screwing up his eyes and against the wind, before returning to the job of steering the cog to its moorings.

It was a while before the ship was anchored and we disembarked, walking unsteadily down the gang plank to where the crew were offloading our meagre luggage. Matilda sat down tiredly on one of the trunks with Walter on her lap, keeping an eye on the wooden palisade out on the island as if she expected the drawbridge might suddenly be lowered and King John's men would emerge to row across the Suir and arrest us.

'Now then, Moll,' William said, seeing the direction of her gaze. 'You heard what the skipper said. The Fitzgeralds are not in residence at the moment and I doubt if King John and his spies even realise that we have fled Wales yet. Have no fear.' Then he turned impatiently away to take charge. 'Robert, you will accompany Reginald and William into Waterford and see if you can find horses. Make some discreet enquiries about the fellow that owns that manor over there,' he said, nodding towards a large imposing building set on the hill beyond Waterford.

When the men had left to do as William bid, he seemed to relax a bit, pleased to have put some distance between the king and ourselves. He even ruffled Giles' hair and swung him up onto his shoulders for a while so that that the little boy might watch a fishing boat approach the jetty to unload its shimmering catch.

It was late when the last of our coffers were lowered alongside the others. Will had managed to purchase a horse and cart from a man whose consignment of hides was now on a ship bound for England. Between them he and William loaded our meagre possessions onto it under the interested eye of a couple of doxies who were plying their trade on the wharf. Robert and Reginald finally returned, holding the reins of three mangy looking mares and several packhorses acquired in Waterford. I was no judge, but I reckoned that whoever had sold the animals to them had fared better out of the transaction than they had, given the sorry appearance of the beasts.

William was still in good spirits as he helped the women mount, before turning and lifting the children and their nurses onto the waiting cart with me, and whilst he slung a bag of provisions across his saddle, Will told us that his enquiries had revealed the manor on the hill was owned by a family called Fitzwarren who, like the Fitzgeralds, were also sympathetic to the king, and so it seemed that we couldn't seek refuge there.

We were finally packed and ready to leave when a lanky fellow lounging silently against a warehouse suddenly unfolded himself and stepped out in front of William's horse.

'Get out the way, man!' William shouted. 'What the devil do you think you're doing!'

Ignoring him, the man took hold of the horse's bridle, halting him firmly in his tracks. 'Your William de Braose, if I'm not mistaken,' he said in a soft Irish accent that did nothing to hide challenge that lay behind the words.

'Who wants to know?' William asked rudely.

For a moment Matilda's face gleamed white in the ghostly evening light, and somewhere in the distance a dog began to howl; a strange, mournful sound setting half a dozen other dogs barking in unison.

For a long while nobody spoke. Then the man said softly. 'Oh, I think King John will!' And without another word, he released the bridle, and disappeared into the deep shadows of the warehouses before anyone thought to stop him.

'Did you know him, Father?' Reginald asked sharply.

'I don't know. I … I don't think so,' William replied in a shaky voice, shocked that he might have been recognised so soon into our flight.

'But he knew you,' Matilda whispered. 'John has his spies everywhere; there will be one in every port in Ireland reporting back to him wherever we go. Oh, why ever did we think we could escape him?' She cried, her voice rising in anguish as she finished.

'Well, it's no good standing around and debating the matter,' Reginald concluded, picking up his reins and peering worriedly into the gloom after the man. 'We must ride towards the safety of Kilkenny immediately - mayhap we will be there on the morrow if we ride through the night.'

'Yes, you're right,' William, said numbly. 'I'll take the front. You, Will and Robert take the rear. Keep checking behind. Alert me if you have any suspicion that we are being followed!'

And without another word he gave spurred his mount into a trot, eager to be on the road to Kilkenny and safety before anyone else recognised his face.

✝

Kilkenny Castle, Ireland, October 1208

A blanket of rain followed us from the port as we rode for Kilkenny. William sent Robert ahead to scout the land. If it was a choice of a main highway or a narrower, more secluded track, then we took the latter if the cart could manage it. The family remained quiet and apprehensive as we wound our way down yet another waterlogged trail. The only sound was the sucking of the horses' hooves in the mud, or the howl of a wolf in the distance as darkness fell. We rode hard through the night, careful to keep our heads low when a fellow traveller passed us in case we were recognised again, and although I was still tired from the previous night's lack of sleep, I stayed awake whilst the nurses and children dozed. Gradually, the night turned into a misty grey morning, followed by a cold, drizzly afternoon. Then at last we were picking our way through some cotters' cottages and a small village until we were at a fording point on the River Nore. Ahead of us towered a large, imposing grey walled stone castle, its four large circular corner towers still under construction. Those, we learned later, were the new fortifications commissioned by William Marshall to withstand the notoriously ferocious attacks from unfriendly Irish Lords.

As we approached, the clip clop of the horses' hooves on the wide stone path alerted the lookout, and a group of knights on horseback wearing the Marshall's livery cantered to meet us, led by a distinguished grey-haired man with a neatly trimmed beard that I recognised as the Marshall himself.

'Christ's bones, Marshall! I can't tell you how good it is to see you. It has been a devil of a journey to get here,' William gasped, his relief evident as he sheathed his hurriedly drawn sword and slumped over his saddle in exhaustion.

'You're welcome, Sir William, Lady de Braose. Word travels fast and we have been expecting you. It appears we share a common fate in that we are both out of favour with the king,' he said, his brown eyes roaming Matilda's drawn white face and William's anxious one, looking for any sign that he might be mistaken.

William forced himself to smile, mumbling a few short, incoherent words that appeared to confirm the Marshall's assessment of the situation, before turning back and watching the rest of the bedraggled wagon train limp up the track behind us.

For a moment the Marshall's eyes followed his, before returning to the children, now beginning to wake and grizzle in the waggon alongside me, and I thought he might say something. However, he merely turned away and shouted commands to his men before turning his horse around and spurring it towards the castle, leaving his knights to gather around us and take charge.

It was only as we followed him across the drawbridge and towards the gate that led to the castle's inner ward, that I looked down into the massive ditch and then up at the walls towering above us and wondered if I was the only one feel the strange, oppressing coldness of the place. A feeling that, once inside the castle walls, the Marshall did nothing to dispel by immediately jumping off his horse and disappearing up a short flight of steps and into the keep without another word.

For a while we waited patiently. I could see Matilda looking around, a puzzled look on her face as she stared up at the tall windows, empty and vacant. Nobody had come to greet us and the feeling that we were unwelcome seemed to hang over the bailey like a cloud. Then suddenly she let go of the reins and slumped forward onto its neck in exhaustion, her hair, now free from its restraining pins, falling in wild abandonment around her shoulders.

Immediately, Will leapt from his saddle, and pushing aside the few hapless, gawking, stable lads milling around her helplessly, he was at her side with William standing by seemingly at loss as what to do with his wife. 'It's all right now, Mother, we shall soon be safe and warm,' I heard Will say as he lifted her down. 'May we be shown the hall?' he called to the Marshall who had left the warmth of the castle and was now crossing the yard towards us with his steward and several liveried servants in tow.

'A thousand apologies,' the Marshall began, his voice trailing off as he looked around in embarrassment, taking in the cold, pinched faces surrounding him and the look of challenge on Will's face as half pushed, half held his mother upright. 'What must you think of me? You must be exhausted and in need of sustenance, and here was me leaving you standing out in the cold. But if you follow me now, I shall see that the guest quarters are made ready for you whilst provision is made elsewhere for the rest of your servants and family. Then,' he added, glancing dubiously behind him towards the doors, 'when you are feeling quite well, I shall introduce you to my wife, Isabel, who I am sure will be only too happy to see to your needs.'

Tension blanketed the great hall like woodsmoke as we jostled together by the fire with the Marshall and half a dozen dogs for warmth. Seeing that the children were fractious and tired, the Marshall had dispatched them to the nursery whilst the rest of our accommodation was being prepared.

'Ah, Isabel, my dear,' the Marshall said turning to a poker thin, tight-lipped woman some years his junior who made a sudden and silent appearance at his side. 'You remember Lord and Lady de Braose from court, do you not?'

Isabel frowned at William and Matilda, and she didn't rush forward to greet them. She didn't appear pleased to see her unexpected guests at all, but if anybody noticed it was quickly forgotten as we were joined by two of their sons, William the Younger and Gilbert, whom I recognised from amongst the group of knights that had escorted us to the castle.

'But you must be famished,' the Marshall said, looking over his shoulder at the servants bustling about setting the tables for dinner and then Isabel Marshall who, throwing him a glare, disappeared only to return some moments later with the steward carrying a pitcher of wine and some sweetmeats.

'Thank you, my dear,' the Marshall said, ignoring the stony looks she threw our way as he directed William and Matilda and the rest of us towards the dais where they could talk more privately.

'Tomorrow we will write and beg one more audience of the king,' I heard him say to William as he pulled the chairs haphazardly around the table and took charge of the wine which Isabel had plonked unceremoniously down on its surface.'

William ran his hand through his hair tiredly. 'Do you think that will do any good?' he asked uneasily. 'Surely it will only alert him to where we are hiding?'

The Marshall sighed and I saw him throw a puzzled glance at Isabel who, despite her obvious disapproval, was still hovering nearby. 'As you know, John has spies everywhere and he will have been told of your whereabouts by now. But having the knowledge doesn't mean he can invade Ireland. To do that would cause unrest and uprisings that he can ill afford to suppress amongst the Irish lords. Anyway, for now you are safe – and you can rest assured that you will be safer still when we deliver you to your daughter in Meath where you will be under the protection of both her husband and his brother in Ulster. John will think twice before directly attacking such great magnates on Irish soil,' he finished.

I saw Matilda shiver as she recalled the man at the port who had recognised them almost as soon as they had stepped off the boat. She, like I, knew that we would not be safe anywhere for that was not the way that fate worked. Mistress Destiny's plans were laid and they were already working their way to fruition, even as we sat in the Marshall's hall. We were no safer here in this castle than a rabbit was trapped in the sight of a fox.

'But he can, and will, dispossess those who help us,' William continued, his voice rising strained and worried above the noise of the hall as it carried on around him. I glanced at the Marshall's wife, and her tightly compressed lips, still clearly displaying her dislike of the situation that her husband had presented her with, made me shiver.

'I wonder if I might be excused to my chambers to get some rest?' Matilda's voice cut through my thoughts, addressing the Marshall as she eyed the servants scuttling around with platters loaded with what looked like some sort of game swimming in grease. The smell of the meat was so strong that she had covered her nose with her hand and she looked as if she might be sick.

Immediately the Marshall jumped to his feet. 'My dear lady, forgive me I almost forgot. Your chambers must be ready by now, and of course you'll be wanting nothing more than to bathe and rest after your arduous journey!' he cried, beckoning Isabel forward to escort us before turning back to William who was now engaged in deep in discussion with Gilbert and Reginald over the content of a petition to the king.

Matilda stood slowly, and together we followed Isabel out of the hall and into a corridor lit by rows of sconces. The flames flickered wildly up the walls as we passed, throwing strange, elongated shadows in are wake, until finally we came to the set of chambers that the Marshall had had made up for his guests. Matilda sat down on the bed tiredly, and after thanking the squire I set about plumping up the pillows for her. Then, noticing that the door was still ajar, I went to close it.

Outside in the passageway I saw that Isabel had stopped to talk to someone partly concealed in the shadows. The man, for I was certain it was a man, seemed to be listening intently. Then he raised his head and looked in the direction of our rooms. Hastily, I pushed the door to. When I opened it to look again the man was still standing there, though Isabel had continued on back down the corridor towards the hall. For a moment our eyes met, then, pulling his mantle around him, he turned swiftly on his heels and disappeared into the darkness, leaving me with an odd feeling of dread in the pit of my stomach.

With a shiver, I pushed the door firmly shut this time. Then with a quick look at Matilda asleep on the bed, I threw the metal bar into place for good measure. There was only one thing for it, I must tell William what I'd seen in the morning ...

Kilkenny Castle, Ireland, November 1208

We were sitting down to a simple meal of cold meats, pottage and frumenty when the justiciar of Ireland, John de Grey arrived, accompanied by two of the king's officers. They were unarmed, having relinquished their swords to the Marshall's steward as was the custom when invited into another man's hall.

The Marshall rose slowly from his seat on the dais and flanked by his sons he stepped down to greet them. 'John,' he said, 'this is a pleasant surprise! Pray, come join us for some supper.'

I sensed that his jovial greeting was forced. Beside him, his sons looked like coils ready to spring should the need arise. There was clearly no love lost between the family and the justiciar.

De Grey did not reply immediately. Instead, he looked around until his narrow, shifty eyes fixed themselves on William and Matilda seated on the high table. I saw Matilda's knuckles grow white as she gripped the stem of her goblet, certain that they were about to be arrested.

'I didn't come for small talk or supper,' de Gray said, turning back to the Marshall. 'The king demands that you hand over de Braose and his family immediately.'

'Oh, come now. Surely that's not necessary, man,' the Marshall responded a little testily, putting a restraining hand on the collar of a large Irish Wolfhound that had padded silently over to his side, and was now baring its teeth.

'Indeed, it is,' John de Grey replied, his face impassive. 'You must know that you're shielding fugitives? They are in a great deal of debt to the treasury, and King John requires an audience with them immediately. They are to come as hostages.'

'Well, I know nothing of any quarrel with the king. My wife and I have merely extended our hospitality to them as our feudal duty requires, and I will not have them harried and threatened in my hall.'

The room had fallen silent. All eyes were on the Marshall, the atmosphere so thick that you could have cut it with a knife; a feeling enhanced by Will and Reginald who'd appeared from nowhere and were now making their way towards him with their hands deliberately resting on the hilts of their swords.

John de Grey, however, was not intimidated by their show of solidarity. 'I must insist, *sir*, that they come with me at once,' he said, holding the Marshall's gaze defiantly.

'And I must insist, *sir*, that you leave this hall immediately!' the Marshall thundered. 'Or else I shall have you thrown out like the dog you are!'

Another silence fell over the hall, broken only by the sound of a goblet being knocked onto a metal platter where it spun noisily before someone stilled it with a hand.

Then William himself stood. For a moment he hovered uncertainly, and I thought that he might flee, but then he seemed to make a decision, and making his way unsteadily across the dais he descended the steps and addressed de Grey himself.

'Tell King John that it will take an army to arrest my family, and not one ferrety little justiciar and a couple of foot soldiers who've yet to have their first shave. You may also tell him that he's made many enemies, both here and at home, and should he raise an army he will encounter the fiercest of resistance,' he finished, the bravado in his voice fading as he heard the gasps that were beginning to ripple around the hall.

John de Grey didn't move for a long time after William's little speech. The only sign that he'd heard was the tell-tale tide of red that showed above his collar as he turned and addressed the Marshall again.

'Anyone who threatens the king will suffer for it. I strongly recommend that you reconsider your position whilst it's not too late – you're already low in his favour as it is'. Then turning on his heel, he gestured to his men, and with his head held high he marched out into the bailey. Minutes later we heard the jangle of harnesses and the sound of horses' hooves crossing the ward, followed by the clash of metal on the drawbridge as the Marshall's captain of the guard, not trusting the men, ordered their arms to be flung out after them.

At once the hall erupted, with the Marshall's loyal retainers and the knights of his mesnie outraged at the implied threat to their Lord, imploring him to send troops in pursuit of the men as a lesson to the king. But the Marshall held up a hand and ruled that killing John de Grey, one of John's favourites, was not an option.

Behind him, Matilda rose shakily from her seat. Then, giving a little sob, she flung down her napkin, and twirling on her heels she ran down the length of the hall, blindly pushing past people as she went. Before she reached the doors, however, she crashed into a man standing concealed deep in the shadows along the wall. For a moment her eyes widened in shock, then, backing away from him fearfully, she burst into tears and ran up the narrow, winding flight of stairs that led to the guard room instead.

The man watched her go, making no attempt to follow. Then he began to push his way impatiently past a group of people, making for a door in the wall used by the servants to carry food to and from the bakehouse to the hall, and for a moment I glimpsed his face.

The man was Faulkes de Breauté. And he was undoubtedly the man that I had seen in the corridor the first night.

Isabel Marshall stood before her husband with William and Matilda standing alongside him looking shaken and ill. Will, Reginald, and some of the Marshall's foot soldiers were out, scouring the countryside searching for de Breauté. It had taken some time to calm Matilda, and for the Marshall to realise that one of John's mercenaries had already infiltrated the castle. But it took no time at all to work out that it was Isabel who'd let him in. For it was written plainly on her face.

'Why, Isabel? These are our friends, for pity's sakes. I expected better of you!'

Isabel Marshall held her head high. 'They are fugitives and traitors, not friends, William. And you're a fool to harbour them. I shall not!' She said, stamping one small foot defiantly.

'And what did you think to do?' William interrupted sarcastically. 'You surely didn't think that de Breauté and his small band of men would pick a fight with the man who has the reputation of being the greatest knight in Christendom in his own castle, did you?'

'He was waiting until you left. You would have been ambushed on the road - en route to Meath,' Isabel said, ignoring her husband and looking directly at Matilda.

Matilda shivered. *They had made plans to leave in two days' time and de Breauté would have been waiting for them on the road ...*

At that moment the door opened and Will and Reginald entered the chamber. 'He and his men are nowhere to be found!' Will said, throwing Isabel a look of disgust and crossing to put his arms protectively around his mother's shoulders.

'They left by the postern gate some hours ago – they had a key!' Isabel sneered.

'You must leave at once,' the Marshall said with a sigh. Then, opening the door, he beckoned a guard into the room. 'Keep her locked up until I get back. And double the watch tonight.'

'But surely you can see –' Isabel protested.

'No. No, I cannot see, and that is where my failing lies, for I did not listen to my intuition and therefore I did not see what a duplicitous, scheming, wretch of a wife you really are!' Then, with a final glare in Isabel's direction, he ushered them out of the chamber, bidding them to make haste and pack ready to leave for Meath immediately.

Chapter 31

Trim Castle, Ireland, November 1208

It was late afternoon, some days later, when our small company finally reached the castle at Trim, having left Kilkenny as soon as possible after Isabel's revelations. Trotting over the drawbridge, I saw Matilda take in the details of the large imposing castle within which her daughter Margaret and her husband the Earl of Meath lived with Gilbert, Egidia and Petronilla, their son and two baby daughters. Only when they were in the bailey, and the massive gates had been closed behind us, did I see Matilda let out a breath. We would be safe here, I thought, trying to forget the horror of Kilkenny as I watched a group of sparrows, unperturbed by our sudden arrival, squabble noisily over the remains of a loaf lying on the cobbles beside her.

After a moment Margaret came running out of the keep and, catching the bridle of Matilda's mare, she led it towards a mounting block where she helped her alight. Once on her level, I watched Matilda gave her daughter a fierce hug before holding her at arm's length so that she could inspect her. Despite Matilda's fears that word of Kilkenny might have proceeded our small party and that we might no longer be welcome at Trim, Margaret did not seem unhappy to see us - or at least she put the matter aside for the time being as one by one she hugged Annora and her brothers before beckoning a groom forward to help her father alight.

It seemed like an age before, having dispatched Walter off to the nursery with a freckled faced young maid called Sian, and made sure that our escort had provisions enough for the long journey back to Kilkenny, we were able to follow Margaret and the others into the great hall where Walter de Lacy was waiting to greet us.

'Lady de Braose, you are most welcome,' he said, coming forward and raising her hand to his mouth gallantly, though I noticed that he made no attempt to hide the pity in his shrewd brown eyes as they roamed her face, taking in the lines of worry around her eyes and mouth, and the streaks of grey at her temples where she had hurriedly pulled back her hair and coiled it beneath her veil before entering the hall.

'My lord, you are most kind. I fear that our visit here is not conducted under the most pleasant of circumstances.' Matilda murmured, flushing with embarrassment, and I could see her remembering a time when her daughter's husband's eyes would have held nothing but admiration for her.

'My dear lady,' Walter said as he took her arm and led her over to the fire where Margaret now sat with Annora, fussing over Gilbert, who, disturbed by all the noise, had been brought to the hall by his tutor, 'surely you must know that my wife's kin will always welcome here ... whatever the circumstances may be. And you can rest assured that we will do whatever is necessary to see that you remain safe and sound under our protection.'

Throwing a grateful glance at her husband, Margaret stood. 'You must listen to Walter, Mother,' she said, kissing him on the cheek and reaching for one of her furs over so that she could place it over Matilda's thin shoulders. 'You will be safe here, and before long the danger will have passed and, God willing, you may return to England.'

Matilda looked around and sighed. 'Well, as I am sure you are aware, John has already had John de Grey track us down and try to arrest us. You should also know that Isabel Marshall didn't agree with harbouring us. She made it quite plain. I know that if John does sail for Ireland, she would gladly offer him a safe house and troops to hunt us down which would put you in danger.'

'I am sure that it won't come to that,' Walter said, but even I did not miss the worried look he threw his wife. 'Personally,' he continued, 'I think John is calling your bluff. It is one thing to send the justiciar of Ireland to arrest you when he is already on Irish soil, but it is quite another to finance a costly expedition to cross the Irish sea in order to do it himself. But, in the unlikely event he does sail, we will get you on the first boat to France where John has no influence anymore'

'I'll second that!' We all turned. The voice belonged to Hugh de Lacy, Walter's younger brother, the Lord of Ulster, who had entered the hall unannounced. 'John de Grey will not make another attempt to arrest you,' he continued, handing his sword to his squire and looking around fiercely. 'He would be a fool to try and challenge the combined might of the lords of Leinster, Meath and Ulster, and from what I hear the king already has enough to worry about in England what with all the discontent and unrest that is beginning to surface in the north. Why, there is even talk that the Northern barons might throw their lot in with the Scots, which is more than enough to distract him from his pursuit of you – even without the cost of doing so.'

I sighed. Despite Hugh's reassurances Matilda still looked uncertain, and I thought that, like me, she was probably unable to rid herself of the image of John marching to port and crowding on to a ship with his troops and doing just that.

Over in the doorway, Maude appeared, flanked by Will who'd left to deal with the content of the wagons and the horses. Beside them John, Phillip and Giles stood looking around confused. I could see that the long hours on the road had taken their toll.

At once the subject of King John and his pursuit of them was forgotten as Margaret held out her hands. 'Maude,' she said. 'Come! Introduce me to your children, then, when you're ready, I shall take you to the nursery. Walter is already asleep there with Egidia and Petronilla, but your boys can share with Gilbert in his room. They'll all get along famously, I am sure!' I heard her say as with a nod from Matilda I followed them out of the hall.

Trim Castle, Ireland, August 1209

The freezing winds and snow that had marked Christmas and the New Year slowly gave way to a wet and dreary spring, followed by a lukewarm summer in the months following their flight from Kilkenny. It was as Hugh had predicted: the justiciar, John de Grey, could not take on the might of the lords of Leinster, Meath, and Ulster combined, and King John was too taken up with troubles along the Welsh borders and in the north of

England to plan an invasion. And so, for a while, there was a stalemate.

Then, in the August one of Walter's messengers arrived bearing news from the king's court. Walter listened as the mud splattered youth stuttered the message out over the noise of the hall, whilst throwing quick darting looks at the dais where William and Matilda were breaking their fast. When the messenger had finished, Walter sent him to the kitchens to get some food. Then, in a few short strides, he crossed the length of the hall and began to relate what the boy had told him.

'You must prepare yourselves,' he said carefully. 'I'm sorry to tell you that it's not good news. Word has come that John had resolved his problems in the north. He is now mustering his Flemish mercenaries together at Margram Abbey for an expedition to Ireland in the New Year to arrest you and your family,' he said, his voice grim. 'I never thought it would come to this, but the messenger assures me that it has. The king has raised an army against you, William. He is planning to invade us.'

Walter paused for a moment. William's face looked blank; registering neither shock or outrage and for a moment he wondered if the man had had some sort of seizure. 'Hugh and I have been talking,' he continued after a while, keeping his voice low. 'We think it would be best for everyone if you write to the king and beg one last audience. Say you wish to return to England and settle your debts with the him. You must do this for all our sakes; the king is threatening to attack our castles and dispossess us of our lands here in Ireland because we are harbouring you.'

'No!' William banged his fist down so hard that it shook the table sending food flying and making both Matilda and the page who was serving her jump. 'Damn it, man! You know I can't do that. For a start, I have no money or possessions with which to pay him!' he thundered, paying no heed to the eyes beginning to turn in his direction as, galvanised out of his stupor, he reached for the nearest pitcher of wine and with a shaky hand began to top his goblet up to the brim.

'Calm down, man!' Walter barked, glancing quickly around the hall before continuing in a more reasonable tone. 'Think on it, William. You must write to John. Implore him to allow you to return. It's the only course open to you now, else all will be lost. You have already lost Limerick. Whatever happens, we must hold on to Meath and Ulster because we cannot afford to be weakened in Ireland any further.

William stood so suddenly that he found himself nose to nose with Walter. 'And where does your loyalty lie, eh? When you first harboured us, you made us a promise of loyalty. You stood in this very hall and said that you disagreed with the king's treatment of my family. And now you wish me to return and beg to the very same king for one last chance to repay my debts. Even though I cannot!'

'I have to look at things from our perspective,' Walter said, gesturing towards Hugh who had just stepped up to the dais with a grim look on his face. 'We cannot afford to lose our lands and fall out of favour with the king, William.'

Hugh coughed. 'I think we should discuss this somewhere else, Walter. Somewhere more private, perhaps,' he said, looking at the sea of interested faces now turned their way.

For a moment neither man gave any indication that they had heard. Then, nodding in agreement, Walter turned and without another word began to make his way to the chancery.

The chancery was deep in shadows when they arrived. Above Walter's head, dust motes danced in the little bit of sunlight that filtered through the only window in the room. William immediately crossed to a table and poured himself a goblet of wine, leaving Matilda and Hugh hovering in the doorway. Walter seemed at loss what to say now that they were alone and so he busied himself instead with lighting the single rush light in the corner before fiddling with a sheaf of papers lying discarded on the desk.

It was Hugh who finally spoke. 'Think on it, William,' he said, picking up on the conversation as if they had not left it in the hall, 'it's the only option left to you now. If you write to John, and if he agrees to an audience, the rest of your family can remain here with the children whilst you go. Hopefully, John will have seen sense by then and he will deal leniently with you. After all, with the feeling of unrest amongst his barons high he needs to make a compromise somewhere, and where better to start than by pardoning one of their own. Write to him, William. I urge you. For the sake of your family, write and have one last go at reconciliation!'

William said nothing for a long time following Hugh's speech, paying little heed to anything apart from topping up his wine again, but it was plain from the expression on his face, and the veins standing out on his neck, that he was apoplectic with rage. Then, before anyone could think of anything to break the silence, William flung down his goblet and stormed out of the room, leaving the three of them staring unhappily after him.

Hugh sighed and, going to Matilda, he laid a hand on her shoulder. 'I am sorry that William has taken on so. But you must persuade him that writing to the king is the right thing to do. In fact, it's your only chance,' he said. Then giving her shoulder a squeeze, he turned to Walter and the pair of them left the room, leaving Matilda standing alone, her world once more crumbling around her.

✝

Trim Castle, Ireland, May 1210

Matilda glanced wearily around at the ashen faces of her family.

They were gathered together in the great hall to urgently to discuss the latest news from England. The king had finally granted William one last audience in the Spring, and he had reluctantly returned to England as demanded, along with a messenger from Walter assuring John that this time William would comply with his wishes. However, unaccountably, instead of meeting with the king at Hereford as planned, William had fled instead to Wales. Once there, he'd immediately rallied together those men who were still faithful to him and set about harrying the countryside in yet another attempt to seize back his lands by force.

'But why would he do such a thing? Matilda whispered looking from Will to Reginald, and then to Walter who had just joined them. 'Why can he not see that fighting the king again will only make matters worse?'

Wordlessly, Reginald put an arm across her thin shoulders and guided her to a seat, where she sat feeling the fear wrap itself around her like an iron band.

It was Walter who finally spoke, his normally pale face showing blotches of angry red along the cheekbones. 'Apparently de Ferrers eventually interceded and managed to persuade William to meet with the king in Pembroke on his way to Haverfordwest, where his forces are gathering to leave for Ireland. It seems that after much negotiation your husband promised to pay John the sum of forty thousand marks.'

'Forty thousand marks!' Matilda exclaimed in a shocked voice. 'William knows full well that we don't have that kind of money!'

'Well, that's as maybe,' Walter said, turning to look at her with pity. 'But there's something else you should know. John also told William that he will only deal with you from now on. He claims that it is you, and you alone, who is responsible for the debt. In fact, he went so far as to extract a promise from William that he would return to Ireland with him and make arrangements to meet you in Meath. But instead, William fled again and resumed his campaign in the Marches. Seemingly, with the support of Llewellyn ap Iorwerth, the Prince of Gwynedd.'

Behind Matilda, Hugh entered the hall his face set in haggard lines. 'It's too late for all that now, Walter! All is lost! I have just been told that King John's fleet is about to set sail from Haverfordwest as we speak – it appears we are all to pay for William's mistakes! I am also told that it is Annora's own husband's father who has provided men for the expedition, caring not, it seems, that it is his own family they are pursuing,'

'No,' Annora whispered, turning her stricken face away and going to stand by the hearth. Matilda, mortally afraid now and powerless in the face of such news, simply covered her face with her hands and let out a little sob.

Groping for a chair, Walter sat down. 'We must be prepared. We need to flee now – before John and his fleet set foot on Irish soil,' he said, looking around the hall desperately for escape.

There's still a chance that he might not, though? Despite the fact that he has gathered his forces,' Matilda whispered, looking first at him and then up at Hugh, still grasping at straws.

Walter looked at her incredulously. Then standing, he turned on his heels and strode from the room with orders to his steward to start organising their retreat from Trim immediately.

Chapter 32

The Port of Waterford, 20th June 1210

Crossing the Irish Sea had been a much more pleasant experience than King John remembered from his past expeditions to Ireland, and now that he was here he felt elated – like a fox that had got wind of a rabbit and was ready for the chase. Oh yes, he was impatient to be on the road and in pursuit of his quarry. In his mind's eye he could see her standing before him. Matilda de Braose. He shivered. Once he had captured her and defeated the de Lacys it would be alright. Then he would have banished his ghosts and she would no longer haunt him.

Witch. Sorceress ...

Impatiently, he pushed the voice away and turned to William the Marshall standing alongside him. 'How many days journey until we make Dublin?'

'A sennight, I should say,' the Marshall said, eyeing the bands of Flemish mercenaries and foot soldiers that now occupied the wooden key with distaste. John smiled. He knew that William had not wanted to answer the summons that had arrived on his doorstep the previous year. The one that demanded that, *he,* personally attend King John in the business of making preparations for an expedition to Ireland. An expedition in which they would hunt down and capture the de Braoses who, even knowing that they were outlaws, William had given shelter to whilst they were on the run to the de Lacys in Meath. Indeed, John knew that the conflict between himself and the Marshall was not over yet, for William deeply resented the fact that following his act of treason, John had forced him to return to court to account publicly for his actions, leaving his lands open to invasion by his rival Meilyr Fitz Henry, who had then burned the town of New Ross. He also knew that the Marshall now harboured a deep resentment for his wife. Not only for her betrayal of the de Braoses when they were in his shelter, but also for the fact that it was Isabel that had written to him in England saying they regretted their actions in shielding the outlaws, and that William wished once again to be his loyal servant. And so, here the Marshall was, cursing both his King and his wife, but knowing that to refuse the king in his request to hunt the de Braoses down would be to commit suicide along with the de Lacys.

Turning away from the Marshall, John stood fiddling with the jewel encrusted hilt of his dagger as he watched more of his men embarked unsteadily from the ships, trying to find their land legs. The din was enormous as sailors shouted down to the quay to make room for the coffers that were being lowered. Some were packed with his personal possessions: jewels, gold, silks and furs, but other, much larger chests, contained swords, longbows, chain mail, and the countless other items of war that he had deemed necessary for his men. He had not wanted to leave the acquisition of anything to chance. He had come prepared to lay siege to the de Lacys.

'Here comes Noir.' It was the Marshall again, for once looking impressed as John's great black war horse was led blindfolded down the gangplank by his groom. John nodded, pleased to see that the beast seemed unfazed by the journey. Once on dry land the groom paused to remove the blindfold. Then, when the horse was ready, he led him over for inspection with an undisguised look of relief on his face. For had anything happened to the horse, everybody knew that the groom would have been the first to suffer for it.

Much later, as the train of men trailed out of the docks, the foot soldiers and the overloaded carts bringing up the rear, they were met by John de Grey with a company of Irish troops. As John greeted the man, he noticed the Marshall watching him closely. His jaw was clenched, his eyes unfriendly, unguarded. For a moment their eyes met. They had once been friends, but now he could see that William thought him mad; thought him a cruel and vengeful king, and all because he could not understand the all-consuming hate that had led him to muster an army on Irish soil to capture one woman and her family. Then suddenly the shutters came down on the Marshall's face and, giving John a short, mocking bow, he turned and climbed onto his horse.

Moments later he was heading in the direction of Dublin, his golden spurs winking in the sun.

Trim Castle, Ireland, 25th June 1210

We were gathered in the hall where Hugh's messenger stood panting with exertion after a hard ride, armed with the latest information on the king's progress. 'It's the worst news, I'm afraid. King John is now in Dublin residing with the Marshall,' he said after taking a few gulps of the wine proffered to him by Hugh's squire.

Hugh ran his hand across his face tiredly. It was obvious that he had not really expected John to carry out his threat of invading Ireland. It seemed impossible that he had got this far and so quickly.

Walter walked into the hall. 'I have sent five of my principle tenants to Dublin,' he listed their names quickly, ticking them off on his fingers as he went. 'They have instructions to place my castles and land in the king's hands. He can do as he wishes with them!'

'God damn it, man, why did you do that! That is to give in to the king's tyranny once and for all!' Hugh shouted, making me jump and sending the dogs scurrying under a table.

'I had no choice,' Walter said, wiping sweat from his brow with a napkin. 'Our men are deserting us and flocking to the king. Word is out that half the Irish lords are in bed with John. Donough Cairbrech O'Brian met him at Waterford and got the grant for the castle and lordship of Carrickogunnell. Once rumour spread that King John is being generous with Irish lordships, they flocked to him in droves. We are lost, Hugh. Face it. Our troops are deserting us and, unlike King John, more are not flocking to join us!'

For a moment there was silence. I could see the desperation in the two men's eyes. Then Walter turned away to address Matilda who was huddled in a corner with Margaret, Annora, Maude and the children. 'Pack, but bring little. We will ride for Carrickfergus Castle immediately. From there we will get a boat to France. Or Scotland. Whichever is available.'

'You must hand me over to John.' Matilda, rousing herself at last, stumbled her way forward to where Walter and Hugh stood. 'It's the only way, can't you see! It's me he wants, Walter. Take the children to Carrickfergus. I beg of you. Get them to safety. At least that way you too will have a chance!' She swayed for a moment and I thought she would faint, but between us Walter and I grasped her around the waist and led her towards a chair.

'*No!*' Margaret pushed me aside and dropped to her knees at Matilda's feet. 'No, we will not desert you, Mother,' she said, turning her eyes imploringly to her husband.'

'Nay, we shall not leave you to the king's mercy,' Walter said sarcastically. 'Despite that you are the instrument of our destruction. Go now. Pack your bags so that we may leave with haste.' And with that he turned angrily on his heel and strode from the hall to organise our departure.

Only when Hugh had hurried after him did Matilda and I begin to organise the tearful group of women and collect what little belongings we had. Walter would not have us weighed down unnecessarily, and so the sad sum of our baggage when we eventually finished was a small pile of leather satchels, a couple of coffers, and a few battered cooking pots for good measure. Finally, under the cover of night, we left the castle. Will and Reginald led, with Maude trotting disconsolately behind, Walter in her arms and a tearful John sat in front of her. Walter followed, with Gilbert riding a sturdy pony, and Margaret squeezed into a cart with the remaining children and their nurses. Annora, Matilda and I brought up the rear, along with some of Walter's trusted soldiers. Hugh had refused to accompany us, saying that he would prefer to face the king than flee. And so, it was on bad terms that the brothers parted.

As we crossed the moat into the outer ward of the castle, I saw Margaret looking back at the gatehouse.

There were tears in her eyes as she raised a hand in final farewell. She was beginning to understand, as we had understood for so long, that Mistress Destiny was never to be denied. Mistress Destiny was unwavering in her ruthlessness. And careless of those that got in the way of her plans ...

Carrickfergus Castle, Ireland, July 1210

Matilda stood at the window and gazed down over the lough. In the distance, a flock of gulls wheeled and dived above several small fishing vessels approaching the quay with the daily catch, a churning mass of silver in the bottom of their boats. Turning away, she crossed herself and prayed once more that such a boat could be found to take them to France where they might find safety with Giles. But no word had come that this had yet been achieved, and the tension in the castle was almost unbearable.

For perhaps the millionth time she wondered why William had deserted them and taken up arms against the king. He must know that that would only make John more determined to capture her. Picking up an old mantle of his that Reginald had kept she fingered the material. She had never liked William. He had always been a cruel and vicious man. But now her hate for him gnawed like a canker in her stomach, and hurriedly she put it down lest it reminded her of worse things about her husband.

After a while the door opened and Will strode into the chamber. Fear was etched deeply in his thin lines of his face, and he looked like he was going to be sick.

'What is it?' Matilda asked, her voice rising in alarm as she ran to him and frantically shook his arm.

'The king has made it to Dundalk,' Will said. 'Hugh is burning his castles. Worse still, many of Walter's soldiers who made promises of fealty to him have deserted their posts and joined King John's troops.'

Matilda swayed and all colour left her face. Quickly, Will put his arm around her skeletal shoulders and guided her to a chair by the window where she sat shaking while he went to pour her a goblet of wine. The smell of the lough drifted in from below; salty and heavy, mingling with the screams of the children as Annora and Margaret chased them round and round the bailey and, in the distance, she could see the hot, still air hanging languidly over the top of the hills. Everything seemed normal, and for a moment she wondered what it would be like to be a nobody: a peasant in a field, or a milkmaid in a cowshed. Anybody, but the most wanted woman in the land.

'Walter has doubled the lookout now, for word is that King John is marching towards Carrickfergus as we speak,' Will's voice cut through her misery. 'I just wish we could get a ship. It's not for want of trying, Mother, but each time we try they ask exorbitant prices that we cannot meet. Still, Walter says that he's had word that Hugh is making his way to join us – he managed to sell a lot of plate and some of his decent horses for coin, and so we will be able to pay eventually and get out of this God forsaken place.'

Matilda sighed as, not for the first time, she anxiously scanned the far side of the Lough for any sign of the king's troops. The sun was dipping in the sky and she had to strain to see. Her eyesight wasn't as good as it once was, and neither was her health she thought as she laid a hand on her breast where her heart fluttered like a timid bird.

'You can't sit up here forever, Mother. You must come downstairs and eat with us now, otherwise you will not have the strength to endure the journey when it does come,' Will said, his fear turning to compassion as he saw her distress. 'We will eventually get transport to France where we will be safe – King John cannot pursue us forever, you know,' he added, feeling her tremble as he reached down to help her stand.

For a moment Matilda stilled, then she turned her troubled face up to his. 'I fear that he can, Will,' she said sadly. 'I fear that he can.'

I dreamed *the* dream again. The dream that I always have: the one in which Matilda stands on the edge of a deep precipice, her arms outstretched beseechingly to me as I desperately try to wade through a sea of thick sticky treacle to reach her.

In my dream, I see King John laughing. He is so clear now that I am afraid to look at him for there is hate etched on each and every one of his features; it oozes from his pores in a tide of stinking rottenness that spreads around him, engulfing everything and anyone that it touches. He laughs again. It's a cruel laugh that twists his face making him look ugly, and once again I feel a band of fear grip me so tight that I can barely breathe, and his blue eyes glitter with such malice that I am afraid. Afraid now for myself as well as her.

And as I watch he makes her dance. She is dancing with her son Will, and the music is the devil's music. It is the devil's jig. Faster it goes, the devil's jig. Faster, and faster still, as they spin and wheel nearer and nearer to the darkness that is the precipice, until I feel dizzy just watching them. Such is my fear for them that I cry out loud, but the words are stuck in my throat as is the manner of dreams, and King John looks at me with his cold, cold blue eyes and he smiles that cruel, cruel smile, for he knows that I am powerless to stop them dancing to his tune.

I woke suddenly with Annora shaking me. Her lovely blue eyes were fixed on mine anxiously, and for a moment they reminded me of King John's eyes. But then I realise that, unlike John's, they are not cold blue eyes, instead they are full of warmth and love, not hate and jealousy and greed. For Annora is a child of the light, in the same way that King John is a child of the dark. And suddenly everything seems so much clearer to me ...

✟

Carrickfergus Castle, Ireland, August 1210

Hugh stood in the great hall and looked around dully. He was a shadow of the man he'd once been, and where once they had been merry, his eyes, when he turned them on Matilda, were now like the shattered windows to his soul. The strain of the last few weeks had taken its toll, and he was ruined. We are all ruined, Matilda thought, as she stared numbly across at her sons who stood huddled together over a map, urgently planning their escape with Walter and the only three knights that had remained loyal to them over the course of the last few months.

Sighing, she turned away and crossed to the window. High above the keep, a gull wheeled and shrieked, before sweeping down to join its fellow gulls dipping and diving above the hidden shoals of fish in the dark waters of the lough. Beyond them the little harbour lay still, the water unmoving in the uncustomary August heat. But still Matilda felt cold, for news had come with Hugh that King John was a day's ride from Carrickfergus. Only a day hovered between them and their capture. She shivered. John had done the impossible. In his attempt to capture her he had subdued Ireland, ruined the de Lacys, and brought the Marshall back to his side. He was truly earning his Earldom, the Marshall, she thought bitterly, wondering that he had ever taken the trouble to help them at all. Rubbing a hand over her face tiredly, she turned towards the doors, steeling herself for more bad news as yet another anxious messenger entered the hall.

For a while the messenger conversed with the men, throwing the odd worried look her way now and then. Then suddenly they seemed to come to a decision, and moments later Will was at her side. 'Come, Mother,' he said gently. 'Hugh has brought enough coin for us to get passage to Scotland, but not enough for passage to France, and the messenger warns that John will be here by the end of day. It's the best we can do for now with John so close,' he added apologetically.

Stunned, Matilda pushed the hair out of her face and stared at Will. 'Scotland?' She whispered. 'But surely that is too dangerous ... To place ourselves back within John's reach in England, I mean ... Surely that is to put ourselves in mortal danger!'

'It is the best we can do, Mother! We have no coin, no means –

'*No!*' Matilda's voice had risen to a shriek.

'Mother!' Annora, hearing her above the din as Walter threw orders to anyone who would listen to collect their belongings, made her way across the hall. 'Mother. Please calm yourself and think. It is the only way. Think of the children! We have friends there who would help ...' Annora tailed off, her voice wavering as if remembering that those that they had called friends, the Marshalls, and others, even members her own family, had already deserted them.

'Scotland, though,' Matilda whispered, running her hand across her face in despair. 'Can we not afford passage to France?' she pleaded. 'We would be safer there with Giles and the girls.'

'I know!' Will said fiercely. 'I know. And I wish that we could. But you must understand that we have no choice now. It's Scotland or submit to the king. We simply cannot afford passage for France. And I for one,' he said, throwing an anguished look over her head at Annora, 'am pretty sure I know which fate I prefer!'

It was dark by the time our small party left by the postern gate and headed towards the quay. The water was black and deep, and Matilda gripped my arm tightly when she saw the first signs of fires being lit across the Lough. There was no doubt that if we had not made the decision to leave now, by morning King John would be laying siege to the castle.

Walter glanced around him fearfully as he began to lead the way, keeping to the shadows of the castle wall, with Margaret clutching their two babies to her chest and Gilbert trailing behind, holding his nurse's hand. Moments later Maud followed with John, Giles, Phillip and Will carrying Walter nestled gently against his shoulder. Matilda, Hugh, Annora and I came last with our small escort of knights carrying what provisions and baggage we could manage between us, picking our way carefully through the rocks towards where the little fishing boat that Walter had hired waited in the shadows of the harbour.

The skipper of the fishing boat was a shrewd, taciturn looking little man, with a mass of wrinkles etched onto a weather-beaten face, and eyes that darted everywhere. After inspecting the purse that Walter handed him, he nodded to a pile of blankets in a heap at the broad prow of vessel and turned to watch impassively as Hugh directed the knights to help us on board. It seemed like an age before the two sailors, the sum total of his crew, had cast the moorings off and coiled the rope neatly on the flat floor of the little boat and we on our way.

Nobody dared speak as the boat slowly nosed its way out towards the sea. In the distance we could see the light of hundreds of camp fires on the horizon and hear the shouts and laughter of the men gathered around them as it was carried on the wind towards us. Softly, Margaret began to sob. Above us the castle loomed and, where once it had offered safe haven, now it hung huge and menacing in the darkness, like a hungry beast ready to pounce. Only Hugh and Walter stood staring back as it slowly retreated into the distance, twin looks of anger and regret on their faces.

Then suddenly a strong gust caught the sail and we were moving in earnest, leaving the dark rocky coast of Ireland behind us. Heading for Scotland. Above us the stars winked eerily in the inky sky, and in our wake the echo of Mistress Destiny's laugh floated on the wind ...

Matilda couldn't sleep. Instead, she stood watching the frothy white crests of water fanning out at the rear of the craft as it cut through the deep channels of the Irish Sea. Above her, the stars shone bright in the dark, cloudless sky, and apart from the odd splash of a fish alongside the boat, all was quiet. After a while she glanced at Annora. She was asleep on the blankets with her long fair hair fanning her thin oval face. Occasionally it lifted in the breeze, and Matilda was reminded of the wings of the swans that had floated on the river Adur. Beside Annora the children slept with the ease of those that are too young to worry, and a few feet away from them Margaret and Maude sat with the babies and their nurses and, as Matilda watched, one of them lifted Edigia to her breast and settled her down to feed, crooning to her gently as her little mouth worked unconsciously on her breast.

The men had spent a lot of time staring worriedly behind them as if expecting at any moment to see the bows of King John's ship loom out of the darkness full of mercenaries with the moonlight glinting on their lances ready to capture them. But now they sat hunched on a pile of ropes curled at back of the broad vessel having a quiet discussion as to what they would do when they reached Scotland, and after a while Matilda went to join them.

'The best thing to do when we get there is to enquire about passage to France,' she heard Will saying as she approached them.

'For Christ's sake, Will, you know as well as I do that we don't have enough for passage to France, and what little we do have will have to be used to acquire horses!'

Matilda hesitated, she could see Reginald's eyes glinting in the light of the lantern hanging above him as he spoke.

They were desperate.

'I say we should head for the Marches and join with Father? Persuade him to meet the king again and offer terms. Mother could retrieve the gold plate and jewels she hid before we fled Hay ...'

'*No!*' Matilda's voice cut in on the conversation, stopping it abruptly. 'No.' She repeated when they all looked at her. 'It is too late for that. It's no longer a question of money. No amount of money or gold plate would appease the king now. And as for William,' she paused, 'well I can never forgive him for deserting us in our hour of need,' she finished bitterly.

Matilda hadn't realised that she had spoken so loudly but hearing her, the skipper handed the steering oar to his pilot and crossed over to the little group. 'You'll be looking for horses when you arrive,' he observed, and although his enquiry seemed innocent enough, it held a hint of menace and his dark eyes darted about constantly as if seeking something, and Matilda quickly made a note not to sleep until they had their feet on dry land in case he planned to rob them of what little they had left. Will obviously had the same thought, for his hand went to the hilt of his sword as if to check it was still there, before looking around to making sure that the guards were still at their posts.

'Well if you are,' the skipper continued nonchalantly. 'Ask for Red Derrick in the village - he'll sell you a couple of old nags for a high price!' He wheezed with laughter at this, showing a row of ragged brown teeth with large gaps between them, then he held out the stone jar of rum he was clutching towards the men. 'You'll make for England then ... when you get there, I mean?' he asked, watching as Hugh and Will took several large gulps each before handing it back.

'We have no idea yet,' Matilda said before anyone else could open their mouth to speak. 'And even if we did, then *you* would be the last person that we would tell. Now, kindly leave us to our business whilst you get on with yours,' she finished tersely, knowing that if they gave him any information about their destination - even if they knew it - he would have no qualms about sailing back to Ireland and selling it to King John. For a moment the old man looked like he would say more, but instead he merely grinned, and turning he disappeared back into the shadows to resume his steering leaving them standing staring nervously after him.

After that progress was slow because of a lack of wind, but still the little boat cut through the water like glass carrying them nearer to their destination, and for that Matilda was thankful although she was beginning to feel distinctly unsafe.

'I'll be glad to be off that odious little man's boat,' Will muttered. Then looking to the horizon, he said. 'At least the dawn is coming – we must be near the Rhins of Galloway by now, for I think I see land.'

Matilda turned her head and followed his gaze. In the middle distance the sky was turning a misty grey tinged with pink, and she could just make the faint outline of the rugged Scottish coast rising out of the sea before them, and suddenly she found she was crying. Crying for all that they had lost. Crying for her children, and the fear of what would become of them in the future. Crying because of the ache that lay deep in the pit of her stomach. The ache which would never leave her, and which she would carry with her to the grave.

Chapter 33

Degannwy Castle, North Wales, August 1210

William stood high up on the ramparts of Llewellyn's castle, shielding his eyes with his hands as he gazed in the direction of Ireland. Even now, even though he knew that they were losing the fight, he knew that he would never return there. He knew that he would never return to try and save his beautiful, feckless, unfaithful wife. In his mind's eye he saw her staring back at him, her green, cat like eyes full of reproach. He shivered. King John was on Irish soil in pursuit of her and he wondered if she was afraid. He knew that he would be and that made him angry, but then he knew what King John was capable of. He gripped the edge of the stone battlements as he remembered a pair of wide, grey eyes fringed with dark lashes. Grey eyes full of fear as King John plunged a red-hot poker into them, whilst he and de Breauté stood by and did nothing. Suddenly he felt sick with remorse, remembering the terrible screams and the smell of burning flesh, and felt again the weight of the boy's dead body as he and de Breauté disposed of it in the Seine. He would go to the chapel and pray. Perhaps if he prayed hard enough, God would forgive him for his part in the boy's murder.

But what of King John? Will he forgive you for your wife's outburst ...?

William pushed the voice away; his anger rising once again to the fore. All this suffering was Matilda's fault of course. She had ingratiated herself with the king, and then she had fallen out of his favour for reasons he did not understand. But it was her outburst that had brought about his current predicament. Of course, he didn't consider that his own sins of pride and greed might also have played a part in his downfall. William de Braose was not that much changed.

Port Patrick, Scotland, August 1210

The sun was high in the clear blue Scottish sky, a backdrop to the rolling hills that curved protectively around the wide harbour. Margaret, Annora, and I were helping the nurses with the babies who were tired and fractious after the long boat trip in the stifling August heat. Above us, the gulls shrieked like harridans, fighting each other as they swooped to gobble up the odd fish that had escaped from the nets of a fisherman unloading his catch, and now flapped on the quay in a bid for freedom and the sea. A bit further down the quay, Matilda stood watching the little fishing boat sail away into the distant blue horizon, glad to see the back of both it and its skipper, whilst beside her, her grandsons stood solemnly clinging to her skirts, gazing up at their father who was deep in discussion with Hugh, Walter and Reginald about the acquisition of horses and food. Only Maude sat alone, perched on the edge of a small coffer, looking desolately out to sea.

When at last the little boat had disappeared from sight, Matilda pulled the wimple from her hair and began to use it instead to wipe the sweat from her face. I followed her gaze as she regarded the smattering of small, chalk white cottages that wound around the harbour, and the half a dozen or so sheds where the local fishermen stored their nets and pots. After a while a small boy approached us, and in exchange for a few pennies he handed Will a piece of waxed cloth containing four herrings and a handful of prawns, and for another penny a plump fishwife sitting outside one of the cottages gutted and grilled them on her open fire. I watched Matilda scrape the last of the white flesh from the bones with her small eating knife and hand it to John as we sat under a tree sheltering from the sun. We could have been any little family out for the day to get the sea air. But we were not. And I was afraid. For despite the sun blazing high in the sky, I had seen the dark shadows slowly gathering around us ... *watching ... waiting ... whispering ...*

Matilda obviously felt it too, for she suddenly stilled and looked around fearfully. Then her attention was diverted by a loud wail as a seagull swooped down and relieved Giles of his last morsel of herring. And the moment of tension was gone.

Seeing that we had finished eating, the fishwife crossed over to us bearing a pitcher and two wooden cups. I could see that they couldn't understand each other, for the fishwife spoke only Scots, but Matilda accepted the offering and thanked her in English when she would not accept payment. We drank the mead in silence, passing it around and savouring the underlying taste of heather. Matilda looked almost content as she watched Reginald drain the last of it. I knew she was enjoying her freedom, thinking that all we had to do now was to find horses and a safe house with one of the many barons in the North who were still opposed to John, but still I could not shift the butterflies of apprehension that were gathering in my stomach: I wanted to tell them to stop. To tell them not to get horses, but instead to get on another boat to France. Now! Immediately! Before it was all too late! But each time I opened my mouth the words would not come, they simply remained lodged in my throat. And so, I sat helplessly by saying nothing. And knowing everything. For I was the seventh child of the seventh child. And I had the Sight ...

It was mid-afternoon before it was finally agreed among the menfolk that the women and children would, under the protection of Will and our three trusted knights, travel onto the shrine of St Ninian's. Matilda had expressed a desire to make the pilgrimage, saying that she felt it would bring us luck if she had the blessing of the Saint to sustain her on her journey. And so, it was on a whim that it was decided, for whilst we were eating Reginald had managed to acquire a rather old pony and cart upon which we would travel. He had also brought some supplies in the way of food and drink which, together with our belongings, he had already loaded onto it. I listened fearfully as Will told us that Reginald and Hugh were to make their way to the castle that lay in the distance to see if they could purchase some decent horseflesh, leaving Walter to set about making discreet enquires in order to try and find out where the occupant's sympathies lay regarding King John. When they had concluded their business, they would then catch us up on the road to the shrine, Will said, shielding his eyes and staring worriedly out to sea as another boat approached.

My head told me that Will's plan was all very straightforward, but somehow my heart told me it was not. And so, I watched them leave with my head buzzing and my tongue stuck fast to the roof of my mouth, desperately wanting to call out and tell them to stop. Wanting to do anything to change their destiny. For I had a terrible certainty that the wheel of fate was turning and we would never see them again…

Matilda stood and watched as the three men left on foot for the dusty path that led to the castle. Something didn't feel right, and for a moment she was tempted to shout at them to stay. But suddenly they were gone. Disappearing round the bend. A hazy mirage in the shimmering summer heat, and before she knew it Will was at her side and helping her to clamber onto the cart.

'They will be fine, Mother,' he said climbing onto the cart beside her as she turned and gazed back in their direction once more. 'As soon as they have word of the occupants of the castle and have procured us decent horses, they will return to us.' Suddenly he caught Matilda to him and held her tightly. 'This is our reality now, Mother. We have not come this far for John to catch us yet,' he said fiercely. Then, as swiftly as he had caught her to him, he released her, and with a deft flick of the reins he bid the pony to begin the journey to the Holy Saint.

The road was clear, and they had been travelling for a while when Margaret announced that the little ones needed to visit the bushes. Moments later she had disappeared into the undergrowth in a rustle of leaves and twigs with the children trailing disconsolately beside her. With a sigh, Will handed the reins over to Maude and announced that he would walk with Walter's knights for a bit. Watching him go, Matilda decided she too needed to stretch her legs, and so she stepped down and looked around. It was still. Hardly a cloud moved in the sky. But suddenly, standing alone, she found herself almost preternaturally aware of the strange, almost ethereal landscape that surrounded her: the rolling hills were topped with purple heather, and all around her the chirp of the sparrows vied with the sound of the bees bobbing lazily among the wild flowers. It was still unbearably hot, and in the cart Annora had rigged together a make shift sun canopy using some branches and old sacks under which she and the babies dozed contentedly. But still, there was something eerie about the place that she could not put her finger on.

For a moment she hesitated. She felt dizzy. Everything seemed to have tilted of its axis. Then suddenly there was a loud buzzing in her head and, although she couldn't be certain, she thought she could hear the sound of hooves thudding on the hard earth and the jingle of harnesses in the distance.

'There are riders approaching!' It was Will, shouting as he ran to her side, shielding his eyes with his hand as he indicated to a dust cloud on the horizon moving rapidly towards them. 'Lots of them by the look of it! And not from the right direction for it to be Reginald and the others!' Matilda, jarred out of her trance like state, grabbed the arm of one of the knights who had run forward and was shading his eyes, trying to pick out some clue as to who they were.

'We know no one in Scotland,' Matilda said in a shaky voice.

'Hush, Mother. Just remember we're simply a group of pilgrims to them. Nothing more,' Will said, reaching instinctively for his sword.

Quickly, Matilda stepped back behind the knights who had formed a line in front of her. Her heart was beating hard. She felt helpless, as though she was falling. Nothing seemed real anymore; it was as if she was someone else and this was happening to them and not her, and she began to look around wildly for escape.

But it was too late. The horsemen were close enough now to make out the blood red chevron emblazoned on their tunics and the hilts of their swords glinting in the sun. 'Some Scottish lord's mesnie,' Will muttered under his breath. 'Move to the side of the road,' he said. 'They must have no reason to slow. And slapping the rump of the pony, he quickly led it as far off the path as he dared without the wheels of the cart getting lodged in one of the deep, dry ruts along the bank from which it might not be freed.

As the riders drew nearer the small group, the leader held up his hand and his men came to a rearing halt behind him. He had coarse, copper coloured hair and tawny brown eyes set under bushy eyebrows. The rest of his face was obscured by a ferocious looking beard, but what Matilda could see of his features beneath it were set in a puzzled frown as he regarded the bedraggled group of strangers before him.

'Well, well, well, it's Lady de Braose, is it not?' he said, drawing the name out in a lazy, Scottish drawl. 'And here was us travelling to port to make ship to join my cousin King John at Carrickfergus, and I find myself lucky enough to intercept ye on the same road. That's verra fortunate for my cousin, I think. And I canna help think that it's verra fortunate for me, too!' He threw back his head and laughed delightedly, showing a row of decaying brown teeth. Behind him his men milled about looking uncertainly between their Lord and the other occupants of the road. Matilda looked around fearfully, her eyes finally fixing themselves on Annora, sitting as still as a statue in the cart with her eyes on Margaret who'd just reappeared out of the bushes with the boys. Nobody spoke. Only Maude, who sat alongside the nurses huddled with Petronella on her lap, dared to shush the babies fearfully when they began to cry.

'Please allow me to introduce myself to ye,' the copper haired man said, leaning forward in his saddle, his face so close to Matilda's that she could feel his breath warm on her cheek and smell the decay. 'I'm Duncan of Carrick, King John's cousin and devoted friend, forbye, at your service, my lady!' he said.

Matilda felt her heart pounding in her breast, and the pressure of the red-hot blood rushing to her ears made her sway. Immediately, Will put his arm about her. 'You are mistaken, sir. We are but simple pilgrims travelling to the shrine of St Ninian's,' he said affably, hoping to deflect the man's gaze away from his scrutiny of them.

After a few moments, Matilda gathered herself together as best she could and, shielding her eyes, she looked up at him. 'Sir, it is true, we are but simple pilgrims on our way to the shrine of St Ninian's - to pray that my daughter be cured from the chills that beleaguer her each winter. Pray let us proceed, sir. I beg of you. As a good Christian man please let us pass so that we may make her well.'

'Aye, my lady,' he said wryly, 'and I'm a wee bitty haggis! Noo, I kent well enough who you are when I first slapped eyes on ye,' Duncan said more firmly. 'I was just taken by surprise seeing ye on the road like a gaggle o' geese waiting for Christmas. So now, let's have no more games, aye, and weel all get on well enough,' he finished.

There was a long silence in which he drew his sword and rested it across his saddle as he regarded Matilda from under his bushy brows. Will, too, rested his hand on the hilt of his sword, reluctant to draw it just yet for the odds were clearly against him, but eager not to lose face in the threat of a fight.

'Your hair is the giveaway, ye really should never have left it uncovered, I recognised it at once from my days at court,' Duncan said conversationally, producing an old leading rein from his saddle bag with his free hand. 'Aye,' he said. 'Ye are most certainly the Lady de Braose that my cousin is seeking. And ye will now have the pleasure of joining us on ship whilst we return ye to Carrickfergus where King John can confirm my findings!' Then, lifting his sword arm, he signalled to his men and before they could react the little group was surrounded.

For a moment nobody moved. Then Will leapt back and, pushing Matilda behind him, he pulled his weapon from its sheath with an almighty roar. The screech of metal as Carrick's men drew their swords in response galvanised Walter's knights into action, but they were outnumbered and one of them took a blow to his arm, cutting it through to the bone, before he was run through mercilessly by the sword. Behind Matilda, Annora screamed as she was plucked from the cart and hauled over the saddle in front of one of the mounted men. Maude too let out a cry as she was dealt with similarly, leaving Margaret and the nurses to fight the men who were trying to stop them fleeing into the undergrowth with the children. The fight went on a few moments more before Will was finally knocked to the floor, stunned by a blow to the head with the flat of a sword. Matilda ran to him as the remaining two knights flung down their weapons and raised their hands in a gesture of defeat. She could feel the hot tears streaming down her face as she fell to her knees beside him, wondering where the others when they needed them, but at the same time knowing that it would have made little difference had they been there, for the might of Carrick's men was too great to fight.

Satisfied that he had everything under control, Carrick signalled to one of his men to pull her to her feet and, dropping out of his saddle, he cut the leading rein into pieces and personally bound her hands behind her back. Then he knelt by Will and did the same to him before he could regain consciousness. Finally, he gave the order for his men to secure the rest of the women and children. Only when Will was deposited onto the cart, and Matilda was seated on the horse in front of him, did he issue instructions for the party to make its way back to Port Patrick where they would join a ship and be transported back to Carrickfergus. Only this time as prisoners of King John.

Matilda looked around numbly one last time at the purple heather topped hills that were Scotland, knowing that even if she survived her ordeal she would never return there, for the horror of her treatment at the hands of Duncan Carrick would stay with her forever. Far behind them there was a rumble of thunder, followed a sudden flash of lightning, and somewhere in the distance she thought she heard the sound of laughter ...

Chapter 34

Portpatrick, Ireland, August 1210

It was late afternoon. The little party of prisoners sat huddled miserably in a group under some trees, watching Duncan of Carrick's men throw up a makeshift camp. Each of them had been interrogated separately by Duncan. It had not taken him long to extract the information from a tearful Maude that their party had travelled with the de Lacys and another of Matilda's sons who were still at large. Down in the harbour, a ship bobbed lazily on the water. Above them, a gull shrieked. Matilda had an urge to do the same. They had been so near to freedom. She felt tears pricking the back of her eyes, but instead of giving into them she dashed them angrily away. She would not let them see her cry.

After a while Duncan strode over and stood regarding them steadily, his narrow, tawny brown eyes dark in the dull afternoon light. 'I'm surprised ye didn't head for the safety of France,' he commented. 'Old Garbh is King John's man now,' he said, referring to the aging King William of Scotland. 'He claimed he received a divine warning not to go to battle wi' John again. So, I dinna expect you would have got support from him - if that's what ye were here for. He's no' too eager to stir up another hornet's nest wi' the King o' England.'

Then, changing the subject, he looked around him. 'Your companions canna ha' got far. I shall send out a search party at first light. We canna leave for Ireland yet anyway as I dinna think the tide is right, or so the ship's master says,' he said, shielding his eyes as he looked down at a ship bobbing on the water by the quay: the very same one that had been approaching the port as they left earlier that morning. Then, nodding to them dismissively, he spun on his heels and went to bark orders at a group of his men hopelessly attempting to erect a canvas tent in the middle of the field.

They spent several days guarded noon and night at the makeshift camp, whilst Duncan sent troops galloping the length and breadth of Galloway, scouting the land and making enquiries as to the whereabouts of the de Lacys and Reginald. Matilda was relieved when each evening he returned without them, hoping that they had found safe harbour with friends despite Duncan's prophecy.

At last, as dusk fell two days later, Matilda found herself being summoned to Duncan's tent. 'I trust ye are well,' he said, handing her a goblet of wine and indicating to a chair standing by a small trestle table strewn with ink, quills and parchment. 'It seems that Reginald and his companions have escaped me,' he continued, regarding her face impassively. 'Although we have William, and for now that will have to suffice.'

Matilda lowered her eyes and said nothing. Although they had been separated from Will, she knew he was being treated well, though for what purpose she wondered bitterly – for them to be returned to John to deal with as he saw fit.

'Verra well,' Duncan said without demur, seeming to read her mind. 'I have no alternative but to return ye to Carrickfergus. I have news that the castle has fallen to the king. I am sure that he is eager to renew his acquaintance with ye.'

Matilda shivered despite the cloying heat of the tent as John's cruel face came unbidden in her mind. He would have no mercy she knew. Then draining her cup with a shaky hand, she nodded to Duncan and walked dazedly out into the open air.

The next day they were on a ship and speeding back through the Rhins of Galloway towards Ireland. Once underway Duncan had them released from their fetters and allowed them to roam the deck under the watchful eyes of several big, burly guards. Matilda remembered with humiliation the look of pity on the fishwife's face as she watched them being prodded like cattle onto the waiting ship. But still, she knew that there would be worse humiliation before long, for she would have to fall on her knees and beg King John to give them one last chance.

Carrickfergus Castle was bustling with activity when the little party was ushered into the great hall. From the dais, King John regarded them impassively with his cold, blue eyes, taking in the bruises on Will's face and arms and the bandage around his head. By his side, a huge grey wolf hound lounged, its tongue lolling from its mouth whilst it panted heavily. Outside, the rain poured relentlessly down. Wearily Matilda ran a hand through her hair, conscious that it was still wet and tangled from the sea spray, and she wondered what John must be thinking of her now, before wondering why she even cared.

It was several minutes before he rose and, dismissing all the servants save his clerk, he crossed over to where they stood. Immediately Matilda fell to her knees. The others followed suit.

'So, what have we here,' he mused. 'A bunch of fugitives brought to heel – except that we don't yet have your husband, madam. Nor yours,' he added, addressing Margaret, 'for it seems he had a lucky escape with his brother. It's of little consequence, though,' he continued almost conversationally, 'as I have confiscated their lands. If they show their faces again I shall have them hanged as traitors.'

Margaret let out a little sob.

'Still,' John continued, ignoring Margaret's distress, and looking from one frightened face to another. 'You have done me a favour in a sense, for I have subdued Ireland at last. The Irish lords will no longer defy me. And to think my original plan was simply to capture *you*,' he said, bringing his gaze back to Matilda who flinched openly at the malice that lay there.

'Sire. Please hear me.' Matilda lifted her chin enough so that she could meet his gaze squarely. 'I can get money. I have some hidden away along with some gold plate and jewels. I will get it for you if you will let me. And I will beg William to come and swear fealty to you once more. I shall not let you down again,' she finished, hating herself for the pleading tone that had crept into her voice suddenly.

Twin spots of anger burned on John's cheeks. 'I believe your husband is too busy beleaguering Wales along with Llewellyn and your son Phillip to pay heed to you!' he snapped. 'But, no matter. I shall deal with them upon my return!'

'No!' Matilda looked up at him with desperate eyes. 'I beg of you, sire, please! 'Just give me one more chance to get the money. I can repay you, I promise. From now on both William and I shall be your dutiful and loyal subjects to the end of our days. I know that I can speak for William on this. If you will just give me time to find him!'

John did not reply immediately. The only sound in the room was the panting of the dog and the sound of the children's voices drifting in from the bailey. Matilda felt small and afraid as she knelt, waiting for John's reply. John turned and went and stood by the dais, studying a wall mounted tapestry that showed a hunting scene. Matilda knew exactly how the frightened hart felt as it stood trapped in the gaze of the hunter, and she shivered, making the small hairs on the back of her neck rise in response.

At last John turned back to them. 'I shall give you one last chance, madam, to repay your debts to me. 40,000 marks as William agreed, 10,000 of which must be paid by Michaelmas at the latest. If you fail, then 10,000 marks more will be added to your debt. You will of course remain my prisoner until then'.

When he'd finished his speech, he signalled to the clerk who had been seated silently in the corner during the proceeding drawing up the terms of their agreement. At his bidding the clerk rose and, blowing off the sand that he'd sprinkled on the document to dry the ink, he crossed the room and handed it to John. Matilda watched as he spent a few moments reading it through carefully. Then, when he was satisfied, he crossed to a table laden with books and writing instruments to prepare a quill. 'You will sign this, my lady. Upon our return to England, your husband will sign it, too. If he does not –' he left the implied threat hanging in the air.

Matilda stood, awkward and stiff from kneeling so long. Her head, light and dizzy from lack of food, swam alarmingly. Duncan, who'd been watching the proceeding with interest, reached out a meaty hand and steadied her. 'Now lass don't take on so,' he said softly. 'I dinna think it's unfair terms, considering.' Then taking her elbow he led her over to where John was waiting.

Her eyes, sore with unshed tears, could not focus on the wording. But still, with a shaking hand, she dipped the pen into the ink and put her name to the agreement, knowing in her heart of hearts that William would never put his own signature alongside hers willingly. Then, feeling sick to the core with fear at what she had just done, she replaced the quill on the table.

I sat in the chamber allotted to us by King John, thinking wryly that not much had changed. Carrickfergus had been a dismal place when the de Lacys had still clung to it before our flight, and it was no better or worse now that we were locked up in this godforsaken room. A maid had been in earlier and left a tray of meats and cheeses, a loaf of bread and a jug of water, along with a bowl of soft milk sops and some thin gruel for the babies. We had pallets to sleep on and blankets. Beyond that our comfort was ignored. The floor was bare of rushes, and the musty smell in the air assured me that the chamber was seldom used.

Matilda, Will and the girls had just returned from their audience with the king, and I knew that it was not good news. Margaret's face was blotchy from crying and the others were blank with exhaustion and shock. Matilda was the first to stir. Picking Walter up from the floor she hugged him, ruffling his head of baby hair absently as she tried to disguise the fear that was etched on her brow.

Taking her cue, Margaret crossed the room and lifted Petronella from the arms of one of the nurses in charge of the babies, who'd been snivelling since she'd heard the heavy clunk of the wooden bar falling across the outside of the ancient oak door. Will just sat quietly on a pallet, ashamed that he had not been able to prevent our arrest. At his feet, John, Giles, Phillip and Gilbert sat on the bare floor with Maude and Annora, playing listlessly with some carved soldiers that a sympathetic maid had found for them.

Outside, the door was heavily guarded. King John was not going to give his quarry another opportunity to escape.

After a while Matilda came and perched beside me on the window embrasure, clutching Walter to her breast. We sat in silence as she peered helplessly down into the bailey below where tiny figures milled going about their everyday tasks.

'What will become of us, Ailith?' she asked in a low voice. I saw her bottom lip tremble, and I felt helpless for there was nothing I could do. We were caught in a trap of King John's making. 'I was made to sign an agreement that upon our return to England William will honour the debt,' she continued after a moment. 'The first instalment of 10,000 marks is to be paid by Michaelmas. I have written to William under the king's instruction and told him where I hid the jewels and gold plate. I can only hope that he will come.'

She sighed. 'I have lived a lifetime trying to run from my destiny, Ailith. Since the night of the Abergavenny murders I have known that my fate has been decided for me by some far greater power. It only needed an orchestrator; and that person is King John. And Will,' she glanced sadly over to where he sat miserably on the pallet, pulling at the straw stuffing angrily. 'Well, Will had the misfortune to be born on that cursed night and so his destiny has been marked too.'

I recalled the red dream, and shivering I pulled my cloak tighter around me. It was getting cold and outside the light was fading. One by one I could see the stars lighting up in the sky as the shadows grew deeper in the chamber. I could not save Matilda, William or Will. But the rest of her family would survive. I knew now that they had destinies that could only be born out of a greater sacrifice. If I tried to do the impossible and change that, then the results would be disastrous. And so, instead, I concentrated on the future, for the past would soon be just that. The past.

As if sensing my anguish, Matilda gave me a small smile and took my hand where it lay balled tightly on my lap. 'Thank you, Ailith - for being here when I needed you,' she whispered. She said no more, and after a moment I let the hot tears squeeze out from under my lashes and roll down my face, where they fell unchecked onto the bare floorboards at my feet.

That night I lay on my pallet listening to the faint snores around me, and it was a long time before I finally fell into an uneasy sleep.

The dream, when it came, was shadowy. There was a meadow, bright with summer flowers: tall white daisies, and blood red poppies. In the distance, the brightly coloured pavilions rippled in the early summer breeze in front of Windsor castle. Overhead, the first swallows of summer wheeled in the blue sky, swooping occasionally to skim the surface of the river. Then suddenly the shadows cleared: I could see a host of King John's barons jostling for a view; many of them older now and more careworn in my dream of the future. I could see the stooped figure of William the Marshall who was with the king, and the broad shoulders of Richard de Clare who'd once forsaken Matilda to side with him. Then there was the face of the Earl of Arundel, the Earl of Salisbury, and Eustace de Vesci, mingling with many other important and influential barons all gathered together in this meadow to one end: to witness King John put his seal to a charter to protect the rights and liberties of all freemen. A charter designed to bring an end to the abuses of the king, and all future kings. Once and for all. And, as they watched, King John stepped up to a podium draped with gold cloth bearing a roll of parchment, and a wax mould of the great seal of England. Then, conscious of the hushed silence around him, he attached the great seal to the greatest document of the future to come: a list of promises such as had never yet been extracted from a king whose tyranny had been the source of so much hate and violence. And in my dream, I saw John's lips move in the twilight of the future as he recited the clauses one by one to his barons, pausing only at clause number thirty-nine:

> *No man shall be taken, imprisoned, outlawed, banished or in any way destroyed, nor will we proceed against or prosecute him, except by the lawful judgement of his peers or by the law of the land.*
> *The Magna Carta*

Bristol Castle, Bristol, England, December 1210

They had been returned to England in the balmy heat of August. As soon as they had arrived at the port of Fishguard in Wales, Matilda and Will had been separated from the others and taken to Bristol Castle. Margaret had managed to hug her mother once whilst the tears coursed down her face, before a guard had stepped forward and pulled her aside with an iron grip. The last she had seen of them was when they were being ushered away from the quay in the opposite direction with the nurses and children in tow. Nobody would tell her where they were being taken. She later heard that they were being confined at Corfe Castle, King John's favourite place of imprisonment for those that had crossed him.

Matilda had spent many hours pacing the small chamber that served as her prison, begging William silently to come and save them. But she knew that he would not. She knew in her heart of hearts that he had abandoned them to their fate.

Michaelmas had long since past when the doors to their chambers were opened, and John's clerks and a lawyer stepped into the room, followed by the king himself. He was dressed richly in a purple tunic lined with ermine and trimmed with gems. At his side hung his jewel encrusted sword. On his head was a gold coronet, a symbol of his power. Matilda raised her eyes and met his cold, blue gaze defiantly. But she had been the first to look away, afraid of the undisguised hate that she met there.

It had not taken long for the lawyer to outline the gravity of their situation. He was a tall, thin man, with legs like a stork and lank, greasy hair that he kept pushing nervously out of his face as he paced the length and breadth of the room, explaining in sonorous tones that her husband had finally gone too far and attacked one of the king's own castles. When the sheriff had tried to apprehend him, he had fled to Bramber. From there he had taken the first available ship to France dressed as a beggar. He was, the lawyer gravely told her, now officially an outlaw.

Matilda let out a small sob and, falling to her knees, she had begged John for more time to pay. But the lawyer had interrupted sternly and told her that the king was not prepared to extend more time. William's actions, he said, had made it plain that he no longer felt beholden to his debts to the king, and therefore she must be prepared for the final sentence to be carried out upon her and Will.

For a moment Matilda thought she saw a flicker of sympathy in John's eyes and a faint candle of hope burned in her breast. Perhaps he would offer a reprieve? But this was quickly snuffed out when he nodded to the lawyer, who proceeded to read out the sentence, throwing nervous little glances her way as he did. She and Will would be taken to Windsor Castle. Once there, they would be incarcerated and left until they were dead. There was a long silence when the lawyer finished speaking and Matilda felt curiously detached as if the sentence was being read out to another person. Then she felt her legs buckle beneath her.

The last she saw of King John was his cold blue eyes staring down at her on the ground before, with a swish of his cloak, he turned on his heel and left the chamber.

Windsor Castle, Berkshire, England, December 1210

Matilda stood alongside Will, staring down into the shadowy depths of the oubliette that lay beneath the floor of the old Norman keep. 'So, this is to be the place that I die,' she whispered. She raised her head slightly, wanting to see her son's face clearly one last time before being thrust into the inky darkness below. Will's eyes shone with unshed tears and, reaching out a shaky hand, he pushed a lock of the once bright chestnut hair off her brow and kissed it gently. The silence stretched for long moments, then suddenly an icy wind spilled into the room from nowhere and the sconces flickered wildly, throwing ghostly fingers up the wall. Beside her, the constable jumped like a spooked cat and sketched the sign of the cross over his chest. Then beckoning a guard forward with a smoking torch, he poked it quickly down into the chamber, sketching a hasty circle into the blackness below, checking their prison one last time before their confinement. Finally, with one last glance at their white faces, he nodded to the jailors and indicated that they were to proceed with the sentence King John had pronounced.

Will was first. He landed awkwardly, his legs buckling beneath him as he hit the cold stone floor. For a moment he lay stunned, but then a wave of excruciating pain shot through his side, rendering him unconscious before he could drag himself out of the way for Matilda to be lowered down after him. Sending a silent cry to God that in his mercy he might spare them, Matilda found herself being tied and pushed, only slightly less roughly, into the darkness after him, followed by a couple of sheaths of straw, their yellow ears dusty and dry from storage, and a fur lined cloak that smelled of woodsmoke and sweat, and had seen better days.

For a moment Matilda lay curled up where she had landed, pressed against Will with the cloak across her legs and the straw strewn around them. Above her, the smoking torches hovered for a while, illuminating the rough features of the constable and his men as they stared down pityingly on their faces one last time. Then without another word the heavy trapdoor was lowered with a resounding bang, shutting out the world beyond. All that remained was darkness, and the faint, thin slivers of light that shone through the gaps in the trapdoor. Soon, even that was gone.

For a while Matilda listened numbly to the sound of the men's boots growing fainter as they crossed the room above and headed for the door. Suddenly desperate, she dragged herself to her feet and called out to them. But her voice simply echoed around the bare cell until all that was left was its memory; a ghostly thing that hung in the air, mocking her silently in her despair. Softly, she began to cry. Then, groping for Will, she tucked the cloak around him with shaking hands and pulled him towards her, holding him tightly as he cried out in pain. She didn't know how long she sat there but a sudden drop-in temperature indicated that night had fallen. Slowly, she stood and began to feel round the walls, and even knowing that there was no escape other than from above she tore at them with her hands until her fingers were raw. The sound of something scuttling in the corner made her cry out, and with a little shudder she gave up her search, before dropping to her knees again and burying her face in her hands. 'Sweet Virgin. Holy Mother,' she whispered. 'Let King John have mercy,' then, curling up alongside Will, she pulled him into her arms once again and tried to prepare herself for the long night ahead.

She must have slept, for when she woke the cell was a little warmer. She could hear the shouts of the maids in the distance through the cracks in the trapdoor and she knew they were preparing the first meal of the day and laying the fires. For a moment she wondered if they would bring her some, but then she knew they would not. To them she and Will were already dead. Incarcerated and forgotten.

'I shall not forget ...'

It was a sigh. A whisper in the wind. Ailith.

'You did not fail me, Ailith.' Matilda's lips moved, as though she could see her friend standing in the bailey, see her standing there with the cold winter wind stirring her hair as she stared up into the keep. She would not let King John forget. Matilda smiled sadly. So that was her vow, her pledge. It had been from the day she had arrived at Bramber. And would be until the end of time.

She groped for Will. He was burning with fever. It would not be long now she thought, as she sat cradling his feverish head on her lap, rocking him gently as one by one he called out for Maud and his children. The day passed in a fog of delirium and dreams, but still no food or water was sent to show that John had relented, and gradually any hope that he might faded with the glimmer of light from above, as once again the temperature dropped and darkness fell. When it was truly black once more, Matilda tucked some of the straw around them, then desperately she tried to eat some of the dried ears of wheat, but without water to wash it down it lodged in her throat. When finally she slept, it was with no hope left in her heart. The next morning, she woke to find Will stiff and cold beside her. With an agonised cry of despair, she stood and began clawing at the walls of the cell in grief, only stopping when fingers where bloodied ribbons of flesh, and her nails had been ripped from their beds. Finally, exhausted, and all out of tears, she crawled back to where Will lay, and gathering him in her trembling arms she began to rock him.

She didn't know how long she sat there with Will's stiff body by her side. The growing cold then the slight rise in temperature was the only indication that day had turned to night then back to day again. The only company she had was silence, deep and dark, and the odd rustle in the corners where something shared her cell. Once she thought she felt a furry object brush against her hand and she shuddered, but she didn't have the strength to move it, not even when she heard it begin to gnaw on Wills arm. Memories drifted in and out with her consciousness now: of happier times with her children, bright pictures of smiling faces stuck in the long distant past. She tried to whisper their names, but her lips were chapped and dry, and her swollen tongue was firmly stuck to the roof of her mouth. Then blackness, blessed blackness beckoned ...

It was the hour before dawn she knew instinctively when she next opened her eyes. She could feel them there waiting for her: those that she had loved and had loved her. They waited in the shadows. She need only to step over to be with them, but they must wait a few moments more. Above her, from a long way away, she heard the sound of a door opening and closing, and after brief hesitation footsteps slowly began to cross the room. Moments later they came to rest on top of the trapdoor, then a bright light flooded down through the gaps and her fading eyesight made out a shadowy form above; she could feel weight of a pair of cold blue eyes boring down at her through the heavy oak.

'So, you came at last,' she whispered through dried lips. Then, turning her head, she kissed her son's cold cheek one last time, and closing her eyes she let them come and take her …

EPILOGUE

Wigmore Castle, Herefordshire, 12th October 1216

Annora stood in front of the metal plate that served as a mirror. Her reflection stared back at her: blue eyes framed by thick black lashes, incongruous against her pale skin, the long, fair hair that fell untamed down her back almost to her waist, and the elfin chin. A legacy from her mother. Around her, the silence hung heavily in the air. Her husband preferred to hunt and frolic rather than spend any time in her company since King John had released her from her captivity in Bristol Castle.

King John. *Your father* ... a small voice whispered ... *The man who murdered your mother and Will* ...

Around her, dust motes swirled in the dull light of the afternoon. Slowly she blinked. Willing it to come as she had trained herself to do in the long, cold, lonely nights of her imprisonment. Keeping her gaze steadily on the mirror, she concentrated on her breathing until it was deep and rhythmic and her limbs began to feel heavy. Then, when she was ready, she crossed to her solitary bed and lay down.

Long minutes past before she felt herself rise like a phoenix from the flames. Then suddenly she was free again: soaring across the rolling hills of Herefordshire, looking down upon the carpet of autumnal leaves spread across the valleys below and on, further still towards the gorse topped mountains of Wales in the distance glowing like fire in the late October sun. Below her, her sharp eyes caught the movement of a tiny field mouse, the little creature stopped and sniffed the air before scuttling hurriedly away, afraid that she might swoop. But she flew on. Seeking. Searching. Her wings beating faster and faster still as she went, carrying her swiftly along on the currents.

Only when she was over the East Anglian marshes did she slow down and hover for a while. Then her sharp eyes spotted the baggage train, heading directly across the marshy Wash, departing from the main train that was picking its way along the longer route to avoid the rebels that dwelled there. With a thin cry she swooped down, and then down still further, dropping on the wind currents until she was immediately above the trailing stream of men and horses.

And the huge mass of water that was heading their way.

King John felt his guts gripe again, and he wished that he'd not partaken of so many lampreys at Lynn. He had sent his baggage train, which included his precious crown jewels, directly across the Wash against the advice of his captain of the guard. Now he was beginning to regret it for it was causing him anxiety. And anxiety was making his gripes worse.

He rode on for a while, making his way around the relative safety of the shore, but still keeping an eye on the estuary in the distance. It was getting near to dusk, and he was hopeful of his chances of making it to Swinehead Abbey before dark, where he hoped he would be offered some rest and respite from his illness, when suddenly he heard a shout. From his position at the rear of the column, one of his sergeants was waving his arms wildly above his head, dancing around and trying to attract his attention. Then all at once the entire guard was milling around in confusion. It was pandemonium. Their shouts carried across the sands like the sounds of a distant battle. From where he sat, perched on his great black war horse, John didn't understand what was happening. Then, with a dawning horror, he saw the huge torrent of foaming water that was speeding towards the precious baggage train from the rear. Out in the estuary the frantic men tried their hardest to turn the wagons and horses, but within moments they were engulfed in the roaring mass of sea, and as John and his entourage watched speechlessly, it spilled over the baggage train, sweeping it away and sending men, horses and wagons cart-wheeling into the quicksand beyond, which opened its fickle embrace and quickly claimed them for its own.

For several long moments John just stared in horror at the devastation. Then his bowels twisted once more in an agonising spasm, and slowly he fell forward onto his saddle, just as they voided themselves in a rush of blood and faeces. So appalled were his attendants that none of them heard the hoot of the owl, or saw the great white bird circle the sky above them before it turned and headed for home …

Hereford Castle, Wales, 14th October 1216

Margaret de Lacy stood looking down at the charter she was holding in her hand, before sinking into the chair that one of her ladies, concerned by her sudden pallor, had hastily dragged over for her. In front of her the messenger stood waiting for instructions. The only sound in the room other than the crackling of the logs in the hearth, was the rustling of the rushes as the woman returned to her distaff, throwing concerned glances her way every now and then.

After a moment Margaret allowed herself to read the creamy parchment again, not really believing that at last her wish had been granted. It was from King John, and it was dated 9th October and addressed Kings Lynn in Norfolk. News had travelled that John had been warmly greeted and lavishly feasted by the people of Lynn who had been the only ones to lend him their support in the darkest days of the baron's war, despite his failure to abide by the terms of the Magna Carta signed at Runnymede the previous year. As far as she could tell the letter was in the king's own hand and it looked as if it had been scrawled in haste. Unaccountably, she felt the hairs on the back of her neck rise as she read the words again:

Know that for the sake of God we have conceded to Margaret de Lacy three carucates of land to be assarted and cultivated in our forest of Aconbury, to build there a certain religious house for the souls of William de Braose, her father, Matilda, her mother, and William her brother. And we instruct you to assign those three carucates of land in the aforesaid forest to the same Margaret.

Margaret's eyes blurred and there was a lump in her throat as she carefully rolled the precious parchment and placed it on the table alongside her. 'Well,' she whispered to herself. 'It seems that King John does have a conscience after all.' Then standing she picked up her skirts and went to find her husband to give him the good news, slipping a generous payment to the messenger as she went.

Six days later, on the 19th October 1216, King John was dead.

Author's note:

I am not a historian, I don't even pretend to be one. However, I have a complete and utter fascination where the de Braoses are concerned, particularly when it comes to the fate of Matilda de Braose. I like to think perhaps that if there had been an Ailith a little bit of her still lives on through me, and thus Matilda's tale is told again. But again, I must stress that this is a work of historical fiction, and therefore any errors are my own.

Acknowledgements:

Many thanks to Sarah Green, keeper of the keys of Bramber Castle, for her insight and knowledge on all things to do with Bramber Village, its castle and history.

Also, I owe a debt of gratitude to Nicky Galliers who kindly took me under her wing and spent so much of her own time editing and critiquing my second novel, Call of the Raven. Unsurprisingly, many of the observations and comments she made in relation *to Call of the Raven* were true of *Storms and Shadows* as well, and so I can honestly say that she had a hand in its final creation! Thank you, Nicky!

Glossary of Terms:

Bliaut: A bliaut or bliaud is an overgarment worn by both genders from the eleventh to the thirteenth century in Western Europe, featuring voluminous skirts and horizontal puckering or pleating across a snugly fitted under bust abdomen.

Barbette: The barbette was worn from the 12th century and was a band of linen that passed under the chin, as a chin strap, and was pinned on top of the head. The barbet was worn with a linen fillet or headband, or with a linen cap called a coif, with or without a couvrechef (kerchief) or veil.

Chemise: Woman's under garment sometimes known as a shift.

Coffer: A chest to house and transport clothing/linen/personal effects.

Galanas; A Welsh term for the payment of a blood feud, compensation levied against a person/family who has harmed another person/family – probably extracted in many ways, not necessarily, or even, simply by the exchange of money because the terms seems to be mostly applied to blood feuds.

Garderobe: A historic term for a room in a medieval castle. The Oxford English Dictionary gives as its first meaning a store-room for valuables, but also acknowledges "by extension, a private room, a bed-chamber; also a privy". Its most common use now is as a term for a castle toilet.

Kirtle: A kirtle (sometimes called cotte, cotehardie) is a garment that was worn by men and women in the Middle Ages. It eventually became a one-piece garment worn by women from the late Middle Ages into the Baroque period.

Madder: A red dye derived from the root of the (genus Rubia) plant.

Mummer: Medieval travelling entertainer.

Marchpane: The forerunner of marzipan.

Peliçon: A cloak worn predominantly by women, though there is evidence it was at some point worn by men too.

Subtlety: A subtlety was a type of medieval food sculpture, mostly made out of marzipan/marchpane.

Terce: An hour denoted by the canonical bell: Matins; Prime; Terce; Sext; None; Vespers; Sunset; Compline.

Teulu: A term used to refer to a medieval prince/chieftan's or leaders Welsh body guard, retinue or war band

Tournament: A tournament is where what we refer to as jousting took place.

Trencher: A plate made out of slices of stale bread or rounded loaves hollowed out to hold food.

Select Bibliography:

Gerald of Wales, The Journey through Wales and the description of Wales. (Penguin Classics 2004)

Bartlett, Robert, Gerald of Wales. A voice of the middle ages. (Tempus Publishing Limited)

Turvey, Roger, The Welsh Princes, The Native Rulers of Wales 1063-1283, (Pearson Education)

Weir, Alison, Eleanor of Aquitaine, (Pimlico)

Herbert, Norris, Medieval Costume and Fashion, (Dover Publications inc)

Labarage, Wade, Mistresses, Maids and Men; Baronial Life in the Thirteenth Century, (Eyre and Spittiswoode 2003)

Hammond, Peter, Food and Feast in Medieval England, (Sutton Publishing Limited, 2005)

Hudson, Roger, Hudsons English History, A Compendium, (Weidenfudd & Nicolson, 2005)

McLynn, Frank, Lionheart & Lackland, King Richard, King John and the Wars of Conquest, (Vubtage Books, 2007)

Hindley, Geoffrey, A Brief History of the Magna Carta, (Constable & Robinson, 2008)

BV - #0019 - 050719 - C0 - 197/132/25 - PB - 9781916440036